RHAPSODY OF LIGHT

BOOK 4

OF

MIRRORS OF THE WORLD

BY

KAI STORMHAVEN

Published by Kai Stormhaven LLC
www.kaistormhaven.com

ISBN: 978-1-972065-10-5

1 – HARNKETI 5

2 – FREEDOM 18

3 – NOURISHING LIGHT 29

4 – TRAIN 41

5 – ANGELS 53

6 – HOLD ON TO YOUR BUTTS 65

7 – PARTY 77

8 – INSATIABLE 91

9 – LEVELING SYSTEM 101

10 – RESURRECTION 108

11 – EVIL BASTARDS 120

12 – RESURRECTION PARTY 132

13 – MELODY 144

14 – ETHERIC BEAUTY 157

15 – CRISIS AVERTED 168

16 – LIVE IN THE NOW 180

17 – HELPLESS 192

18 – LEXI 204

19 – RECALL 216

20 – DANCE OFF 229

21 – RESET 242

22 – THE END OF EVERYTHING 254

23 – ONE LAST GIFT 266

EPILOGUE 280

1 – HARNKETI

Harmony shivered as her bedroom vanished, replaced by the entrance to Yggdrasil. Teleportation was a strange sensation, like dropping through a layer of icy water for a split second.

"It's even more beautiful when you can see it properly, isn't it?" Rhapsody said softly, clasping her hand.

She stood next to Harmony, her face glowing with affection. She wore a green summer dress that revealed her long, toned legs to mid-thigh and left her arms bare.

The previous night had surprised her. Exploring the limits of her mirror-touch synesthesia had been enjoyable in a way she'd never imagined. She'd spent her life wishing it gone, yet for the first time, she welcomed every extra sensation it brought.

Harmony nodded with a dazzling smile. "It really is beautiful. Everything in my world became more beautiful when you entered my life."

Rhapsody floated up and embraced Harmony, her eyes growing moist. "I love you, Harmony. Rhapsody spent so many years enjoying the *idea* of someone like you, who she could fall in love with, knowing it would almost certainly never happen outside her imagination. It's kind of ironic how you focused on living vicariously through your characters to experience love, too. I'm glad we came down here and gave Rhapsody a chance to have this experience."

Harmony blinked when Rhapsody referred to herself in the third person. It reminded her of the day Rhapsody had visited Harmony in her garden in what seemed like a lifetime ago. She threaded her fingers through Rhapsody's crimson hair, luxuriant and warm beneath her touch, and asked softly, "Why haven't you tried to have a relationship before now?"

Rhapsody leaned back to look into Harmony's eyes. The fairy studied her face with a serious expression, her large, lavender eyes like pools Harmony could lose herself in.

"A world tree can see a person's physical body, their thoughts, and their hopes and dreams. Those aspects of a person are primarily driven by the spirit piloting their body. Even though mortality filters out most of the spirit's memories, it doesn't change the root personality. Most spirits are young and frivolous, exhibiting selfish traits like a toddler. There aren't very many old spirits who've been through dozens of incarnations."

Rhapsody sighed, smiling sadly. "Mortality's a brutal place, and after a spirit's experienced it once, they'll move on to less difficult places. Occasionally, a spirit understands that mortality requires many iterations to truly grow and mature. They know the pain they'll endure but continue anyway."

Rhapsody caressed Harmony's cheek fondly. "It takes a special kind of spirit to return to a place as difficult as the mortal realm. You're one of those indomitable spirits, Harmony. Your body is young, but your spirit is old—and your soul makes your spirit seem young. That's why you spent your childhood going out of your way to take care of everyone."

Rhapsody leaned her forehead against Harmony's, gazing into her eyes lovingly. "Your spirit is blindingly beautiful, something she couldn't ignore even if she wanted to. From the first time Rhapsody saw you, she could feel the radiance of your spirit. She knew you were someone she could fall in love with and not feel like she was bonding with the equivalent of a child. You're someone as old as me, forged by the fires of experience through countless lives. That's why Rhapsody hasn't had any interest in anyone else. You don't remember now, but we've known each other for a very long time."

Harmony couldn't stop a playful smile from stealing across her lips. "Are you calling me an old lady? And what's with all this third-person weirdness?"

Rhapsody raised an eyebrow, her expression stern. "Do you have a problem with old ladies? You know I'm over half a million years old, right?"

"Touché," Harmony grinned. She leaned forward and kissed those expressive lips, shivering with delight as her synesthesia mirrored the sensations.

Rhapsody leaned back, smiling wistfully. "I'm referring to myself in the third person because I'm not truly Rhapsody. Like you, I'm here to help save this world. I'll explain in more depth when you're ready. For now, just know that you and I have been together for more time than you can imagine in your current state."

She finished with another lingering kiss that set Harmony's insides on fire.

"Didn't you two reach peak saturation last night?" Taxti asked dryly.

She'd appeared out of nowhere, Serenity and Aurora each holding one of her hands. She stood in front of the two of them with a languid smile.

Rhapsody shook her head, giving Harmony a hungry look. "Not even close."

Harmony looked at her nieces curiously. "Where's your grandma?"

Taxti sighed lustily. "She's talking with Nidhogg. The oversized bat stole her when I had my back turned for one second. He wanted to ask her about the world of mortals."

Serenity and Aurora both wore huge grins. They looked completely energized, even though they hadn't slept the previous night. Rhapsody had assured her yuccas fitter completely removed the need for sleep, rejuvenating the body even more than eight hours of slumber could achieve.

"Aunt Harmony," Aurora said excitedly. "Taxti's been showing us how to teleport! We can do it by ourselves now. It's *super* easy."

"Really?" Harmony glanced at Taxti in surprise. "I thought teleportation would be some kind of advanced magic."

"Nope," Taxti shook her head with an indulgent smile down at Serenity and Aurora. "Displacement magic is one of the easiest kinds of magic to learn. It still takes a level of comprehension for abstract concepts, but these two are really clever. I've been impressed with just how fast they catch on. Older souls always have a natural affinity for magical theory."

Harmony smiled affectionately at her nieces. "I'm going to guess these two are a special case. They keep surprising me with how much smarter they are than I was at their age. What else have you learned besides teleportation?"

A second Serenity appeared next to the first one, grinning at Harmony excitedly. "I learned how to make an illusory clone of myself that has enough substance to feel solid to other people."

Aurora sighed enviously. "I haven't figured that one out yet." She brightened. "I did figure out how to levitate, though!"

She slowly rose into the air until she was at eye-level with Harmony. "It's not really like flying," Aurora informed her matter-of-factly, eyes tight with concentration. "You have to focus on weight and density to make this work. Taxti says flying is harder to learn but easier to maintain once you figure it out."

Harmony smiled wryly. "Now I know who to call when I can't reach something on the higher shelves in the garage."

Rhapsody raised an amused eyebrow. "Since when is there anything you can't reach, Miss Six Feet Tall?"

Harmony shrugged. "We have shelves that are ten feet high in our garage." The sight of her nieces' happiness left her with a warm glow. Their lives had improved so much since Rhapsody had appeared.

Serenity suddenly giggled. "We saw someone with a jet pack try to fly over the wall. You should have seen his face when Harnketi suddenly appeared in front of him in the air. She pointed her finger toward the outside of the wall, and he decided he had something important to do elsewhere."

Harmony's eyes widened. "He actually made it inside the circle?"

Serenity shook her head, eyes sparkling with mirth. "No, he was still between the outer and inner walls."

Harmony looked at Rhapsody inquisitively. "Have things chilled out yet, or are they just getting crazier?"

Rhapsody shook her head. "They keep trying to elevate the bar for crazy," she said with a short laugh. "Some of the nutjobs showing up at the outer wall were trying to make shrines or offer sacrifices of flowers—self-proclaimed druids and witches. Then there were the UFO enthusiasts demanding we release all the abductees I've supposedly taken over the last few decades."

She giggled mischievously. "They brought a megaphone and stood just beyond the EM field shouting demands. I decided to extend the EM field by a few hundred feet. The cries of chagrin when all their devices crashed could be heard for miles. There was one guy working on an honest-to-god catapult to try and launch himself over the walls. I had to dissolve it before he got himself killed."

Rhapsody's mirth faded as she continued. "The military finally sent more soldiers and forced everyone away from the circle, then blockaded all the roads in the area. They have drones patrolling the perimeter outside the new EM field in case anyone gets past them."

Harmony's brow creased with concern. "Is the military trying to get in again?"

Rhapsody shook her head with a small smile. "No, not at the moment. They've decided to take a more cautious approach this time—now that they understand this place isn't defenseless."

Harmony scowled darkly. "I'm surprised they haven't tried nuking it yet."

Rhapsody smiled grimly. "Oh, that's *definitely* on the table. It's more of a last resort, however. They don't want to destroy what they think could be a treasure trove of advanced technology."

Harmony chewed her lip worriedly. "I wonder how Mystery is doing. Do you think the government is bugging her?"

"Yep," Rhapsody confirmed with a nod and a roll of her large eyes. "The FBI showed up at her house shortly after she got home. They dragged her off to a field office, then flew her to DC before she even got a chance to have a relaxing bath."

Harmony frowned anxiously. "That doesn't sound good. Do you think she's in any kind of danger?"

"No, she'll be fine," Rhapsody assured her confidently. "Azeban's with her in case she *does* run into any trouble. She's been assigned a protective detail. The CIA, DIA, FBI, and members of the cabinet are all meeting with her to discuss what she knows about the inside of the circle. For now, she's the most important person in the world."

Harmony sighed, running a hand through her hair. "I guess we're kind of trapped here then, aren't we? The moment we end up outside the circle, we'll have some government agency snatching us up."

Rhapsody caressed her cheek and smiled reassuringly. "No, you won't have to worry about that. I've set up wards around your house and another one that surrounds you and the kiddos anytime you leave the circle. Anyone with ill intent entering the field won't recognize you or remember anything about the circle."

"Wow," Harmony breathed in amazement. "That's pretty damn precise. How do you even make something like that?"

Rhapsody smiled mysteriously. "Those are secrets about the universe you'll learn in time. I'll introduce you to some angels I know when the time comes."

Harmony stared at her disbelievingly. "Like, actual angels from biblical times?" she asked skeptically. She suddenly remembered the time Rhapsody had turned into an angel when she was a child. Had it been a trick of her imagination?

Rhapsody laughed scornfully. "No, nothing like that. *Definitely* not like that. You'll just have to wait for that introduction. It will probably be a few years before you're ready for that kind of information."

Harmony eyed Rhapsody shrewdly. "I'm assuming you wanted Mystery to talk to the intelligence agencies. Otherwise, you would've warded her as well. Or is that against those rules you were telling me about?"

Rhapsody smiled approvingly. "Well spotted, Harmony. I actually *do* want the leaders of this world to know about us, as well as the calamity that awaits if we fail to revive the other circles. If they understand the continued survival of this world depends on us being left alone, they'll be less likely to cause trouble."

She smiled dryly. "Of course, it won't be that easy. They aren't just going to believe everything Mystery tells them. They're a suspicious bunch and will suspect an ulterior motive. They'll try to use her to arrange a meeting with *me* if all goes well."

Harmony snickered. "That would be an interesting meeting to watch. All those uptight bureaucrats trying to throw their weight around. They're used to being the most powerful people in the world. It'd be interesting to see how their attitudes change when they realize they're just footnotes."

Rhapsody sighed, shaking her head. "They'll act with fear and make poor decisions if I don't handle them carefully. Fear shuts down higher cognitive reasoning. I'll probably need to accept an ambassador inside the circle to keep them from doing anything stupid."

Harmony gestured at a Yuccus Fitter tree. "I'd suggest never letting them learn about the immortality fruit. The last thing the world needs is those clowns living forever."

Rhapsody chuckled. "Yeah, that'll be our little secret."

Harmony tilted her head curiously. "What happens if they react out of fear anyway?"

Rhapsody smiled brightly. "I'll have to be a little more heavy-handed if that happens," she said cheerfully. "There are limits to what I'm allowed to do without inviting interference from other entities, but if it's in direct response to a threat to me, I have a lot more leeway."

Aurora sighed discontentedly and looked up at Taxti hopefully. "This is boring grown-up speak. Can we learn some more magic?"

Before Taxti could respond, the gigantic form of the dragon, Nidhogg, flew down to hover near them. Joline stepped off his head and floated several hundred feet down to the ground next to Harmony.

Nidhogg's voice shook Harmony's bones as he spoke, his booming voice shaking the leaves of the trees. "Thank you for the stimulating conversation, Joline. It's been a long time since I've learned so many interesting things about the world."

Joline's smile was radiant as she replied, "The pleasure was all mine, Nidhogg."

Harmony still couldn't get over how young her mother looked, almost like a shorter version of Harmony.

She watched in awe as the dragon flew back up into the higher branches of Yggdrasil. "I still can't wrap my mind around how large Nidhogg is."

Rhapsody stared at her pointedly. "You'll notice I'm *significantly* bigger than Nidhogg."

Harmony looked Rhapsody up and down with pursed lips. "I'm just not seeing it."

Aurora folded her arms, giving Harmony a pointed stare. "She's the world tree, silly. She's *way* bigger than Nidhogg."

"Oh!" Harmony exclaimed in mock surprise. "I do believe you're right, Aurora. How silly of me."

Serenity turned a disapproving gaze on her, mouth turned down into a small frown. "Are you back on the sarcasm train?"

Harmony smirked. "Choo choo."

Joline looked up at the looming branches above them in wonder. "You wouldn't *believe* how amazing the world looks from high up in Rhapsody's branches. It's a good thing I don't need to breathe anymore and don't feel the cold."

Harmony smiled when she heard her mother refer to them as *Rhapsody's* branches, rather than Yggdrasil's.

Joline looked back at Harmony, then cast an appraising glance at the sun rising above the eastern horizon. "Are we going to get these two back to school before classes start today?"

"No!" Aurora and Serenity shouted in sync, consternation thick in their voices.

Harmony stared at the two of them thoughtfully before glancing inquiringly at Rhapsody. "What do you think?"

Rhapsody gave her a flat look. "Sure, make *me* the bad fairy."

Taxti looked between the two of them hopefully. "Can't we just teach them here?"

"Yes!" her nieces exclaimed eagerly.

Harmony shook her head firmly, ignoring their pleading looks. "Kids need other kids to interact with. You can still come here and be with us, but only *after* school. There'll be plenty of time for you to be inside the circle—especially since you don't need sleep anymore."

Their expressions wilted. She decided to throw them a bone.

"How about this: I'll let you teleport to and from school instead of taking the bus, but only *if* you find a good spot where nobody will see you appear and disappear."

Her nieces perked up, and their expressions became considering. "Would we be allowed to do any magic at school?"

Harmony paused, chewing her lip as she thought. "No showing off," she said firmly. "You can use magic if it's subtle and other people can't see you using it. Would that be okay, Rhapsody?"

Rhapsody nodded, biting her lip to hold back a grin.

Harmony turned back to her nieces expectantly. "Okay, how does that sound? Deal?"

"Deal," they chorused, grinning.

Harmony toyed with a strand of hair as she thought. She glanced at Taxti and Rhapsody speculatively. "Is there some kind of scrying spell that'll allow them to view an area before teleporting so they can make sure nobody's around to see them arrive?"

Taxti nodded. "Teleporting isn't just about movement; it's about awareness. As you reach for a location, sentient minds glow like sparks around your exit point. If you know the area well, you'll even feel the weight of where they're directing their gaze."

Harmony nodded approvingly. "That sounds perfect. Okay, just be careful about not letting other people see you do magic. I know you'll want to show off to your classmates, but please show some restraint and avoid anything that'll bring more attention down on you."

She paused and nodded toward Rhapsody. "She put a kind of force field around you that'll keep anyone with ill intent from remembering who you are, so you should be safe from any threats."

Rhapsody floated around behind Harmony, arms encircling her waist, breasts pressing against her back. Harmony's brain briefly short-circuited as her synesthesia mirrored the sensations.

"Declan offered to go with them as well," Rhapsody told her reassuringly. "I'm pretty sure he just wants to experience life outside the circle, but he'd definitely keep them safe if anything broke through the ward."

Harmony let out a relieved sigh. "That makes me feel a lot better about things. Not that I don't trust your wards, Rhapsody—I'm just always anxious when they're not under my eye."

Taxti sighed petulantly. "Aw, I want to be on guard duty. How come Declan gets to do it?"

Rhapsody looked at her with an artful expression of disappointment. "I was hoping you could start giving Joline some history and magic lessons. I suppose you could go hang out with Declan instead."

"Oh, no, that's perfectly fine!" Taxti blurted out, glancing at Joline with a wink. "I'm sure Declan can handle it."

Harmony bit her lip to keep from laughing as she watched the faun backpedal, recalling how well Taxti and Declan got along—like oil and water.

She glanced at the sun. "What time is it? I'm so used to checking the time on my phone that I feel helpless without it."

Rhapsody released Harmony's waist and held out a hand. "Let me have your phone for a sec."

Harmony handed her phone over, raising a questioning eyebrow. The fairy held it in front of her face for a moment. After several seconds, the Apple logo appeared on the screen.

Rhapsody handed it back. "There, now your phone has an exclusion zone around it and won't get shut down when it comes close to the circle."

Harmony eyed Rhapsody curiously. She just casually added an exclusion zone that would somehow stop her phone from being affected by the EM field. Was this how magic actually worked? It seemed so strange to see magic act more like a program than what she thought of as traditional magic.

She remembered Rhapsody quoting Arthur C. Clarke, and that sufficiently advanced technology would be indistinguishable from magic to humans. Rhapsody was clearly using technology *significantly* more advanced than humans. How were Aurora and Serenity using magic, though, if it was just some kind of advanced technology? She had *so* many questions.

She glanced at her phone and noticed that class started in a few minutes.

"Serenity and Aurora, time for school," Harmony called to her nieces, tucking her phone into her back pocket. "Remember, make sure nobody sees—"

She broke off when her nieces both teleported away, giving her an impish grin before they vanished.

Harmony sighed in exasperation. "Those little punks."

She stared levelly at her smirking mother, then shook her head with a wondering laugh. "I'll never get used to how young you look, Mom."

"Me either," Joline agreed with a pleased grin. "I really like being young again."

"Me too," Taxti added, looking Joline up and down appreciatively.

Rhapsody rolled her eyes at the faun, an expression that looked particularly expressive with her enormous eyes. "You're shameless, Taxti."

"This is true," Taxti agreed pleasantly. "We feel no shame."

Rhapsody playfully smacked Taxti on the shoulder, and the two of them shared a smirk that was oddly symmetrical.

Harmony looked at Rhapsody and bit her lip. "There's something I've been meaning to ask you," she began hesitantly.

Rhapsody smiled invitingly. "By all means, ask away."

Harmony took a deep breath. "I'm not sure if it would be a rude question to ask," she said tentatively. "I don't suppose you could just read my thoughts?"

"It's not rude," Rhapsody assured her with a dimpled smile. "Harnketi wouldn't mind telling you where she came from either. The answer will *certainly* surprise you. The only record you have of who she was as a mortal is her title: The Lady of Cofitachequi."

Joline gasped. "*That's* who Harnketi is? And Harnketi was her name? That sounds more like a Pueblo name."

Rhapsody snorted disdainfully. "She was driven out of her native Puebloan homeland in the Southwest after being accused of witchcraft. The healer of her tribe became jealous of her success in healing some of their sick when she enlisted my help. After she was driven out, Azeban accompanied her to the Southeastern tribes, where she used her intellect and natural charisma to climb the ranks until she ruled over most of the Southeastern tribes."

Rhapsody's face darkened. "When the Spanish explorer Hernando de Soto visited the area, he threatened to use their superior weapons to murder the children of the tribes unless Harnketi accompanied them in their travels to act as a guide. She agreed to their demands in order to save the children of the tribe."

Her lip curled in disgust. "You can imagine what they *really* wanted her for. Harnketi's a beautiful woman, and they only had one thing on their minds when they coerced her into leaving with them. They killed her a few months later, after she continually attempted to escape, killing several explorers in the process."

Rhapsody paused again, smiling in satisfaction. "After her death, she was given the choice to reincarnate, move on, or return as a Baykok and exact revenge on those who prey upon women. She chose to become a Baykok. She joined me here after the European colonizers wiped out the majority of the indigenous population. Her purpose became less compelling after the nineteenth century. She's been trying to decide if she should give up her life as a Baykok and resume mortality."

"That's terrible," Joline murmured sadly. "Humans can be such cruel creatures."

Harmony frowned. "When you say, 'resume mortality,' do you mean be reborn, or would she just transform into a human?"

Rhapsody absently tucked a lock of Harmony's hair behind an ear as she spoke. "She'd resume her life from the moment of her original death. She was thirty years old when she died, so she'd resume mortality at the same age."

Harmony struggled to follow the conversation as Rhapsody continued caressing her skin. She tried to rein in her desire, but it was an uphill battle.

Joline tilted her head curiously. "Who gave her the option to become a Baykok?"

"That was me," Rhapsody admitted with a shrug. "I felt bad for her and wanted to give her a chance for vengeance. I couldn't do anything directly without having other entities ignore our agreement. I intercepted her spirit on its way out and made her the offer."

Joline gazed at Rhapsody in fascination. "Has she just been hanging out inside the circle ever since?"

Harmony smiled at the eagerness on her mother's face. She'd been a professor of linguistics for ten years and had a passion for Native American languages in particular. Having someone like Harnketi, who was a native speaker of the old languages, was like a shiny treasure Joline would be unable to resist.

Rhapsody sighed. "She's not a huge fan of Western civilization. She's watched her beautiful land become tortured and disfigured by endless expansion and plunder of natural resources. She retreated here and stopped going out into the world back in the 1950s. Occasionally, she'll visit places that were special to her, just to see if they're still there."

"Poor Harnketi," Harmony sighed, feeling a sense of loss on behalf of the Baykok. "I wish there was something we could do for her."

Rhapsody cupped her cheek gently. "She's made peace with the state of the world. She's not an unhappy person. We party it up pretty hard in here. She's an amazing singer and a marvel on stringed instruments. The one thing she actually *does* love about Western civilization is the amount of literature produced and how easy it is to obtain. I connected your laptop to the internet and showed her where to find free fiction stories. She's been as happy as a conservative at a gun rally ever since."

Harmony blinked. "How did you connect it to the internet? I didn't think they had cable internet out here. Or are you hacking into satellite internet?"

Rhapsody grinned impishly. "I just opened up a tiny portal next to your Wi-Fi router. Thanks for the internet, Harmony."

Harmony snorted a laugh at the mundane explanation. She'd half-expected some kind of magi-tech that hacked into satellites or cell towers. Opening a small portal certainly seemed like a much less complicated solution.

Harnketi suddenly appeared out of nowhere. "I think I'm ready now. Thank you for giving me the opportunity to find closure and to experience a new aspect of reality."

Harmony's heart pounded in her chest at the unexpected appearance of the Baykok. She was a skeletal frame draped in a transparent film of skin; her eyes were red embers in a skull that would've haunted Harmony's dreams, if she still slept.

Rhapsody smiled jubilantly. "Okay, one human coming up."

Harmony expected a flash of light or the familiar crackle of red and blue sparks. Instead, the change unfolded slowly. The thin, translucent skin stretched and thickened as muscle and fat formed beneath it. The skull reshaped itself, softening, rounding, and then long black hair spilled down her back. It was unsettling to watch the monstrous visage resolve into something unmistakably human, and strikingly beautiful.

Dark brown eyes regarded Harmony with calm intelligence. Tan skin, scattered with faint freckles, replaced the pallor she remembered. The woman's beauty rivaled Mystery's, a fact Harmony noted with wry amusement. She really did attract remarkable women. Taller than her mother and only slightly shorter than Harmony herself, the woman's height alone suggested how imposing she must have seemed to the first Europeans who encountered her.

Harnketi shuddered. "This feels so strange. I feel so *heavy*."

Rhapsody laughed, her eyes full of affection. "I'll bet you do. You're more than just skin and bone now."

Joline studied Harnketi curiously. "What are you going to do now?"

Harnketi smiled eagerly, "I want to experience the world as a human once again."

Harmony watched Harnketi, fascinated. She radiated charisma, drawing everyone's attention when she spoke. Something in her voice's timbre and pitch, along with her expressive face, naturally drew people in. Harmony could see how she had risen to become chief of so many tribes in her last life.

"Where will you go?" Joline asked, her expression rapt, already ensnared by Harnketi's magnetism.

Harnketi's smile turned thoughtful. "To start, I want to visit what remains of my people. I want to hear their stories and record them in a book. I feel a burning desire to reconnect with them and offer what help I can."

Harmony cleared her throat. "My neighbor, Eileen, would *definitely* love to talk with you. She really wants to meet Rhapsody, too."

Harnketi nodded musingly. "I know of this Eileen. Rhapsody sends her dreams when she needs something done in the outer world. I think I'll go meet with her."

Harmony pulled her iPhone from her pocket. "I have her number; I can call her and see if she's available to meet, if you like?"

Harnketi nodded, smiling warmly. "That would be wonderful, Harmony. Thank you."

Harmony tapped the call button. It only rang once.

"Harmony?" Eileen's voice answered, sounding startled. "Are you back outside the ring?"

Harmony grinned. "No, I'm still inside. I just wanted to see what your schedule looks like today."

Eileen paused. "My schedule? Aside from picking up my kids from school in five hours, I'm totally open. Are you doing okay?"

She felt a quiet warmth at the other woman's concern. "I'm doing great, thank you. There's a woman here named Harnketi who wants to meet you. When would be a good time for her to drop in?"

Eileen's voice grew curious. "Any time would be just fine. Should I meet her at the ring?"

Harmony raised a questioning eyebrow at Harnketi. "No, I think she can just teleport to you." At Harnketi's nod, she continued. "Yeah, she can. And yes, Eileen, this is the same skeptical Harmony from the other day, telling you someone's going to teleport—I get the irony."

Eileen laughed, a rich, happy sound that reminded Harmony how easy she was to talk to. She smiled as she continued.

"I'm here with Rhapsody, my mom, and some other locals. How are things in the real world?"

Rhapsody scowled at her indignantly. "Are you trying to say this place isn't real?"

Harmony smirked. "I meant out in the asylum," she amended.

Eileen laughed easily. "Things are a little crazy, as you can imagine. I haven't seen Mystery interviewed by any news stations yet, so I'm assuming she managed to dodge the reporters camped out at her house."

Harmony smiled wryly. "She got whisked away by the FBI. They took her to D.C. for questioning. Rhapsody's keeping an eye on her."

"You seem pretty well informed," Eileen noted questioningly. "Also, aren't your nieces with you?"

Harmony sighed. “I made them go to school. There aren’t any kids here, and they need to interact with people their age.”

“Are you sure that’s safe?” Eileen asked, concern thick in her voice. “There are a *lot* of people looking for you. If word gets out your nieces are at school, they could be in danger.”

Harmony smiled faintly. “Rhapsody took care of that. They’ll be completely safe at school—or anywhere else for that matter.”

Harnketi cleared her throat. “Can you ask her to say my name out loud?” she asked quietly.

“Can you say Harnketi out loud, Eileen?”

“Harnketi?” Eileen asked hesitantly.

Harnketi vanished, followed a second later by a startled gasp from the phone.

“Thanks, Eileen,” Harmony said gratefully. “I’ll talk to you soon.”

Joline smiled wryly. “Well, that was anticlimactic.”

Harmony arched an eyebrow. “What were you expecting? Fireworks and dancing girls?”

Joline gave her a level look, and Taxti snorted a laugh. “I was hoping to pick her brain before she left.”

“She’ll be back,” Rhapsody assured her with a soft smile. “If for nothing else, then to get some yuccas fitter.”

“So...” Harmony bit her lip. The desire she'd held at bay returned, filling her like a drug. "The kiddos are gone to school for the day, and the house is empty..."

Rhapsody’s slow smile turned Harmony’s knees to butter, and a swarm of butterflies tried to fly away with her stomach. “We’ve got four hours. Let’s make them count.”

2 – FREEDOM

Mystery sighed as she waited for the agent on her protective detail to inspect the safe house before allowing her to enter.

It had been a grueling two days. She'd been grilled by senior intelligence analysts, counterintelligence specialists, and a team of psychologists, as well as a group consisting of physicists, anthropologists, and parapsychologists. They'd put an fNIRS helmet on her head for monitoring her brain waves throughout the entire process.

They'd even brought psychics in, though they called them Cognitive Anomaly Researchers. They hadn't spoken to her at all—they just sat in the room and tranced out.

Partway through one of the interviews, the CARs, as she referred to the psychics, suddenly all gasped and ran out of the room with expressions of pure terror. She wished they would tell her why, but information was only flowing in one direction.

She regretted declining Rhapsody's request to become a world tree more by the minute. The agent who'd spoken to her the most had told her she was currently the most important person in the world, and that foreign intelligence agencies would have been after her if the FBI hadn't reached her first.

Anxiety wormed its way through her gut as she fretted about how long she'd be the equivalent of a political prisoner.

She hadn't tried to hold anything back during the interviews. She was confident there wasn't any technology on Earth that could threaten Rhapsody's ring. While the analysts had remained professional for most of the interrogation, they'd been unable to hide their unease when she revealed the imminent destruction of the world if Rhapsody failed. The revelation of world trees, dragons, mermaids, spirit walkers, fauns, and leprechauns had been met with varying degrees of skepticism.

She could understand that. If she hadn't seen it with her own eyes, *she* would have doubted it as well. However, the growing evidence of Rhapsody's power had made them more open-minded than they might have otherwise been.

The National Security Advisor had only stepped into the conference room once, after she revealed Rhapsody's ability to teleport people wherever she wanted. She could understand his concern—teleportation would be nearly impossible to defend against.

Special Agent Michaels finally exited the front door of the safehouse and beckoned her to enter. His partner, Special Agent Reinhart, had been waiting next to her with a barely concealed scowl of impatience. He'd exhibited irritation and even disgust since being assigned to her. She wondered if it was an internal matter or something personal. Michaels had grown increasingly uncomfortable with his partner's behavior.

A special task force had been created to handle the "Rhapsody situation," made up of representatives from most of the alphabet agencies, with the FBI tasked with handling Mystery's protective detail.

"The room's clear," Michaels informed her with a nod. "Be advised that everything inside is under constant surveillance, including the bathroom."

Mystery's face flushed, and she glared at him indignantly. "Why, *exactly*, do you need to watch me in the bathroom? This is starting to feel more like a prison."

Michaels' expression didn't change, but he suddenly gave off the air of a babysitter dealing with a whiny child. "Nobody's watching you in the bathroom. An AI monitors all the surveillance. A human only looks if there's something the AI escalates as a cause for concern. All access to the surveillance feed is logged, and alerts are sent to leadership when it's been accessed. Anyone accessing the surveillance feed had better have a damn good reason for doing so."

Mystery sighed, slightly mollified. It still rankled to know that some grubby agent could watch her shower. She was really starting to regret not accepting Rhapsody's offer. Was it too late? Rhapsody was essentially part of the entire planet, with her root system going right through the center and connecting to four other world trees. Would Rhapsody hear her if she asked for help? She was pretty sure she would.

"What about my brother?" Mystery asked anxiously. "When can he visit? Or at least talk on the phone?"

"Probably never," Reinhart said bluntly. "You don't seem to understand the seriousness of your predicament. Assuming you've told us everything you know, you're now nothing but a security liability that foreign governments would love to exploit. Get used to the idea that your old life is over and that you'll be spending the next decade in secure facilities with no contact to the outside world."

Michaels gave his partner a flat look but didn't deny Reinhart's assertions. Mystery didn't try to hide the dislike in her eyes as she glared back at him.

"Thank you for helping me make a tough decision, Agent Reinhart," she said icily. "I have no intention of being a political prisoner for the rest of my life."

He stared back at her with a bored expression. She had an overwhelming desire to stick her tongue out at him. She resisted the urge and turned away, walking through the door.

The inside was sparsely equipped. The furniture looked uncomfortable and cheap. The small kitchen was stocked with paper plates, cups, bowls, and plasticware. She shook her head in disbelief as she continued touring the small area. The bed had a four-inch mattress and a thrift store nightstand and dresser.

She went back into the kitchen and opened the small fridge. Empty. The three cupboards had a combined inventory of one empty saltshaker, a partially full pepper shaker, and a half-bottle of instant coffee that was expired by eight years.

Were all their safehouses this crappy, or were they just trying to send her a message? Maybe it was an experiment to see what happened to a person surviving on pepper and stale coffee. Did they really expect her to eat takeout food indefinitely?

The large apartment building the safehouse was located in looked at least seventy years old. She wondered how many of the other tenants were idiots like her, forced into a kind of witness protection. Did they even have regular tenants, or was the whole building full of political prisoners? And were their apartments as disgusting as this one?

She sighed dejectedly and continued walking through the time capsule of an apartment. The lack of windows was disturbing. How was she supposed to get any vitamin D?

What the hell was she supposed to do all day? She wandered over to the stiff couch to look at an old CRT television dubiously. It had the old telescopic antennas sticking up from the back. She doubted they worked anymore, since everything was digital now. She turned the television on, more out of morbid curiosity than any real interest. She was greeted with white and black fuzz. She turned the analog knob to switch through the channels with the same results. The knob made a plastic clicking sound for each channel. Just how old *was* this TV?

Just before she reached to turn it off, she noticed a shape moving through the fuzz. She tilted her head curiously, trying to make sense of the distortion. It looked like a raccoon, if raccoons were made static fuzz. It turned and appeared to be looking at her expectantly.

"What the hell is going on?" Mystery muttered under her breath. "Did they dump me in a haunted apartment?"

The raccoon shrugged its shoulders in a manner that looked almost human. Could this be something related to Rhapsody? Or was this some kind of prank that bored, spiteful feds did to amuse themselves?

"What the hell are you?" Mystery whispered, mindful of the constant surveillance in the rooms.

She stumbled back in shock when the raccoon began stepping out of the fuzzy television. Her calves hit the couch, and she fell down onto the hard cushions. She winced as she felt a bruise in the making on her left ass cheek.

Damn these cheapskates! she thought in irritation, briefly forgetting the fact that a raccoon was climbing out of her television. It stood on hind legs and stared at her curiously, its head tilted to one side. It would've been cute if the manner of its arrival hadn't been so damn creepy.

"How long are you going to stare at me, mate?" an Australian man's voice said from the raccoon, though its mouth didn't move.

"Uh... um," Mystery stuttered, staring anxiously at the talking raccoon. "Are you, um, a friend of Rhapsody's?"

"That's right, mate," the raccoon confirmed with a nod. "Name's Azeban. Rhapsody asked me to keep an eye on you; we figured these clowns would try to use you to secure a meeting with her if things went well. Unfortunately, things didn't."

"What do you mean?" Mystery asked faintly, feeling like her stomach had lost its attachment to gravity. "Did they do something stupid?"

"You could say that," Azeban answered dryly. "They're convinced she's a demonic entity. There's a vocal group of paranormal advisors who are convinced all manifestations, whether aliens or ghosts, are demons in disguise. The geniuses running the core intelligence agencies are all fundamentalists who want to use you as bait to try and capture Rhapsody."

Azeban shook his furry head in disgust. "She feels bad for putting you in this position, so she's put a ward around you that'll make you unrecognizable to anyone with ill intent. That won't help you get out of here, of course, since anyone unrecognizable is going to be seen as a threat. I'll create a distraction to allow you to leave the building. There's a train station not far from here. Go there after you leave this dump. We'll talk more on the way."

Mystery watched Azeban with a frown. That would explain the disdain from Reinhart. It would also explain the crap accommodations they'd dumped her in. She wouldn't be surprised if she met an accident in the near future to save them the expense of locking her up indefinitely.

She chewed her lip anxiously. "How do I get to the train station? Which direction is it? I don't have my phone, so I'm basically blind when it comes to finding anything."

Azeban snorted a laugh and shook his head. "Your generation is hopeless without your tech. When you walk out of the building, take a right and just keep walking until you see a sign that says Train Depot. Good luck."

As soon as he finished speaking, he vanished.

Her pulse spiked as she stared nervously around the room. Wasn't she being watched on surveillance? What about Azeban's diversion? How long was she supposed to wait?

Gunshots sounded in the distance, followed a moment later by pounding feet as someone ran away from her door. Taking a deep breath, she quickly walked over to the door and tried to open it. It was secured with an electric combination lock on both sides. She really was a prisoner.

As she stared at the lock in consternation, there was a click, and the door slowly opened. She reached out with a shaky hand and opened it all the way, poking her head outside. There was no sign of either agent.

She tentatively walked outside and moved down the stairs. She noticed another person exiting an apartment on the second floor. They had a shopping bag and wore casual clothing. So, she really was in a regular apartment complex.

She continued down the stairs, confidence growing as she put more distance between herself and the prison she'd just escaped. The sun was just dipping below the horizon, reminding her she was two nights short on sleep. She wished she had some yuccas fitter.

The thought of the delicious fruit triggered a pang of longing. She'd only been with Rhapsody and her friends for a few hours, but they were such nice people that it had been easy to form an attachment to them.

She sighed regretfully, wishing she were with them now, instead of sneaking away from a federally sanctioned citizen prison. There'd been something so compelling about Rhapsody and Harmony she couldn't put into words. She'd been such an idiot to leave, letting her fear control her better judgment.

Michaels appeared on the stairs as she descended the last flight of steps. She watched him warily. He scowled as he moved up the stairs, muttering about poor life choices. He didn't even look at her when she passed him.

She let out an explosive breath when she reached the ground. Apparently, she really *was* as good as invisible as far as the agents were concerned. She'd only moved a block away from the apartment when she was interrupted.

"Hello dearie," an old woman with a bandana wrapped over her head said brightly. She was hunched over in a permanent slouch, leaning heavily on an ornate cane. Her long, gray hair was frayed and snarled, easily reaching her waist, though with her hunch it hung down in front of her. Her face was lined like dried and cracked leather, and one of her eyes was a milky white, while the other was a milky blue. "Do you mind helping me find my cat? Lord Borris is such a scamp. He's always sneaking outside when I have to take the garbage out."

Mystery groaned inwardly as she smiled back at the old lady politely. She really wanted to get out of this place, even if she *was* disguised. The cat would probably come back on its own when it got hungry.

"What does he look like?" she heard herself ask. She was such a sucker for hard-luck cases.

"He looks like a dairy cow, but you won't get any milk out of *him*," the old woman cackled at her joke, banging her cane on the ground in her mirth.

Mystery smiled awkwardly. "Okay, so black and white splotchy patterns. Does he come to his name when you call him?"

Her maddening reply was, "Only if he wants to, or if it's time to eat."

Mystery suppressed a sigh and looked around at the buildings and alleyways surrounding them, feeling a sense of hopelessness set in. They weren't going to find Lord Borris until he got hungry.

"Okay, I'm going to check that alley," Mystery said, attempting a cheerful tone.

"Oh, bless your heart, dearie," the old woman said with a gap-toothed smile.

There wasn't a lot of traffic on the three-lane road, allowing Mystery to quickly cross the street and move into the alley. There were several garbage cans and two dumpsters haphazardly arranged along the walls. Garbage was scattered all over the narrow space, and the smell of feces was strong in the air. Mystery scrunched her nose in disgust as she moved further into the alley.

"Here, kitty kitty," Mystery called out hopefully. "Come here, Lord Borris."

Dodging a fire escape at the last second, she nearly bumped her head. At six feet and four inches, she found the world contained more hazards than it did for shorter people. Peering over the edges of the garbage cans, she nearly gagged at the stench. Behind one, a golden, short-haired cat looked up at her in alarm, startled from its nap.

"Have you seen a dairy cat anywhere?" Mystery asked the golden furball conversationally.

"He's two alleys down," the cat answered, its mouth making cat sounds while translations appeared in Mystery's head. She groaned and put her head in her hands.

"What's the matter?" the cat asked curiously.

"I've finally lost it," Mystery told it sadly. "I knew I probably didn't survive that crash. I'm probably in a coma in a hospital somewhere."

"I'm not sure what most of that meant," the cat said critically. "Maybe stick to smaller words that would make sense to a cat."

"Okay, sure," Mystery agreed in a bemused tone. She turned and began walking toward the street. "Two alleys down then. Fine."

She wasn't too surprised to find the missing cat in the second alley—if she was dreaming, at least it was a consistent one. Lord Borris was a friendly cat, apparently. He ran right up to her, arching his back and rubbing against her legs. Hesitantly, she picked him up. He began to purr as she carried him back to the street where she'd left the old lady.

"So, are you a talker too?" Mystery asked him with a raised eyebrow.

"With a voice like mine, who wouldn't be a talker?" the cat answered self-importantly, preening in her arms. "Is Nanna looking for me again?"

"Yep, Nanna's looking for you," Mystery confirmed, still dazed. She crossed the street and saw the old woman talking to a group of older children, describing Lord Borris. Before Nanna could finish, the children broke away and hurried off without a backward glance.

"Found him," Mystery called out to the woman. The old lady was staring after the children with disappointment on her leathery face. When she heard Mystery, her face brightened, and she tottered toward her.

"Oh, my word, I can't believe you found him so fast," she exclaimed in amazement. "It usually takes hours of searching."

"So, this is a pretty common routine, huh?" Mystery asked, scratching Lord Borris's ears, much to his delight. "Maybe you should get a collar with a bell, so he jingles when he walks."

The old woman beamed at her. "That's a brilliant idea, dearie. I wonder where I could find something like that."

"You should be able to find one online—" she broke off when she realized she was about to tell an ancient old lady to try and use the internet for shopping. "What I mean is, there should be some pet stores around here somewhere."

"Would you mind carrying Lord Borris back home for me, dearie?" the old woman asked hopefully. "He's a little hard to carry with my cane."

"Sure, no problem," Mystery's mouth answered, while inside she groaned.

"When you get me back to Nanna's, watch out for the guy with the pokey thing," Lord Borris warned her in a contented tone. "Every time she brings someone back, they fall asleep after he pokes them with his metal tooth."

Mystery stopped dead, turning to stare at the old woman warily. "Where do you live?"

"It's not too far, dearie," the old woman assured her with a gummy smile. "Just a few more alleys down, and we can go in through the back door."

Mystery frowned at the woman doubtfully, trying to imagine her being involved in some kind of human trafficking operation. Of course, the fact that she had so much trouble imagining it might be why she could get away with such a disgusting scheme. She seemed so sweet and helpless.

She suddenly recalled the children the woman had been trying to lure into finding Lord Borris. If Mystery walked away from this, there would be more victims. She couldn't exactly call the cops. Even if they didn't recognize Mystery, what could she say? “The cat told me the nice old woman is a human trafficker?”

She needed to do *something*. She wasn't completely helpless. She’d been pretty good at kick boxing before she lost her leg. Now that she had it back, she might still have enough skill sitting in her brain somewhere to make the difference in a confrontation.

As they continued, sweat slicked her palms, and her heart rate spiked. Even if she could overpower the person responsible, it wasn't likely to stop them from doing it in the future. Without law enforcement to witness it, they’d be free to do it again after they recovered.

"How long have you been selling humans for profit?" Mystery asked the old woman conversationally.

The woman froze for a moment before continuing, confirming Mystery’s suspicions. "What on earth are you talking about, dearie?"

"I've seen some strange things in this world," Mystery informed her tersely. "I've seen some terrible things. I've never seen anything as disgusting as what you've dedicated your life to, though. Using people's kindness to hurt them the way you do is the kind of blot on your soul that’ll probably never come clean."

The woman's sweet visage vanished, replaced by a derisive glare. "You know nothing about life, you privileged little bitch. Life is a despicable place where you do whatever you can to survive. Don't talk to me about souls, you pampered powder puff. This life is it, and it's survival of the fittest. Now get in front of me, or I'll put a hole in your pretty little head."

The cane's handle detached, revealing a pistol. She pointed it at Mystery and gestured for her to move ahead.

"No," Mystery shook her head disdainfully. "If you're going to kill me, you'll have to do it right here. You're in for a big surprise when you die and realize what you’ve done to so many other souls."

The old woman sneered. "Nobody's going to believe an old lady killed you. Get walking, or I’ll put a slug in your self-righteous face."

"Then you're going to have to kill me," Mystery said indifferently. She’d nearly committed the deed herself so many times that it held no fear for her.

She shook her head sadly, feeling a pang of sorrow that this woman had found a way to ignore her conscience to such a monumental degree that she was willing to harm children.

The woman aimed the gun, her eyes filled with hate. As she squeezed the trigger, Mystery closed her eyes and smiled, ready for the end. A click echoed as the bullet failed to fire. Mystery opened her eyes to see the woman staring at the gun in confusion, pulling the trigger again and again to the same result.

"What happened to you to make you so callous to the suffering of others?" Mystery asked the woman sadly.

The old woman grimaced at her, smacking the gun with her cane, as if she could bash it into a functional weapon. "What does it matter? The past is in the past, and this is who I am now. I'm not about to start fussing about morals this late in the game."

"I'm sorry for whatever trauma you experienced to make you like this," Mystery told the woman with a mixture of sympathy and disgust. "There's plenty of good in the world still. Every time someone gives in to their darker side, it becomes that much bleaker. How many parents lost the laughter of their children after you stole them away? How many other old ladies will suffer because they will no longer be trusted? I'm sorry for the monster you have become and whatever it was that turned you into this ghoul preying on the weak and innocent."

The woman lifted her cane to strike Mystery, her face twisted with rage and self-loathing. As she raised the cane high into the air, her back suddenly gave out, and she collapsed to the ground with a cry of agony.

Mystery shook her head in disappointment. "You really are a monster."

She put Lord Borris down and turned away, walking toward the train station. The woman began yelling curses at her back, her voice lit with fury. Mystery ignored her.

She was joined by a raccoon when she reached the other side of the street. She glanced down at Azeban curiously as they walked. "Are you responsible for her gun jamming?"

Azeban nodded. "Do you have any idea what Rhapsody would do to me if anything happened to you?" he asked laconically. "Being turned into a hat would be the least of my worries."

A warm glow lightened her heart at the knowledge the beautiful fairy was watching out for her. "Why does she care what happens to me?"

Azeban began skipping on his hind legs, looking ridiculous. "Do you remember the offer she made for you in the circle?" he asked cheerfully.

Mystery nodded, her voice subdued. "To become a world tree."

Saying it out loud made it sound even stranger than thinking it did—actually *becoming* a world tree and projecting an avatar like Rhapsody. "I'm curious why she doesn't just find somebody else for the role. There must be better candidates than me somewhere on Earth."

"Do you think that's really true?" Azeban asked pointedly. "Do you think she wouldn't have picked someone else if there *was* a better candidate than you? If there were even *any* candidates besides you?"

"Wait, hold up," Mystery exclaimed, her stomach churning with sudden anxiety. "What do you mean, if there were even any candidates *besides* me? There must be a ton of other people who could fulfill these roles."

"You know that world trees are transitioned stars, right?" Azeban asked expectantly.

Mystery nodded nervously. "Yeah, Rhapsody mentioned that. What does that have to do with anything?"

"A *regular* spirit can't become a world tree," Azeban explained, glancing up at her significantly. "It takes a mature spirit to become a world tree. You and Harmony are some of the first mature spirits to visit this world since Rhapsody arrived. Harmony has lived through more incarnations than I can imagine, as have you. Your average human might make it to three incarnations before they move on to find easier places to grow spiritually. Harmony and her family are some of the only mature spirits on this world, besides you. I'm sorry to put the world on your shoulders, but without you, this plan is going to be precarious."

Mystery shook her head disbelievingly. "That can't be right. You're telling me that in the hundreds of thousands of years Rhapsody's been on this world, Harmony and I are some of the *only* mature spirits to visit this place?"

Azeban turned to face her, looking absurd as he walked backwards on his hindlegs. "You don't understand how rare it is for spirits to visit mortality repeatedly," he told her gravely. "Mortality's a difficult and painful place. When given the choice to move on to a place without pain, almost every spirit takes that option. Some will visit one or two more times, but that's it. There are a few other mature spirits here *now*, but it takes a special kind of spirit to become a world tree."

"If it's so rare, how are there five of us all within two generations?" Mystery asked shrewdly. "Those odds seem pretty astronomical."

"You came at her request," Azeban said simply.

Mystery stopped walking, pressing her hands against the sides of her head as she stared at the ground. Could she really be here by direct request? Her breath quickened as her anxiety went into overdrive. She felt trapped, a feeling that terrified her.

Losing her leg had brought her close to madness, triggering intense bouts of claustrophobia. It felt as if her freedom had been stolen. As a teenager, she'd been an avid runner and hiker. Eventually, she pushed herself to resume those activities with her prosthetic, but it didn't replicate the freedom she remembered with her real leg. The idea of being trapped in this mortal realm for eons, with her black depressions, made her want to crawl under a rock and hide.

Now, she felt like her choices had been taken. If she didn't accept Rhapsody's request to become a world tree, untold billions would die—possibly even the planet.

That old fear of being trapped crept back into her heart as she looked into the future and only saw one possible option her conscience could live with. She would be stuck with her messed up mental issues forever.

"It's not certain the world will fail without your help," Azeban said reluctantly. "Four world trees would probably be enough to stabilize this world for tens of thousands of years."

Mystery paused, feeling her anxiety ease up a little. They wouldn't fail if she didn't join them—not for a long time, anyway. Tens of thousands of years should be long enough to find another mature soul to incarnate and become a world tree. Hell, that should be enough time for a star to transition and provide the real thing.

Taking a deep, calming breath, she began walking again. She looked down at her fully functional leg and smiled. She'd been whisked away by the FBI too fast to actually spend any time enjoying her restored leg. She broke into a run for the last mile to the train station, grinning as she finally felt the freedom she'd missed so dearly.

She received some odd looks as she passed other pedestrians, her face lit with a radiant smile, but she didn't care. She was finally *free.*

3 – NOURISHING LIGHT

A persistent blush warmed Harmony's cheeks as Rhapsody watched her dress. The fairy lounged on the sofa, her smile suggesting she was mentally replaying the highlights. It was absurd, really—after everything they'd just done, the simple act of pulling on a shirt felt strangely vulnerable.

At least she could breathe again. Something had shifted overnight, as if Rhapsody's touch had finally silenced the frantic hum of Harmony's nerves. For the first time in years, the crushing weight of her anxiety had simply... evaporated.

Rhapsody was like a drug she just couldn't get enough of. Four hours had disappeared far too quickly. The shapeshifting bundle of energy had been full of surprises that made Harmony blush just to think about.

She glanced quizzically at Rhapsody as she pulled on a pair of white shorts. The cold didn't affect her the way it had before her transformation, dramatically opening up her wardrobe options. "How's Mystery doing over at the FBI?"

Rhapsody shook her head in disappointment. "She's having a rough time of it. Turns out the intelligence agencies are run by fundamentalists who are convinced I'm some kind of demonic entity. They locked Mystery up in a rundown apartment in an attempt to lure me over to them. They have a couple of silly psychics who think they can trap me Ghostbusters-style. It's hard for me to imagine just how little these people understand the etheric realm. They're like toddlers walking into a corner to do something they know is wrong—while looking surreptitiously over their shoulder at you."

Harmony's brow furrowed with worry. The thought of Mystery in danger triggered something primal and intensely protective. "Seriously? What are we going to do? We're not going to leave her there, are we?"

"Of course not," Rhapsody scoffed, scowling indignantly. "Azeban already broke her out. She's on a train back here now; I'm hoping the journey will give her a few days to clear her head. I dumped a lot of crazy information on her, and she needs time to process it all. She suffers from severe depression and fears being trapped as an eternally depressed immortal."

Harmony frowned as she slipped her socks on. "What about the intelligence agencies? Are they going to cause us any trouble?"

She sat up and adjusted her shirt self-consciously. She'd skipped the bra, remembering Rhapsody's comment about not being ashamed to be female. She felt too exposed with the protrusions on her chest signaling her state of arousal to the whole world—but Rhapsody liked it, so she'd deal with it.

Rhapsody smirked. "They'll *try* to cause us trouble—they simply lack the capacity to do so. We'll probably need to do something about them eventually. They're already discussing how to vilify us—like convincing the world we're demons. Normally, that wouldn't matter to me because I wouldn't interact with them. However, we have Aurora and Serenity to worry about, as well as Mystery. Until they decide to join us, they need to be able to exist out in the world with some level of normalcy."

"What did you have in mind?" Harmony asked intently. "To deal with the fundies, I mean."

Rhapsody tilted her head to the side, eyeing Harmony with a small smile. "I have a fantastic plan. Are you ready for it?"

Harmony arched an amused eyebrow. "Hold up, let me sit down first." She stepped over to the vanity and sat, watching Rhapsody expectantly. "Okay, I'm ready to be amazed. What's your plan?"

Rhapsody grinned impishly. "I was going to ask *you* what we should do. You were human recently enough to have some ideas for dealing with these kinds of people. Just imagine you're writing one of your novels—what would your protagonist, Rhapsody, do to deal with a secret government full of religious fundamentalists?"

Harmony snorted a laugh. "And here I thought the half-million-year-old fairy would conjure up a brilliant plan, drawing from her enormous pool of knowledge."

Rhapsody's smirk deepened, dimpling her cheeks. "I *did* come up with a brilliant plan. I plan to have *you* come up with a plan. So? How are we going to deal with their smear campaign?"

"Well," Harmony began, bending down to slip on her shoes. "I suppose we already have some positive media on our side. There are plenty of videos showing you rescuing people from human traffickers, as well as rescuing me from David. Maybe we can combat their smear campaign with more heroics. Although, they probably control most of the internet, so they might be able to shut down uploaded videos and censor comments portraying us in a positive light. I guess a lot depends on the extent of their control."

Rhapsody curled up on the sofa, leaning a cheek on her fist and watching Harmony with a mysterious smile. She didn't have to dress the slow way; she simply magicked her clothes back on. She wore dangerously short white shorts that showcased her long, glorious legs.

"Let's assume we have a method to override their censorship," she said, eyes sparkling.

Harmony paused in the act of brushing her hair to stare at Rhapsody's reflection in the vanity mirror. She knew Rhapsody possessed advanced technology but had always thought of it as a kind of magic, not something computer-related. Staring into Rhapsody's twinkling lavender eyes, however, she began to doubt her assumptions.

"Okay," Harmony said slowly. "Who has more control over the internet? You or them?"

Rhapsody winked, causing Harmony's heart to skip a beat. "Let's just say your computers are more like punch cards compared to what I work with."

Those large, expressive eyes were even more communicative than her lips. Harmony occasionally spaced out, that captivating gaze pulling her into a softly glowing trance. She could stare into those huge lavender eyes for hours. Something as simple as a wink was so much more expressive when delivered with the fairy's large, luminous gaze.

"Hi, Harmony," Rhapsody grinned, eyes twinkling with amusement. "Are you back with me yet?"

Harmony shook her head and blinked several times, the trance breaking. A blush crept up her neck as she looked ruefully at Rhapsody. "Sorry, I was just... I mean, I was thinking about..."

She trailed off as she got lost in Rhapsody's beautiful eyes again. The moment stretched out before Rhapsody closed her eyes with a small smile.

Harmony narrowed her eyes suspiciously. "Are you mesmerizing me on purpose? Or is this fairy glamour?"

Rhapsody smiled tenderly, her eyes still closed. "You're just a deeply passionate person, Harmony. It's flattering, I'll admit. I never imagined someone staring at me like you are right now—as if you're seeing your first sunset."

"Sunsets have nothing on you," Harmony told her truthfully. "I just can't help myself. Your eyes and lips are so intensely expressive that I lose track of everything else. It's your fault for making yourself so damn perfect."

Rhapsody threw her head back and laughed her golden laugh, filling Harmony's insides with warmth. She cursed quietly when her alarm notified her school was out. She just wanted another day alone with Rhapsody—ten at the most.

Rhapsody stood and walked over to her. Taking the brush, she began to draw it through Harmony's hair in long, rhythmic strokes, the action feeling oddly familiar.

"Okay, so you want to perform more heroics for the world in hopes of pushing positive sentiment our way," Rhapsody spoke quietly, almost a whisper. "Now I want you to put that creative brain to work and think outside the box. Imagine you have vast magical powers. What would you do if you had access to less conventional resources? Don't put any boundaries on what you think is possible. I'll tell you if it can be done *after* I hear your ideas."

Harmony closed her eyes with a smile, enjoying the sensation of the brush stroking her hair. Rhapsody's soft voice sent tingles rippling up and down her spine and into her head.

"If imagination were no object," Harmony began languidly, "I could think of countless ways to make the problem disappear. I couldn't live with most of them, though. Teleporting all the troublemakers into active volcanoes, for example, probably isn't a good look for heroes."

"Probably not," Rhapsody whispered, her mouth right next to Harmony's ear. Harmony shivered as tingles powerful enough to charge her phone shot down her neck.

Harmony's lips curved into a mischievous smile. "What if we forced everyone to speak the truth? What if, for one week, no one on Earth could tell a lie?"

Rhapsody broke the spell with a burst of golden laughter that filled the room, bouncing off the walls like rays of sunlight. "Harmony, I think that might just collapse civilization."

"Probably," Harmony agreed, smiling as she imagined the fallout for cheating spouses, marketing conglomerates, and politicians. "Okay, my next idea is pretty wild."

Rhapsody raised an eyebrow, a curve of anticipation playing on her lips. "Go on."

Harmony glanced into Rhapsody's eyes in the mirror, then quickly looked away before she got lost again. "I've read this new genre of fiction called LitRPG. A common element in these stories is a leveling system: an overlay that appears in everyone's vision, displaying character information like health, skills, class, and reputation. After I read one a few years ago, I thought humans might be more proactive in making the world better if they had a similar system in real life. Something as mundane as taking the trash out would increase your cleaning skill. And if the leveling system were skewed to reward people for good deeds and not at all for bad ones, the world might just end up with more good people."

She paused, brows creasing in thought. "As far as combating the smear campaign, our reputation and character would be visible to everyone. They'd know we weren't demons. They'd also know we were good people because our reputation would reflect our deeds—not the opinions of the easily influenced masses."

Harmony glanced up into Rhapsody's calculating eyes. "Pretty wild, right?"

Rhapsody beamed at her proudly. "That's why I asked *you*, my beautiful author. I knew you'd devise something far more interesting than playing ping pong with the news media."

Harmony frowned doubtfully. "So, are either of those even possible?"

She couldn't imagine a way to force everyone on Earth to speak only the truth for a week. That still seemed more feasible than implementing a worldwide leveling system.

Rhapsody nodded confidently. "They're both totally possible. The second option would require a good deal of planning, though. You'd need to define all the rules and logic for how different interactions are evaluated. If you're just creating a reputation system to let people observe each other's decency, that's fairly simple. If you want people to actually gain abilities based on the leveling system, that would be more complicated—but still totally doable."

"How?" Harmony asked incredulously. "How could you possibly make a change that affects everyone on Earth with a system like that? We'd need nanobots augmenting our bodies, data centers constantly monitoring and adjusting people's stats, and a way to stay connected to all of them."

Rhapsody smirked and booped her nose with a finger. "You're falling into the same trap astronomers trip over when they say aliens couldn't visit Earth because of the distance to other stars. You're assuming we'd be working with all the knowledge available to *you*, when we'll actually be working with the knowledge available to *me*. There's a great deal you don't understand about how this reality works, so your idea of what's possible is limiting you."

Harmony shivered with growing awe as she stared into Rhapsody's beautiful, impossible eyes. "You're telling me you really could make some kind of leveling system that appears in everyone's vision?"

Rhapsody nodded with a sanguine smile. "Yep, I really can—and I can do it without breaking a sweat."

"You really are somewhere above the gods, aren't you?" Harmony breathed, seeing the small woman in a new light. "Is there *anything* you can't do?"

"Uh-huh," Rhapsody confirmed with a mischievous grin. "I can't fix stupid. Nobody's ever figured that one out."

Harmony dissolved into giggles as she gazed in the mirror at the goddess behind her. She still couldn't fathom how she'd ended up with someone so wonderful—someone so far out of her league. Of course, nobody was really in Rhapsody's league. She truly was several orders above godhood.

Harmony felt a strange buzzing, as if a high-voltage line were vibrating within her bones. The sensation lasted only a split second before disappearing.

"Aunt Harmony, are you home?" Serenity called from outside the room. "And are you decent?"

Harmony sighed regretfully, wryly eyeing Rhapsody in the mirror. "As decent as a politician's campaign promise, Serenity."

"So, you're butt naked and doing things no child should witness?" Serenity asked, her voice filled with apprehension.

Harmony shook her head sadly as she walked over and opened the door. "You're too young to know so much about the harsh realities of politics, Serenity."

Serenity raised an eyebrow pointedly. "I'm thirteen, Aunt Harmony. Besides, with how frequently you mocked politicians and corporate capitalism when I was younger, how could I *not* be aware of the disgusting state of politics?" She drew in an eager breath and actually *bounced* with excitement. "Let's go back to the circle now, okay? I wanna learn more magic!"

Harmony nodded with a smile. "Okay, but you have to tell me how school went when we get there. I'm curious what it was like with the ward surrounding the two of you. Oh, and good job on your eyebrow—you've mastered the arch to the point that it's hazardous to low-flying aircraft."

Serenity's only response was to arch an unimpressed eyebrow, sending Harmony into fit of giggles.

Rhapsody's eyes danced with mirth as she watched Harmony with open adoration. The fairy took Harmony's hand, and a moment later, they appeared near the entrance to Yggdrasil.

Under Rhapsody's affectionate eye, Harmony slowly recovered from her giggle fit. She'd always had a low threshold for what her sister called "Harmony Episodes"—bouts of hysterical laughter that would seize her for up to five minutes, leaving her sides and cheeks sore for hours.

Joline and Aurora were waiting near the entrance to Yggdrasil, along with Taxti and Declan.

Harmony hid a grin as she listened to Taxti and Declan trade barbs.

"So, Aurora," Taxti said, directing a malicious smile at Declan, "were there any reports of students' Lucky Charms disappearing?"

Aurora blinked. "How did you know? Did you come to the school, too?"

Taxti's grin vanished. She stared between Declan and Aurora in sudden consternation. "Wait... someone actually *did* lose their Lucky Charms?"

Declan watched Taxti flounder, a look of supreme satisfaction on his face.

Aurora gave Taxti a peculiar look. “Yeah, Denice couldn’t find hers at lunch. She always brings them as a snack to eat with her lunch. How did you know someone took them?”

Taxti stared at Declan disbelievingly. “You *didn’t*.”

Declan nodded with a smirk. “Aye, that I did.”

Taxti spluttered, momentarily at a loss for words.

Rhapsody began laughing as she watched them. "That one really backfired on you, Taxti."

The faun finally seemed to recover. “I can’t believe you *actually* stole that girl’s Lucky Charms.”

“Really?” Declan asked derisively, hitching up his large belt buckle. “Because the first thing you asked was if someone lost their Lucky Charms. It seems like you actually *could* believe it.”

Taxti took a deep breath. “I was *trying* to insult you.”

Declan watched her struggle smugly. “I had a feeling you would say something stupid like that at some point. As soon as I smelled the Lucky Charms, I knew it was time for a preemptive maneuver. Go ahead and ask her about the rainbow now.”

Taxti blinked, then narrowed her eyes, studying Aurora and Declan suspiciously. Aurora’s lips twitched as she fought to keep from laughing. Taxti let out a sigh of disappointment, watching Aurora sadly.

“You’ve joined the other side already, I see. I thought we’d really hit it off, Aurora.”

“We did!” Aurora assured Taxti brightly, running over and hugging her. “We can play jokes on Declan, too.”

Harmony smiled fondly as she felt the hug through her synesthesia. Rhapsody glanced at her with a knowing smile and a wink.

The disappointment left Taxti’s eyes at Aurora’s embrace. Her lips twitched as her eyes met Rhapsody’s. Harmony squinted at her suspiciously. How much of Taxti’s surprise had been an act?

“I’m still curious about the rainbow part,” Joline announced with a questioning look at Declan.

Rhapsody snorted. “The two of them have been around each other for hundreds of years. They know each other better than they know themselves. Taxti was going to ask Aurora if they found any gold at the end of a rainbow. Something tells me Aurora has some gold in her pocket she was going to pull out if the conversation made it that far.”

Aurora sheepishly reached into her pocket and pulled out some heavy golden coins. “Declan said it’ll disappear at sunset, so it’s kind of worthless.”

Joline glanced between Rhapsody and Aurora doubtfully. “So, *were* there any missing Lucky Charms or not? Or has Aurora been practicing artistic license?”

Aurora hung her head, smiling contritely. "Sorry, Grandma."

Harmony grinned at her niece proudly. "Well done, Aurora. We'll make an author out of you yet."

Joline attempted to maintain a stern expression, but it was marred when she had to bite her lip to keep from smiling.

Rhapsody smiled sardonically. "Okay, now that we've corrupted the children, let's hear about how school went today."

Serenity suddenly giggled. "There were lots of guys in suits who looked really confused. They kept getting phone calls that seemed to confuse them even more. Mr. Anderson said they were with the government but didn't know why they were there. The principal tried to question them a few times as well, but they kept losing track of what they were saying halfway through a sentence. The principal finally called the cops and asked them to escort the government guys off the property, but the cops said they couldn't force federal agents to leave. Declan started tying their shoes together, so they tripped every time they tried to move. It felt like being at a circus where all the clowns wore suits."

Even Taxti laughed as Serenity finished speaking. It sounded like Rhapsody's wards were working as intended, but it was still comforting knowing Declan was there to help if something went wrong.

Harmony smiled gratefully at the leprechaun. "Thank you for going with them, Declan."

Declan winked roguishly. "The pleasure was all mine, lass. I haven't had so much fun in centuries."

Serenity cleared her throat, running her hands through her long hair anxiously. "Susan invited me to her birthday party. I told her things were kind of crazy, so I probably couldn't make it."

"Of course you can go," Harmony insisted after a quick glance at Rhapsody. The fairy gave her a firm nod. "When is it? We need to go gift shopping."

"Really?" Serenity asked in surprise. "It's tomorrow after school. Her mom works on weekends, so she has to do it on a weekday."

"That's no problem at all," Harmony assured her with an encouraging smile. "Do you know what kind of stuff she likes? We can probably get her something generic if not."

Serenity hesitated, glancing at Rhapsody and then quickly away. "Well... there was something she wanted. She asked to meet Rhapsody. I told her that wasn't an option, but that maybe I could bring you, Aunt Harmony, and you could sign one of their books."

Harmony groaned inwardly. She hated the very idea of signing books—it seemed so pretentious. However, if it was for her niece, she'd just have to suck it up and deal with it. Her nieces had suffered enough in their short lives. Harmony wanted to give them every chance to balance out the negativity they'd experienced with positivity.

"I can do that," Harmony beamed at Serenity, willing her face to look enthusiastic.

"Really?" Serenity exclaimed, running over and throwing her arms around Harmony. *"Oh, thank* you, Aunt Harmony! I know how much you hate this stuff. I'll do something super nice to make it up to you."

Harmony shook her head. "You don't need to do anything to make it up to me, you goose," she chided Serenity fondly, shivering slightly as her synesthesia played both sides of the embrace. "Seeing you happy is more than enough of a reward."

Serenity stepped back and smiled up at her radiantly. "You really are the best, Aunt Harmony."

Harmony rested an affectionate hand on Serenity's shoulder. "We have a lot of good memories ahead of us. I'm glad we have this chance to start making some."

Serenity stared at her with a wondering grin. "It's still so weird to see you and Grandma with lavender-colored eyes. That's definitely going to get some attention."

Harmony smiled ruefully. "Oh yeah, I'd almost forgotten about that. I guess I look more fairy than human right now, don't I?"

"All but the ears," Serenity agreed enviously. "I can't *wait* until Aurora and I can become fairies, too."

Harmony patted her head fondly. "You just focus on having as much fun experiencing the rest of your childhood as you can."

Rhapsody stepped forward with an expectant grin. "Are you two hungry for some yuccas fitter?"

"So ready!" Serenity blurted excitedly.

"Yes!" Aurora chimed in enthusiastically, bouncing on her toes.

Rhapsody snapped her fingers, and a yuccas fitter suddenly appeared in her hands. She twisted the stem off and offered it to the two girls. They eagerly took turns drinking from the large fruit, making ecstatic sounds of appreciation as they drank.

Harmony sighed in disappointment as she watched. "I'm guessing Mom and I don't need to keep drinking yuccas fitter anymore?"

She'd only had it one time, and it had been the most mind-blowing taste she'd ever experienced. She hadn't felt any kind of hunger pangs since her transformation. She was pretty sure she no longer needed to eat. She felt just the barest hint of fatigue, so slight it almost wasn't noticeable.

Rhapsody smiled mysteriously. "I'll show you two what fairies eat. I dare say you'll like it more than yuccas fitter."

Harmony blinked. "Anything better than yuccas fitter will make me explode," she declared, and she was only exaggerating a little.

"Follow me, you two," Rhapsody instructed them with a smile full of promise.

"Can we watch too?" Aurora asked hopefully.

Rhapsody shook her head regretfully. "Sorry, Aurora. It wouldn't be safe for you. You'll get the chance when you're older, if you decide to become a world tree."

"Not if," Aurora said firmly. "*When.*"

"I'm confident that'll be the case too," Rhapsody agreed, casting an indulgent smile over her shoulder as she led Harmony and Joline inside the tree.

"Who's up for a run?" Rhapsody asked playfully. "Joline, I haven't seen you take advantage of that new body yet. Let's see what you've got, old lady."

A loud guffaw escaped Harmony's mouth before she could stop it. "Oh, that's rich, coming from you."

Rhapsody shoulder-bumped her—though at Rhapsody's height, it was more like an elbow bump on Harmony. "Quiet, you," she ordered with a smirk. "Okay, let's boogie!"

She took off like a missile, her legs a blur as she shot ahead of them.

Harmony grinned at her mother and took off after Rhapsody. She poured all her energy into her legs as she shot forward. Her eyes widened when she realized just how fast she was going, her hair flying out behind her, rippling like a banner in the wind.

She'd thought Rhapsody was fast when they'd raced by the beach a few days ago, but the fairy had clearly been holding back—a lot. Harmony reached the chasm in less than ten seconds. When they'd walked the same distance the day before, it had taken fifteen minutes.

Rhapsody was waiting for her near the chasm, a radiant smile dimpling her face. Harmony flushed when she saw that smile. She was glad she no longer had trouble breathing, or she would've been seeing spots. Her fairy looked *so* damn beautiful. The wind had scattered Rhapsody's scarlet hair around her, strands trailing down her shoulders, back, and chest. She was like a fairy tale princess—well... just the fairy part.

Joline arrived a few seconds later, beaming with exhilaration.

"It's been so long since I could run without pain that I'd forgotten how enjoyable it is."

Harmony looked at Rhapsody curiously. "How fast were we running? It felt close to a hundred miles per hour."

"Pretty close," Rhapsody acknowledged, slowly looking Harmony up and down with an appreciative smile. "It's great for the mussed hair look."

"I'll second that," Harmony fervently agreed, eyeing Rhapsody hungrily.

Joline let out an exasperated laugh. "Just chill out, you two. I'm sure you'll have more alone time tonight at some point."

Harmony sighed, shoulders slumping in disappointment. It was so hard to keep her hands from roaming all over Rhapsody. She was the embodiment of the word 'appealing.'

"*Fine*," Rhapsody grumbled petulantly. She took a deep breath and then gestured at the beam of light shooting into the chasm. "That's where we feed. Get ready, 'cause it's intense."

Harmony raised an eyebrow at her word choice. Before she could ask any follow-up questions, the shaft of light intensified. An ocean of liquid light flooded over the edge of the chasm and washed over them.

Harmony gasped in shock as waves of euphoria enveloped her. The faint sense of fatigue she'd noticed vanished, replaced by a torrent of vitality. She quivered with the sudden surplus of energy. Joline looked as oversaturated as Harmony felt, practically bursting at the seams. She half expected light to leak out of their ears and mouth as the exquisite pressure swelled inside them.

Rhapsody soaked up almost all the liquid light. Harmony stared at the fairy in awe as she witnessed just how much power Rhapsody was capable of consuming. Harmony and Joline had become gorged on a tiny fraction of the energy Rhapsody absorbed.

As the last of the liquid light disappeared into Rhapsody, the chasm returned to normal, the beam of light continuing its circuit into the planet.

A blissful moan escaped Harmony's lips. "That was... something," she whispered in amazement, still overflowing with the supercharged light.

Bright-eyed and radiant, Rhapsody beamed at them. "I told you it was better than yuccas fitter."

Joline nodded, dazed. "It sure was. How often do we recharge?"

Rhapsody stretched, arching her back and running her fingers through her thick hair. An erotic moan of contentment escaped her lips, a sound that went straight to Harmony's libido. "It depends on how much energy you expend. I usually visit once a week. The two of you'll need to return daily until you've fully transformed. That supercharged feeling is the light stretching your meridians. They'll need to continue expanding until you reach maturity."

"Oh, darn," Joline complained dryly. "Don't make me do it every day, please."

Rhapsody laughed, watching the two of them fondly. "I know you two don't remember me right now, but we've known each other for a long, long time. It's so good to be with you again. I've missed you so much."

Harmony stared at Rhapsody curiously. She was clearly referring to their spirits. Just how long had they known each other? After all, what was time to an immortal?

Rhapsody stretched again, arms reaching outward and sending Harmony's pulse into the red. "Now that you've had your first charge, you'll start to feel some of the powers inherent to your character. Most of them will need to remain dormant while you grow, but there are a few you can use without expending energy. The one you'll want to start practicing is the ability to shapeshift. When the time comes to revive your world trees, you'll need to be able to project your own avatar. It can be difficult to master, so you'll want to start now."

Harmony’s cheeks flushed as she remembered the previous night. “I’m ready to learn.”

Rhapsody’s lips twitched as she watched Harmony with a sparkle in her lavender eyes. “Good girl.”

4 – TRAIN

Mystery drew a lot of attention as she stood in line at the train depot. Her face had been plastered all over social media and the news for several days now, and the raccoon sitting at her feet only amplified the effect. She stood stiffly, knowing it was only a matter of time before someone started questioning her about Rhapsody and the circle.

"Excuse me," a man in a MultiCam military jacket said beside her.

She stifled a sigh and turned to face him. His dark eyes studied her intently. She took in his mop of dark-brown hair and tan face, dominated by a prominent, beaklike nose. He was several inches shorter than her—though, admittedly, most people were.

"Yes?" Mystery answered, her tone polite but preoccupied.

He glanced down at Azeban, then met her eyes with open fascination. "Are you the one who crashed inside that fairy ring?"

All eyes focused on Mystery, the dozen other customers making no attempt to mask their interest.

Mystery offered a hopeful half-smile, though her tone was doubtful. "Um...would you believe me if I said no?"

He blinked, then grinned conspiratorially. "I won't tell anyone."

Mystery barely stopped an eye roll, glancing at the other people who probably *also* wouldn't tell anyone. *Yeah, right.*

He leaned forward excitedly. "I've heard a ton of crazy rumors about what's inside the rings. Is there really a skeletal demon who harvests souls in there?"

"You mean Harnketi?" Mystery asked, frowning. "She doesn't harvest souls, and she's not a demon. She's a Baykok."

"Harnketi?" he repeated the name slowly, seeming to taste it. "What's a Baykok?"

"Harnketi is a Baykok," Mystery replied with a shrug. "Now you know about as much as I do about Baykoks. I think Rhapsody said Harnketi hunts men who prey on women."

Another man stepped closer, his face dubious. "I've heard a lot of people claim Rhapsody is really a demon in disguise."

Mystery turned to face the middle-aged, balding man, who sported a gold tooth and a bullseye tattoo on his forehead. *Who puts a bullseye on their own head?*

Mystery scowled, planting her hands on her hips. "Who's claiming she's a demon? We were the first humans to enter the rings, so where's this information coming from?"

The man shrugged with a wry smile. "Psychics, supposedly. I've never had so many psychics pop up in my YouTube feed. I'm not a conspiracy theorist, but it seems a little contrived."

Mystery glanced at the curious faces watching her, wondering if she should tell them about her ordeal with the intelligence agencies and what she'd learned. It's not like it would make any difference—nobody would believe them anyway.

Mystery sighed, shaking her head in disgust. "The people in charge didn't like what I told them about Rhapsody. Rather than grow up and accept the truth—even when it's hard—they decided it must be a lie and that she was a demon."

"What truth?" he asked intently. You could've heard a pin drop in the large room. Even the clerk was watching, customers forgotten.

Mystery took a deep breath. "Rhapsody is a projection of the world tree, Yggdrasil. She's the only thing keeping this planet alive right now, and the clock's ticking. She has a plan to save the world, but it depends on other people."

She sighed dejectedly, then inspected the suddenly anxious faces watching her. She tried to see them as individuals, with their own hopes, dreams, struggles, and triumphs. These were the people depending on her to make the right choice: to accept Rhapsody's request to become a world tree.

"I don't understand," a young mother with a toddler said apprehensively. "How is she keeping the planet alive, and why does she need to?"

"It's complicated," Mystery said wearily. "To keep it short, an opportunistic alien destroyed the other world trees on this planet around a thousand years ago, and Rhapsody's the last one. It's getting harder every year for her to keep the world alive. She needs certain people to take on the role of new world trees to take the strain off her shoulders. There aren't very many people who can fulfill that role."

The first man looked at her shrewdly. "Is that what she wanted you for?"

Mystery flinched, her shoulders hunching. She turned away and walked to the ticket counter, ignoring the line of people watching her.

"I was told you have a ticket waiting for me," she told the clerk expectantly. "Could I please have it now?"

"Mystery Donovan?" the clerk murmured, nodding slowly. "I'd ask for ID, but I don't think there's anyone who wouldn't recognize you. Here's your ticket. It was nice to meet you."

"Thanks." Mystery took the ticket gratefully and hurried past the silently watching crowd.

Mystery replayed the conversation in her head, wishing she'd just kept her mouth shut. She couldn't shake the image of the young mother's worried expression—worried for her child's future.

Her eyes filled with tears, and her throat tightened as she sat on a bench to wait for her train. She wished more than anything that her brother could be here right now. He was an idiot, but he was the only one who'd ever been able to guide her through the land mine of her tangled thoughts.

She'd always been moody, certain triggers sending her spiraling downward until she could barely function. Something as trivial as failing to assemble a piece of boxed furniture correctly would drive her into a tailspin of self-loathing.

She'd struggled with suicidal thoughts since her fourteenth birthday. The idea of being trapped in an immortal tree with her melancholy thoughts for millions of years was terrifying. Sometimes she could barely make herself finish the day. Being stuck in the form of a giant tree for eternity was nightmare fuel.

She put her face in her hands, trying to hide the tears that began spilling down her cheeks. She knew the decision should be easy. What did her suffering matter, compared to billions of lives? Yet no matter how she framed it, the thought of being trapped in this living hell filled her with stark, unshakable terror. She would become a giant tree, unable to die while she watched her brother age and expire, leaving her utterly alone.

"What made you want to become a pilot?" Azeban asked quietly.

Mystery jumped, nearly letting out a yelp of surprise. She'd forgotten he wasn't just a raccoon. Awkwardly, she wiped away the evidence of her meltdown, sniffing loudly as she tried to pull herself together.

Azeban just waited, patiently watching from the chair beside her.

"It was like the ultimate expression of freedom," Mystery muttered, her throat still tight. She could feel more tears just waiting for a chance to escape.

"I could leave the world behind and go anywhere I wanted—no roads or boundaries. It was an indescribable feeling every time I took off and watched the ground shrink below me. All my cares and worries faded, left behind on the two-dimensional surface. I'd put on a playlist of my favorite music or an audiobook and just lose myself in the freedom of the third dimension."

Azeban raised an eyebrow, an expression that, on a raccoon, nearly brought a smile to her lips. "Rhapsody told you about spirit walkers, right, mate?"

Mystery gave a short nod. "She told us about a spirit walker who killed the other world trees."

She wished she had some tissues. The FBI had taken all her possessions, leaving her without a phone, money, or even ID. She was glad the clerk had recognized her.

Azeban grabbed his chin in his paw thoughtfully, which brought a welcome surge of humor and a smile to Mystery's face.

"You may or may not have made the connection when Rhapsody told you about the time she hunted that spirit walker down. World trees are also spirit walkers. You aren't just a giant tree on planet Earth. You can go to any world you want, unconstrained by things like physics. If you think flying an airplane is amazing, you should try flying through outer space or traveling to the other side of the galaxy—*without* a vehicle. There are no boundaries or roads for a spirit walker. In fact, you won't find a being with more freedom than a world tree. Just some food for thought."

Mystery nodded, humiliation still clinging to her after her public breakdown. She looked around discreetly but couldn't see anyone in the distant benches watching her. Maybe she'd only made a fool of herself in front of Azeban.

A train pulled into the station, its brakes squealing. An announcement confirmed her train had arrived. She stood, a fresh wave of embarrassment washing over her as she realized she had no luggage. She had no way to get clean clothes or bathe. She was going to be stuck in the same outfit for a week of travel.

Maybe she could borrow someone's phone and contact her brother, but what good would that do? He couldn't ship clothes to a moving train, and she couldn't simply get off and go shopping. Sighing, she resigned herself to growing progressively stinkier as the week progressed.

She showed her ticket and was directed to a cabin several cars down. Maybe she could just stay there and sleep the whole way back. The realization struck her suddenly; she hadn't had a moment to truly consider her situation amid the overwhelming chaos. She had simply been following Azeban's directions.

She glanced around, half-expecting to see the furry raccoon walking behind her.

He was gone.

Feeling suddenly more alone than she had in years, she found her cabin.

Where was she going anyway? She checked her ticket for the first time and saw her destination was San Francisco. So, she was headed toward Rhapsody—back to where her life had begun to fall apart almost fifteen years ago.

She blinked rapidly as tears welled again. A train attendant approached from the far end of the car, and she ducked inside her cabin before the tears overflowed, embarrassing the hell out of both of them.

As soon as she was inside the small cabin, she closed the door and leaned against it, sliding to the floor as another wave of emotion opened the valves on her tear ducts. She stared up at the ceiling as her eyes overflowed. She didn't even know why she was crying.

"Hello, Mystery," a melodic voice said gently.

Mystery drew a startled breath and looked down, finally noticing her cabin mate.

Rhapsody stood across the cabin near the window, a compassionate smile on her perfect face. Mystery inhaled deeply as a fragrance like freshly bloomed spring flowers filled the air.

Rhapsody crossed to Mystery, love and understanding shining in her large eyes. She nudged Mystery's legs flat, then climbed onto her lap, straddling her thighs.

Embarrassment burned on Mystery's face at the intimacy, but Rhapsody smiled reassuringly and pulled her into a tight embrace. The scent of spring flowers intensified, intoxicating.

"You're not alone, Mystery," Rhapsody whispered into her ear. "I'll always be with you. I'll always protect you. I won't let anyone hurt you ever again."

Rhapsody's words were like dynamite dropped onto a dam. Mystery let out a wail, wrapping her arms around the fairy and shaking with heart-wrenching sobs. Strength radiated from Rhapsody, settling around her like a shield. For a moment, Mystery could almost believe she was safe—that Rhapsody really could protect her.

Rhapsody held her comfortingly as Mystery finally released her grief, fear, and anxiety.

She fought the urge to pull away from Rhapsody, finding it difficult, if not impossible, to trust anyone else with her safety. She'd learned long ago that the people meant to protect you couldn't be trusted when you needed them most. Her thoughts shied away from the memory of her parents as if they were hot coals scorching her mind.

She'd pushed herself to become stronger, more independent, more capable, and above all else, untouchable. She would never let her guard down again. There was nobody else who was going to save her—she only had herself to save herself.

Rhapsody's mouth brushed Mystery's ear as she spoke softly. "Can I tell you about Harmony's childhood?"

Mystery's brows knit in confusion as her tears finally slowed. "What about it?"

Rhapsody's voice grew heavy with sadness. "I want to show you, so you can really understand what happened to her. May I?"

Mystery nodded once, feeling an unconscious sense of foreboding. A moment later, images and memories flooded her consciousness. She gasped, witnessing the nightmares Harmony had endured for the eighteen months in her father's lab of horrors. It was worse than any horror movie, more terrible than she would have thought possible.

How was Harmony so normal? How was she able to take care of her nieces and live a normal life at all with those horrors in her psyche? How could someone be burned alive repeatedly and still have any sanity left to cling to?

She thought she'd emptied her tear ducts, but as she witnessed Harmony's brutal violation and torture at the hands of her own father in her early childhood, new tears welled up. She wept for the cheerful, beautiful woman she'd briefly met two nights ago.

The images didn't stop there. She marveled at Harmony's life of unending service, dedicated to raising her nieces when her traumatized sister was too broken to get out of bed. She watched in awe as Harmony cared for her grandmother during the last four years of her life, then in horror as she dealt with the brutal murder of her sister.

How could anyone endure so much pain? How could they continue waking up in the morning, let alone take care of everyone around them? Mystery knew she'd have broken long ago if she'd been dealt the same hand.

Her favorite author had a character that reminded her of Harmony—a woman who'd been through hell and emerged with her spirit still burning brightly. Mystery envied that character and wished she possessed that same unshakable strength, the kind that could face life's horrors and keep going.

"Did I ever tell you Harmony's an author?" Rhapsody asked, a hint of a smile in her voice.

"She is?" Mystery frowned, picturing the blond beauty writing novels. "What's her pen name?"

"You already know it," Rhapsody said, her voice almost bubbling with laughter. "You've been reading her books for the last three years."

Mystery gasped, her eyes widening. "No *way*!"

"Yes way," Rhapsody chuckled, leaning back to look into Mystery's eyes. "Pretty amazing, right?"

"That's *Harmony*?" Mystery demanded in disbelief. "But she's so *young*."

"She might be young in body, but her soul is very old indeed," Rhapsody said softly, her eyes full of love. "Just like you, Mystery."

Mystery struggled to reconcile the secretive author she'd obsessed over for the last few years with Harmony's youthful face. She'd pictured a middle-aged woman, possibly older, as the real face behind the pseudonym.

"How old *is* she?" Mystery asked incredulously. "She can't be over twenty-two."

"Twenty-three, actually," Rhapsody corrected with a dimpled smile. "She published her first novel in high school. I think you've seen enough to understand why her writing carries such depth of feeling. She's a pretty amazing woman—pretty *and* amazing."

Mystery's lips twitched as she stared into the playful fairy's enormous eyes.

Rhapsody's position on her thighs, face only inches away, suddenly registered. She felt the soft curves pressed against her, and a wave of warmth spread from her abdomen.

Rhapsody suddenly grinned mischievously. "Harmony has one more secret for you to figure out when you see her again. And it's a doozy. I wish I could time travel so I could see your face when you find out—I don't wanna wait."

Mystery tilted her head, her lips curving into a curious smile. "What is it?"

Rhapsody snickered. "If I told you, it'd ruin the fun of watching you figure it out. You're just going to have to be extra observant when you're with her."

Mystery's breath caught at the thought of being with Harmony again. She'd liked Harmony before, in a casual kind of way. She was funny, kind, and beautiful. Knowing she was her favorite author pushed her past the acquaintance zone, straight past the friend zone, and right into the naked desire zone—emphasis on naked.

Rhapsody threw her head back and laughed, a sound that would make angels envious, warming Mystery's damaged heart.

Rhapsody's face grew serious as she looked back at her.

"The reason I showed you Harmony's memories is because I want you to know you aren't alone in your traumatic past. Harmony has dealt with her own demons as a result of her trauma. She puts on a normal face, but she has *major* self-esteem issues. Until recently, she would unconsciously hold her breath when she felt overwhelmed—a holdover from her childhood trauma."

Rhapsody leaned her forehead against Mystery's, a soft smile on her face. "The difference between you and Harmony is that she has a loving mother who'd cut off her own arm to keep her daughter safe, someone who's been there to help Harmony on the bad days. I know you have your brother, but it's not the same as having a mother's loving care. With Harmony, you'll have someone who understands the kind of hell you've been through, someone who'll move heaven and Earth to make you smile on your bad days. You'll never be alone with Harmony by your side."

Rhapsody pulled her into a soft embrace, then leaned back, smiling warmly. "I'll leave you to think things over. There are fresh clothes for you on the bed. Your brother will be joining you tomorrow morning. He'll be here with you to talk things over for the rest of your trip."

Mystery almost laughed with relief at the thought of fresh clothes. And her brother?

"How did my brother get out here?"

A pang of sadness struck her that Rhapsody was about to leave. Having her warm body pressed against her felt good in so many ways.

Rhapsody shrugged, the motion triggering a blush. "I'm teleporting him. He doesn't know about this yet, so make sure you enjoy the look on his face when it happens—assuming you're awake when he arrives."

Mystery's shoulders shook as she laughed, jostling Rhapsody in a very distracting manner.

"I can't wait to see his face," Mystery said when her laughter subsided. "Thank you for coming here, Rhapsody. And thanks for the clothes."

"Of course," Rhapsody leaned back, beaming. "I know you don't remember right now, but you and I are very close. We've been together for an extremely long time. There's nothing I wouldn't do for you, Mystery. You, me, and Harmony go way back, in other lives we've lived. Goodbye for now, Mystery. Get some sleep."

"I would *love* some sleep," Mystery announced, trying and failing to stifle a yawn. "I have a feeling these beds are going to be too short for me."

"I fixed it for you," Rhapsody assured her with a dimpled smile. The radiant fairy leaned forward, kissed Mystery's forehead, and vanished.

Mystery blinked as the weight lifted from her thighs. A regretful sigh escaped her lips, quickly turning into a huge yawn. Sleep. That's what she needed.

She stood up with a groan. Sitting on the hard floor for so long had done her tailbone no favors.

With a curious smile, she walked over to the bed. What had Rhapsody meant when she said she'd "fixed it" for her?

She stared in grinning amazement at the foot of the bed. Instead of ending at the wall, a hole in the air led to another bed—this one a *huge* bed. She eyed it thoughtfully. The portal was large enough for her to easily crawl through and just sleep on the larger bed. Was that Rhapsody's intent? Or had she only meant for her legs to go through the hole?

Experimentally, she sat down on the small train bed, frowning at the thin mattress. With an adventurous grin, she crawled through the portal onto the larger bed.

She wondered whose bed Rhapsody had attached to her cabin. Whoever it was, they could throw parties on a bed this size.

She stood up and quickly stripped off her dirty clothes, hoping Rhapsody's mischievous nature didn't extend to dropping her into some stranger's bed.

She crawled under the covers and breathed a contented sigh. This bed was *comfortable*. The thought barely had time to form before she fell into a deep, dreamless sleep.

* * *

"No, I will *not* wait on hold," Michael snarled into the phone. "You've already put me on hold over two dozen times, transferring me back and forth between departments like a hot potato. I want to speak to someone higher up the food chain. Let me speak to your supervisor, manager, director—*anyone* who will talk to me for more than five seconds!"

"I'm sorry, sir, but your tone is extremely combative," the curt voice of an older woman said with a hint of irritation. "Call back when you have better control of your emotions."

"Don't you dare hang up—" Michael screamed in rage as the line went dead.

He'd been fighting his way through the bureaucracy of the FBI and Homeland Security for the last six hours, trying to find out what they'd done with his sister. Her phone went straight to voicemail every time he called. He was beginning to suspect they'd stuffed her into a bunker somewhere, and that she might never see the light of day again.

He was still in Mystery's house, where the FBI goons had taken custody of her almost three days ago. He walked to the coffee maker and started another pot. He hadn't slept since the agents had absconded with Mystery, and he was so tired that his blinks were turning into ten-second naps as he forgot to open his eyelids again.

"Hello, Michael," a melodic voice greeted him from across the kitchen. "I've got a much better pick-me-up than that swill."

Michael whirled around in surprise, freezing when he saw the lavender-eyed fairy his sister had described. She wore a green summer dress that fell to mid-thigh, her long red hair cascading down her shoulders to her waist. Enormous eyes and pointed ears gave her an unmistakably otherworldly beauty, straight out of a fairy tale.

Her softly glowing wings reflected off the black countertops. She watched him with an amused expression, turning a large red fruit in her hands, a variety he'd never seen before.

"Rhapsody?" Michael asked, bemused. Maybe the lack of sleep was finally getting to him.

"Good guess," Rhapsody smirked, walking toward him. She twisted the stem off the fruit, leaving a hole in the top. "Drink this. You can put it in a cup if you don't want to drink it straight from the fruit."

"What is it?" he asked suspiciously.

She firmly pushed it into his hands. "Yuccas fitter. It'll restore your body to a version of you that's one week younger. It also takes care of all the things sleep takes care of, so you'll be fresh and alert. And it's ridiculously delicious."

"Do you know where Mystery is?" Michael asked quickly. "The FBI abducted her, and I can't get anyone to give me any answers."

She smiled at him reassuringly. "She's on a train headed this way. She needed time to work through some tough decisions. I was hoping I could take you to her, so she has a friendly face to talk things over with. She really misses you right now."

He wrinkled his brow in confusion. "How do we get to her if she's on a train?"

Rhapsody looked up at the ceiling musingly. "We could fly, teleport, portal, or go to Harmony's house." She met his gaze with a smirk. "I'd suggest a portal, personally."

"Oh," Michael mumbled, nonplussed.

"Drink up," Rhapsody said crisply. "She won't be able to talk to you if you're asleep."

He peered suspiciously into the fruit, where a nuclear green liquid sloshed. "This is safe for humans?"

"Of course," Rhapsody said patiently. "I wouldn't have given it to you otherwise."

Tentatively, he sipped the radioactive liquid.

He gasped when his taste buds finally sent the right signals to his brain. Eyes wide, he tilted the fruit to his lips and drank greedily.

Rhapsody winced. "You sound like an obscene phone call. I guess 'ecstasy fruit' was a good word for an anagram."

He emptied the fruit, feeling a sense of regret when he'd drained the last drop. He'd never tasted anything even close to as good as that yuccas fitter.

Warmth spread slowly from his stomach, suffusing the rest of his body. His mood shifted from sleep-deprived edgelord to bubbly menace. Everything seemed brighter, richer, as if he'd spent his entire life seeing in sepia.

Rhapsody grinned cheekily. "Okay, ready to go solve a Mystery?"

Michael winced, rubbing his neck. "I wouldn't advise making puns with her name," he warned. "She's heard them all."

Rhapsody tilted her head back with a sanguine smile. "That sounds like a challenge—challenge accepted."

He raised his hands helplessly. "Don't say I didn't warn you."

As his thoughts snapped back into focus, the absurdity of the moment struck him. He was standing in Mystery's kitchen, talking to a fairy.

He couldn't stop staring; there was something undeniably beautiful about her, alien and otherworldly in a way no human comparison quite fit.

He jumped as a hole in the air opened in front of him, revealing the cabin of a passenger train. He stared, wide-eyed, as the ground moved past the cabin window. The small bed was empty, and there was no sign of his sister.

"Here, take this with you." Rhapsody snapped her fingers, and another yuccas fitter appeared in her hands. She handed it to him with a severe expression. "This is for *her*, not you. And watch your head; these trains weren't made with giants in mind."

Michael stared at the empty cabin, confused. "Where's Mystery?"

Rhapsody nodded at the bed, an amused twinkle in her eyes. "She's probably on the other side of the portal at the end of the bed. Just shout through it and she'll come crawling back—especially if you tell her you have some yuccas fitter."

Michael walked through the portal, ducking his head as he entered the small cabin.

"See you soon," Rhapsody waved cheerfully just before the portal closed.

Michael shook his head, wondering if he'd fallen asleep and was having a lucid dream.

He walked over to the bed and found the portal Rhapsody had described. His sister was dead to the world in a giant bed. He frowned, wondering if he should let her sleep—she could probably use the rest. He looked down at the yuccas fitter and grinned ruefully. Nope, she wouldn't need *any* sleep if she had some of this.

"Hey, Mystery!" Michael called through the portal.

She jerked awake, looking in surprise at the foot of the bed where the portal opened.

"Michael?" she asked, rubbing sleep from her eyes. "Did Rhapsody bring you?"

He snorted. "No, I made my own portal."

Mystery chuckled, snapping fully awake. "I deserved that. Go find something interesting to do in the cabin while I get dressed."

He rolled his eyes and went to the window. He'd never been on a train. It was a lot smoother than a bus or car. They were passing through a rural farm town, the train horn blaring as they neared a crossing.

"I've got some yuccas fitter for you!" he called, watching a line of cars waiting at the crossing.

He heard rustling and turned to see her quickly crawling through the portal, her face alight with eagerness. He laughed and handed the fruit over to her.

She took it and hugged him tightly.

"It's so good to see you, Michael," she said, her voice thick with emotion, right on the edge of a meltdown. "Thank you so much for coming."

5 – ANGELS

Harmony felt a warmth bloom in her chest as she watched Taxti instruct Serenity and Aurora in the use of magic. The three stood at the lake's edge, eyes fixed on the water's mirror-smooth surface. The two girls wore expressions of eager fascination, their dark eyes sparkling with delight. It was so good to see them happy.

The moon was a sliver, barely worth calling light—not that Harmony needed it; her second sight painted the world in layered energies that bled softly into the physical, turning the night into something akin to an overcast day.

Inside the circle, the air was thick with the scent of exotic flowers and ripe fruit. Unlike most lakes Harmony had visited, there was no trace of lake mud rot or fish tainting the air. Shimmering lights reflected off mermaids in the distance. She wondered how deep the lake was, remembering her mother's claim that the moat between the two rings was bottomless.

A fond warmth replaced the usual seductive tone in Taxti's voice as she instructed the two girls.

"Technically, you can use any surface for this—even sand or air—but for the best results, find something reflective. First, think of the person, place, or object you want to view. Hold it steady in your inner eye. Then project it onto the surface of the water."

She paused, letting the words settle.

"And when I say project, I mean use your will. You're commanding an image to appear the same way you command your arm to move. Start thinking of everything as an extension of your body, something you can order around like your limbs."

Taxti lifted her chin toward the lake. "Go ahead. Try it."

Aurora and Serenity turned and eagerly stared into the water, their faces tight with concentration. After a few seconds, two separate streams of video appeared on the lake's surface, overlapping at the edges.

Serenity grinned in satisfaction. The water showed a girl her age asleep in a bedroom that had been completely conquered by stuffed animals.

"That's Susan," Serenity said. "And she's clearly in a committed relationship with plushies."

Aurora's scrying feed locked onto the inside of a passenger train cabin. Harmony's breath caught when she saw Rhapsody wrapped around a weeping Mystery.

The moment was heavy with grief, and yet Harmony felt a spark of amusement. Rhapsody's idea of personal space had always been nonexistent.

Aurora's brow furrowed as Mystery wept into Rhapsody's shoulder. "Why's she so sad?"

Taxti smiled wistfully. "It's probably years of grief being released. Rhapsody's had a lot of experience pulling repressed emotional toxins out of people."

Harmony shifted nervously. "I'm not sure we should be spying on Rhapsody and Mystery like this."

Taxti shook her head wryly. "There's no spying on Rhapsody. If you can see her, it's because she's *letting* you."

Harmony swallowed as she watched Rhapsody hold Mystery tenderly. She'd expected a stingy part of her mind to object at seeing her fairy in such an intimate embrace with the beautiful woman, but all she felt was sympathy for Mystery.

When Rhapsody asked if she could share Harmony's traumatic childhood memories with Mystery, Harmony frowned, glancing worriedly at her nieces. She didn't want them to hear the horrors she'd endured. She breathed a sigh of relief when Rhapsody used some kind of mental link to show Mystery instead of speaking aloud.

Aurora and Serenity looked at Harmony with concern when Mystery began weeping again, clapping a hand to her mouth in horror.

Harmony's father had never been a part of her nieces' lives—she had no idea where the bastard even was, assuming he wasn't in prison. She never wanted them to discover just how monstrous the sadistic prick truly was.

She bit her lip to hold back a smile at Mystery's disbelief when Rhapsody revealed Harmony's profession as an author. A flutter stirred in her abdomen at Mystery's growing eagerness to meet her favorite author again.

The image abruptly vanished, eliciting a startled yelp from Aurora.

"It just collapsed," Aurora informed Taxti in confusion. "It felt like a thread getting cut."

Taxti glanced at Harmony in amusement. "That's because Rhapsody kicked us out. I'm sure she has something private to discuss."

Serenity's eyes widened. "She knew we were watching the whole time?"

"What do you think?" Taxti asked archly, planting her hands on her hips. "Nobody spies on Rhapsody without her permission."

"Yeah, I guess not," Serenity agreed with a rueful smile.

Aurora nodded, grinning. "I knew she knew."

Taxti rubbed her palms together, her eyes bright. "Now that you know how to scry, it's time to learn how to detect when someone is scrying on *you*—and how to prevent it."

Joline leaned closer, smirking as she spoke quietly. "Seems you have another fan."

Harmony remembered the excited look on Mystery's face when Rhapsody revealed that Harmony was Mystery's favorite author. She fixed her mother with a stare, searching for a retort, but nothing came.

She stood there with her mouth open, grasping for words. Her mother's smile widened at Harmony's inability to articulate a response.

Harmony settled for a huffy silence and turned back to Taxti, pretending she hadn't just short-circuited.

"You'll need to practice this regularly, until it's second nature," Taxti was saying to her nieces.

Her dark hair glowed softly in Harmony's second sight. What special properties made it glow on the EM spectrum? She shelved the question for later and focused on what Taxti was saying.

"You need to visualize a shield surrounding your mind," Taxti continued. "The more complex and creative, the more resistant it'll be to someone breaking through. However, added complexity requires increased focus. Imagine each layer representing a thread of thought; you'll need to essentially think of multiple concepts simultaneously. I'd suggest starting with something very basic, then increasing the complexity as you grow more proficient."

Taxti paused and looked over at Harmony and her mother. "This doesn't require any magic expenditure, so you two can practice this as well. It'd be a good idea to add this to your daily routine during meditation."

"When we meditate?" Harmony repeated, tilting her head curiously.

Taxti blinked. "Oh, Rhapsody hasn't started you on meditation yet?" She suddenly smirked, eyeing Harmony wryly. "I suppose she's been busy with other... lessons."

Harmony tried to will her face not to blush, but her body ignored her commands. Joline and Taxti laughed as a deep red flush crept up her neck.

Her nieces joined in the laughter, making her blush even harder. Weren't they too young to understand what Taxti was implying? Harmony tried to think back to when she was thirteen, but those memories were a bit of a blur. She'd spent most of her time alone, lost in imagination games with characters from her favorite books.

Taxti directed Harmony and Joline to practice mental shields while Serenity and Aurora attempted to break through. As long as Harmony maintained the thought of a bubble shield around her consciousness, her nieces' scrying attempts failed. The moment she became even slightly distracted, her face would appear on the surface of the water.

Harmony sighed in frustration when her shield failed for the tenth time, allowing her ecstatic nieces to spy on her. "How in the world do you train your mind to *always* have a mental shield active?"

Taxti smirked, her voice dry. "That's what the meditation you've been missing is for. You'll learn to partition your mind and think with multiple threads of consciousness. Without your transformation, it would take decades to learn how to split your thoughts. Luckily for you, it'll probably only take a few sessions to unlock the ability."

Harmony cringed internally at the thought of meditation. She'd tried it a few times and hated it. The idea of emptying her head of thoughts was the *opposite* of what she wanted as an author. It was so damn *boring*. She hoped they had a different method than what she'd found on YouTube.

"Okay, let's move on to light weaving," Taxti suggested, smiling approvingly at the two girls. "You two are extremely quick learners. I'm impressed with how well you're progressing."

Harmony's nieces preened under the praise, their faces beaming as they looked at each other excitedly. Harmony smiled gratefully at Taxti, knowing the faun was deliberately building their self-esteem. She reflected again on how lucky she was to have befriended Rhapsody and her companions.

Harmony froze, a familiar buzzing sensation erupting in her bones. She'd begun associating it with certain kinds of magic, like teleportation. She looked around warily, searching for whoever had triggered her magical sixth sense.

Taxti stopped speaking when she noticed Harmony warily searching the area. "What's the matter?"

"I felt someone using magic nearby," Harmony explained distractedly. She couldn't see anything out of the ordinary, but the electrical resonance in her bones persisted.

Taxti frowned. "What do you mean, you *felt* someone use magic? How does one *feel* magic?"

Harmony shrugged, speaking quietly so as not to alert whoever was nearby. "It feels like my bones are buzzing when someone uses certain types of magic, like teleportation. I can still feel this one, though, so it's not teleportation."

Taxti studied her for a moment, then closed her eyes and took a long, deliberate breath, her chest rising like punctuation.

Harmony felt another low-level buzzing in her bones at whatever Taxti was doing. A moment later, Taxti opened her eyes and smiled excitedly.

"Emily!" Taxti called out. "Oh gods, it's so good to see you! Where have you been?"

A moment later, an *angel* materialized in front of Harmony, her eyes full of curiosity. She had dark hair and the face of an... angel. Her eyes were swirling purple galaxies. Harmony felt an aura of power emanate from the angel, a presence that was both benevolent and protective. Her wings looked as though they were made from clouds, and Harmony could feel how soft they were just by looking at them.

"I had planned to just spectate," Emily said dryly. "Apparently, I'm going to have to find a new method for stealth. I'm not sure how she detected my presence."

"It's her synesthesia," Taxti said musingly. "It seems to be some kind of sympathetic response to magic."

Harmony gaped at the angel in front of her. An *angel*! She was beautiful in a way that could only be described as transcendent. Rhapsody was the only other person she'd ever seen who possessed the same type of fantastical beauty, though Taxti came close.

She hoped like hell this didn't mean all the nonsense from religious dogma was valid.

"Girls, this is Emily," Taxti introduced the angel with a delighted smile as she embraced Emily tightly. "She already knows who you are."

"Please tell me this doesn't validate any of that nonsense from religions," Harmony begged.

Emily and Taxti laughed, releasing each other.

Emily smiled at Harmony, her eyes full of love. "Luckily, that's not the case in *this* universe. We're just regular people, like you. We just come from another realm."

Rhapsody suddenly appeared next to Harmony. "Well... look what the cat dragged in," she said playfully. She floated up and embraced Emily warmly. "Words can't describe how good it is to see you, Emily. What kept you?"

Emily nodded at Harmony. "We lost track of her about twenty minutes ago and got worried. Another node appeared and overclocked time, so we started freaking out. Luckily, it looks like only twenty years have gone by. What's been going on while we were in slow time?"

Rhapsody's face lost its exuberance as she stared back at Emily, her eyes suddenly filled with pain. "Let's talk about this somewhere else."

Emily's eyes tightened with concern. She nodded, and they flew away.

Harmony stared at the others, blinking slowly. "Okay, did anyone else just see an angel? I'm pretty sure that yuccas fitter is still affecting me."

Taxti shook her head, smiling wryly. "We hadn't intended to introduce you to people from other realms for a few more years, but your ability to detect magic sort of fast-tracked that revelation. I don't suppose I could persuade you to forget what you saw?"

Harmony laughed incredulously. "How am I supposed to forget a being like *that*? Her presence was *insane*."

Taxti snorted. "It's a good thing she was holding back, then. We wouldn't want you drooling all over the ground for the next hour while you recover."

Harmony froze. The presence she'd felt earlier suddenly blanketed the area in a towering rage so intense that her knees buckled, and she fell to the ground. The fury was so hot that she half-expected the world to combust around them. The aura fluctuated wildly between rage and soul-crushing sorrow for several seconds before vanishing.

"What was that?" Aurora demanded anxiously. She and Serenity had both fallen to the ground as well and were hesitantly getting back to their feet, eyes fearful.

"I'm guessing Rhapsody just told her what's been going on here for the last twenty years," Taxti answered, looking sadly at Harmony.

Suddenly, Emily was standing in front of Harmony, her face covered in golden tears, and wrapped Harmony in a tight embrace. "I'm *so* sorry, Harmony. I failed you!"

Harmony gasped as waves of overpowering love charged her soul to overflowing. She closed her eyes and soaked up the wonderful feeling.

Confusion flooded her mind as she tried to make sense of the last ten minutes. Was this woman some kind of guardian angel assigned to protect her? Had Rhapsody told Emily about Harmony's childhood, and that's what triggered the emotional storm?

Harmony tentatively wrapped her arms around Emily, which turned out to require different arm placement when the person had wings.

"It's totally fine, Emily," Harmony assured her gently. "You haven't failed anyone. Just look at me! I've never been happier in my life. If having a different past meant losing this, I wouldn't change a thing."

Nothing Harmony said consoled Emily. She was completely devastated, her grief sharp and jagged. Harmony looked over Emily's shoulder at Rhapsody helplessly. Rhapsody's expression was almost identical to Emily's, but when the fairy saw her looking, she quickly changed it to one of commiserating sympathy.

Harmony stared at Rhapsody anxiously. Had she been hiding this kind of soul-crushing grief from Harmony and putting on a happy face the whole time? Why did they feel so responsible for Harmony's childhood trauma?

Harmony struggled to feel anything but happiness as the angel's embrace charged her system with radiant love.

"What happened to Aunt Harmony?" Serenity asked Taxti quietly, her young face determined.

Harmony gave Taxti a warning look, though it wasn't necessary.

Taxti smiled down at Serenity with a mixture of sadness and regret. "When she thinks you're ready, she'll tell you."

After another minute in the emotionally charged embrace, Emily vanished. Harmony stood in shock, her arms still raised where she'd held Emily.

"Where did she go?" Harmony asked, confused. She slowly lowered her arms and looked around.

Rhapsody smiled reassuringly. "She went back to her own realm. She's probably with her husband. Certain disasters are so complete that any attempt at description is just an insult to the wreckage."

"What disaster?" Harmony asked intently. "Rhapsody, what the *hell* is going on?"

"I actually can't tell you, I'm afraid," Rhapsody said regretfully, her large eyes full of repressed emotion. "Just trust me when I say it will all make sense someday. The important thing now is to live your life to the fullest. We're here for you now, and we aren't going anywhere. Can you accept that, Harmony?"

Harmony stared into Rhapsody's pleading eyes, her thoughts a turbulent mess. She could tell there was so much more going on that she should somehow know. She could almost *feel* the knowledge waiting behind locked doors, if she could only find the key.

She took a deep breath as Rhapsody teetered on the edge of her own emotional cliff. She would do anything for her beautiful fairy.

"Okay, Rhapsody," Harmony finally said, smiling with love in her eyes. "I'll do anything for you."

Rhapsody closed her eyes as a large tear formed and ran down her cheek. "Thank you, Harmony."

Joline shared a curious look with her, clearly sensing the vast emptiness of all the unspoken words.

"I do have a request to make of you," Rhapsody said softly. "Would you mind spending some time with Mystery on the train tomorrow?"

Harmony's eyebrows rose. "Sure..." she agreed slowly. "But why?"

Rhapsody exhaled, her smile pained. "Because she's drowning, Harmony. She has been for years. And tomorrow, she'll be trapped on a train with her thoughts, convinced the future is just an endless version of the worst days. Becoming a world tree... living forever... it terrifies her."

Rhapsody sighed, a hint of the pain she felt reflected in her eyes. "She doesn't really have anyone. Not like she needs. I was hoping you could just...

be there. Be a friend. Someone who reminds her there's still beauty in living, even when her mind insists otherwise."

Harmony smiled warmly as she gazed back at Rhapsody. "I would love to spend some time with Mystery."

Everything Rhapsody did seemed to be to help someone else. Harmony wasn't sure Rhapsody wasn't secretly an angel in disguise. She still remembered that childhood memory she'd recovered, of Rhapsody transforming into an angel. She'd never met anyone as selfless as her sweet fairy.

Rhapsody suddenly grinned, all eagerness. "In the meantime, I thought I'd discuss some ideas Harmony had with the whole group. I think this could be a totally epic change to the way the world works."

Joline leaned forward, looking intently between her and Rhapsody. "What change?"

Rhapsody's grin turned wry. "I asked Harmony to come up with some ideas for dealing with the intelligence agencies demonizing us—and I mean that literally. They're trying to convince everyone we're actually demons intent on destroying the world."

Rhapsody shook her head in disgust, then grinned as she continued. "One of Harmony's ideas was to implement a heads-up display that showed character information for everyone. There'd be a leveling system allowing people to track their abilities as they improved their skills. It'd also show other information, such as species, alignment to good or evil, and reputation. People would gain levels from activities that had a positive alignment, while they'd *lose* levels for negative actions."

Joline stared, eyes wide. "And you could actually make a system that could do all that? How would that even be possible?"

Rhapsody smiled faintly. "Just think of it as magic. And yes, I can do that."

Joline stared at Rhapsody with the same awe Harmony had earlier. Aurora and Serenity were watching her with hope in their dark eyes.

Rhapsody's tone grew serious. "We need to come up with some rules, though. Like, what kinds of things are considered positively or negatively aligned? How much grinding would it take to level up, and what kind of abilities should we give people for reaching those levels?"

Joline gaped. "You're seriously talking about turning life into a game?"

Harmony nodded, moving behind Rhapsody. The fairy twisted her head to look back at her curiously. Harmony just smiled and threaded her hands through Rhapsody's thick mane, then began kneading her scalp. She needed to give something back to the gregarious fairy, and this gave her an excuse to touch her.

Rhapsody let out a contented moan and leaned her head back, smiling blissfully. Harmony groaned contentedly at the sensation of ghostly fingers kneading her own scalp.

"It makes sense, Mom. Look how much time kids will spend clicking on a cookie on a screen repeatedly just to see their level go up. If they could get the same positive feedback in life, people would *willingly* do their chores, their homework, and even help the old lady carry the groceries out to her car. People might actually get back out into the real world and interact with each other in person."

Joline frowned contemplatively, then laughed, her blue eyes sparkling. "The idea just seems so wrong, but I can't fault your logic. You're basically going to prove all those quotes and adages about life being a game correct."

Rhapsody laughed softly, closing her eyes as Harmony massaged her scalp. Her mirth faded, and she took a deep breath. "The first thing we need to isolate is what's considered a good or bad deed. After we've mapped those alignments, we can come up with classes and the skills assigned to those classes. Do the rest of you think people should be rewarded with innate skill knowledge after leveling up, or should the level system merely be a visual display that allows people to see their progress?"

"Rewards!" Serenity exclaimed, grinning. "There should definitely be some kind of reward system. If I practice running until I reach level five, I should get a reward, like greater speed or stamina. Rewards would keep people from getting bored."

"Yes!" Aurora agreed excitedly. "If I get good at cleaning my room, there should be a reward that makes cleaning easier after I level up."

"Hmm..." Rhapsody stared at them thoughtfully. "I suppose there could be a dexterity system that makes it easier to just toss your stuff in the general direction of where it goes, and it automatically ends up in the right place."

Harmony pursed her lips. "What about intellect? Should we actually increase intellectual acuity based on breadth and depth of knowledge acquisition? How significant should the intellectual reward be? Should intellect increase incrementally, or should there be a specific concept that they'll immediately understand as a reward, without having to learn it the slow way? Would that even be possible?"

Rhapsody leaned her head back further to smile up at her, cheeks dimpling. "Just assume anything is possible for now. I'll interrupt if I hear something that I don't think is possible."

Harmony eyed her appraisingly. "You're really playing up this goddess vibe, aren't you?"

Rhapsody arched an eyebrow, her lips curving seductively. "I'll be your goddess anytime, anywhere."

Harmony flushed as desire flared, sending heat to all the right places.

Joline groaned at the look in Harmony's eyes. "Focus, Harmony. Let's try to get through a few more hours of planning before you go play peekaboo."

"Peekaboo?" Harmony demanded indignantly. "That phrase is now on the banned list."

She looked down at Rhapsody hopefully. "Can we add a ban feature that makes people forget what they were going to say if it's on the banned list?"

Rhapsody shook her head, an amused smirk on her face. "I'm afraid that's a line we don't want to cross. We offer extra abilities for positive actions and take those abilities away for negative ones. We *don't* take away people's inherent abilities or freedom of speech. We're not dictators, after all."

"I guess not," Harmony sighed regretfully, glaring at Joline. "There should be exceptions, though. Peekaboo indeed."

Taxti laughed as she observed Harmony's disgruntled expression. "Now I'm curious where you came up with peekaboo as a word for... you know..."

Taxti caught herself before finishing, glancing at Serenity and Aurora.

Serenity folded her arms, giving them all a pointed stare. "Can we get back to the task at hand? So, you're able to add intellectual rewards, but what about the other types? For instance, Aurora just saved a kitten from certain death, then rescued a cricket from a sliding door track, and then saved a beetle from getting stepped on. Would those actions be rewarded? If so, what class would they fall under, and how many levels would someone need to climb to receive a reward?"

"That definitely sounds like the vegan class," Joline declared, grinning at Harmony. "And I'd suggest an ability to speak with animals. There's probably a gamer term for it already."

"You mean like a beast tamer?" Aurora asked excitedly. "Yeah, I want to be a beast tamer!"

They spent several hours discussing classes, rules, and abilities, finally breaking off the discussion near morning before Aurora and Serenity got burned out.

Serenity stretched dramatically. "I need to grab my toothbrush from Aunt Harmony's bathroom."

Rhapsody reached out to stop her, but she'd already teleported away.

Rhapsody giggled mischievously. "Well, this might be awkward."

"What?" Harmony asked curiously, her lips twitching in anticipation.

Before Rhapsody could answer, Serenity was back, eyes wide.

"Aunt Harmony, there's a woman in your bed!"

"There is?" Harmony asked, brow furrowing in confusion. "Did you recognize her?"

Serenity shook her head quickly. "No, she was covered in blankets and had a pillow over her head. Do you think it's some kind of drifter who found an empty house and decided to sleep there?"

Harmony raised an eyebrow at Rhapsody. "Something tells me there's another explanation."

Serenity looked at Rhapsody expectantly.

"Well," Rhapsody began slowly. "Do you remember how tall Mystery is?"

"That's *Mystery*?" Serenity gasped in surprise. "I thought she was on a train?"

"She is... sort of," Rhapsody said, biting her lip as she tried not to smile. "So, have you ever seen the size of the beds in those trains? Well, I kind of felt bad for Mystery, so I put a portal at the end of the bed on the train, so her feet had somewhere to rest. I sort of made the portal big enough so she could just climb through and use Harmony's whole bed if she wanted."

A slow blush crept up Harmony's neck. She wasn't even in her room, but the thought of another beautiful woman in her bed seemed to trigger her libido.

Rhapsody tilted her head backward, watching her with a small smile on her expressive lips, causing the blush to flood into her hairline.

"It's not my fault!" Harmony exclaimed defensively, staring back at Rhapsody worriedly. "It's just this overactive imagination. It's *your* fault for putting the portal into *my* bed."

Serenity stared at her in bewilderment. "What are you talking about, Aunt Harmony?"

"Do I look jealous?" Rhapsody asked dryly. "I'm not the thought police, you know."

Harmony watched Rhapsody cautiously. She *didn't* seem jealous that Harmony's first thoughts had immediately pictured an intimate scene with her unexpected guest—but Rhapsody was also highly skilled at controlling her facial expressions. The last thing Harmony wanted was to hurt Rhapsody; she didn't even know where the stray thought had come from.

"Did you get your toothbrush?" Rhapsody asked Serenity, her smile never fading.

Serenity folded her arms defensively. "No, I panicked as soon as I saw a stranger in Aunt Harmony's bed."

"It's totally fine," Rhapsody assured her. "You've been drinking yuccas fitter anyway, so you don't *need* to brush your teeth. It rewinds your biological clock, remember?"

Serenity's brows drew down. "I thought that only happened if you were older."

Rhapsody nodded patiently. "It won't make you any younger, true, but it does make you invulnerable—including your teeth."

"Hey, you two," Taxti called out to Serenity and Aurora as she began walking up the beach. "Are you ready to learn how to fly?"

Aurora and Serenity stared at each other, wide-eyed, then let out squeals of excitement and raced after Taxti.

"I don't want to miss this," Joline declared with a wry grin, eyeing Harmony and Rhapsody appraisingly. "I'm going to go watch, somewhere out of earshot."

Harmony snorted a laugh as Joline jogged after the other three.

"So..." Harmony began awkwardly. "Why is everyone leaving us alone like there's something private to discuss?"

Rhapsody turned to face her, floating into the air and drifting toward Harmony until their chests were touching. "Because there *is* something private to discuss."

Harmony gasped as her synesthesia sent double shockwaves of sensitive stimulation through her system when Rhapsody pressed against her tightly.

"What do you think of a three-way relationship?" Rhapsody whispered into her ear, sending tingles down Harmony's spine.

"Three-way relationship?" Harmony repeated, uncomprehendingly. "With whom?"

Jealousy seared through Harmony, sharp and furious. Who was Rhapsody talking about? One of the angels?

"Mystery," Rhapsody answered in the same seductive whisper.

The jealousy vanished. Harmony blinked in surprise. *Why don't I feel any jealousy if it's Mystery?*

"Do you remember how I said the three of us have been together for more years than you could imagine?" Rhapsody asked softly. "We weren't just friends."

6 – HOLD ON TO YOUR BUTTS

Mystery sat across a table from her brother in the observatory car. At six feet eight inches, he was in even more danger of hitting his head than she was.

He frowned, staring out at the flat farmland flowing past, his dark eyes troubled. She'd just finished recounting her experience with the "Rhapsody taskforce" and her subsequent escape from their "safehouse."

She'd also told him about Rhapsody's request for her to become an immortal world tree. She'd remained clinical in her description of her time inside the rings, but he'd zeroed in on her fear of being trapped in an immortal body forever.

He turned to face her, his tone conversational as he slid further down the bench, attempting to find more leg room.

"I'm not saying anything you don't already know, but you're a pretty miserable person most of the time. I can tell you're worried about being stuck in Debbie Downer mode until the sun swallows the planet. However, did you ever wonder if the person who healed your leg might just be able to heal your mind as well?"

Mystery blinked, turning her gaze from the endless farmland to regard him consideringly. "Actually, I did. Do you remember the other woman I told you about—Harmony?"

He grinned, eyes sparkling playfully. "Yeah, your favorite author. The one you wanted to meet someday."

She gaped at him. "How did you know that was Harmony?"

He barked a short laugh at her shock. "It's been all over the internet for a few days now. Someone was videoing Rhapsody when the four of them were at a Walmart, and Harmony's niece asked why someone else's name was on one of her books at a kiosk. Apparently, her nieces helped her design the cover illustrations but had never seen her pen name."

"Oh," Mystery deflated with a disappointed sigh. She'd hoped to be one of the only people to know her favorite author's true identity. Now there'd be hordes of people competing for Harmony's attention—people who weren't emotional wrecks most of the time.

Michael raised a curious eyebrow. "Why'd you bring Harmony up? I assume you were going somewhere with that."

Mystery shook her head, trying to focus her scattered thoughts. "Rhapsody showed me some of Harmony's memories from when she was about three years old that I'm going to have nightmares about for a long time. I don't know how someone can keep going after living through that kind of hell. She seemed so normal and sane when I talked with her. I just don't understand how she can be such a happy person while I'm such a train wreck."

He snorted dryly and tapped the window. "Was that pun intended?"

Her eyes refocused as she glanced around the train. She smiled faintly, shaking her head. "Nope, but we can pretend it was."

He leaned onto the table, his expression serious. "I should point out that you've only seen Harmony *after* she'd been with Rhapsody. Who knows what she was like before that? She might have been just as miserable and moody as you are. I suggest you learn more about her and consider what kind of help Rhapsody can offer you to deal with your own issues."

Spend time with Harmony—the author she venerated like a goddess?

"There's that smile I love," Michael grinned approvingly.

Mystery blinked in surprise when she realized she *was* smiling. Come to think of it, she felt more positive than she had in a long time. Just thinking about Rhapsody and Harmony seemed to buoy her spirits. Would being a world tree really be so bad if she had Rhapsody and Harmony as companions?

She remembered that the two of them seemed closer than just friends. But what if they weren't? Would she have a chance? She felt like she already knew Harmony, after reading her novels so many times. She was almost positive Harmony played for the same team.

Even if Rhapsody and Harmony were together, she could always try to find someone else. She'd be immortal, with all the time in the world to search for the right person.

Of course, therein lay the problem: finding a person who'd complement her personality and not be an opportunistic jerk.

The thought of her ex-boyfriend, Todd, flared through her mind like a caution sign. She'd thought they had something special when they first met.

He'd showered her with attention, gifts, and affection. It'd been her first relationship, and it felt wonderful for the first few months. It wasn't until three months in that the real Todd started peeking through the façade.

He'd started questioning her about everything. If she wanted to play guitar in her sound studio, he wanted to know why it was more important than him. When she had emotionally taxing days, he'd suggest she just *think* herself happy, then get frustrated when she claimed it wasn't that easy. If she wept, he left the room because the sound of crying made him anxious.

Long before their one-year anniversary, she'd begun to dread coming home, knowing she'd be questioned like it was the Inquisition. Why was she so late? Why was work more important than him? Why did she need so much space? The questions just went on and on until she had to leave the house to escape the nonstop harassment.

Shortly after their one-year anniversary, everything finally came to a head. She came home early after an air tour was canceled and found him in bed with another woman. It was the proverbial straw that broke the camel's back.

She wasn't a screamer. Her rage was always cold and unyielding. She immediately started packing all his belongings and setting them out next to his car, ignoring his attempts to justify his infidelity.

The girl he'd brought over had been livid that he was already in a relationship. She screamed the house down before calling an Uber and leaving, apologizing profusely to Mystery on her way out.

Mystery hadn't noticed; she was already spiraling into one of her dark moods. She drove to the airfield and took to the air. She'd done a quick preflight check but wouldn't have noticed if anything was wrong.

When her plane stalled, she felt a moment of peace, knowing the end was near. Discovering a lake beneath her, she was half-convinced she'd already passed into some kind of afterlife, since there shouldn't have been any lakes in that area.

She smiled, recalling her shock at seeing several mermaids waiting for her when she exited her sinking plane. That had been the beginning of the strangest night of her life.

She vividly recalled the electric shock that surged through her when she first made eye contact with Harmony, as if she'd stumbled across a sibling who'd disappeared as a child.

Mystery took a deep breath and unconsciously began wringing her hands. "What if they *can't* help me? What if I'm stuck like this forever? I'm so damn scared of being like this for millions of years."

He shrugged. "Don't commit to anything yet. Just be with them for now. If it seems hopeless, decline the request."

She threw her hands up with a helpless growl. "If I decline, everyone's going to die—including *you*. I don't really have a choice, and I think that's what's driving me so crazy."

He shook his head, his voice firm. "There's always a choice. You said she told you your soul is old. If we have souls, even if everyone on the planet dies, they're just going to end up reborn somewhere else or moving on. Don't get hung up on the idea that the world needs you in order to survive. Everyone alive right now is going to die eventually anyway. It's that simple."

Mystery stopped wringing her hands, pondering his logic. It was hard to argue with, but it was also hard to accept when she could so clearly remember the fear on the face of the young mother in the train station.

"I don't want to die," Michael told her gently, "but that's not going to stop it from happening. We're hard-wired to fear death. I know that look. You're worrying about someone else and thinking you could save them. Stop thinking like that and start thinking like an eternal being who's on an expedition with other eternal beings, and this is just a short connector flight on a much longer journey."

Mystery gazed at her brother fondly. "You sound like a sage."

"I'm the Great Sage," Michael declared magnanimously, spreading his arms wide and accidentally smacking a woman in the ass as she walked past. She spun around, her eyes narrowing into a glare that could have punched through Kevlar.

"I am *so* sorry, ma'am," Michael apologized, his face flushing scarlet with mortification. "I didn't see you there, and I have these gorilla arms."

She stared at him hard for a moment longer before wordlessly turning away and continuing down the aisle.

Mystery bit her lip, nearly drawing blood as she tried to restrain her laughter. Her shoulders shook as she watched her brother flounder. He was usually pretty smooth with the ladies, so it was entertaining to see him so off-balance.

He glared at her warningly. "Not. One. Word."

Her voice tight with the effort of suppressing her laughter, she responded, "Nope, I have a lot more than one. I never took you for the type to slap random women's asses. Is this a new trend, or are you just trying it out while I'm with you in case you need protection?"

He sighed in exasperation, waving his arms at the train. "It's these cramped quarters. I'm going to start a new colony on an island, and everything will be sized for tall people. I feel like I'm trying to move around in the Shire everywhere I go."

"I hear that," Mystery agreed with a laugh, eyeing him fondly. One of her biggest reservations about becoming an immortal was watching her brother grow old and die. She suddenly remembered something that might change that.

"So... Michael, if I decided to become a world tree and offered you the ability to stop aging, would you take it?"

He smiled wryly, returning her speculative look with one of his own. "Why? Does Rhapsody have a potion for immortality stashed away somewhere?"

She nodded, noting his oversized irises. "As a matter of fact, she does. And I can tell by the size of your irises that you've already tasted it."

His eyebrows shot up. "You mean the yuccas fitter? Am I immortal now?"

She shook her head, leaning forward with sudden hope. "You have to keep drinking it. It takes one week off your age every time you drink it. So? Would you stay with me?"

He snorted derisively. "Of course, I would. Who's going to turn down immortality? Besides you, that is."

Mystery let out a relieved breath as one of the biggest roadblocks in her mental highway to becoming a world tree vanished. She knew having her brother around wouldn't be enough. She needed to find a way to stop the dark mood swings from happening at all. Maybe Rhapsody *could* heal her mental illness. She couldn't even imagine what the world would look like without the constant shadow of her dark moods threatening to ruin each moment.

Michael looked up when someone entered the observatory car behind Mystery, his eyes widening before a broad grin spread across his face.

She raised an amused eyebrow. "What are you so excited about? Did your favorite chick band just walk in?"

His expression went blank, and he shrugged. "Nothing. Nothing at all."

She raised her other eyebrow, considering turning around to see for herself. Before she could, a pair of long, toned legs in white shorts appeared next to their table.

Mystery slowly looked up to see Harmony smiling down at her. Harmony wore a white button-up, open low enough to reveal her stomach and a generous amount of cleavage, seemingly without a bra. Her hair was pulled into a messy bun, pale strands escaping to frame her cheeks. Her eyes, much larger than Mystery remembered, held her in a warm gaze, lavender irises glinting like polished amethyst.

Harmony had already been beautiful, but now she seemed mythical, enchanting.

Those large eyes studied her with more than just affection, holding curiosity and a hint of familiarity. Mystery's breath quickened as she stared up at Harmony. There was something *so* familiar about her, just out of reach.

"Do you two mind if I join you?"

She hadn't even glanced at Michael, her focus solely on Mystery.

"Not at all," Michael answered when it became clear Mystery wouldn't. He kicked her under the table, breaking the spell.

"Sorry, Harmony," Mystery apologized with a sheepish smile.

She cringed inside at her fangirl behavior, mentally slapping herself as she scooted over to make room for the gorgeous author.

She couldn't stop staring, still unable to believe this was *her* author. She'd reread all her books so many times that she felt like she knew all the characters personally—they'd been so relatable while also being *likable*. Sometimes, she thought those books were the only thing keeping her sane, giving her the determination to keep trying, even on her worst days.

Harmony sat next to her, twisting in the seat and tucking one leg under herself so she could face Mystery, just inside her personal space. Mystery noticed she smelled like sweet flowers, an intoxicating scent that made her pulse quicken.

"I just wanted to say how much your books meant to me," Mystery blurted, her face earnest. She felt a driving need to explain that Harmony's characters had been so much more than just stories to her. "I felt like I knew your characters. I fell in love with them, especially Riah. They helped me through some of the most difficult days of my life. It was like an antidepressant I could run to when I just couldn't stand reality anymore. I'd bury myself in their lives and adventures and forget all about the world around me. Thank you, Harmony, for creating something so wonderful."

Harmony's face reflected a shy pleasure. "I'm so glad they meant so much to you, too. To be honest, they were all like family to me. Every time I sat down to write, I felt like I was peeking into their universe to see what happened next. It just wrote itself, for the most part. I felt more like a historian or documentarian than an author. Everything flowed so smoothly from one experience or conversation to another that I never struggled to figure out what to write. Sometimes I think my brain is just picking up a frequency from some other world, and I'm just documenting their adventures."

Mystery smiled, her fingers absently curling a strand of hair before she stopped herself. "I'd love for that to be true. I swear, I'd find a way to portal over to their universe and meet them in person."

Michael watched them quietly with an indulgent smile. Mystery ignored him, focusing her attention on her beautiful author. She absently brushed the strand of hair behind her ear. As she did so, Harmony shivered, and her cheeks reddened slightly.

Harmony clasped her hands in her lap and leaned closer, triggering a wave of nervous excitement in Mystery's abdomen.

"Mystery, can you tell me about yourself? All I really know is that you're a pilot and that you were hit by an asshole in high school. I'd love to know more.

What do you do for fun? What kind of hobbies do you have? Aside from having great taste in fiction, what else do you like?"

Harmony finished with a wink that sent the butterflies in Mystery's stomach into a frenzy. She licked her lips, eliciting an even more violent shiver from Harmony, followed by a deep blush. Mystery bit her lip, then took a deep breath.

"Well, I love music with a passion. I've been playing the guitar and piano since I lost my leg. I was going nuts being stuck in a bed after several surgeries, so I decided to learn guitar and piano. I've been obsessed ever since."

Harmony's eyes lit up, and she laughed delightedly. "Rhapsody must have a knack for finding musical people. One of my hobbies is learning new instruments. Once I feel like I've reached a passable proficiency with one, I find another to start learning. I have a studio at home where I love to layer tracks with all the instruments I've learned." She paused, laughing ruefully. "Of course, Rhapsody showed up and made what I play sound like a toddler banging on pans."

Mystery's lips curved into an excited smile. "Seriously? Oh my god, I would *love* to hear what you make!"

Harmony returned her smile with an eager grin, then pulled out her phone and began swiping through the screens. "I don't have anything of mine with me, but let me show you something Rhapsody made in my studio while I was at the women's shelter."

Mystery stared at Harmony, wondering if she'd heard correctly. She volunteered at a women's shelter in addition to everything else she did? Where did she get all the motivation to constantly help others?

"Here it is," Harmony announced triumphantly, tapping her screen one last time.

Mystery sat frozen as she listened to the beautiful voices harmonize. She'd never heard anything so moving. Tears streamed down her cheeks as the song ended; she wouldn't have believed *anything* could be so sublime. It struck a chord in her soul, leaving her breathless with wonder.

"*Wow*, that was incredible!" she exclaimed, her eyes wide with admiration. "I would *love* to see you two play sometime."

Harmony smiled disarmingly. "It sounds like we should all *three* be playing together. I've never actually played with other people, so it'll be a new experience. I have a feeling it will be a very *good* experience."

Warmth suffused Mystery's cheeks at Harmony's prediction. She was so personable, so genuinely kind, that Mystery felt comfortable with her in a way she'd never felt with anyone else.

She suddenly remembered the signs of attraction between Harmony and Rhapsody she'd noticed in the ring. The thought doused her in a metaphorical bucket of cold water, cooling her growing attraction. She couldn't hope to compete with Rhapsody for Harmony's affection. She reined in her heart and settled for having her author as a friend. She hadn't had any real friends since high school, so this would be a fresh experience.

"I haven't ever played with other people either," she said shyly, trying and failing to stop her heart from throwing itself at Harmony's feet. "I think you're right—it'll be fun."

Harmony coughed delicately. "So, um, what happened with that guy who cheated on you? Still exiled?"

Mystery scowled. She tried to school her features, but they were as rebellious as ever. She began wringing her hands as she remembered just how miserable her life had been with Todd.

"Exiled is too soft a term," she muttered darkly, her positivity plummeting. "I'm not sure why it took him cheating on me to end things. It was a miserable relationship for most of the time we were together. I'd never been in a relationship before, so I thought I was doing something wrong. I know I'm not the easiest person to deal with."

Harmony placed her hand on Mystery's, gently stopping her from wringing them. Mystery blushed at the contact and looked up into Harmony's compassionate gaze.

"I've only known you for a day, but I can confidently say you've done nothing wrong. You're a wonderful person, Mystery, and I'm so sorry you had to deal with an asshat like Todd. I'm glad he's history."

Mystery thought her hands might combust where Harmony's rested on hers. Conflicting emotions warred within her as she looked up at Harmony with a hesitant, warm smile. The chemistry between them was undeniable—hell, a blind person could see it. But what about Rhapsody? She was almost positive they were more than friends.

"Are you and Rhapsody... um... together?" The question escaped before she could stop it. Blood rushed to her face as she stared at Harmony, unable to look away.

Harmony squeezed her hands gently, her voice soft. "Rhapsody said the three of us have been together for more years than we can imagine. I think she must be right, to a degree. The thought of sharing her with anyone else fills me with insane jealousy—but when I think of sharing her with you, there's nothing but a warm glow."

Mystery's pulse skyrocketed as she stared back at Harmony with sudden hope. She felt that odd sense of familiarity again as she gazed into Harmony's lavender eyes, as if reconnecting with a long-lost lover. She licked her suddenly dry lips and watched Harmony shiver, a slight blush rising on her cheeks. Curious, she slowly licked her lips again, watching Harmony closely. Harmony sucked in a breath and let out a small whimper.

Michael cleared his throat, eyeing them with amusement. "Maybe I should give you two some privacy."

Mystery suddenly realized what she'd been doing and how it must have looked. Her face flushed crimson as heat flooded her head.

She picked up a wrapper and threw it at him as he began laughing at her burning face. He just laughed harder, causing the blush to creep into her hairline. She covered her face with her hands and bent over the table, trying to hide her flaming head.

She felt a gentle hand on her back, sending tingles down her spine. The hand began drawing designs, triggering even more tingles.

"Do you have mirror-touch synesthesia?" Michael asked curiously.

She felt Harmony flinch and raised her head to look at her. Harmony's face was suddenly full of trepidation, and she avoided their gaze.

Mystery looked at her brother with a puzzled frown. "What's mirror-touch synesthesia?" The way Harmony was reacting, it sounded like a virulent disease she was afraid people would flee from.

Michael watched Harmony in confusion. "It's an odd effect—some people can feel what others are feeling. A friend of mine has it and has to avoid places like hospitals or violent contact sports. She acts the way you do, so it was kind of obvious, since I knew what to look for. It's nothing to be ashamed of, though. Why the guilty expression?"

Harmony's eyes darted around nervously as she sat stiffly next to Mystery, her whole body radiating discomfort.

"I'm still struggling not to see it as a major handicap," Harmony finally said with a sigh. "My nieces have dealt with enough mental instability in the family without me bringing more uncertainty. Rhapsody's been trying to convince me it isn't a burden, but it feels like a burden on everyone around me, once they know about it."

Mystery studied her in fascination. "So, you feel what other people feel? When I was licking my lips, it felt like—" She broke off, unable to say that it felt like she was licking Harmony's lips.

Harmony nodded, her face turning a light shade of pink. "It used to only happen when I could see what someone was doing, but when Serenity found out about it, she was convinced it was some kind of psychic ability. She discovered that just thinking about me watching her when she does something will trigger it, even if I'm not able to see it."

"Seriously?" Michael asked incredulously. "That definitely sounds psychic to me."

Harmony laughed ruefully. "Yeah, I kind of gave up on my skeptical side after seeing a unicorn and a phoenix, followed shortly after by a fairy and a world tree. You couldn't find a bigger skeptic on the planet than me before that."

Harmony paused and stared at Michael levelly. "Do you mind?"

"Sorry!" he said quickly, a boyish smile on his face. "I just had to test it. Not that I didn't believe you, but I still had to try it."

Mystery stared between the two of them, uncomprehending. "Huh?"

Michael rubbed his neck sheepishly. "I decided to try and trigger her synesthesia by scratching my knee under the table while thinking of her watching it. I'll admit, I didn't expect it to work."

Mystery couldn't stop her thoughts from straying to the bedroom. What was it like for Harmony to sleep with someone if her synesthesia mirrored what they were feeling, too? Her face reddened as she saw Harmony watching her shrewdly.

Mystery attempted to empty her mind of the thoughts of her and Harmony in the large bed she'd been sleeping in. "So, how long have you had this... ability?"

"Since I was five," Harmony answered quietly, a haunted look in her eyes.

Mystery suddenly remembered the memories Rhapsody had shown her of Harmony's childhood. She felt a fresh wave of horror at the memories, and even more so at seeing that haunted look in Harmony's eyes.

"I'm so sorry, Harmony," she blurted, placing a hand on Harmony's. "I didn't mean to bring up bad memories."

"It's fine," Harmony assured her with a warm smile. "Rhapsody locked them away so completely that they no longer have an emotional hold over me."

"She can do that?" Mystery asked, sudden hope filling her eyes.

Harmony smiled fondly. "There isn't very much she *can't* do. She says the only thing she's never figured out is how to fix stupid."

Mystery glanced back at her brother, feeling a sudden ray of hope for the first time since childhood. If Rhapsody really could fix or lock away mental issues, life might just feel worth living.

Harmony smiled at her reassuringly, her eyes full of understanding. "If she can fix *me*, then I don't think there's anything she *can't* fix."

Elation flooded her like a wave of liquid hope as she glimpsed a future free of the despair and self-loathing that had plagued her life for the last thirteen years. She was finally going to be free.

"So," Harmony began with a teasing smile. "Has my bed been comfortable enough?"

Mystery stared at Harmony in growing alarm. "Oh my god, is that *your* bed? Where have you been sleeping?"

Harmony laid a reassuring hand on Mystery's arm. "My mom and I no longer require sleep or food."

"Oh," Mystery blinked, then tilted her head curiously. "What's it like, not sleeping or eating? Don't you miss it?"

Harmony's eyes glowed with a kind of ecstasy as she answered. "The replacement *more* than makes up for it."

"What is it?" Michael asked curiously. "Or is it a secret?"

Harmony frowned. "I don't think it's a secret. Hey, Rhapsody, is it a secret?"

Michael and Mystery exchanged a startled look and began searching the train for the fairy. When there was no sign of Rhapsody, they looked back at Harmony in confusion.

"Come on, Rhapsody, I know you're watching," Harmony declared with a playful smile. "I can feel it in my bones."

"Well, aren't you Miss Observant," Rhapsody suddenly appeared next to their table, grinning sheepishly.

There was only one other person in the observatory car: the woman Michael had accidentally gotten too familiar with as she walked past. She was sitting at the other end of the car, staring at her phone screen. Rhapsody's appearance seemed to pull her attention away from the screen. She gasped when she saw Rhapsody, wings and all. Rhapsody glanced down the aisle and winked before turning back to face the three of them.

"You can tell them what we do for sustenance," Rhapsody allowed with a mischievous smile. "Or I could just share the memory. The memory's a lot more fun. However, I'm only showing Michael—I want it to be a surprise for Mystery when the time comes."

Michael raised a hand. "I'll take the memory, for 200."

Harmony laughed, eyeing him speculatively.

Rhapsody glowed brightly for a moment, then Michael's face went slack.

As the memory ended, Michael slumped in his seat, a comical expression of bliss on his face.

"*Wow,*" Michael breathed. "That's how fairies eat, huh? I wanna be a fairy."

Rhapsody laughed—a sound like golden light.

She sobered quickly and raised an eyebrow at Mystery. "So, what do you think? Do you want to continue on the train for the rest of the trip?"

"I think I'm ready," Mystery said, feeling lighter than air as she gazed at Rhapsody and Harmony, hope shining in her dark eyes. "Can you help me with my mental issues?"

Rhapsody smiled at her affectionately. "Your mental issues are *because* of us—or the *lack* of us. Our souls are linked, and the physical separation has interfered with your mind's natural ability to heal after trauma. Now that you're with us, we'll get you all healed up."

Mystery felt like she knew both women, as if she had somehow just forgotten their names. They seemed so *familiar,* like a dream she had every night but forgot upon waking.

She took a deep breath and tentatively faced Rhapsody. "Can I keep my brother? With yuccas fitter?"

"Michael will *always* be welcome," Rhapsody declared with an affectionate wink. "Let's boogie—or, as Harmony would say, hold on to your butts."

Mystery frowned, confused. She'd never heard that phrase before—so why did it sound so familiar?

The last thing she saw before they vanished was the woman at the other end of the train car watching them in fascination. And, of course, she was videoing them.

7 – PARTY

Harmony watched with concern as Mystery began to wring her hands as they stood before the chasm. Rhapsody appeared on the opposite side of Mystery and floated until she was eye level with her. Harmony could tell Mystery was still hesitant to undergo the initiation, her face displaying an incongruous mixture of excitement and dread.

Rhapsody rested a reassuring hand on Mystery's shoulder. "We don't have to do this right now. You can hang out with us until you feel more comfortable with the decision."

Mystery shook her head firmly, her jaw tightening. "No, let's do it. Deep down, I know this is right, and I'll be happier for it."

Rhapsody's concern vanished, replaced by an excited grin. "Okay, bottoms up."

The light beam shooting down the chasm intensified until Harmony couldn't see anything with her physical eyes. Using her second sight, she watched Mystery's spirit morph, layers of complexity weaving and warping it to Rhapsody's blueprints.

Mystery felt a moment of fear as the full power of a world tree connected to her freshly minted immortal body. It only lasted a split second before Rhapsody placed the limiter between the power source and Mystery's consciousness.

Harmony couldn't keep track of the billions of threads of energy connecting Rhapsody to Mystery. It was awe-inspiring to watch the fairy work with forces more complex than Harmony could comprehend.

When the process was complete, the light from the chasm diminished to a solid beam again. Mystery stood in stunned amazement, mentally cataloging all the changes to her body and spirit.

"Not bad," Rhapsody said warmly, studying Mystery appreciatively. "Not bad at all."

A mirror sprang up in front of Mystery so she could observe the changes. Her eyes had increased in size, like Harmony's, and changed to a deep shade of lavender. Her eyelashes had grown longer, and her face had softened. Already stunningly beautiful, she was now transcendently radiant.

She stared into the mirror intently, studying her new body. After a moment of silent inspection, an approving smile lit up her face.

"Okay, I've got to admit, I'm pretty hot. I'm guessing the fairy ears come later?"

Rhapsody orbited Mystery like a small moon, reviewing her work. "They do if you want them. After all, you'll be a projection of your world tree—a shapeshifter. Technically, you can make yourself look however you want."

Harmony grinned. "Yeah, we never have to shave our legs again."

Rhapsody glanced at Harmony with a small smile, inducing an immediate blush.

Mystery looked at the floating fairy curiously. "Do you ever change your appearance? I noticed you wear the hat and glasses in public. Can't you just make yourself look like a human?"

Rhapsody grinned mischievously. "I absolutely could make myself look like a human—but where's the mystery in just looking like a normal human? It's more fun to look like someone hiding their true appearance. It certainly got Harmony's attention."

Harmony stared at Rhapsody in surprise; the thought had never occurred to her, though it probably should have. She knew Rhapsody was a shapeshifter, yet she'd never questioned why the small woman didn't just appear as another human. The more she thought about it, the more sense it made. Harmony probably wouldn't have responded to another normal-looking human the same way she had to the mysterious fairy.

She rubbed her neck sheepishly. "I feel like I should have thought of that before now. It never even occurred to me to ask why you didn't just shapeshift into a human."

A faint smile tugged at Rhapsody's lips. "It's all about the narrative. Harmony's a fantasy author—I knew she couldn't pass up that kind of mystery. Hmm... that could have an interesting double meaning."

Harmony shook her head, smiling ruefully at Mystery. "I think your name's going to be dragged through every kind of literary device imaginable, Mystery."

Mystery shrugged, unable to stop looking at her new face in the mirror. "That's why I started going by Misty in high school."

"Well, it's too late now," Rhapsody said with a satisfied grin. "We already know your name is Mystery."

Mystery finally pulled her eyes away from her reflection. "So, what now? I have a feeling going back to normal life might be a little difficult with all the attention on us now—especially looking like this."

"We have a plan," Rhapsody informed her with a barely repressed smile. "Harmony's plan."

Harmony raised an amused eyebrow at Rhapsody. "You're not going to claim it was your plan, since your plan was to let me come up with a plan?"

Rhapsody looked at her sternly, hands on her hips. "You shouldn't raise your eyebrow like that without Serenity here to witness it. I don't think she knows you're a master of the raised eyebrow."

"The plan?" Mystery reminded them, her face a mixture of amused patience.

"It's her fault," Rhapsody said, pointing at Harmony accusingly. "She sidetracked me."

Harmony gave Rhapsody a level look, then turned to gaze at Mystery calculatingly. "How familiar with video games are you?"

Mystery shrugged. "I know you play them on a computer or something. I've been more of a readaholic my whole life—I just never got into games."

"Ah," Harmony pursed her lips as she studied Mystery. "Well, this might take a little bit of explaining, then."

Rhapsody tilted her head, the act sending Harmony's adorable meter into the red. "Maybe you should just show her a game using the mechanics we're planning to use. A picture's worth a thousand words and all that jazz."

Harmony nodded, her heart fluttering as she looked back and forth at the two gorgeous women. "Maybe you're right—though my house isn't the best place to show her an example. We aren't real big on video games. I think Serenity might have some games on her tablet we could use for examples."

"Let's go fetch it when she gets here, then," Rhapsody decided, glancing appraisingly at Mystery. "It's time for Mystery to see what her new body can do. Try to keep up."

Rhapsody sprinted away, disappearing into the long passageway leading out of Yggdrasil. Harmony grinned at a stunned Mystery before bolting after Rhapsody at full speed.

The chasm vanished as Harmony accelerated. She reached the opening in less than five seconds, nearly plowing into her mother as she exited. Laughing, Rhapsody grabbed Harmony's wrist at the last second and pulled her aside.

Mystery emerged only a few seconds later, bursting out of the opening in a blur, a radiant smile on her face. She nearly went into the lake before slowing down, then turned and ran back up to them, her smile never dimming.

"Wow," Michael breathed in amazement. He'd been talking to Joline when Harmony exited at full speed. "I guess you probably don't need cars anymore."

Rhapsody eyed him speculatively. "It might attract a little attention to sprint down the highway at over a hundred miles per hour. We should do it just to see people's reactions. Great idea, Michael!"

Mystery shared a look with Harmony, then erupted into laughter.

Rhapsody smiled at them fondly, her large eyes full of nostalgia.

Harmony gestured at her shorts. "We'll need to find something more durable to wear for any serious sprinting. These just aren't made to deal with that kind of friction."

Michael nodded, smiling appreciatively. "Yeah, I suppose you could just run around starkers. It's not like anyone will get a good look at you at those speeds." He paused, studying his sister curiously. "You look like a fairy in training wheels. How do you feel?"

"I feel *amazing*," Mystery said ecstatically. "I wish I'd made this choice sooner."

Michael let out a relieved sigh. "I was afraid you were going to come out filled with regrets."

"Nope," Mystery smiled giddily. "I'm *definitely* not having any regrets. I don't know if it's the upgraded body or what, but my head feels clearer than it ever has. It's like the cloud of doom that follows me everywhere just evaporated."

Michael beamed at her, his eyes growing moist. "If you only knew how good it is to see you actually happy."

Mystery laughed exuberantly and gave him a quick hug. "I can assure you, I know how good it is to *feel* happy. And being able to run again... it feels *amazing*."

Michael faced Harmony with a wistful smile. "She used to be an avid runner and hiker before the accident. She never walked anywhere—it was always a full sprint if she was moving."

Harmony studied Mystery intently, their connection having grown into a much stronger bond. She felt as though she could close her eyes and point to Mystery, a sense that went beyond merely knowing her physical location. It was almost as if she could *feel* Mystery's happiness, a sensation similar to the warm glow she felt when Rhapsody was nearby.

Rhapsody regarded them thoughtfully. "We have some time before Serenity and Aurora get out of school, and a birthday party to crash in a few hours. How about we get some more introductions out of the way?"

Joline rubbed her hands together eagerly. "I was wondering when we were going to meet some of the others. I was pretty sure there were more people here than just Taxti, Declan, Nidhogg, and Ikle Chikle."

Rhapsody smiled at Joline's exuberance. "Declan's the king of the leprechauns—though it's mostly a ceremonial title since they don't actually have a kingdom. Taxti's the queen of the fauns, and Nidhogg's the clan chief of the dragons. All the other leprechauns, fauns, and dragons live here as well, but they didn't want to overwhelm you, so they've remained out of sight until now. Would you like to meet some of them?"

"*Yes*!" Joline exclaimed, eliciting a laugh from Rhapsody.

"Hell yeah," Michael grinned.

"Sure," Harmony agreed, her curiosity piqued. She hadn't even considered where the other leprechauns and fauns were, too distracted by her own life events to question the lack of a larger populace within the circle.

Rhapsody put her hands on her hips. "Okay, Leesha, Eimear, Niall, and Cormac, would you like to formally meet our new friends?"

Four leprechauns materialized out of thin air: two women and two men, all slightly shorter than Declan. They weren't wearing traditional leprechaun outfits like Declan, making Harmony wonder if he wore it as some kind of prank.

"This is Leesha," Rhapsody said, gesturing to a petite, blonde woman with almond-shaped eyes.

Harmony was immediately charmed by the dusting of orange freckles across Leesha's nose. Leesha wore a simple yellow dress that fell to her knees, and bright green eyes sparkled from her youthful face. A long, blonde braid draped over one shoulder, nearly reaching her waist. She stood only about three and a half feet tall, her small feet clad in simple sandals.

"She was Declan's niece and can outdance anyone else in the circle," Rhapsody added with a grin.

Leesha blushed at the compliment, a pleased smile appearing on her face. "It's nice to meet you," she greeted them in an Irish dialect that made Harmony smile; she loved Scottish and Irish dialects.

"This is Eimear," Rhapsody continued, indicating another slight leprechaun.

Eimear had long, brilliant orange hair and a smattering of freckles across her cheeks. Like Leesha, she wore a simple dress, though hers was green. More buxom than Leesha, she shared the same brilliant green eyes. "She was also one of Declan's nieces. She has a mischievous spirit, so watch yourselves around her."

Eimear gave Rhapsody an innocent smile, though her eyes sparkled with mischief. "It's nice to finally meet you," she said in the same Irish dialect as Leesha. "Don't let Rhapsody fool you—she's the chief mischief-maker around here. The rest of us can't even compete. She suddenly caught the mischief bug about twenty-five years ago, and now she's the mischief-maker in chief."

"I resemble that remark," Rhapsody declared impishly. "Moving on, this is Niall, the voice of reason in a place that can get a little silly occasionally."

Niall was a stocky leprechaun, just under four feet tall. His bright orange hair was cut short, framing a square jaw and a face that radiated dependability. He wore brown trousers and a green button-up shirt, which accentuated his bright green eyes. Simple sandals adorned his feet, which seemed disproportionately large for his height.

"I'll correct Rhapsody and point out that I'm the voice of reason in a place that is occasionally *not* silly," Niall said dryly. "It's nice to meet you. I'm sure we'll be seeing a lot of each other from here on out."

"And last, but *maybe* least, this is Cormac," Rhapsody gestured grandly at the final leprechaun. "He's Eimear's partner in crime and should definitely *not* be trusted if he's not under your eye—and even then, only a little."

"I'll repeat what Eimear voiced and point out that we learned everything we know from you, Rhapsody," Cormac declared, leveling an accusing glare at Rhapsody. "But it's nice to see some new faces. I'm pleased to make your acquaintance."

Cormac was dressed in the same style as Niall. Permanent dimples creased his cheeks, and a perpetual look of mischief shone in his green eyes. His blonde hair was longer than Niall's, reaching just above his shoulders.

Harmony nodded at each of them with a forced smile as they were introduced. She hated introductions—they were so damn awkward. Maybe they would be a thing of the past when they implemented the new overlay.

Harmony turned to Rhapsody with a curious frown. "So, what's with Declan's outfit? Is it some kind of formal attire that royalty wears?"

Cormac and Eimear started laughing before Harmony finished speaking. Rhapsody joined them, her eyes sparkling with amusement.

Harmony shook her head, smiling. "Okay, so it was what my gut first told me—he did it as a joke because that's what humans think leprechauns look like."

Rhapsody nodded, lips quivering. "He wanted to see how long it took for one of you to question him. He's going to be *so* disappointed he wasn't here when you asked. Technically, they're not leprechauns—that's just one of the many names they've acquired over the ages."

Mystery watched them with an amused smile. "I get the feeling this place makes its own entertainment." She nodded at the leprechauns. "It's wonderful to meet you. If you don't mind my asking, how old are you?"

Eimear glanced at Cormac, raising an eyebrow. "Three thousand twenty-four? I can't remember the exact year, but I like the sound of twenty-four, so we'll go with that."

"Aye, that's about right," Cormac agreed with a nod. "I'm sure I could figure it out with a little time."

Leesha raised a small hand. "Five thousandish. When you live as long as we do, you stop keeping track after the first century."

"Twelve thousand," Niall offered with a nod. "Like Leesha said, we don't really keep track past a century."

"Are you immortal?" Mystery asked in surprise.

"Aye, that we are," Cormac confirmed with a grin. "We just keep on ticking in spite of all the kicking."

Rhapsody facepalmed, shaking her head sadly. "That was pathetic, Cormac. I'd say you need to work on your rhythm and meter, but if you haven't figured it out by now, I don't think there's any hope you ever will."

"Well, what would you have said?" Cormac demanded in an injured tone.

Rhapsody grinned impishly. "We just keep on trying, in spite of all the crying?"

Cormac grimaced. "You're a cruel fairy, Rhapsody," he accused her with a sad sigh. "Nay, cruel doesn't do it justice. You're a *hurtful* fairy."

Rhapsody adopted an expression of faux concern. "It's for your own good, Cormac. I'm sure you'll keep on ticking—like a bomb waiting to destroy aphorisms."

Cormac shook his head ruefully, looking at Eimear beseechingly, but she just grinned back at him mercilessly, her lips quirking into a small smile.

Mystery shook her head in bemusement. "I'm getting the strangest sense of déjà vu."

"You are?" Rhapsody asked quickly, all signs of amusement gone.

"Yeah," Mystery nodded slowly. "Is that a problem?"

Rhapsody chewed on her lip for a moment before responding. "I'll be back in a sec."

She vanished, leaving Harmony and her companions to stare at the empty air in surprise.

Joline folded her arms, looking around nervously. "I wonder what that was all about."

Niall shrugged. "I wouldn't worry about it. She does this kind of thing occasionally. She gets depressed if she doesn't have something dramatic going on every few weeks."

Harmony frowned. "She's had plenty of drama already. It feels like something's wrong."

Niall eyed her speculatively for several seconds before responding. "Let's assume it *is* a problem of some kind. What are you going to do? Rhapsody will either be able to handle it, or not. There's nothing *we* can do to make a difference, so why worry about it?"

Harmony grimaced, conceding the point. Rhapsody's abilities were so far beyond their own that there really wasn't anything they could do that would amount to anything. She *hated* feeling helpless.

Rhapsody reappeared in front of Harmony, looking annoyed. When she saw the look of worry on Harmony's face, however, her expression shifted to amusement.

"You just can't help being a worrywart, can you, Harmony?" she asked fondly.

Harmony raised a dubious eyebrow. "I don't suppose you'd tell me the truth if I asked what was going on?"

Rhapsody shrugged, then reached up and fondly caressed her cheek. "If I told you the truth about what was going on, one, you wouldn't believe me, and two, you wouldn't understand—not yet, anyway. In general terms, I'm dealing with some bugs in reality. It's taken care of, though, so no worries, mate!"

Harmony once again felt like she was glimpsing a world far beyond her understanding. She sighed and nodded reluctantly, resolving to be patient. She had time—lots of time. She'd find out, eventually.

"You okay?" Mystery asked, watching Harmony with concern in her large, lavender eyes.

"Yeah, I suppose," Harmony replied with another sigh. "I'm just too curious for my own good. I can tell Rhapsody is trying to get me to take this slowly for reasons I don't understand, but it's hard for me not to dig into any mystery I find."

Mystery's face colored. Harmony rolled her eyes when Rhapsody started giggling madly. Cormac and Eimear were struggling not to laugh, quickly turning their backs as if they'd found something fascinating to observe. Joline made no effort to hide her chortling.

Mystery bit her lip, struggling not to laugh as she observed Harmony's disgruntled expression.

Harmony was saved from any more abuse when her nieces teleported a few dozen feet away, along with Declan. The two girls hurried over to them, studying the leprechauns in fascination. Declan raised a questioning eyebrow at Rhapsody when he arrived.

"You missed it, Declan," Rhapsody informed the leprechaun king with a grin just short of laughter. "Harmony already asked why you were dressed like a... leprechaun."

Harmony shook her head as he began laughing loudly, shoulders shaking. "I'm sure you can show me the memory later. I hated this outfit at first, but I've actually grown fond of this oversized belt buckle. It adds a whole new range to my expressions when I hitch it around for emphasis."

"I've joined a comedy troupe," Harmony muttered in disbelief. "That's what this is—a comedy troupe."

Niall scowled at Declan and Rhapsody, his expression morose. "Try dealing with them for thousands of years. Those two are the worst of the lot, but they have little mimics everywhere in the circle trying to emulate them."

Rhapsody introduced Serenity and Aurora to the four leprechauns, much to their delight. Harmony smiled indulgently as she watched her nieces. Each leprechaun got a hug from Aurora, triggering Harmony's synesthesia and earning her a wink from Rhapsody. Serenity stood awkwardly, too tall to hug them without kneeling.

"Rhapsody says Leesha's an amazing dancer," Harmony told Serenity with an encouraging smile. "I remember how much you used to love dancing. I bet we could watch their next celebration and pick up some tips."

Leesha nodded, smiling invitingly at Serenity. "We have celebrations several times a week. You should *definitely* join us—you won't regret it."

Rhapsody turned to the two girls, her expression expectant. "Are you two ready for some yuccas fitter?"

"*So* ready," Aurora exclaimed eagerly, her dark eyes lighting up with anticipation.

Serenity grinned. "We're *always* ready for yuccas fitter."

With a snap of her fingers, Rhapsody conjured a yuccas fitter and tossed it to Serenity.

"Ah, the food of the gods," Eimear commented enviously. "I could deal with being mortal all the time if it meant yuccas fitter every day."

Serenity blinked. "Can't you have it whenever you want?"

"Nay, lass," Eimear sighed regretfully. "We're only mortal for one night each year. As immortals, we don't have the anatomy to digest mortal foods."

Joline tilted her head. "How do you sustain yourselves as immortals?"

Declan nodded toward Rhapsody. "We receive our energy from the world trees. I'm sure she's mentioned she was a star before transitioning into a world tree. Instead of broadcasting light for planets, she broadcasts magic for magical creatures. That's why we're all here with her in the circle. Without Rhapsody, all magical creatures would wither and go into stasis. As you might guess, we're eagerly looking forward to your transition to world trees."

Harmony stared at Rhapsody in wonder. She was singlehandedly keeping the entire planet alive. So much depended on this amazing creature. She could still hardly believe she was in a relationship with such a glorious being. She felt a moment of unworthiness as she gazed at her perfect fairy. How could she possibly hope to be a partner to someone so far above her? All of Harmony's accomplishments and abilities amounted to next to nothing in comparison to Rhapsody.

Mystery turned to Harmony, concern in her eyes. "Hey, what's going on in that head of yours?"

Harmony blinked, looking back at Mystery in confusion. "Can you hear my thoughts, too?"

"No, not your thoughts," Mystery said, shaking her head. "I can feel... I don't know how to describe it. It's like I can feel what you're feeling."

"Synesthesia?" Harmony asked doubtfully. "But you're talking about emotional feelings. That can't be synesthesia."

"It's more than just emotions," Mystery told her quietly, blushing as she glanced at the watching faces. "I can feel the same things you're feeling with *your* synesthesia."

Harmony's eyes widened in shock. She turned to Rhapsody and raised an eyebrow that would have won an award from Serenity. "Okay, my little keeper of secrets, what's going on?"

Rhapsody flashed her a dimpled smile. "I mentioned earlier that the three of us have been together for a long time. Well, a long time ago, we linked our spirits. You haven't awakened your spirit connection yet, so you aren't affected as much. In time, you'll start to notice us in ways similar to your synesthesia, but on a deeper level and all the time."

Harmony considered the explanation. She didn't know anything about spirits, so she couldn't really make any guesses about what that really meant. She felt slightly better about her relationship with Rhapsody, with the reminder that they'd been together so long. She couldn't help wondering how Rhapsody knew about their linked spirits and previous incarnations. Wasn't forgetting your previous lives part of reincarnation? Was there a way to access soul memory and have some kind of recall? Clearly, there must be. It would certainly explain why she felt so comfortable around Mystery.

Rhapsody turned to Serenity with a mischievous grin. "It's time to crash a birthday party."

Serenity's eyes widened with sudden hope. "You're coming, too?"

"Of course I'm coming," Rhapsody declared imperiously. "I never miss a chance to crash a party."

Serenity rushed forward and embraced Rhapsody. "You're the *best*, Rhapsody!"

"Don't I know it," Rhapsody agreed, returning Serenity's hug with an affectionate smile.

Declan rubbed his hands together eagerly. "I want to see that memory when you return. I'm pretty sure *everyone* will want to see it."

"We'll have a movie night," Rhapsody promised with a bright smile. "It'll be fun to show the dome to our new members."

Taxti materialized next to Rhapsody, glancing around at the gathering with a critical eye. When her gaze landed on Michael, a slow, sensual smile spread across her face. Michael blinked at the seductive expression directed his way.

"Behave," Rhapsody commanded Taxti firmly. "We're going to a birthday party, so we'll be away for about an hour. Can you catch Mystery up on some world history and mental training while we're gone?"

"Like the training you've been giving Harmony?" Taxti asked with a smirk, turning to look Mystery up and down appreciatively. "Yeah, I think I can handle that."

Rhapsody rolled her expressive eyes but couldn't keep a smile from forming. "Just behave. She's mine."

"You're a greedy fairy," Taxti complained bitterly.

Rhapsody grinned at Serenity and Harmony. "Okay, you two, ready?"

"As we'll ever be," Harmony replied, doing her best to keep the trepidation out of her voice. This kind of thing was her worst nightmare. If it wasn't for Serenity's sake, it would definitely never happen. She would do anything for her nieces though, including attending birthday parties.

The land around them vanished, replaced by a green lawn in front of a modest house. It was located in a cookie-cutter neighborhood, with houses adjacent on both sides. Harmony already missed her house in the forest.

"Shall we knock?" Rhapsody suggested with a wink at Harmony. She took Serenity's hand and walked up the stone steps to the front door.

Before she could knock, the door opened, and a woman started to step outside. She jerked back in surprise when she saw the fairy standing on her porch, wings and all.

"Hello, Tiffany," Rhapsody greeted the woman with a bright smile. "Serenity said Susan had a birthday today. Are we early?"

Tiffany stared at Rhapsody in disbelief, her eyes bugging. She tried several times to speak, but the words caught in her throat. Rhapsody waited patiently, her large eyes full of mischief as she gazed at the flustered woman. Tiffany finally shook her head, blinked several times, and started over.

"Rhapsody?" she said in a reverent voice. "You're really real?"

"I'm really real," Rhapsody confirmed with a nod. "Do you need any help with anything? What were you coming outside for?"

"Outside?" she repeated, dazed. "Oh, um, I was going to get the balloons from the car and tie them to the mailbox."

"Say no more," Rhapsody sang, gesturing first at the car, then at the mailbox. Harmony felt the buzz of magic in her bones as the balloons vanished from the car and reappeared tied to the mailbox.

Tiffany goggled at the display, her face resembling a fish out of water.

Harmony bit her lip, trying not to laugh at Rhapsody's antics. Deciding to take pity on the poor woman, she walked up behind Rhapsody and offered her best friendly smile.

"Hi, Tiffany, it's nice to meet you," she greeted the floundering woman. "Serenity's been so excited to come to Susan's party. Thank you for inviting us."

Tiffany looked at Harmony and gasped. "Harmony? You're the author of—of—of..."

"Yep, that's me," Harmony agreed with a nod, her smile never faltering. "Is there anything else we can help you with?"

"Um, I don't think so?" she said, making it sound more like a question.

Harmony heard another car pull up to the curb and turned to see a small economy car in front of the house. The woman in the driver's seat was staring up at the porch in disbelief as her daughter quickly exited the car and ran toward them.

"Mom, is anyone here yet?" a girl asked from inside the house. When her mother didn't reply, the girl came to the door and gasped. Several inches shorter than Serenity, she had shoulder-length brown hair, and her brown eyes stared at Rhapsody in delight.

"You must be Susan," Rhapsody smiled up at the girl. "Happy birthday, Susan!"

"Rhapsody, you came!" Susan exclaimed, beaming.

"I love parties," Rhapsody said with a small laugh. "When Serenity said you invited us, we were overjoyed. Is your mom going to be okay?"

"Mom, snap out of it," Susan tugged on her mother's elbow. "Come on in, please."

Tiffany finally came out of her trance and blushed a sunset. "Yes, please come in. I'm sorry, I'm just a little flustered."

"You're totally fine," Rhapsody assured her with a winsome smile.

Harmony followed them into the house. The front room was decorated with balloons and party ribbons, and a large HAPPY BIRTHDAY sign hung from the ceiling between the dining room and front room.

Harmony hadn't been in many other people's houses before, having spent most of her time at her sister's after Serenity was born. Always a loner, her synesthesia only worsened her awkwardness in social situations. She was just glad nobody at school found out about it. As cruel as kids could be, she would've been tormented mercilessly. Instead of making friends, she spent most of her time in her imagination or reading.

Rhapsody looked around the room, her smile wide. "Wow, this place looks *awesome*. Your mom rocks, Susan."

"Uh, yeah, thanks, Mom," Susan said weakly. "It looks great."

Rhapsody rubbed her hands together eagerly. "So, what's on the agenda for today's party? Any games, or is thirteen too old for that kind of thing?"

Susan answered for her shell-shocked mother. "We have Twister and croquet set up in the backyard. We were going to play Cards Against Humanity."

"The family edition," Tiffany hastily added, smiling at Harmony, then quickly looking away.

Rhapsody grinned confidently. "I'm *so* getting in on a game of Twister. I'm the undefeated champion in the circle. One of Declan's nephews almost beat me once, but leprechauns have a habit of trying to tickle you, which I call cheating."

"There are leprechauns inside the ring?" Susan asked, her eyes wide with wonder.

Rhapsody nodded nonchalantly. "Leprechauns, fauns, dragons, mermaids, sentient trees, and of course, a fairy. The dragons have to stay up in the branches of Yggdrasil, though—they're too big to land without destroying things."

Harmony glanced at Rhapsody in surprise, not expecting her to reveal the inhabitants of the circle. As she thought about it, though, she realized it didn't really matter—nobody was going to get past Rhapsody to bother any of them.

"That is *so freaking cool*," Susan exclaimed, her eyes staring into space, imagining the mythical races. She turned to Serenity, her eyes intent. "Have you ever seen any of them?"

After a quick glance at Rhapsody, Serenity nodded. "Yeah, I've seen all of them. We just met four new leprechauns today. They're even shorter than Rhapsody, and they have the coolest dialects."

Susan sighed enviously. "You are *so* lucky."

The girl who'd arrived while they were on the porch had followed them inside, her mother trailing a minute later. They were gawking at Rhapsody and Harmony with wide eyes. Harmony remembered her own face now looked more fairy than human.

Susan waved at her mother. "Oh yeah, Mom, go get that book you wanted signed."

Tiffany blinked, her wondering gaze slowly returning to the present as she looked at Harmony hopefully. "Oh yeah, um, if you wouldn't mind?"

"Of course," Harmony agreed, keeping her expression clear of her distaste for the practice of book signings.

Tiffany hurried off to her room, glancing back as she went, as if needing to reassure herself that they were really there.

Harmony had a feeling her mischievous fairy was enjoying this way too much. As the thought crossed her mind, Rhapsody grinned and winked at her. Harmony laughed, shaking her head. There were no secrets with Rhapsody around.

The new girl shyly stepped forward to greet Rhapsody. "Hi, I'm Amber."

"Hi, Amber," Rhapsody smiled warmly. "It's nice to meet you. And yes, I can fly."

Amber blinked. "Can you hear what I'm thinking?"

"Yep, she can," Harmony assured her with a resigned sigh.

Amber's mother's eyes widened at the revelation, her face adopting the shuttered look of a DMV clerk five minutes after lunch.

"Would you like to see?" Rhapsody asked Amber expectantly.

Amber nodded, her eyes bright.

Rhapsody's wings began to glow brighter, and a moment later she rose into the air until her head was near the ceiling.

Rhapsody grinned triumphantly. "There, now *I'm* the tallest one in the room. I've been surrounded by giants ever since Harmony and Serenity showed up."

Harmony snorted. "We all know who the real giant is."

"Quiet, you," Rhapsody commanded with a wink.

She floated back down to the floor as Tiffany returned to the front room. Seeing the book Tiffany was bringing to Harmony, she grinned.

"That's one of my favorite books, too," Rhapsody told her brightly. "You have great taste in books, Tiffany."

Tiffany tittered nervously, tentatively handing the book to Harmony. She'd forgotten to bring a pen.

Harmony arched an eyebrow at Rhapsody. "I don't suppose you have a pen in some nebulous pocket dimension somewhere?"

"It just so happens..." Rhapsody's playful eyes grew brighter for a second, and then a pen appeared in her hand. It was a heavy, golden pen that didn't seem to have an ink cartridge, looking more suited for calligraphy than book signing.

Harmony eyed the pen suspiciously. "Do I dare ask where the ink comes from?"

"It's a magic pen," Rhapsody shrugged, the playful sparkle in her eyes never dimming. "Be careful what you write."

Harmony paused, taking the pen from Rhapsody and narrowing her eyes. Deciding to take Rhapsody at her word, she opted for a simple autograph rather than a message. She opened the book to the title page, quickly signed her name, and handed the book to Tiffany, who accepted it with trembling hands.

"Thank you, Harmony," Tiffany said effusively, smiling gratefully.

"I'd hang on to that book for a long time," Rhapsody suggested with a smirk. "I doubt there will ever be another book with her signature again."

"*You've got that right,*" Harmony thought dourly.

"*Chin up, Harmony,*" Rhapsody's voice echoed in her head. "*You've done a good deed here today. Tiffany's going to be the talk of the town for weeks to come.*"

"So, who's up for a game of Twister?" Rhapsody asked, eyeing Harmony challengingly.

"You're on," Harmony grinned, not bothering to say aloud how much fun it would be to tie herself in a knot around her fairy—not with the kids present.

8 – INSATIABLE

"Those wings are going to make this really difficult," Harmony observed critically from her position in front of the Twister mat in Susan's backyard. "It's no wonder you always win against the leprechauns."

Rhapsody's wings vanished, and she stared haughtily back at Harmony. "I don't use my wings with the leprechauns, so you won't have that as an excuse when I win."

"No magic," Harmony added firmly, eyeing Rhapsody suspiciously.

A small crowd had gathered. Two more girls had arrived, along with their parents, who had decided to stay when they learned Rhapsody was there. They watched silently as the fairy faced off against the much taller Harmony.

"I won't *need* magic," Rhapsody declared airily, "'cause I'm just *that* good."

Harmony narrowed her eyes. "If I feel any magic vibrating in my bones, you're in big trouble," she warned sternly.

"Oh yeah," Rhapsody grinned suddenly. "I forgot you could feel magic. Good, that means you can prove I'm not using magic next time I play against Cormac."

Rhapsody turned a challenging gaze to the watching crowd. "Is anyone else going to play?"

Serenity immediately stepped forward, grinning confidently. Susan seemed conflicted but ultimately decided to just watch. Amber joined them, her eyes sparkling with excitement as she smiled at Rhapsody.

The game started simply enough but quickly became more difficult with each turn. Rhapsody purposely chose colors that would block Harmony, her hand or foot darting to the spot before Harmony could reach it.

It didn't take long for Harmony to lose, once Serenity started cheating. When Serenity reached a point where she couldn't move to a new color, she rolled off the mat and made a wager with Susan that her friend couldn't tickle her. Susan enthusiastically attempted to prove Serenity wrong, and Harmony suddenly felt ghostly fingers tickling the life out of her as she tried to balance in a twisted backbend. She immediately collapsed, curling up and holding her sides while laughing uncontrollably. She took Amber down with her when she collapsed, leaving Rhapsody the winner.

Serenity immediately held up a hand to Susan, admitting that she was wrong, grinning at Harmony the whole time.

Harmony scowled at her niece. "There's going to be payback for that, young lady," she threatened ominously.

Serenity's eyes widened with innocence. "Why, whatever do you mean, Aunt Harmony?" she asked, her eyes darting to Rhapsody for a fraction of a second.

Harmony narrowed her eyes and turned to face Rhapsody. "You're a shameless cheater."

Rhapsody raised her hands defensively, a shit-eating grin on her face. "Hey, I didn't use magic."

Harmony gave her a flat look. "And that whispered conversation with Serenity before we came out here didn't involve the word 'tickle,' right?" she asked levelly, wishing she could reverse the direction of her synesthesia.

"Come now, Harmony," Rhapsody chided with a smug grin. "Don't be a sore loser."

Harmony tried to maintain her ire, but the small fairy was so outrageous that it was hard not to laugh at her expressive face. She struggled to keep the thin line of her lips from turning up into a smile, but it was a losing battle. When Rhapsody waggled her eyebrows suggestively, Harmony lost it, giggling helplessly.

"You're a *bad* fairy," she declared between giggles.

Rhapsody froze, a moment of shock flashing across her face before it split into a wide grin. Her eyes shimmered golden, fighting back tears as she stared at Harmony, love in her eyes.

"What?" Harmony asked, suddenly concerned. She could tell something she'd said had deeply affected Rhapsody.

"It's just wonderful to have you back," Rhapsody explained softly. "I've missed you *so* much."

"Can you show us some magic?" Amber asked hopefully, breaking the moment.

"You betcha," Rhapsody said brightly. "What would you like to see?"

Amber bit her lip. "What kind of things can you do?" she asked excitedly.

The adults stood a dozen feet away, making no attempt to socialize, their eyes fixed on Rhapsody.

"If you can imagine it, I can probably do it," Rhapsody told Amber with a wink. "What can you imagine, Amber?"

Amber's eyes glazed over as she considered the question. Given that she was thirteen, her response was fairly predictable. "Could you make it so I can fly?"

Rhapsody nodded toward Amber's mother. "That would depend on whether your mother is amenable."

"Is it safe?" Amber's mother asked hesitantly.

"Absolutely," Rhapsody nodded with a reassuring smile. "I can make her invulnerable so that even if she fell from orbit, it wouldn't hurt her."

Amber's mother stared at her in amazement. "You can do that?"

Rhapsody smiled confidently. "Like I told Amber, if you can imagine it, I can almost certainly do it."

"Okay... if you're sure," Amber's mother said slowly.

"Alright, Amber," Rhapsody said, turning back to Amber with a more serious expression. "When I give you the ability to fly, the knowledge of how to do it is going to be included. For the next twenty minutes, you'll be invulnerable. Just stay fairly close, okay? We don't want you running into any airplanes."

Amber's eyes widened with excited anticipation as she realized she was actually going to fly, nearly bouncing in place as she waited.

Rhapsody waved a negligent hand. "Okay, go get 'em, tiger."

Grinning widely, Amber slowly began to rise into the air. Susan and her friends stared in wonder, their eyes filled with hope.

Amber began zooming around the neighborhood, letting out loud whoops as she swooped through the air a hundred feet above the houses.

Harmony looked at Rhapsody curiously. She knew Aurora and Serenity were learning how to fly using magic. How was Rhapsody giving Amber the ability to fly *without* magic? And why would her nieces even need magic if they could gain the ability without it?

Rhapsody was immediately swarmed by four more girls asking for the ability to fly as well. Their parents hesitantly agreed, and soon the air was filled with girls zooming around the neighborhood, their excited screams echoing as they dove through the air. Serenity joined them, flying without Rhapsody's help. Harmony could feel the telltale buzz in her bones when Serenity lifted off the ground. As far as Harmony could tell, Serenity was the only one using magic.

She sidled up to Rhapsody, close enough to talk without being overheard.

"How are they flying without magic?" she asked quietly.

Rhapsody shrugged. "It's a different kind of magic. You'll learn all about it someday."

Harmony glared at her playfully. "So, you could have been cheating without Serenity's help."

"Technically, yes," Rhapsody admitted with a small smile. "But... I didn't. I'd give you my word, but I've already used my monthly quota of integrity."

"You're just *so* mysterious," Harmony mocked in a patronizing tone.

Rhapsody gave her a slow wink. "I heard you can't stop yourself from digging into any mysteries you find, so I thought I would try to be one."

Harmony rolled her eyes but couldn't stop a smile as she stood next to a mystery she *definitely* liked digging into. "You're such a goof."

The girls spent about twenty minutes flying around before Rhapsody brought them all back down, much to their dismay.

"I'm pretty sure there's still a cake that needs to be lit, and presents delivered," Rhapsody said, gesturing toward Susan's mom. "Don't make Tiffany go through all this work for nothing."

With much grumbling and sighing, the girls trooped back into the house. Harmony was pretty sure Susan would never live this birthday party down and would certainly be the envy of her classmates when they found out the next day. Harmony suspected a number of neighbors had noticed the flying teens zooming around the neighborhood as well.

Rhapsody discreetly handed Serenity a small, ornate flask. "Tell Susan that one drop on her palm is equivalent to a thirty-minute deep-cleaning shower—perfect for those days when she wants to skip showering but still feel super clean. There's about a year's worth of drops in there."

"This thing is *priceless*," Serenity whispered in awe.

"That's because it's not for sale," Rhapsody pointed out dryly.

"How do you even *make* something like this?" Serenity asked in amazement.

"With lots of practice and lots of patience," Rhapsody answered with a long-suffering sigh. "It will only work for her, though, so anyone who thinks they can steal it will find that it's just regular water."

"You're pretty amazing, Rhapsody," Serenity told the fairy admiringly.

"I have my moments," Rhapsody admitted with an airy toss of her head. "Now let's go get you some cake. Isn't that why people go to birthday parties?"

"You're not wrong," Serenity agreed with a giggle.

Harmony followed Rhapsody into the house to light the cake. The children's parents seemed too nervous to engage with Rhapsody, though they clearly wanted to. Several times, they looked on the verge of approaching her but chickened out at the last second. As they waited for Tiffany to light the cake, Rhapsody turned to the watching parents.

"Hi, Trish," Rhapsody greeted a stout woman who was only a few inches taller than Rhapsody. "No, I'm not a demon. The government didn't like what Mystery told them about fairies, so they started a campaign to turn public opinion against me. There actually is a core group within the intelligence agencies who believe I *am* a demon."

Rhapsody turned to another woman with a sallow face and a large wart on her nose.

"Hello, Nida," Rhapsody nodded at her with a smile. "Yes, I can take care of your illness. Do I have your permission?"

Nida's eyes widened, and she nodded, too nervous to speak, as she stared at the seemingly omniscient and omnipotent fairy.

Harmony wondered what was wrong with her.

"Great, let's get started," Rhapsody said with a gentle smile. She didn't make any hand motions or gestures, and Harmony didn't feel the familiar buzz of magic in her bones. Nida gasped, her already wide eyes growing wider. A moment later, the wart on her nose disappeared. Her skin darkened to a healthy tone, and Harmony sensed vitality pulsing brighter within the woman.

"All fixed," Rhapsody declared with a satisfied smile. "Stop using whatever detergent you're using for your clothes—you're allergic to it."

Nida's lips trembled as she stared back at Rhapsody, gratitude shining in her eyes.

"And Gloria," Rhapsody smiled at the last woman. She was only a few inches shorter than Harmony and had chestnut hair that reached her shoulders. "Are you sure you want me to wipe that memory? They say we're doomed to repeat our mistakes until we learn from them, and if you can't remember it, you won't be able to learn from it."

Gloria nodded mutely, her eyes full of determination.

"Very well," Rhapsody said sadly. "It's done."

"I remember wanting a memory removed, but I don't know which one," Gloria murmured in amazement. "Is that because you removed it?"

"That would be why," Rhapsody nodded, her lips twitching as she struggled not to laugh. Harmony bit back a smile of her own at the obvious response.

"Okay, I've granted lots of wishes today," Rhapsody said with a sinister smile. "Now your souls are *mine*."

The women stared at her in sudden trepidation until she dissolved into giggles. "Sorry, I'm an irredeemable tease. When you live as long as I have, it's hard not to start making jokes about everything. Your souls are safe."

Harmony watched Rhapsody with bemusement, wishing she could be so comfortable around others. Her introverted nature made small talk with strangers a struggle, while Rhapsody treated everyone like acquaintances and teased them like old friends. She was so gregarious and likable that it was difficult to see her in a negative light. Harmony wondered if this was part of her plan: to show the world that if she *was* a demon, then she was a *fun* demon.

On multiple occasions, two of the women had surreptitiously recorded video, attempting to make it seem as though they were simply filming their daughters. Harmony was fairly certain those videos would be posted to social media within an hour of the women returning home.

The candles were lit, awaiting the happy birthday song. Harmony shuddered inside as she sang along with the rest of the group. She *hated* singing the happy birthday song. Something about it just felt so *lame*. She was determined to come up with a better song for Serenity's and Aurora's birthdays.

Rhapsody winked at her roguishly as they sang, clearly enjoying Harmony's dark inner grumblings. Harmony scowled back until one of the mothers glanced her way, and she hurriedly plastered a smile back on her face. Rhapsody's smile widened as she sang, her eyes never leaving Harmony's.

When Susan blew out the candles, a huge jet of flame shot up into the air above the cake, eliciting several shocked screams. The women relaxed when they saw Rhapsody giggling herself silly, their expressions varying degrees of disgruntlement. Harmony felt an odd sense of nostalgic fondness as she watched the mischievous fairy. There was something so familiar and comforting in her behavior.

The five girls and their parents made short work of the cake. When Tiffany tried to convince Harmony and Rhapsody to try a piece, Rhapsody created another stir.

"We don't have stomachs, so we *can't* eat it," Rhapsody informed her, patting her narrow waistline for emphasis. "We eat energy. Well... *absorb* energy—what you would probably call magic."

Tiffany nodded. "You know, I always knew Harmony must be from some kind of magical society," she confided. "The way she described magic and the secret societies hidden in plain sight seemed too close to the truth."

Rhapsody smirked at Harmony. "Yeah, Harmony's been head over heels for magic for as long as I've known her."

Serenity quickly turned away to hide her grin.

Harmony felt a strong urge to tell the woman just how skeptical she'd been about all things magical until a few days ago. She opened her mouth to announce her agnostic position, but Rhapsody subtly shook her head, her large eyes full of hidden meaning. Harmony slowly closed her mouth, fixing Rhapsody with a level stare that demanded answers later—answers that had better be good.

When Serenity gave Susan the flask of liquid and explained its purpose, Susan squealed with delight, excitedly telling her mother that she could sleep in for twenty more minutes every day now.

It was the little things.

As the party wound down, Rhapsody thanked Tiffany for inviting them before taking Harmony's hand and teleporting them back to the circle. Serenity stayed behind to spend a few more hours with her friend and play Cards Against Humanity... the family edition.

Harmony and Rhapsody reappeared on the beach near the lake. Aurora was with Taxti and the group of leprechauns she'd met before the party, standing around a small pool on the beach. Aurora held her hands above the water with a look of intense concentration. Mist began rising from the pool, taking shape as it ascended into the air.

"Is that a gryphon?" Harmony asked quietly, not wanting to interrupt Aurora.

"Looks like it," Rhapsody confirmed with a pleased smile. "She really is brilliant—her and Serenity both. They're prodigies when it comes to magical theory, which isn't uncommon for older souls."

"And we've known them for a long time, too?" Harmony asked curiously.

"Yep, they're the equivalent of close family in the cosmic age of our souls," Rhapsody said with a fond smile.

Mystery glanced up from Aurora's gryphon. Her lavender eyes met Harmony's, and she smiled warmly, sending butterflies through Harmony's insides. Mystery's smile widened as she sensed Harmony's attraction through the mysterious spirit bond Rhapsody had told them about.

"She's doing a lot better now that she's with us," Rhapsody said in satisfaction. "I'm glad she didn't take longer to decide to join us. It wasn't pleasant watching her suffer so much."

Harmony glanced down at Rhapsody sympathetically. Rhapsody could likely feel *both* of their emotions, similar to how Mystery seemed to feel Harmony's. When Harmony concentrated, she could sense a bright feeling of wonder and happiness inside Mystery. It was strange to think they were linked by some kind of metaphysical bond that had formed who knew how long ago.

"I'm sorry you had to deal with that, Rhapsody," Harmony murmured softly.

"I'm just sorry *she* had to deal with that," Rhapsody said wistfully. "That's okay though, because it's all rainbows and roses going forward."

The gryphon suddenly flew up into the air and began flying in circles around them. As it flew, the shape filled in with color, becoming more lifelike. Aurora's face was tight with concentration as she stared up at her creation. After a minute of flying around, the gryphon dissolved into mist. Rhapsody and Harmony moved over to join them.

"That do be the quickest lesson I ever did witness," Leesha announced in an awed voice. "Aurora, are you sure you haven't been learning magic for a few decades?"

"I'm only a decade old, silly," Aurora replied with a pleased smile.

"You say that, but you seem pretty tall for a ten-year-old," Eimear noted doubtfully. "Are you sure there isn't another digit or two in there?"

"That's because I'm a *human*," Aurora said, a smile teasing her lips. "I've been around Aunt Harmony long enough to recognize sarcasm."

Mystery glanced at Harmony, amused. Harmony shrugged, a wry smile on her lips.

"What's this sarcasm you speak of?" Eimear asked with an artfully innocent expression. "I'm intrigued."

Aurora looked a little less sure of herself until she saw Eimear's lips quirk. "It's her superpower."

All eyes turned to Harmony with varying degrees of humor.

"It's true," Harmony assured them with a wink.

Mystery's smile widened as she stared at Harmony, sending shivers of delight down her spine. Between Rhapsody and Mystery, she felt like she was being kept on a low broil, her insides heating up with desire.

"How was the party?" Declan asked with a grin. He was no longer in the stereotypical leprechaun outfit depicted by Western tradition, but garbed similarly to Niall and Cormac, with the exception of the large belt buckle. His thumbs were tucked behind it in a relaxed manner, apparently planning to keep it as an extension of his expressions.

"She told the parents that she was taking their souls," Harmony replied, chuckling. "The intelligence agencies have been claiming she's a demon, so they had a moment of terror."

Eimear and Cormac joined Declan as he roared with laughter. Rhapsody grinned mischievously when Niall gave her a flat look.

"So, are they convinced she really is a demon now?" Joline asked with an amused glance at Rhapsody.

Harmony tilted her head consideringly. "If they do, they have a fresh take on what a demon is," she said dryly. "She performed several miracles for them, including healing one of them, so they'll have a difficult time seeing demons as evil entities at this rate."

"Are demons real?" Michael asked curiously.

Rhapsody shrugged. "Depends on which universe you're in, but there aren't any in this one."

Michael's eyes lit up. "How many universes *are* there?"

Rhapsody frowned, her eyes calculating. "That I know of? Around three millionish."

They all stared at Rhapsody curiously, though some showed more suspicion than curiosity.

"Have you ever been to any of them?" Joline asked intently.

Rhapsody nodded, smiling at Joline fondly. "I've been to all of them—as have you."

Joline blinked. "I have?"

"Yep," Rhapsody nodded firmly. "So have Harmony, Mystery, Michael, Aurora, and Serenity."

"What about Taxti and the others?" Aurora asked, glancing inquisitively at the faun and leprechauns.

"Declan's been to a few," Rhapsody said, nodding at the leprechaun king. "While you might be young in this world, your soul is much older than almost anyone else here. You'll understand someday."

"And you just *love* dropping tantalizing hints, don't you," Harmony accused her with a playful glare. She noticed Rhapsody had avoided disclosing how many universes Taxti had visited.

"I might enjoy it a little," Rhapsody admitted with a wink.

Harmony stared into Rhapsody's beautiful eyes, feeling a hint of the connection they shared—a connection going so far back into the past that time became meaningless. Rhapsody's lips quirked up as Harmony stared, entranced by those gorgeous eyes.

"She's off in la la land again," Harmony almost heard her mother say with resignation. "Somebody step between her and Rhapsody."

Harmony's trance ended as Taxti stepped in front of Rhapsody, grinning widely. "Welcome back, Harmony."

Harmony blinked, trying to recall what they were talking about. "Millions of universes?"

She frowned when everyone started laughing, including Niall. Aurora giggled up a storm, watching her aunt fondly. Mystery watched her with a small smile that sent another flutter through her abdomen.

"We asked if tonight would be a good time to roll out the leveling system," Joline supplied, amusement twinkling in her eyes. "We've established enough of the governing mechanics that Rhapsody thinks it's ready."

"Oh," Harmony blushed, realizing how long she'd been mesmerized by her beautiful fairy. "Um, did we ever figure out how to do it safely, so people don't get into accidents when the overlay suddenly appears in their vision?"

"It'll appear the next time they wake up," Taxti said, still fighting back a grin. She watched Harmony with a look of affectionate delight.

"I still want to know how in the world you can just make something like this work in a few hours," Harmony declared, stepping sideways to look at Rhapsody. Taxti mirrored her movement, continuing to block her view. "Do you mind?"

Taxti just smirked, maintaining her position.

"Trade secret," Rhapsody said impishly. "You'll just have to wait a couple of years before you learn about *that* little nugget."

"I'm still not sure what this leveling system is," Mystery confessed, brows furrowed in confusion. "Weren't we going to get Serenity's tablet or something?"

"Oh yeah," Michael said sadly, shaking his head. "You never tried any video games. It was all books for you—especially books by a certain author."

Mystery's gaze found Harmony's, and she smiled shyly. Harmony's pulse quickened at the adoration and respect in Mystery's luminous eyes.

"My turn, I guess," Joline muttered, stepping between Mystery and Harmony. She was too short to block their view of each other, though.

"Aurora, can you please come float in front of Mystery?" Joline asked tiredly.

Harmony heard her mother but didn't process the words, completely captivated by Mystery's beauty. She blinked when Aurora's grinning face suddenly replaced Mystery's.

"What?" Harmony asked, blinking at the amused faces observing her.

Michael chuckled, watching her with an approving smile. "I didn't think stuff like this happened outside of stories."

"It's their fault for being so damn *perfect*," Harmony declared defensively, folding her arms like a shield.

"I'm sure that's it," Joline agreed sardonically. "That's why the rest of us are struggling so much—oh, wait, we're not."

Harmony scowled at her mother as the others laughed. She knew there must be a clever retort, but try as she might, she couldn't think of one.

Michael pulled out his phone. "If Mystery needs a demo, we can use my phone—assuming there's a way to make it work inside the circle."

Rhapsody took the phone, then handed it back. "It should work now."

He nodded gratefully. "I have a few games on here with leveling systems," he said, walking over to Mystery. "I'll give her a quick tutorial."

Harmony tried to focus on the imminent rollout of the leveling system, but she couldn't stop thinking about getting Rhapsody alone. It was a burning hunger she couldn't ignore. She snuck a look at Rhapsody and was met with a slow, sensual wink and a seductive smile. Heat bloomed beneath her skin as she stared at the beautiful fairy hungrily.

"I just remembered there's something Harmony and I need to discuss before we move forward," Rhapsody announced, never breaking eye contact with Harmony. "We'll be back in a while."

The world around them vanished, replaced by Harmony's bedroom. Rhapsody floated over and wrapped herself around her.

"You're insatiable," Rhapsody whispered into Harmony's ear, sending shivers down her spine. "Now I'm going to tell you what I'm going to do to you."

Harmony's knees grew weak as Rhapsody continued.

9 – LEVELING SYSTEM

Susan groaned as her alarm beeped. She stretched with another groan before sitting up and opening her eyes. She blinked in surprise when she saw Rhapsody's head floating in front of her, beaming cheerfully.

"Good morning, Susan. My name is Rhapsody," she greeted her with a wink. "We've decided to add a leveling system to your world to make life more interesting. For those of you unaware of what a leveling system is, keep watching, and I'll explain. If you don't have time for explanations right now, just focus your thoughts on the time of day you want to postpone this tutorial to replay. The tutorial will take about five minutes."

Rhapsody's disembodied head tilted to the side. "Still here, huh? I guess we'll move on with the tutorial, then. For those of you unfamiliar with leveling systems—a term from modern games and LitRPG fantasy novels—it provides a metric for ranking your skills in any activity. For instance, if you're learning how to garden, you'll gain experience points for the time you put into gardening. When those experience points reach a certain threshold, you'll gain a level. Each time you gain a certain number of levels, you'll receive a bonus reward. These rewards vary depending on the classification of the skill you're working on. For a gardener, level one might unlock a skill called *Deft Touch*. This skill increases the odds of your crops reaching maturity and producing a harvest by ten percent."

She suddenly grinned. "Remember all those boring, annoying tasks in life, like school and work? Well, there are skills for anything, whether it's cleaning your kitchen, doing schoolwork, or learning to play a new instrument. You'll get more than just money or degrees for completing these tasks going forward. If you're a programmer, you'll receive leveling bonuses like syntax proficiency for different programming languages. If you're a carpenter, you'll receive boosts to your accuracy and efficiency. If you're a janitor, you'll find boosts to how easily a surface is cleaned, or your productivity may increase. If you're a graphic design artist, you might receive increased creativity bonuses."

Ghostly hands suddenly appeared next to her head, pointing up. "You'll also notice an overlay that appears at the top of your vision, commonly called a heads-up display. The icon at the top left is a picture of your face and is where you go to access all the information regarding your class, progress, and abilities. The small bar at the top is your level progress bar, which shows how far you have to go to reach the next level. The heart on the right is your health. Keep a sharp eye on this—if you don't take care of yourself, you'll notice it starts to change from red to black. Focus your attention on it to see more detail on what's causing you to be unhealthy, along with tips on how to rectify the issue. Physicians will love this feature—no more guesswork."

"When you look at other people, you'll see pop-up bubbles appear above their heads, displaying their name, species, and, if they choose, orientation. It will also show their alignment to good or evil. Yes, you will be called out for being a bastard from now on. I'm looking at you, politicians."

"You can make your overlay disappear or change its transparency by focusing your intent on it. You can also disable it for the rest of the day, and it won't reappear until the next morning. For a more detailed tutorial, focus your intent on the words: **more detailed tutorial**. The detailed tutorial explains how to use the chat feature, class options, friend requests, and instructions on how to use any abilities you gain."

"Now that the basic tutorial is out of the way, I'll tell you a little more about myself. I'm known by many titles, but in your current culture, the most familiar is fairy. However, this is just a projection of my true form, which is the world tree known as Yggdrasil. I'm sure most of you are aware of the Circle of Dominion in Northern California by now. Space is warped around this circle, so it is much larger on the inside. For the most part, the magical creatures of the world live inside these Circles of Dominion. Nearly a thousand years ago, an unscrupulous spirit walker destroyed the other world trees of this world. I'm in the process of restoring them, so those Circles of Dominion will once again bring life to the arid regions of the world and share their magic with its magical creatures, as well as humans."

"I want to make it very clear to the governments of the world that any interference will not be tolerated. This world will die if the world trees are not restored soon. I have found five humans who have the capacity to transition into world trees. The process has already begun for three of them, so there is hope."

"This concludes the intro for the new leveling system. I hope you enjoy it! We'll stay in touch." Rhapsody's head had started to fade, but it suddenly returned, grinning mischievously. "Oh yeah, PS: This was Harmony's idea."

The floating head of Rhapsody vanished, and the overlay Rhapsody had described appeared in Susan's vision. She stared in shock for a moment before grinning delightedly. She bounced out of bed and ran to her mother's room.

Her mother's eyes were staring into space from where she sat on the edge of her bed, clearly interacting with her new interface.

"This is so cool, Mom!" Susan exclaimed, her grin stretching across her face.

"I guess so," her mother answered, sounding much less confident. "How could she do something like this to everyone on Earth? Just how powerful *is* she?"

"She said she was a world tree," Susan replied with a shrug. "That seems pretty powerful."

"Yeah, I suppose so," her mother murmured distractedly.

Susan looked around for something to do, anything to show some kind of level increase. She went back to her room and began cleaning, curious if that counted as a skill. As soon as she finished picking everything up and making her bed, a firework appeared in the overlay, along with the words:

LEVEL UP!!! You are now at Level 1 for the skill: **Cleaning**.
You will have the option to choose an ability at level 5.
Note: Each level increase requires increased work—also known as grinding—in order to reach the next level.
Well done, Susan! You rock!

She gasped as a euphoric glow enveloped her, lighting her up brilliantly for several seconds. When the effect ended, she stood panting. Was this how it would feel every time she leveled up?

Susan grinned manically, already planning her next skill. This was going to be so freaking cool!

* * *

Eileen woke with a start at the sound of Harnketi cackling loudly in their guest bedroom. She blinked when Rhapsody's disembodied head appeared in front of her. As she listened to Rhapsody's introduction and brief tutorial, her eyes widened. When it was over, she went to the living room to find a grinning Harnketi and her equally delighted oldest son, Tiacan.

"I had a feeling Rhapsody was going to do something crazy after Harmony showed up," Harnketi declared with another laugh. "She didn't disappoint."

Bemused, Eileen stared at Harnketi, trying to wrap her mind around the implications of what Rhapsody had done. "Harnketi, I knew Rhapsody was powerful, but this... I can't even imagine how she could have done something like this to every human on Earth."

"Oh, this isn't just for the humans," Harnketi told her wryly. "This will affect all the magical creatures, too. Knowing Rhapsody, there will be some augmented wildlife as well. As far as her power goes? There really is no limit to what Rhapsody could do. I spent almost six hundred years with her and learned things that would seem unbelievable if you heard the least of them. She's very respectful of how she uses her power, though. She tries to work within the natural laws of this world, instead of just making things work the way she thinks they should. She doesn't want to be a dictator."

Harnketi paused, then grinned. "To put it into perspective, the Creator walks carefully when Rhapsody's around. They're pretty good friends, but I've heard her thank Rhapsody for allowing her to keep her autonomy. Whatever Rhapsody is, she's somewhere above the Creator of our universe."

Eileen nodded slowly, feeling a growing sense of awe for the fairy she'd always revered in legends as a magical spirit walker. Apparently, she was much more than that.

Her husband, Tyee, walked through the front door looking harried. He'd worked the night shift at the fire department. Tall with a medium build, he wore his long, black hair pulled back into a ponytail. Wrinkles fanned out from his eyes from frequent laughter. He was a wonderful husband and father, filling their home with love and cheer.

"You wouldn't believe how crazy things were this morning," Tyee said, shaking his head in disbelief as he walked over and kissed her. "People are having mass hallucinations. We had hundreds of calls for EMTs from people saying they saw a woman's head appearing in front of them."

"They weren't hallucinations," Eileen told him calmly. "I'm guessing you haven't seen it yet because you haven't gone to sleep. They appeared as soon as I woke up."

Harnketi nodded. "Yeah, Rhapsody would have done it that way to prevent people from getting hurt if they were driving or operating dangerous equipment. Go to sleep, Tyee—you'll see the same thing when you wake up."

Tyee looked at them curiously. "What did Rhapsody do?"

Eileen laughed. "I wouldn't want to ruin the surprise. Go get some sleep. I want to be there when you wake up."

Tyee's lips quirked into a smile as he stared into her sparkling eyes. "Okay, fine. I'm not sure how I'm going to get to sleep now."

"I can put you to sleep when you're ready," Harnketi offered, wiggling her fingers dramatically.

"I think I'll have to take you up on that," Tyee nodded, his eyes alight with curiosity.

Eileen's phone rang. She walked back into her bedroom and answered it. It was an automated announcement that school was canceled for the day. She snorted a laugh, imagining the superintendent trying to decide how to manage a school full of kids who were playing in their heads-up displays all day. Rhapsody's new system was certainly going to have far-reaching effects.

* * *

World Reels from New Leveling System

The world is reeling as what was initially dismissed as mass hallucinations has now been revealed to be a gaming overlay appearing in people's vision upon waking this morning.

While the phenomenon has primarily affected the Western Hemisphere due to time differences, individuals on the other side of the world who were asleep during the day have reported experiencing the same vision upon waking. A figure identifying herself as Rhapsody, a fairy who is the projection of the world tree Yggdrasil, has appeared in this overlay, providing a tutorial and introduction to what she calls a leveling system. She said the other world trees were destroyed by a spirit walker a millennium ago and that, without new world trees, the world will end.

She claimed to have found five human candidates to become new world trees, and that three were already undergoing the process. We believe Harmony and Mystery are two of these candidates, as both women are known to have been inside the ring in the Northern California redwoods where Rhapsody allegedly resides. The third candidate is likely Harmony's mother, Joline, who was also believed to be within the fairy ring. We assume Harmony's two nieces, who are in her custody, are the remaining candidates.

Experts are baffled by this unprecedented event. Given Rhapsody's capabilities in the week prior, many suspect the cause involves either magic or advanced technology.

We have contacted the White House for comment but have received no response as of this article's publication.

In the days leading up to the event, numerous social media videos featured psychics claiming Rhapsody was a demon. If this is true, her influence extends to both religious and secular individuals, as even prominent religious leaders worldwide have reported seeing the new system.

We have reached out to Vatican City for comment but have not received a response as of this publication. Several televangelists have claimed the new system is the work of the devil and have warned people against using it. Oddly, the system's alignment indicator, which is supposed to show whether a person is good or evil, has identified these same televangelists deep in the negative. They claim that the system is a devilish attempt to turn the faithful against God's shepherds. When asked why God would allow the devil to create such a system, they responded that it was a test of their faith. Based on this response, it remains unclear whether God approves of the system.

We will be posting regular updates at alicenominas.com *as events unfold. Now, if you'll excuse us, we have some leveling to do.*

* * *

Harmony laughed as she finished reading the latest article aloud on her laptop. Rhapsody had been reading over her shoulder. They were in Harmony's front room with Serenity, Aurora, Mystery, Michael, and her mother.

"Well, this is certainly going to be a fun year," Michael noted with a broad grin. "The world is about to get really interesting."

"Just how powerful can a person become?" Joline asked Rhapsody curiously. "How far up can they level something like strength?"

"It's set to peak at level one hundred," Rhapsody answered distractedly as she skimmed through the comments with Harmony. "That's to encourage people to find new things to level up and not just focus on one thing."

Michael rubbed his chin. "How strong would a person at level one hundred be compared to the strongest human alive today?" he asked. "Are they going to have Incredible Hulk-type strength?"

Rhapsody squinted thoughtfully, her eyes calculating. "About five times stronger than the strongest human on record. That's within the range that other strength-based classes could still handle, especially since law enforcement will likely offer a bonus to officers working on that class. So, we shouldn't see a tide of overpowered humans taking the law into their own hands, because people will lose levels when they do things that are negatively aligned."

"Oh yeah, I forgot about that," Michael murmured, looking up at Rhapsody curiously. "You didn't mention that in the tutorial. Why not?"

Rhapsody grinned mischievously. "I want them to figure it out on their own. I plan to have the system automatically record their expressions when they realize they've lost a level."

The room erupted in laughter. Harmony shook her head ruefully, looking back at Rhapsody.

"You are a *bad* fairy."

Rhapsody kissed her forehead. "You have no idea how good it is to hear you say that."

"You are one odd duck," Harmony said with a wink.

"I'm feeling more like a goose right now," Rhapsody whispered seductively.

Harmony blinked, a distant memory from what felt like a dream floating into her consciousness. "Because they honk?"

Rhapsody's smile widened. "And why do geese honk?"

Harmony burst out laughing. "Because they're horny."

Rhapsody's eyes gleamed. "That's right, Harmony."

10 – RESURRECTION

"I want to see the tutorial," Harmony demanded, narrowing her eyes at Rhapsody. "Eileen called and thanked me for coming up with the idea after her kids started cleaning the house, and I know I didn't tell her about it."

Rhapsody was leading them on a tour to other parts of the circle. They walked along a wide trail that began a few hundred feet from the world tree's entrance. Joline, her nieces, Mystery, Michael, and Declan followed. Taxti had run off on an errand she'd been very vague about, and the four leprechauns they'd met were off playing with the new leveling system.

"Well, you don't sleep anymore, so there isn't really a way for you to see it," Rhapsody said regretfully. "I'm not sure how it'd work with an actual world tree anyway. I can feel your meridians expanding more than I expected every time you absorb energy from the chasm. At this rate, you'll be ready to complete the transition in months rather than years."

"Oh no," Harmony said firmly. "Don't you *dare* pretend you can't just pull up a holographic window and show me the tutorial."

Rhapsody glanced sideways at her before intently studying the thick Dorekin trees surrounding them. The trees were at least twice the size of redwoods but had bark more like aspens. Rhapsody excitedly pointed to a six-inch hole in one of them.

"Hey, look, an *actual* fairy dwelling," Rhapsody said brightly. "That's what *real* fairies look like. We just copied their form when we made our projections, but we made ourselves a lot bigger."

Harmony tried not to get sidetracked, but her eyes were drawn to the glowing creatures she'd mistaken for fireflies as they flitted in and out of the hole. With her improved vision, she could easily focus on the tiny creatures and see that they were miniature versions of Rhapsody, red hair and all.

"How intelligent are they?" Joline asked in fascination.

"It's a little difficult to compare their intelligence to humans because they're so different," Rhapsody said. "If I had to make a direct comparison, I'd say they're about as intelligent as teenagers. They're very territorial and will unleash the whole hive on anyone dumb enough to intrude on their tree. They're all female and have a group of queens that share authority. They existed on this world before humans and were one of the first creatures I saw when I decided to make a projection for the first time."

"So, they aren't friendly," Joline said with a disappointed sigh.

"Oh, they're *super* friendly," Rhapsody assured her with a laugh. "As long as you don't trespass. They'll talk your ear off for days on end if you let them. They're smart enough to hold a normal conversation, but they don't really grow very much intellectually over time because they don't face any adversity. This also changes their worldview, making it hard for them to empathize with humans. Because they're spawned from transitioning energy-based entities, they don't procreate like humans. They're mostly immortal, but like leprechauns, there's one night a year when they become mortal."

"Why is that?" Harmony asked curiously, studying the fairies with fascination.

"The energy they're created from grows stale," Rhapsody explained, continuing to lead them through the giant forest. "Once a year, they transition to a mortal form while their energy matrices are rebuilt using energy provided by world trees. After their matrices are rebuilt, they transform back into immortal entities. You can tell when their annual renewal is approaching because they start getting sluggish and tired a few weeks beforehand."

"Do world trees have the same issue with stale energy?" Harmony asked, tilting her head curiously. "Do *you* become mortal?"

"No, world trees transition from stars, so we have an unlimited supply of pure energy," Rhapsody replied, glancing at Declan with a nod. "So much energy, in fact, that it's far too much for us, so we radiate it for other magical creatures to use."

"What did you do as a star?" Harmony asked wonderingly, watching the beautiful fairy next to her in fascination. She wore a red knee-length skirt and a silky red blouse that showed a hint of cleavage, along with black boots that almost reached her knees. It was all Harmony could do not to drool. "Since you were essentially stationary, what did you do all day?"

"I observed and interacted with the worlds around me," Rhapsody answered with a reminiscent smile. "I was omnipresent for the worlds around me, able to watch all the lives and activities that occurred over their lifespans. I could project an avatar to interact with the inhabitants, like I do as a world tree. It was never boring."

"Huh," Harmony suddenly grinned. "I guess all those cultures who worshipped sun gods were actually worshipping *you*."

"Yep, that they were," Rhapsody agreed with a short laugh. "They always blamed me for good or bad harvests. My role as a star was to learn from observing the lives around me. I wasn't supposed to directly take any action, aside from verbal interactions through my avatar. Even that was supposed to be incognito, so they wouldn't know I was actually their star."

"You must be quite the expert on human nature by now," Harmony noted, her gaze calculating.

"I've picked a few things up," Rhapsody admitted nonchalantly, a small smile appearing on her face as they continued walking.

Harmony thought back to their first meeting, wondering if Rhapsody had expertly crafted each interaction to draw her out of her shell and give relationships a chance. Had eons of observing human nature given Rhapsody the skills to break through the near-impenetrable walls Harmony had built around herself? She felt a swell of gratitude for whatever forces had put her in Rhapsody's sights. She'd been content as a single person with only her imagination for company, but now she knew how much she'd been missing.

Rhapsody looked up at her and smiled gently, her eyes full of love. Mystery glanced over, tilting her head curiously, likely sensing Harmony's emotions. Ever since Rhapsody and Harmony had returned from their four-hour... interlude, Mystery had blushed whenever she looked at them. Harmony wondered how much Mystery had felt of their intimate exchange through their mysterious spirit bond.

"I was just thinking about how lucky I was that Rhapsody was the one who found me," Harmony said, glancing affectionately at Rhapsody. "I don't think anyone else would've been able to break through all my mental walls."

"She's pretty amazing," Mystery agreed warmly, smiling down at Rhapsody.

"Yeah, Rhapsody's the best," Aurora chimed in, smiling at Rhapsody brightly.

Serenity nodded her agreement, staring at Rhapsody like a favorite older sister.

Rhapsody grinned back and winked. "Stop, you're making me blush."

"You're *always* blushing, though," Serenity pointed out with an envious sigh. "Everyone else has to put on makeup to fake it."

"Being a shapeshifter has its moments," Rhapsody noted blandly, pointedly *not* looking at Harmony. Even so, Harmony's cheeks caught fire. Mystery must have felt the sudden rush of desire through their bond. She took one look at Harmony's flaming cheeks, and her own lit up like a sunset, confirming

Harmony's suspicions that she'd felt at least some of the sensations from their intimate interlude.

"Now *they're* blushing for real," Serenity announced, pointing at Harmony and Mystery. "You can tell because even her forehead is bright red."

Harmony put her face in her hands, trying to hide her glowing cheeks. Serenity was gaining more points in her mental scoreboard than she could hope to keep up with lately. She needed to up her game.

"It's not my fault these silly bodies can't regulate blood flow properly," Harmony complained bitterly. "Whoever designed them was a sadist. Making our faces blush from adrenaline is almost as stupid as making our windpipe share the same passage as our feeding hole."

"Did you really just call your throat a feeding hole?" Michael asked in morbid disbelief as Rhapsody threw her head back and laughed, her golden peels ringing through the air.

Joline shook her head tiredly, watching Harmony with a resigned expression. "Harmony... I don't even have the words."

"That sounds really gross, Aunt Harmony," Aurora commented distastefully, her mouth turned down in a small frown.

"Did you want gills or something?" Mystery asked, her eyes sparkling with amusement.

"*Yes*," Harmony exclaimed in exasperation. "Do you know how many times I've choked on water or food in my life? Do you know how many people actually *die* from choking? It's a poor design, the work of either an idiot or a sadist."

Rhapsody clung to Harmony's arm to steady herself as her fit of giggles robbed her legs of strength.

"Oh, the irony," Rhapsody gasped, trying to catch her breath. "Someday, far in the future, we're going to revisit this conversation."

She felt a faint flare of affection from the glowing corner of her soul she thought of as Rhapsody—the first emotion she'd felt besides an ambient warmth. Was she finally going to be able to feel more of Rhapsody's emotions now?

When she focused on the portion of herself that she thought of as Mystery, she could feel a deep, burning love directed at her. There was also a sense of attraction that had been growing stronger throughout the day, a passion simmering just below the surface. She had to avoid focusing on those emotions, or her easily distracted mind would get derailed. It was difficult, though, with the beautiful woman walking right next to her, close enough that her enhanced senses could feel the heat radiating off her lithe body, and smell the scent of sweet flowers.

Rhapsody finally recovered from her mirth and took Harmony's hand.

"I'm usually the one who derails conversations," Rhapsody said reprovingly, glancing up at her with a smirk as she tugged her forward. "Don't horn in on my turf, young lady."

Harmony rolled her eyes as she let Rhapsody pull her along. The feel of Rhapsody's hand in her own was sending signals to her brain that shut down her ability to think of intelligent retorts.

Ahead of them, in a clearing in the forest, stood a large stone tower. It was easily the same width as Harmony's house, but a lot taller, with large windows spaced every twenty feet. Stone steps led to a large door at its base.

"This is Deighvy's place," Rhapsody announced, walking up the steps. "She's a... spirit walker and spends most of her time on other worlds. I sensed her arrival a little while ago and thought introductions were in order."

Harmony frowned, noticing the hesitation in Rhapsody's voice before naming Deighvy a spirit walker. Was she a spirit walker, or not?

Rhapsody led them up the tower steps and knocked. After almost a minute of silence, the door opened to reveal a middle-aged woman with long black hair. Her eyes were unsettling: black sclera surrounding glowing white irises and pupils. She was completely naked, save for her chest, which was partially concealed by her long hair. She possessed a mature beauty, like a rose in full bloom. Her high cheekbones and delicate chin defined a face of exquisite beauty.

Harmony immediately felt awkward, having already met her quota of nudists after entertaining the soldiers who lost their clothes and equipment when Rhapsody melted them with fog.

Deighvy's eyes flickered toward her, and her lips quirked into an amused smile. It was hard to tell if she was looking directly at Harmony, since her pupils were the same brilliant white as her irises.

Rhapsody had turned to observe their reactions as well, a mischievous smile on her face. Mystery seemed unfazed, as did Joline and Declan. Harmony's nieces, however, looked as uncomfortable as she felt, trying not to stare. Michael, on the other hand, observed the beautiful spirit walker with frank appreciation.

"This is Deighvy," Rhapsody introduced her with an affectionate smile. "She stops by every decade or two for a few days. Deighvy already knows all of you."

Harmony idly noticed the look of respect on Declan's face. Trying to ignore Deighvy's nudity, Harmony focused on her face and activated her second sight, hoping the overlay of energy would obscure the woman's body. She gasped as a brilliant white light blinded her second sight, drowning out everything except Rhapsody. Just what was this woman, to emanate such power?

"It's nice to finally meet all of you in person," Deighvy greeted them with a welcoming smile that filled Harmony with warmth, reminiscent of Emily's embrace, albeit to a lesser extent. Was she an angel, too?

"Please, come inside," Deighvy beckoned, stepping back into the tower.

Intrigued, Harmony followed Rhapsody inside. She could sense power emanating from Deighvy like a supernova. Was she also a transitioned star?

Harmony looked around the large, open room intently, curious about what a powerful spirit walker kept in their wizard-like tower. Circular walls lined with bookshelves wrapped around the entire room. In the center was a twenty-foot-diameter pool filled with what appeared to be mercury, with small, glowing orbs floating in and out of the quicksilver substance. Harmony tracked one of the orbs as it rose through a shimmering portal in the ceiling twenty feet above.

Foot-tall walls surrounded the pool, inscribed with glowing runes that continually changed in brightness, some morphing into entirely different runes.

"How are the rest of your creations doing?" Rhapsody asked Deighvy conversationally. "Anything *new* and interesting?"

"I've been working on creating a light realm similar to what you described last time we talked," Deighvy answered, pursing her lips briefly. "I considered using the same design you suggested, but I decided to change the entry requirements. Only souls that have incarnated at least four times will be eligible, as younger souls lack the comprehension to properly utilize what the realm offers. There are additional karmic requirements as well."

"Wait a minute," Joline said, her voice filled with awe. "You're *that* Deighvy? The creator?"

Harmony blinked, looking at Joline in confusion. Since when was the creator named Deighvy?

"Yep, that's me," Deighvy nodded, offering Joline a faint smile. "I thought you might recognize the name."

Mystery and Michael stared at Deighvy in growing awe. Harmony felt the skeptical monster she thought she'd defeated rear its doubting head to cry fake. She tried to mentally throttle the little demon, but it was like grabbing mist every time she grasped its metaphorical neck with her metaphorical hands.

"So, you created the world?" Harmony asked, struggling to keep the doubt from her voice.

"All of the worlds," Deighvy replied, eyeing her with a slight frown. "All of the worlds in *this* universe."

Harmony once again felt the sense of a tightly compressed supernova blazing within the woman. *If* God was human-shaped, at least she was a girl and not some bearded dude with a dissociative personality disorder who threw temper tantrums when his creations didn't do what he wanted.

"Harmony has some change requests regarding human anatomy she wanted to share with you," Rhapsody informed Deighvy, giving Harmony an impish grin. "I can't remember how she described the person responsible for designing the original human body. Harmony, do you remember?"

Joline's face went white at Rhapsody's words. She glanced worriedly at Deighvy and then back at Harmony.

"I think Harmony was just being facetious," Joline said quickly. "She's always had a sarcastic tongue."

Deighvy shared a look with Rhapsody and then began laughing with as much enthusiasm as Rhapsody had earlier.

"I really want to be there when she finds out," Deighvy told Rhapsody, wiping a tear from her eye. "I think I'll stick around this world for a few centuries so I don't miss it."

Joline let out a relieved breath when no lightning bolts appeared. She stared at the laughing divinity with a puzzled expression, mirrored by everyone except Rhapsody.

"When I find out *what*?" Harmony demanded, narrowing her eyes at the laughing duo.

"Harmony," Joline hissed warningly. "Show some respect."

"I want to know what they're talking about," Harmony declared stubbornly. "Out with it, Rhapsody."

"I'm saying that I want to be there when you finally find out who designed the human body," Deighvy explained, watching Harmony in amusement.

"It better not be the bearded guy," Harmony muttered darkly.

Rhapsody and Deighvy dissolved into another fit of laughter. There was clearly some kind of inside joke that she was the butt of, but try as she might, she couldn't figure out what it was.

"What's with the bubble bath?" Harmony asked, gesturing at the quicksilver pool and the glowing orbs floating in and out of it.

"This is a portal to the place where souls are judged," Deighvy answered, gesturing at the pool. "Mercury is used to bind the spirit to the consciousness from the souls' last mortal form. Depending on their karmic weight, they will be given the choice to pass on to the spirit realm, where there is no more pain, and leave the reincarnation cycle behind."

"Is my sister reincarnated yet?" Harmony asked before she realized what she was saying.

"Your sister has moved beyond the reincarnation cycle," Deighvy replied slowly, glancing speculatively at Rhapsody. "She isn't in this universe anymore. At least, not in a form that I can recognize."

"Mom's not going to reincarnate as a human again?" Serenity asked, her eyes growing wet as she stared at Deighvy with fading hope. "She's gone forever?"

"No, Serenity," Rhapsody walked over and pulled her into a gentle embrace. "She's not gone forever. One of the reasons we are visiting Deighvy today is to see if I can bend a rule in exchange for some information."

Deighvy looked at Serenity and Aurora consideringly before looking down at Rhapsody. "How far are you planning to bend this rule?"

"Not far," Rhapsody assured her with a dimpled smile. "I just want a resurrection."

Harmony and Joline gasped in shock. Harmony's hand flew to her mouth as her eyes blurred with tears.

"Nothing extraordinary," Rhapsody continued conversationally. "Just a restoration to what she was before."

Harmony felt Mystery's arm around her shaking shoulders as silent tears streamed down her face. She leaned into the other woman as hope ignited like a nuclear blast in her chest.

"You could bring Mom back?" Serenity asked in a brittle voice filled with hope.

Deighvy stared at Rhapsody speculatively. "What information are you willing to exchange for my looking the other way?"

"Access to the origin realm," Rhapsody replied quietly, "on the condition that access stays with you and you alone."

"Deal," Deighvy agreed immediately.

"Thank you, Deighvy," Rhapsody said softly.

"Thank you, Rhapsody, for respecting our autonomy," Deighvy replied gravely. "I know you could circumvent our rules, and we all appreciate your temperance."

Rhapsody released Serenity and stepped away from the others. She closed her eyes and remained still for almost a minute. Harmony and her family watched with a desperate hope that was almost painful. A glowing outline of a person gradually grew brighter in front of Rhapsody, then began to fill in as the light intensified. When the light reached a level where Harmony could no longer see, it vanished.

Her sister stood in front of Rhapsody, looking around the room in confusion. She only had a second to stare before Harmony, her nieces, and Joline rushed toward her. Harmony felt like her heart would burst as she pulled her sister into a tight embrace, choking back a guttural sob. She released her quickly so that Serenity and Aurora could reach her.

"Mom!" Serenity and Aurora cried out in elation, tackling her from either side. "Oh, Mom, I missed you *so* much!" Serenity cried, holding her mother tightly.

Aurora couldn't get any words out, her frantic sobs muffled by Melody's shirt as she clung desperately to her mother's arm.

"What's going on?" Melody asked in bewilderment, wrapping her free arm around Serenity. Her voice suddenly became fearful. "Where's David? He has a knife!"

"You're safe, Melody," Joline assured her comfortingly, stepping forward and pulling the three of them into her arms, her shoulders shaking as she held her daughter tightly.

Harmony felt Rhapsody's arms wrap around her waist from behind. "I brought her back from just before the knife attack," Rhapsody whispered into her ear.

"Thank you, Rhapsody," Harmony choked out through her tears, her chest wracked with huge sobs. "I'll never be able to repay you for this."

"You'll never need to, silly," Rhapsody told her gently, resting her chin on Harmony's shoulder.

Mystery watched their reunion with tears in her eyes and a tender smile on her beautiful face as she stared at Harmony. Declan watched with a soft expression and a gentle smile. Michael stared at Melody in confusion, unaware of her recent death.

"Mom, what's going on?" Melody asked Joline in a dazed voice. "Where are we, and how did we get here?"

"It's a long story, sweetie," their mother told her, her voice choked with emotion. "Just give us a minute to enjoy having you back."

"Back from where?" Melody asked, perplexed. "You're acting like I died."

Their mother broke down with a heart-wrenching sob at Melody's words, pulling her daughter in tighter.

"Harmony?" Melody prompted, noticing Harmony's emotional state. "Was I dead?"

Harmony nodded, unable to speak past the tennis ball in her throat, convulsing with large, tearing sobs. She would have never believed relief could feel so strong. She wanted to pull her sister into an embrace and never let her go. All the horrible things she now remembered happening to her sister when they were younger, the horrible marriage she'd been trapped in—they could finally start building happy memories to replace the horrors of her past.

"How did I—," Melody broke off, finally noticing the others in the room. When her eyes landed on Deighvy, she gasped, taking in her strange eyes and the aura of power radiating from her like the sun.

"Rhapsody brought you back to us," Serenity told her tearfully. "She's the fairy with Aunt Harmony."

Harmony was beginning to get overwhelmed by her synesthesia from all the physical contact in the room, but it wasn't unpleasant. She felt like she was hugging her sister by proxy as she felt it through Joline and her nieces. She could feel Rhapsody pressed against her back as well, a reassuring pressure grounding her to something solid.

Melody looked at Rhapsody uncomprehendingly. The fairy still had her chin resting on Harmony's shoulder and her arms wrapped around Harmony's waist. At Serenity's words, Rhapsody released Harmony and floated over to Melody.

"Hello, Melody," Rhapsody beamed at Harmony's stunned sister. "Words can't adequately describe how good it is to have you back. David is gone forever. You're safe, and I won't ever let anything bad happen to you again."

Melody stared at Rhapsody in awe, her eyes pooling with tears. "He's gone?"

"You should have seen it," Serenity told Melody with an exuberant laugh charged with emotion. "Rhapsody beat the living crap out of him. We'll never have to worry about him again."

"How long have I been... gone?" Melody asked hesitantly, unable to say the word.

"Three months," Rhapsody told her gently. "Your daughters have been living with Harmony in your Grandma Dotty's house."

"You wouldn't believe how awesome it's been," Serenity told Melody excitedly, her emotions transposed into manic energy. "It was so good to be with Aunt Harmony again! And then we met Rhapsody and discovered she was a fairy and came inside her fairy ring. She gave us the ability to do magic! Watch this!"

Serenity vanished, eliciting a startled squeak from Melody. Serenity suddenly reappeared next to Melody, an enormous grin on her face. "We can teleport, fly, make clones of ourselves, scry, and create shadow familiars! Just wait until you meet Taxti. She's the queen of the fauns, and she's the one who's been teaching us magic."

Harmony couldn't stop a laugh from escaping through her tears as she observed her niece bubbling with excitement.

"I think we should slow down," Joline told Serenity gently, noticing Melody's stunned expression. "This is a lot for her to take in, especially after waking up so suddenly in a strange place."

Aurora still hadn't spoken, sobbing into Melody's side as Melody stroked her hair comfortingly.

Melody squinted, studying Harmony more closely. "Harmony? Is it really you?"

"It's really me," Harmony assured her with a tremulous smile. "I'm transforming into a fairy, so I look a little different. I don't know if you remember how skeptical I've always been, but apparently magic exists, as do a lot of the magical creatures from folklore. It took me a long time to accept it, even when it was right in front of me."

Melody smiled with relief. "Yeah, that's Harmony. The eternal skeptic."

"If you think *I* look different, take another look at Mom," Harmony said with a short laugh.

Melody finally turned to Joline and gaped. Joline looked a decade younger than Melody. "Mom, is that really you?"

"I'm immortal now," Joline told the dumbfounded Melody with a dazzling smile. "I'm also transforming into a fairy. We'll explain everything, but it will take a little while. A *lot* has happened in the last two weeks."

Melody continued to stare at Joline in stunned disbelief. She looked like a shorter version of Harmony.

Melody had been resurrected wearing the same denim jeans she'd had on the night she died, along with a white blouse that showed a hint of cleavage. Her chest-length blonde hair was the same light color as Harmony's. While not as slim and fit as Harmony, she was still a healthy weight. She was the same height as Harmony and had the same bright blue eyes Harmony once had. If Melody been younger, they could have been mistaken for twins.

"I suggest we go to Harmony's house," Rhapsody said, watching Melody closely. "She needs somewhere familiar to feel comfortable enough to process all these new revelations."

Rhapsody walked up to Deighvy and embraced her with a grateful smile. "Thank you, Deighvy."

"It was worth it to see so much love in one place," Deighvy replied with a wistful smile. "I'll be around if you want to talk."

Rhapsody nodded, smiling again, before rejoining the others. "Declan, are you coming too?"

"You're damn right I'm coming," Declan declared with a snort. "You and Harmony have provided more entertainment than I've seen in a thousand years."

Rhapsody rolled her eyes and turned to Harmony and her family. "Everybody ready?"

Harmony stepped up to Deighvy and embraced her tightly. *"Thank you!"*

"It's the least I could do for you," Deighvy said softly. "After everything you three have done for all of us. It was wonderful to meet you, Harmony."

Harmony stepped back and nodded at Rhapsody.

Serenity teleported ahead. Aurora, however, was unwilling to let her mother go. Rhapsody waved her hand dramatically, and the tower vanished, replaced by Harmony's large living room.

Melody let out a startled squawk as she felt the icy immersion of teleportation. She stared around the front room in surprise, her eyes widening in recognition. Seeing her opening, Harmony quickly stepped over *and* embraced her sister tightly.

"Don't worry, Melody," Harmony said gently. "Rhapsody is going to fix everything."

Melody looked at Harmony searchingly, clearly hearing the hidden meaning in her words.

"Everything," Harmony repeated with a radiant smile.

Melody closed her eyes as tears welled and spilled down her cheeks. Harmony held her comfortingly, feeling the relief flooding out of her sister.

11 – EVIL BASTARDS

"Executive Director Gibson, I'm seriously questioning your continued role on this task force," Vice President Adams declared acidly. "First, you let the only person who has been inside the ring slip through your fingers in an embarrassing display of incompetence. Then, you failed to apprehend two helpless teens from a school, despite having an army of agents at your disposal. It would take a linguistic scholar to adequately describe the level of your failure. Can you explain exactly how Mystery, whom we told you was the most important person in the world, was left in a rundown apartment with just *two* agents to monitor her?"

"We believe magic was involved," Gibson replied, his voice barely above a sullen murmur.

Adams scowled at him. The overlay that had appeared in her vision that morning indicated that Gibson's alignment was far in the negative. Her own alignment was deep in the red, giving her the title: 'Filthy Rotten Evil Bastard,' while Gibson's read: 'Despicable Evil Bastard,' accompanied by an icon of a turd. Her own icon was a whole pile of turds.

"Magic?" Adams repeated in disbelief. "How old are you, Director Gibson? Is there a grown-up hiding inside that thick head of yours? Put on your big-girl panties; there's no place for toddlers in matters of national security. Where the hell is Mystery Donovan right now? If I hear the words, 'We don't know,' you're off this task force by tomorrow morning."

Gibson glared at Adams, all traces of diffidence gone. "We *don't* know where she is, but even a *toddler* could guess that she's in that damn ring."

"Former Executive Director Gibson, you are excused," Adams said coldly. "Deputy Director Beatty, you are now Acting Executive Director of this task force. You will make contact with this *fairy*, this Rhapsody, and you will *beg* her forgiveness in hopes that they will allow open dialogue. If you don't think you can follow these orders, speak up now so we can get a responsible adult in here who *can*."

"Yes, ma'am," Beatty replied with a curt nod, rising from the conference table.

The former Executive Director exited the room, shaking with rage and glaring at Beatty as he passed. Adams felt a sense of grim satisfaction as she watched the incompetent fool leave. A mutiny was taking place in the intelligence agencies, with a core group of senior members trying to impose their ultra-religious beliefs on their colleagues. They were convinced there were literal demons and that only faithful men of God could be trusted to make policy decisions in what they believed was a war between good and evil.

Adams had no patience for such superstitions. They were dealing with entities wielding technology far surpassing their own, and the last thing they needed was a group of fundamentalists provoking them.

A strong push had been made to launch a nuclear strike at the ring, and the President had almost been convinced. Adams had been the sole voice of reason to dissuade the easily influenced leader, as his aides and supposed experts tried to convince him the political fallout would be preferable to allowing a demonic entity to sow chaos unchallenged. She had finally gotten through to him by explaining that an entity who could teleport people, demonic or not, could almost certainly teleport a nuclear weapon into the White House before it reached its target. Fear flashed across the President's face, and all talk of nuclear attacks on American soil ceased.

Adams was no saint, and she knew it. She had skeletons in every metaphorical closet of her house. Initially driven by ambition, she had toed the unspoken line that every politician trod on their climb to power. Her soul was as black as the next politician's, but where many had convinced themselves they were serving a higher cause and that the ends justified the means, she had been motivated purely by selfishness. From everything she'd learned about this Rhapsody character, they were dealing with an entity so far beyond their own technology that they might as well be cavemen. Her motivation to seek peace with the fairy was purely self-preservation.

When she had discovered the overlay that morning, she'd nearly had a heart attack. Seeing Rhapsody's disembodied head appear in her vision, followed by the revelation of the new leveling system, had only reinforced her belief that they were dealing with powers far beyond their capacity to handle.

She sat at the conference table, frowning pensively as she tried to understand Rhapsody's real reasons for implementing the 'leveling system.'

Why give people the ability to track their skills? What were the rewards for leveling up supposed to be, and how would they affect societal stability? Would they be dealing with X-Men-like powers among the general populace as people reached higher levels? It would be anarchy. Was that Rhapsody's goal? If so, why not simply wipe them out in a faster, more efficient manner? If she could install a leveling system in every person's consciousness, she likely could kill them all with equal ease.

She sighed, frustrated by her attempts to understand the mind of a non-human entity. Their reasoning could be far beyond her comprehension. It was a bitter pill to swallow: dealing with entities this advanced meant anticipating their moves would be like a rat in a maze trying to predict the next shock. Maybe that's what this was—some kind of social experiment by an advanced species using humans as lab rats.

She glanced at her Secret Service detail. Two men stood near the door while three more patrolled the room, their eyes scanning the windows.

"Davis, what possible reasons can *you* think of for an advanced intelligence to install this leveling system in humans?" she asked one of her agents, a medium-built man with dark hair. He wore jeans and a polo shirt, looking like a lost tourist as he strolled around the room. "I need a sounding board. I'm almost positive this Rhapsody character could have simply switched our brains off if she wanted. Why give people the ability to level? And why give them rewards that augment their abilities beyond normal human capabilities?"

Davis wandered back to the desk across from her as another plain-clothes agent took his place patrolling the area.

"I only heard about this recently," Davis answered carefully. "But supposedly, if you do things that move your alignment into the negative, you lose levels. If that's true, I'd guess she's trying to get people to be good—or at least, her version of good."

Adams' eyebrows shot up. If true, there wouldn't be a sudden wave of anarchy from supercharged humans taking the law into their own hands—at least not unless they didn't mind losing their levels. Could Rhapsody be trying to improve humanity? The thought made her nauseous. Her success stemmed from exploiting people and navigating the world of questionably legal practices. Would this new leveling system detect such fine distinctions? Based on how far in the red she was on her alignment, the answer was a resounding yes.

"So, this is her way of forcing a moral system on humans," Adams muttered darkly. Still, it was better than angering her and having her clean house—starting at the top.

"It happened shortly after the media began calling her a demon," Davis commented shrewdly. "You've probably noticed the species classification when appraising someone. I suspect the system's primary purpose was to combat that smear campaign, with the other features serving as a convenient excuse to display the species tag. That would prove she wasn't a demon to anyone who appraised her, while simultaneously elevating her to sainthood among the growing number of people worldwide who yearn for a world with gaming mechanics. Add the built-in chat feature, and we have a medium for completely private communication. All the infrastructure our intelligence agencies put in place to monitor communication has just been rendered useless. I was told the chat feature only works for people with a positive alignment, so that may be a silver lining."

Adams sighed tiredly, leaning back in her chair. Most of her Secret Service agents were positively aligned. She wondered about the fallout when the nation learned that almost every politician was deep in the red—not a big surprise to anyone, really. The world was going to change drastically over the next few years. Even if Rhapsody made no further moves, the damage to the established power structure would be crippling.

She idly wondered what the rank and file thought of their leadership now that they could see their alignment. She imagined more than a few organizations were searching for ways to hide their alignments as subordinates viewed the true state of their leaders. It would be embarrassing to be seen negatively aligned—no doubt part of the reason for making it public.

She'd instructed Beatty to find some fresh faces for the task force, people she could work with independently of the fundamentalists running the intelligence agencies. Beatty had found an FBI ASAC to manage Adams's private team, along with two NSA agents Beatty had worked with before. She appointed the agents as Senior Liaison Officers, allowing her to bypass dealing with their bosses. Beatty had sent the two women to secure a meeting with Rhapsody—something Adams doubted was possible at this point. Still, the two agents were just grunts and completely expendable.

"This is going to be a long day," she sighed loudly, closing her eyes to escape the judgmental overlay. "A long year."

* * *

Harmony finally released her sister so their mother could take her place again. She wiped the tears from her cheeks as she turned to embrace Rhapsody.

"Thank you *so* much, Rhapsody," Harmony said, thanking the fairy for the third time. A feeling like a bonfire burned in her chest as she held the beautiful woman. She was so overcome with gratitude and love that she felt like she might combust. "You really are an angel."

Rhapsody stiffened in her arms for a moment before relaxing again. Harmony froze as a thought occurred to her—something she would have never entertained when her skeptical demon was controlling her reality detector. Could Rhapsody actually be an angel for real? She had already met one angel who seemed to be really close to Rhapsody. Could Rhapsody be an angel in disguise, here to save the world as the nodes drifted further out of alignment? Was that childhood memory of Rhapsody transforming into an angel actually real?

Rhapsody's arm slid up her back and began drawing shapes. Harmony shivered at the sensation that wasn't *quite* ticklish, but close. It took her a moment to realize that Rhapsody was drawing words. She focused on Rhapsody's touch, trying to decipher the letters. After a minute of trying to keep track, she was finally able to piece together Rhapsody's secret message: *"You are adorable*."

Harmony dissolved into giggles as her overcharged emotions swung in the other direction. Rhapsody pulled back to stare into her eyes with a smoldering gaze that turned Harmony's insides to jelly.

"I'll bet your sister is hungry," Rhapsody commented, glancing at a slightly befuddled Melody. "She's still mortal, after all."

"I suppose we should figure out some arrangements," Harmony murmured, her insides still a mixture of euphoria and desire. "We have plenty of rooms available here. She's an older soul, too, isn't she?"

Harmony wasn't sure how she could tell, but she had noticed some kind of energy signature from the other humans when she was at Susan's birthday party. It felt different from Melody—her sister's was more complex and mature.

"She is," Rhapsody confirmed with a small smile. "If she's willing to become a world tree, we'll have enough to restore an additional node. I have a feeling she'll accept."

"Can you help her with the trauma?" Harmony asked quietly, cognizant of her sister behind her.

"I sure can," Rhapsody confirmed cheerfully.

Harmony hesitated, sensing a tiny sliver of guilt through their spirit bond. She looked into Rhapsody's beautiful eyes with concern. Was she still hiding the sorrow Harmony had briefly seen when Emily had visited? As Harmony became more aware of their spirit bond, it would become impossible for Rhapsody to hide those feelings.

"Rhapsody?" Harmony prompted softly.

"Yes, Harmony?" Rhapsody asked innocently, her eyes showing no sign of inner turmoil. Harmony focused on the warm corner of her soul where Rhapsody resided. She creased her brow, attempting to probe the glowing corner, but it resisted her efforts. There was a hairline crack at the edges, where the emotions seemed to occasionally leak out.

"What's wrong, Rhapsody?" Harmony asked gently.

Harmony felt the crack hemorrhage crippling pain and guilt for a moment before Rhapsody suppressed it. Rhapsody's innocent expression remained unchanged as she stared back at Harmony.

"Right now?" Rhapsody asked with a slow, sensual smile. "I'm just hungry for Harmony. I guess we should wait for things to settle down a little first."

Mystery stepped up beside them, her expression mirroring Harmony's concern. "You can tell us, Rhapsody."

Harmony marveled at Rhapsody's ability to control her expressions. She feigned puzzlement while the crack in their spirit bond trickled with soul-crushing grief and mind-numbing guilt.

"Tell you what?" Rhapsody asked, feigning confusion.

Harmony glanced at her family and friends around the room. Michael was talking quietly with Declan, while Serenity, Aurora, and Joline continued clinging to a bemused Melody.

"We'll be back in a little while," Harmony told them with a reassuring smile.

She took Rhapsody's hand and pulled her toward the stairs, Mystery following close behind.

"Oh, you're not going to make me wait after all," Rhapsody remarked seductively.

Harmony firmly restrained her libido. Rhapsody seemed to be using every trick she had to prevent Harmony and Mystery from discovering what was wrong.

Rhapsody tried again as they began ascending the stairs.

"You know, your sister's still mortal," Rhapsody said, her voice thick with concern. "We should probably find her some food—she hasn't eaten in three months. Assuming all of your food hasn't expired now that your nieces are surviving on yuccas fitter."

"She'll be fine for another hour or two," Harmony replied dryly, pulling Rhapsody along.

"That's easy for *you* to say, now that you don't need food," Rhapsody said pointedly. "She's probably famished."

"She's with my mom," Harmony said placidly. "If she's hungry, Mom will get her something. Besides, she's a big girl and knows where the kitchen is."

Harmony felt increasing resistance as they neared her bedroom, but she ignored it and pulled harder.

Sensing Rhapsody's intention, Harmony spun around, pointing a finger at her nose. "Don't you *dare* teleport out of here!"

Rhapsody froze, her face a mask of shock as she stared back at Harmony. "How did you know I was going to teleport?"

"I have no idea," Harmony answered with a shrug. "I could just feel it. Quit trying to avoid us and get in here."

Rhapsody reluctantly allowed herself to be pulled into Harmony's room. Mystery followed and closed the door behind them.

Harmony turned and took both of Rhapsody's hands, sitting on the bed so they were at eye level. Mystery sat beside Harmony, watching Rhapsody with a compassionate gaze.

"Okay, Rhapsody, tell us what's wrong," Harmony said tenderly. "I can feel it through the soul bond. You're full of grief and guilt. What's bothering you?"

The crack in the bond trembled, guilt and grief compounded by fear as Rhapsody stared back at them, a puzzled expression on her face.

"Listen, Harmony, Mystery," Rhapsody began softly, "soul bonds can be a little confusing sometimes. You're probably feeling echoes of past sorrow. I'm totally fine now that you're both here. I've never been happier, having all of you back."

She was so convincing that Harmony nearly accepted the explanation, but Mystery's connection was more established. Mystery took Rhapsody's hands from Harmony and pulled Rhapsody into a gentle embrace.

"You don't have to tell us if you don't want to," Mystery said gently, her voice soft with understanding and sympathy. "Just know we're here for you. You can let it out without telling us what it is. We love you, Rhapsody, and nothing you could say will ever change that."

Rhapsody let out a tortured sob as Mystery held her tenderly. The first sob opened the floodgates. Rhapsody clung to Mystery, wailing despairingly, her shoulders shaking as her body was racked with desperate sobs, tears streaming down her cheeks.

"I'm so... so... *sorry*," Rhapsody choked, her voice filled with such agony and heartbreak that Harmony felt her own eyes welling up. "I... I... failed you so... so... badly! I wasn't there when you needed me the most. I... I..." She broke off, frantic, unintelligible sobs overwhelmed her ability to speak.

Harmony ran her hand down Rhapsody's gorgeous red mane, petting her comfortingly as Mystery held her. Time stretched as the weeping storm continued, unabated. Rhapsody radiated guilt and grief, the emotional deluge washing over her like a tidal wave of remorse. Just as she would begin to recover and attempt to speak, her throat would seize up, and guilt would drown out every other emotion but soul-crushing grief.

"I'm so sorry you're carrying this burden," Harmony said through her own tears. "I wish I could take your pain away."

That was the wrong thing to say, sending Rhapsody into another episode of guttural sobs that Harmony worried would tear her apart. Harmony couldn't believe Rhapsody had been able to present such a normal countenance with the ocean of despair that had been hiding just beneath the surface. Why did she feel so much guilt for what had happened to them?

"Let's leave the past behind, okay?" Harmony told Rhapsody gently. "We're here with you now, and we're here to stay. Let's make good memories to banish the bad ones. All I want is to be with the two of you and for you to be happy.

You've brought me so much joy that words can't describe how grateful I am, Rhapsody. Let go of the past and just focus on the now. We have each other, and that will always be enough."

As Harmony spoke, Rhapsody's sobs finally began to slow. Harmony touched Rhapsody's cheek tenderly, staring into her enormous eyes and letting all her love shine through.

Rhapsody took a long, shuddering breath, seeming to soak up the warmth of their closeness. As her tears finally stopped, Harmony leaned her forehead against Rhapsody's, staring into her eyes, a small smile appearing on her lips.

The bundle of emotions tucked away in the corner of her mind that she thought of as Rhapsody was no longer a dull, warm glow. Harmony could feel every emotion as if it were her own. Rhapsody must have tried to block her emotions from flowing through the bond to keep them from feeling her grief and guilt. Now that she had finally let go, she was no longer trying to hide from them. Her love was like a supernova, it burned so brightly. Harmony stared at Rhapsody in wonder as she felt the overpowering love.

Harmony blinked in confusion when Rhapsody's face was briefly superimposed with another: a woman with silky black hair and a heart-stopping kind of beauty. How could *anything* be so beautiful?

The vision faded, leaving Rhapsody's face in its place. "Clarice?"

Rhapsody jerked upright in shock. Harmony felt panic through the bond as Rhapsody stared back at her in sudden anxiety. "What did you call me?"

"I don't remember," Harmony replied slowly, creasing her brows in perplexity. "I just saw another face superimposed on top of yours for a second, and a name popped into my head. I can't even remember it now, though. It's like a dream fading away."

"You said Clarice," Mystery supplied, her face creased in concentration as she looked between Harmony and Rhapsody. "It seems familiar for some reason."

Rhapsody watched her carefully as the panic in the bond calmed. "Do you remember when I said we had been together for a long time before incarnating here?"

"Yeah, that's not something that's easy to forget," Harmony noted wryly. "Is that what you looked like in that other life?"

"Yeah," Rhapsody nodded with an uncomfortable shrug. "You weren't supposed to learn about any of that stuff for years to come. Best-laid plans of mice and angels, I guess."

"Why don't you want us to remember now?" Mystery asked curiously. "Will it cause some kind of trouble?"

"It's one of the rules of this... universe," Rhapsody explained slowly. "We try to honor the rules of the different universes we visit. You need to live a certain length of time before your soul memories are unlocked. You have a few more years before you should be accessing them. It's a hard rule to enforce on souls like ours, so yours are leaking through much sooner than they normally would. Just try to ignore your soul memories and focus on living in this life, okay?"

"I guess you're old enough to access soul memories," Harmony noted dryly, "at half a million years old."

"I can't talk about this yet, but suffice it to say, I've been here close to the same amount of time as you. However, things were a little different for me and the... body I ended up in," Rhapsody told them carefully.

Harmony wrote fantasy novels for a living and could guess what Rhapsody was referring to.

"Stop right there, young lady!" Rhapsody told her sternly, her lips twitching into a small smile of approval.

"Okay!" Harmony laughed, throwing her hands up defensively. "I'm stopping, but it's not easy."

"What did I miss?" Mystery asked, tilting her head curiously.

"Nothing," Rhapsody insisted firmly. "Nothing of importance. We'll tell you when you're older."

Mystery laughed ruefully, watching the two of them fondly. "I really do feel like I've known you two all my life."

"I know what you mean," Harmony agreed with a slow smile as she looked at Mystery. "But I feel like we should get reacquainted."

Mystery blushed as she felt Harmony's sudden torrent of desire through the bond. She stared back at Harmony, lips parted, as her chest began to rise and fall more quickly.

"Sorry, but we're going to have to delay our reunion for a little while," Rhapsody told them regretfully, pushing back on her own desire. Harmony could feel just how hot and wild her desire was for the two of them. She stared into Rhapsody's hypnotically beautiful eyes and tried to think of an excuse for them to get some alone time sooner.

She blinked as a hand broke her view of Rhapsody. She looked over and found Mystery's laughing face watching her fondly. She blushed as she realized she'd tranced out again. Mystery's large lavender eyes were filled with amusement as she smiled at Harmony. Her lips were just as enticing as Rhapsody's, calling out to be kissed.

The world suddenly went dark, and Harmony felt a strip of cloth around her eyes. She finally became aware of the sounds of Rhapsody and Mystery giggling as Rhapsody held the sleep mask in place.

"It *is* kind of flattering," Mystery admitted with warm amusement. "I've never had anyone lose all awareness of the world around them when looking at me before."

"I know, right?" Rhapsody agreed with a delighted laugh. "But I think Harmony is a special case."

Harmony reached up to remove the sleep mask, but Rhapsody gently restrained her.

"Why don't we keep it on until we get you downstairs?" Rhapsody suggested, giggling. "Otherwise, we might never make it."

Harmony grumbled good-naturedly as she let Mystery take her hand and lead her out the door. Butterflies fluttered in her stomach at Mystery's soft touch.

"Is everything okay?" Serenity asked anxiously when she saw Mystery leading a blindfolded Harmony into the room.

"She was having a little trouble focusing with one of us on either side of her," Rhapsody explained, grinning as she removed the blindfold.

"Mom, wait until you hear about all the cool things Aunt Harmony can do," Serenity told Melody excitedly. "She's psychic! She can feel what you're feeling if you think about her watching you—like if you scratch your knee or get tickled. Plus, she gets tunnel vision if she looks at Rhapsody or Mystery."

"Thanks, Serenity," Harmony remarked dryly. "Melody's barely back a day before you tell her what a weirdo I am."

Serenity marched up to Harmony, a stern frown on her face. "You are *not* a weirdo! The things you do are *so* freaking cool—even the tunnel vision! Who wouldn't want to be so in love that they lose track of the real world whenever they look at someone?"

Harmony shook her head ruefully, not answering. She had to admit, she enjoyed being in love to such an extent. She looked over at her sister curiously, joy filling her soul at the realization that Melody was *really* alive.

"Did Mom explain the last three months?" Harmony asked expectantly, walking over to sit on the couch next to her sister.

"Yeah, she did," Melody nodded, looking dazed. "I'm still not sure I'm not in a coma or something. This is all so *bizarre*."

Harmony laughed. "Yes. Yes, it is. But it's bizarre in a *good* way."

"You're in love, aren't you?" Melody asked, noticing Harmony's beaming face.

"Head over heels," Harmony admitted with a wide smile.

"Is it Mystery or Rhapsody?" Melody asked with an indulgent smile.

"It's both of them," Harmony answered with a smirk. She laughed when her sister looked at her peculiarly.

"You're not going to get weird about me being in a three-way relationship, are you?" Harmony asked in amusement.

"I don't exactly have room to judge relationship decisions," Melody replied with a sigh. "I guess I just never really thought of someone being in a relationship with more than one person at the same time. Well, maybe Mormons."

Harmony threw her head back and laughed. "Just call me Jane Smith, with my fairy harem."

Melody chuckled, gazing at Harmony fondly. "It's so good to see you again. I really missed having you around. I don't think I ever properly thanked you for taking care of my little angels during my bad months. And thanks for looking after them while I was...gone."

"It was truly my pleasure," Harmony assured her with a radiant smile. "I was never going to have children, so it was wonderful to be able to have some by proxy. I just wish I'd convinced you all to move in with me when Grandma did. I spent most of my time worrying about you."

"I'll just bet you did," Melody sighed, a faint smile playing on her lips. "You were everyone's mom."

"I like taking care of people," Harmony shrugged, giving a short laugh.

"So, you ended up with the weird touch defect, too, huh?" Melody asked, her expression sympathetic.

"Wait," Harmony breathed in sharply, stared at Melody in shock. "*You* have mirror-touch synesthesia, too?"

"It has a name, huh?" Melody asked sourly. "I'm sorry you ended up with it as well. I suspected, but I didn't want to ask."

"It's not *all* bad," Harmony noted, glancing at Rhapsody. "Though I would have thought so before a week ago. Did you know it doesn't require someone to be in your line of sight to trigger it?"

"Yeah, David figured that out within the first month of our relationship," Melody answered, her voice flat. "He used to think it was funny to smash his fingers in drawers while he was at work and watch me on camera. He got off on the power it gave him over me."

"*Gross*," Harmony exclaimed, looking at her sister in horror. "Melody, I am *so* sorry. I wish I had known sooner. I would have hired a hitman or something."

"That's why I couldn't leave him," Melody sighed bitterly. "He always threatened constant abuse if I did, and since it didn't leave a mark, there was nothing I could do."

Rhapsody's face darkened as she listened to Melody. "I think it's time for me to pay David another visit."

"Isn't he in prison?" Melody asked apprehensively. "What if he finds out I'm alive?"

"He's in the hospital still, which is fitting, since that's where he'll spend the rest of his miserable life," Rhapsody declared grimly before vanishing.

"I told you she would fix everything," Harmony told Melody with a satisfied smile. "When Rhapsody's done with David, he'll probably spend the rest of his life wishing he were dead, but that won't be an option for him."

Melody closed her eyes, a few tears leaking down her cheeks. "I can't tell you how good it feels to be free."

Harmony wrapped her arm around her sister and leaned her head against Melody's. "It's all sunshine and rainbows from here on out."

They all froze when the doorbell rang. Harmony stood and walked to the entryway. On the surveillance camera, she saw two women in suits. Harmony glanced back at the living room, a worried expression on her face. Should she answer the door without Rhapsody here?

"Go ahead," Declan said confidently, stepping up behind her. "I'll take care of any troublemakers."

Harmony sighed with relief. "Thanks, Declan."

Anxiety building, she opened the door and stared at the two women. They both had dark, shoulder-length hair. One looked to be in her mid-thirties, while the other was closer to Harmony's age. The older one had a cute, pixie-like face. Her partner was pretty, though her formal suit didn't do her any favors.

If the wards were still working, only people without ill intent could approach the house. She hoped they were.

"Hello, Miss Conifer," the older of the two greeted her with a friendly smile, studying Harmony's clearly non-human features curiously. "I'm Agent Black, and this is Agent Monroe. We're with the NSA. Would it be possible for us to speak with Miss Rhapsody?"

Harmony had a brief internal debate as she stared at them silently. If she told them Rhapsody wasn't here, they might see her as vulnerable and try to take her. She reminded herself that Declan was right behind her. Still, she couldn't help wondering why they'd sent someone from the NSA. Were they trying to hack the leveling system?

"She stepped out for a few minutes," Harmony finally answered cautiously. "And it's just Rhapsody. She would get weirded out if you called her *Miss* Rhapsody. What do you want with her?"

"We were sent to apologize for any unpleasantness that may have resulted from the former leadership's decisions," Black said smoothly. "Particularly regarding Miss Donovan."

"You mean like telling everyone that Rhapsody was a demon?" Harmony asked dryly.

"Yes, like that," Agent Black nodded agreeably.

"Hello, Agents," Rhapsody said, her voice preceding her as she teleported next to Harmony. "How can we help each other today?"

12 – RESURRECTION PARTY

The two agents jumped as Rhapsody suddenly appeared next to Harmony. It took them a moment to process what she had said. Black recovered first, her smile reappearing.

"Hello, Miss, um, Rhapsody," Agent Black stumbled over her name, remembering Harmony's suggestion to drop the "Miss." "We wanted to formally apologize to you and Miss Donovan for any trouble we have caused."

Rhapsody gave them an innocent smile. "Trouble? I don't remember any trouble."

"Ah," Black hesitated, glancing at Harmony before continuing. "We would also like to apologize to Miss Donovan for the way she was treated. There have been some changes in leadership to address the issue. Would it be possible to start over? We would like to maintain an open line of communication and foster a relationship that is mutually beneficial."

"I'm already in a relationship with Harmony and Mystery, but thanks anyway," Rhapsody replied with a wink. "Don't get me wrong—you're cute, especially with the lady-in-uniform vibe, but I think more than two would start rumors about fairy harems."

Harmony bit her lip as the agents stared at Rhapsody in consternation, clearly floundering.

"You are such a *bad* fairy," Harmony sighed, shaking her head ruefully. She looked at the two agents with an apologetic smile. "Sorry, she's a relentless tease."

The two agents tittered nervously, navigating waters suddenly out of their depth. Black cleared her throat, trying to regain her footing.

"Would it be possible for us to remain in contact with you?" Black tried again, her smile strained. "Perhaps through the chat system in your leveling interface? The Vice President would like to establish diplomatic channels with you in an effort to head off any other... unpleasantness."

"Sure, I'll send Amanda a friend request," Rhapsody offered with a grin. "I'll have to whitelist her, since she's an evil bastard. And I *wouldn't* have teleported the nuke they planned to drop on the circle back onto the White House. I would have just dissolved it."

"Nuke?" Black repeated unsteadily, her eyes widening.

"Your President and his cronies wanted to drop a nuke on the circle," Rhapsody informed her cheerfully. "Amanda convinced them that I'd probably teleport it back to the White House if they *did* try to nuke me. I wouldn't have, though. I'd just eradicate all the remaining nukes in the world—which I'm going to do anyway, but I would have sooner."

Black swallowed, staring at Rhapsody nervously. Harmony felt a little bad for the woman. This conversation was far beyond her expertise or paygrade. Why had they sent NSA agents instead of a diplomat? Wasn't the NSA in charge of electronic surveillance? This seemed way outside their purview.

"I wasn't aware of that," Black replied uncomfortably, nervously licking her lips. "I was also instructed to ask if there was anything we could do for you that could strengthen our... relationship."

She stumbled over the last word, remembering too late how Rhapsody interpreted "relationship."

"Like a double date or something?" Rhapsody asked with a wide grin.

"Stop," Harmony scolded the fairy playfully. "You are too much."

"Too much goodness," Rhapsody replied, smiling affectionately at Harmony. A moment of déjà vu hit Harmony, and she furrowed her brow. Was this another soul memory? She could feel Rhapsody's emotions, filled with nostalgic love, as she gazed up at Harmony.

Black's smile seemed plastered on her face, determined to maintain her affable persona if it killed her.

Agent Monroe stared at Rhapsody, nonplussed, clearly expecting something different than the mischievous fairy on display.

"Are you really a world tree?" Monroe asked doubtfully.

Black winced, then scowled at her partner, who blushed under the fierce glare and looked down at the ground, abashed.

"Yep, I'm the world tree," Rhapsody confirmed brightly. "Do you want to come see?"

The two agents froze, their eyes darting to each other before returning to Rhapsody. Harmony almost laughed at the barely suppressed eagerness on their faces.

"You would let us inside the ring?" Black asked tentatively, staring intently at Rhapsody.

Harmony was pretty sure that getting eyes on the inside of the circle was high on the agents' priority list. Considering that Mystery had already told the intelligence agencies everything *she* had seen, Harmony wasn't sure what they hoped to learn with two more sets of eyes. Confirmation, perhaps?

"Sure, why not?" Rhapsody shrugged, winking again. "We have to get to know each other better if we're going to be in a relationship. Are you ready?"

The two agents hesitated, realizing they were about to be teleported. They exchanged a look, seeming to have an unspoken conversation about how much they could trust the mischievous fairy. They finally looked back at Rhapsody and nodded cautiously.

Harmony's house vanished, replaced a moment later by the entrance to Yggdrasil. The lake ended a few hundred feet away, with the Lost Forest of Choill to their right, its pink leaves painting the landscape with a soft blush.

"Here's the real me," Rhapsody said, gesturing grandly at the mountain-sized tree in front of them.

The two agents gaped at the impossibly large tree, miles wide and towering so high that its upper branches disappeared from view.

"Hey, Nidhogg, are you busy?" Rhapsody called up into the branches. "I want to introduce you to some more humans."

"I'll be right down," a deep, booming voice called from high in the tree, the low bass rumble vibrating Harmony's bones.

"Nidhogg is the Clan Chief of the dragons," Rhapsody informed the two stunned agents. "They live high in the branches because they're too big to land down here without flattening everything."

A rumbling sound came from above, and then the sky was blotted out by Nidhogg's gigantic form. He was over five hundred feet tall, with a head several times the size of Harmony's two-story house. With his wings outstretched, he blocked several acres of sky.

The two agents stood petrified as Nidhogg swooped down to hover a few dozen feet above the ground. Harmony could have walked into one of his large nostrils and still had room to spare.

"This is Agent Shelley Black and Agent Jessica Monroe," Rhapsody introduced the frozen agents, gesturing to the two women. "Agents, this is Nidhogg."

A small squeak escaped Black's throat as she stared up at the enormous dragon in terror. Monroe was too stunned to even make a sound, staring up at him like a bug looking at a playful cat.

"It's nice to meet you, Agents of the United States government," Nidhogg nodded in greeting, eliciting a terrified stumble backward from Black as teeth larger than Mystery briefly came closer. "I understand you may be a little unnerved by our size difference. If it helps, just think of me as a projection."

"Hello," Monroe managed to choke out, her eyes a mixture of terror and wonder.

"Well met, Jessica," Nidhogg boomed in satisfaction. "I can sense the lost wonder of your childhood struggling to reclaim a place in your mind. You will find plenty of wonder here in the circle of dominion. The leprechauns and mermaids are both mischievous, so be on your guard with them. And most wondrous—in addition to the most mischievous—is Yggdrasil, known to you as Rhapsody."

"I guess the legends fail to mention anything about Yggdrasil being mischievous," Monroe noted faintly.

"She wasn't always so entertaining," Nidhogg replied with a rumbling laugh that caused a small earthquake. "That only started about twenty-four years ago."

Harmony turned to smirk knowingly at Rhapsody, who gave one of her trademark innocent stares. Harmony opened her mouth, the threat of words apparent on her face.

"Just don't say it out loud," Rhapsody said quickly, heading Harmony off warningly. "It doesn't break any rules if you're just thinking it."

"What did I miss?" Nidhogg asked curiously, his giant eye watching Rhapsody and Harmony intently. The two agents stopped gawking at Nidhogg to watch the exchange curiously.

"Just Harmony being too smart for my own good," Rhapsody said, smiling fondly at Harmony. She waved at Nidhogg with a grateful smile. "Thanks for coming down to say hi."

"You do realize that it gets rather boring up in low Earth orbit, don't you?" Nidhogg asked, his voice a dry boom. "I'm always up for something to break up the monotony."

"What are you talking about, you oversized bat?" Rhapsody scoffed, though her tone was affectionate. "You're a spirit walker. You spend more time on other planets than you do here."

"That's because this place is usually so *boring*," Nidhogg complained, sighing in a way that would normally have spawned tornados if Yggdrasil wasn't blocking it. "You've certainly made things more interesting for the last couple of decades, though, so thank you. We're looking forward to the festivities later."

Rhapsody rolled her eyes when Harmony stared at her pointedly, but she couldn't stop a silly grin from spreading across her face. Harmony knew that Rhapsody wanted her to live a normal life at a normal pace, but also desperately longed for any trace of her soulmate. Through their spirit bond, she could feel happiness spiking in Rhapsody as she pushed at the boundaries of her soul memory. She stared at Rhapsody curiously, mentally tasting the name she had learned: Clarice.

Rhapsody's head snapped toward her as soon as Harmony thought the name. She narrowed her eyes at Harmony warningly, but Harmony just grinned back. At...Clarice.

Rhapsody threw her hands up in the air with a helpless laugh. The bond flared with happiness each time she said her name. "You are such a troll, Aria."

Harmony froze as she heard the name, feeling like a bell struck by lightning. *Her* name. Her *real* name.

It took Rhapsody a second longer to realize her gaffe. Her eyes went wide, and she quickly corrected herself. "What I meant to say was, are ya Harmony, or are ya a troll?"

Harmony laughed at the look of earnestness on Rhapsody's face as she tried to fix her mistake. "I'm a troll," Harmony smirked, mischief dancing in her eyes. She finished the next part in her thoughts: "*And I learn from the best, Clarice.*"

Rhapsody smacked her forehead and groaned helplessly. "I'm so screwed."

Screwed or not, the corner of her soul she thought of as Rhapsody was burning incandescently with joy.

The agents watched the two of them in bewilderment as a conversation, only partially spoken aloud, took place.

"Let me know if you bring any more humans you need impressed," Nidhogg said dryly as he began rising into the sky. "It's more entertaining than what's going on up in orbit with my clan."

"Do you want to come inside Yggdrasil?" Rhapsody asked the two agents enticingly. "We could show you what the nodes look like that Harmony and the others will be taking over when they become world trees."

"Sure..." Black agreed slowly, her face curious.

"So, we'll be *inside* of you?" Monroe asked in morbid fascination.

Rhapsody burst out laughing, gesturing at Harmony. "God, Jessica, you're as bad as Harmony," she declared, teleporting them into the chasm. "She asked me if it felt *violating*. She's such a goose."

"Honk honk," Harmony said dryly.

Monroe and Black looked around curiously at the chasm and its glowing walls, taking the teleportation in stride. Reaching the invisible field in front of them, they tentatively pushed against it. It wasn't a solid barrier but increased in resistance the harder they pushed, like two magnets repelling each other.

"What is that beam of light?" Monroe asked in fascination. At the very center of the chasm, an enormous crystal pointed down, emitting a beam of brilliant white light that shot into the depths below. "How far down does it go?"

"That's one of the energy nodes," Rhapsody explained, floating near the chasm's edge, unaffected by the force field. "It powers the grid lines around the world, running through Yggdrasil's roots and connecting to the other trees.

There are world trees at the North and South Poles, too. They're responsible for Earth's electromagnetic field. Yggdrasil is more than a single tree; its roots connect to four others across the world. I am the projection of the whole group. Harmony will resurrect the node in Africa, Mystery in the Middle East, and Joline in Australia. We've also found viable candidates for additional nodes in Antarctica and Africa."

"Who's the new candidate?" Black asked tentatively. She seemed to be walking on eggshells around Rhapsody, afraid of causing offense of any kind. "Or is that a secret?"

"Harmony's sister, Melody," Rhapsody answered, smiling at Harmony. "Her soul is old enough to be compatible with powering a world tree."

Black frowned, staring at Harmony. "I was under the impression that Melody was dead, and that's why Harmony had custody of Serenity and Aurora?"

"We brought her back to life earlier today," Rhapsody replied with a fond smile. "You arrived in the middle of a very emotional day."

"You *brought her back to life*?" Monroe demanded incredulously.

"The Creator owed me a favor and promised to look the other way when I brought her back," Rhapsody shrugged, as if it were nothing.

"The Creator of the *planet*?" Black gasped in disbelief.

"No, the Creator of the *universe*," Rhapsody corrected, appraising the two agents. "Do you want to meet her? She's here today."

Their faces paled as they stared back at Rhapsody uncertainly. After a moment, Monroe frowned suspiciously. "Is this more... teasing?"

"Not this time," Harmony said, shaking her head, her expression serious.

"God is a girl?" Monroe asked with a raised eyebrow.

"In this universe," Rhapsody answered with a quick nod, "some universes have dudes while others have... well, never mind. Suffice it to say, creators come in all shapes, sizes, and genders."

"Who created them?" Monroe asked with a frown. "And who created the one that created *them*? And so on and so forth?"

"I only know as far as 'so on,' but I'm not sure about 'so forth'," Rhapsody responded, a steely glint in her eyes. "We haven't found a way to get to 'so forth' yet, but when we do, there's gonna be hell to pay."

"Why?" Harmony asked curiously.

"I'll tell you when you're older," Rhapsody grinned up at her. "Though, you'll probably just remember on your own by then. Suffice it to say, there's a certain entity that knows it's in for a day of reckoning if we ever get our hands on it."

As Rhapsody finished the last sentence, the bond briefly ignited with white-hot fury.

"So, did you two want to meet the Creator?" Harmony asked the agents, tilting her head curiously. "She's really nice."

"I think I'll pass," Monroe said weakly. "I feel like my incredulity meter has already been abused too much today."

Black looked like she might object, but after looking at Monroe's face, she sighed and nodded.

"Okay, so what now?" Rhapsody asked the two women expectantly. "Is there somewhere in particular you wanted to go inside the circle? Besides Deighvy's, of course."

"Nidhogg said there were leprechauns and mermaids?" Monroe said questioningly.

The chasm vanished, and they were suddenly at the edge of the lake at the base of Yggdrasil. Harmony immediately recognized Eimear and Cormac sitting there with fishing poles next to them. Rhapsody took one look at the fishing poles and dissolved into giggles.

The agents stared at Rhapsody in confusion. Eimear and Cormac quickly turned around to see them, then grinned when they saw Rhapsody.

"Marishna is going to be apoplectic when she sees what you've done," Rhapsody commented, grinning.

"I've heard bouts of apoplectic fury are good for magic flow," Eimear replied in her adorable Irish dialect, her green eyes amused.

"This is Black and Monroe," Rhapsody introduced the two agents with a gesture. "Agents, this is Cormac and Eimear. If you hadn't already guessed, they're leprechauns."

"Nice to meet you," Monroe smiled at them, barely repressing the excitement on her face. Harmony thought back to what Nidhogg had said about Monroe reclaiming her lost childhood wonder. Harmony had a feeling Monroe had clung to the hope that magic was real longer than most kids.

"It's an honor," Black nodded politely at the leprechauns, her eyes fascinated. "What are you fishing for?"

The question sent Rhapsody into another fit of giggles, and broad grins appeared on Cormac and Eimear's faces.

"It's more like luring specific creatures," Eimear grinned mischievously. "There's a transparent electric eel that lives in this lake, usually near the south shore. We're luring them over here with a charm that mimics their species' mating call."

"Why do you want them here?" Black asked, eyeing the water cautiously.

"The mermaids frequently swim through this area," Cormac explained with a smirk. "The shocks don't hurt immortals, but they do cause mermaids to hallucinate and become very suggestive. We're going to try to get some of them to fill Marishna's chambers with stink worms."

The two agents blinked, glancing at each other before looking back at Cormac and Eimear.

"So, this is how you spend your time in the Circle?" Black asked with an amused smile.

"When you've been around for thousands of years, you learn to enjoy the little things," Eimear explained with a small smile.

"Let me guess," Harmony said sardonically. "This epiphany occurred about twenty-five years ago."

"Aye, that it did," Cormac admitted, looking at Harmony curiously. "How did you know?"

"Let's just call it a hunch," Harmony murmured with a sidelong glance at a glowering Rhapsody.

"Taxti's almost done setting everything up," Eimear informed Rhapsody with an eager grin. "It should be ready by sundown."

"Perfect," Rhapsody beamed, her face glowing with anticipation. She looked at the two agents speculatively. "Did you two have any plans for the night?"

The two women blinked before exchanging glances again.

"Nothing solid," Black answered after a moment.

"We're having a resurrection party tonight to celebrate Melody's return," Rhapsody informed them with a wink at Harmony. "There will be lots of music, dancing, stories, and games. It will be a night to remember."

Monroe's eyes lit up with eagerness, probably imagining all the fairy tale creatures at such a party. Black hesitated only a moment before nodding her acceptance. They had been sent to smooth things over between Rhapsody and the U.S. intelligence agencies, and accepting an invitation to a celebration would be a clear win to report to their superiors.

"I'll just need to check in with my superiors, if that's okay," Black mentioned cautiously. "Would I be able to go outside the circle so my phone will work?"

"I can fix it so it works inside," Rhapsody said, holding out her hand expectantly.

Black slowly handed Rhapsody her phone, failing to hide her nervousness. Who knew *what* Rhapsody might add to her phone, besides the ability to call out.

Rhapsody's eyes went distant for a moment before she handed the phone back to Black, then raised an eyebrow at Monroe. The younger agent glanced at her partner and received a resigned nod. After all, why would Rhapsody need to tamper with their phones when she could directly affect their brains? Monroe handed her phone to Rhapsody and had it back in seconds. The two agents couldn't suppress their relief when they saw their phones booting up.

"Feel free to go somewhere that feels private for your check-in call," Rhapsody offered, gesturing to the surrounding forests. "Harmony and I are going to fetch the others. It's getting close to sundown."

"When you say somewhere that feels private," Monroe began, her face doubtful, "is there really *anywhere* that is private from you in the ring?"

"My roots stretch all the way through the entire planet," Rhapsody replied dryly. "Do you think there is anywhere on *Earth* that is private from me?"

"I did until you put it that way," Monroe said wryly. "From what you've told us, it sounds like you've been able to listen in on the President's meetings already, so I guess it should have occurred to me before now."

"We'll be back in a few minutes with the others," Rhapsody told them with a parting nod.

"I like her," Harmony commented to Rhapsody just before the world briefly vanished and they appeared in Harmony's house.

"Yeah, she's kind of fun," Rhapsody agreed with a small smile. "Black's a little too high-strung still. Maybe she'll loosen up after some yuccas fitter."

Harmony laughed as she imagined the two women getting their first taste of the radioactive-looking fruit drink.

Melody was sitting on the couch in the front room, petting Juno as the bright green ball of fur excitedly walked around in circles on her lap. Serenity and Aurora made sounds of adoration as they told their mother about discovering the strange creature. Michael and Mystery were watching Juno in bemusement, while Joline stared in fascination.

"I meant to ask you what in the world Juno is back when I was still a skeptic," Harmony told Rhapsody, gesturing at the strange animal. It was completely round and a little larger than a cat, with long green fur and a face that looked more like a sheep than a dog or cat. It had opposable digits on its front hands, though they were barely visible due to how long its fur was.

"That's a Chupacabra," Rhapsody informed her with an expectant grin.

"*What?"* Michael gasped in disbelief, staring at Juno dubiously. "Chupacabras are all scaly with fangs and are as big as dogs."

"They are, if they leave the circle," Rhapsody agreed, a sad look in her eyes. "They're nourished by the energy of the world tree, but sometimes one will stray too far and get lost. After about a year, they start wasting away and go feral, surviving a little longer by draining the blood of creatures like sheep or cattle, but that only extends their life by a few years. I put up some wards a few decades ago to keep them from getting lost."

"Are they immortal, then?" Harmony asked curiously. "And how did this one end up at our house?"

"All magical creatures are immortal," Rhapsody explained, smiling down at Juno. "I asked him to keep Serenity and Aurora company to help with Aurora's night terrors. Chupacabras can influence moods and dreams. He's young for an immortal, only a decade old, and has a lot to learn."

Melody's face had grown sorrowful when she heard about Aurora's night terrors, accurately guessing their cause.

"What's going on with David?" Harmony asked Rhapsody quietly, so her sister wouldn't overhear.

"Remember what I said I'd do if he ever showed his face around here again?" Rhapsody asked, a bleak smile that was strange on her normally cheerful face.

"How could I forget?" Harmony answered with a shiver. "So, he's essentially a vegetable now?"

"Yep," Rhapsody nodded in satisfaction.

Harmony walked over to Melody and sat on the arm of the couch next to her. Melody looked up curiously, a soft smile on her face as she continued petting Juno.

"David is a vegetable now," Harmony informed her grimly. "You'll never have to worry about him again."

Melody closed her eyes and took a deep breath as tears slid down her cheeks. When she let the breath out, it was like an enormous weight had been lifted. She opened her eyes and looked at Rhapsody with naked gratitude.

"Thank you, Rhapsody," Melody said with a fragile smile. "You have no idea how relieved that makes me."

Harmony felt guilt streak through the soul bond; Rhapsody was still blaming herself for not keeping them all safe. Mystery walked up to Rhapsody and knelt, embracing her from behind, wrapping her arms around Rhapsody's waist and resting her chin on Rhapsody's shoulder.

"Don't dwell in the past, Rhapsody," Mystery reminded her gently. "We're all here now, and we're all ecstatically happy. Let it go."

Harmony felt the guilt fade, replaced by a burning love as Rhapsody wrapped her arms around Mystery's arms and leaned her head back to kiss Mystery's cheek.

"Thanks, Mystery," Rhapsody whispered with a sigh.

Harmony felt interesting sensations stir within her as she watched the two of them. She desperately wanted some alone time with them, and soon.

"Aurora, would you mind grabbing a yuccas fitter from the garden for Melody?" Rhapsody asked Aurora, an excited spark in her lavender eyes. "It's almost time."

"Almost time for what?" Aurora and Serenity asked, intrigued.

"I wouldn't want to spoil it for you," Rhapsody said with an impish grin. "Yuccas fitter?"

"I'll go with you," Serenity offered quickly, and the two of them vanished.

"I still can't believe my babies are using magic," Melody smiled ruefully, her eyes full of wonder.

A moment later, the two girls reappeared with a large red fruit. Michael eyed it greedily as Serenity handed it over to her mother.

"If you don't finish the whole thing, I'm sure I could help," Michael offered hopefully.

Mystery laughed brightly, watching her brother fondly. "You're a hopeless addict."

"I would say *hopeful* addict," Michael corrected, his gaze fixed on the bright red fruit as Melody curiously took it from Serenity.

"Just twist the stem off and then drink from the hole that appears in the top," Serenity instructed her mother helpfully. "And I've got to warn you; it's going to make your taste buds explode."

Melody curiously followed Serenity's instructions. When the first mouthful of juice filled her mouth, her eyes went wide, and she moaned with pleasure as she drank it down.

"I would say I miss it, but I like *our* food better," Harmony told Mystery with a grin.

"Like the memory you showed Michael on the train?" Mystery asked curiously.

"Yep," Harmony said with a dreamy expression. "Speaking of which, shouldn't we be refilling about now?"

"Too right, you are," Rhapsody agreed eagerly.

The house vanished as they reappeared in the chasm with Joline. Mystery released Rhapsody and stood up, her eyes radiating curiosity.

"How does this work—" Mystery's cut off as light flooded up out of the chasm and washed over them.

Harmony let out a loud moan of delight as the intense energy flooded her system. Mystery was no better, letting out her own moan of pleasure as the energy filled her meridians and began to stretch them out. Rhapsody once again consumed the vast majority of the light.

As the last of the light was absorbed by Rhapsody, Harmony turned to Mystery with a wide grin. "See what I mean? Better than yuccas fitter."

"Yeah," Mystery whispered, still overwhelmed by the rush of ecstasy. "Being a fairy is *so* awesome."

"And we do this every day," Joline informed Mystery brightly.

Harmony still couldn't get over seeing her mother looking the same age as herself. It reinforced the knowledge that she no longer had to worry about her mother dying from an incurable disease. Everything had become so much better since meeting Rhapsody.

"Okay, let's go pick up the others," Rhapsody suggested, teleporting them back to the house.

Michael was trying to get the last few drops of yuccas fitter that Melody had drained. Harmony and Mystery laughed when they saw him.

"Oh, Michael," Mystery laughed in fond exasperation. "You are *such* a goof."

Melody stood looking around the room with a bemused expression, her blue irises already growing larger as the yuccas fitter took effect.

"The colors are so much more vibrant," Melody observed with a soft smile. "I feel so light and happy. This is *amazing*."

"Much better than that pharmaceutical crap you used to take," Harmony commented distastefully, remembering how little the antidepressants had done for Melody and the horrible side effects they caused.

"It's time," Rhapsody announced with an excited smile. "Let's go celebrate!"

Harmony grinned eagerly as the house vanished, replaced by a large meadow where glowing orbs floated, illuminating the ground with a soft light. Taxti was waiting with Declan, along with a couple dozen fauns, leprechauns, and several extremely tall men who gave off a non-human vibe. One of the tall men approached Rhapsody with a broad grin as they joined the group.

"Hello, Nidhogg," Rhapsody greeted the tall man with a twinkle in her eyes. "You're looking slimmer. Have you lost some weight?"

Harmony gasped as she realized the men were actually dragons in human form. A group of red-haired women joined them as well. Harmony was almost certain one of them was the mermaid who had rescued Mystery the first day they had entered the circle.

"This is your resurrection party, Melody," Rhapsody said to the bemused Melody. "Welcome back to life. We're going to get the first night of your new life off to a great start."

13 – MELODY

Beneath a tree laden with pink leaves, Black waited for her new boss to answer the phone. The ground mirrored the canopy above, the forest floor blanketed in the same pink leaves and casting a rosy glow. She couldn't be sure, but the leaves seemed to brighten as the sun dipped lower on the horizon.

"Miller here," her boss finally answered, her voice distracted and conveying a clear desire to be anywhere but on the phone. Black found it absurd that a pair of NSA analysts had become responsible for contacting Rhapsody. A multi-agency task force—CIA, DIA, FBI, and NSA—had been created to address the Rhapsody situation, but core intelligence leadership, mired in the belief that Rhapsody was a demon, had rendered the command structure woefully inadequate to support her and Monroe. Essentially handpicked by the Vice President, what should have been a massive support network monitoring their every move had devolved into a mom-and-pop kind of organization that had limited resources and reluctant management.

Her current boss, Assistant Special Agent in Charge Miller, had been roped in from the FBI. She had been very vocal about her dissatisfaction with the poor and uncoordinated response from the U.S. intelligence agencies, and even more critical of the decision to send a couple of NSA analysts to make contact with Rhapsody instead of someone from the FBI or CIA.

"This is Black checking in," she said, striving for a professional tone, difficult to maintain amidst the surrounding beauty and fantastical creatures. She had even glimpsed a unicorn upon entering the pink forest, its horn flaring with arcing red and green light.

"You're late," Miller snapped, irritation evident. "You were due to check in two hours ago."

"Our phones didn't work inside the ring until Rhapsody did something to exclude them from the EM field," Black replied defensively.

"Wait, you're *inside* the ring?" Miller demanded, all disinterest gone. "Tell me everything."

Black recounted their last few hours, including Melody's resurrection and the invitation to the party.

"How likely is it that this is really Melody and not just someone they are claiming to have resurrected?" Miller asked doubtfully.

"After what I've seen today, I find it *very* likely that it is the original Melody," Black answered, unable to mask her awe. "We're dealing with godlike powers, from everything I've witnessed. She talked about ridding the world of nuclear weapons like it would be a Sunday outing."

Miller remained silent for several seconds, processing the information.

"Ma'am, did the President really plan to nuke the Ring?" Black asked, her voice hesitant. The idea that their government would drop a nuke on US soil in an act of aggression had upset her more than she thought it would.

"That's above *both* our paygrades, Black," Miller replied curtly. "What's your read on Rhapsody? What kind of person is she?"

Black sighed, unsure where to begin. Cognizant that Rhapsody could hear everything she said, she glanced briefly at her partner as she searched for the words to describe the enigmatic and playful fairy.

"On the surface, she seems caring and protective," Black began slowly. "She doesn't seem worried about humans at all and even refers to the Vice President by her first name. She knew our names immediately after meeting us. I'm pretty sure she can hear our thoughts. Most of her interest is in the humans who joined her. She claims to be in a relationship with Mystery and Harmony. There have been several times when they seemed to imply that in former lives they were more than friends. There's something else they've been alluding to that I can't get a read on. Something happened about twenty-five years ago, around the time Harmony would have been born. From what I've gathered from the other magical creatures, Rhapsody seems to have undergone some kind of personality change around that time."

"If she were to become hostile, what would you say our odds of survival are?" Miller asked carefully.

"At zero, ma'am," Black responded without hesitation. "But I should stress that I don't think that will happen. Even if we did something to provoke her, I believe she would focus on the people responsible, rather than humanity as a whole. She appears to know what's going on everywhere on the planet. Even if she wasn't able to view our activities through whatever technology she uses to monitor everyone on Earth, there's the leveling interface. I imagine she can listen in on any conversation through that."

"What about these other magical creatures you mentioned?" Miller asked pensively. "What are they like? Do they seem hostile at all?"

"The leprechauns seem more interested in playing pranks on the mermaids, from what I've seen so far," Black replied, unable to keep a wry note out of her voice. "We only met the Clan Chief of the dragons, Nidhogg. He was very courteous and friendly, though meeting him was a terrifying experience. He's big in the way that atoms are small. His eye was more than double my height. I still can't believe how big he was. He lives in the upper branches of Yggdrasil because he's too big to land on the ground."

"Could you send me a picture?" Miller asked intently. "I want to see what this world tree looks like."

"I *think* so," Black replied hesitantly, assuming Rhapsody would intervene if she didn't want pictures taken. "Or would you prefer I just switch to FaceTime?"

Instead of answering, her phone started ringing as a FaceTime request from Miller came through. She accepted the call, switched the camera to the front, and held it up to capture Yggdrasil, zooming out to a wide view. Even then, she couldn't capture the entire base of the tree from where she stood.

"Wow," Miller's voice came through the phone as Black slowly panned the camera up and down the tree, then side to side.

"They claimed the creator of the universe is here in the ring right now and offered to introduce us to her," Black revealed, still unsettled at the prospect of actually meeting the Creator. "I was a little overwhelmed by everything and declined. I don't think they were lying. From everything I've seen, having the Creator show up wouldn't be unusual here."

"The *Creator?*" Miller asked in disbelief. "As in, God? And s*he?*"

"Yeah, as in God," Black confirmed with a shiver. "And yes, apparently God is a girl."

"This just went from technologically superior to something else entirely," Miller declared pensively, watching the video feed. "Try to find out more about this Creator. If it really is the Creator, it would be nice to know if any of the nonsense in religion is true."

There was an exasperated sigh from the other end of the line, then Miller's voice snapped, "Jeffrey, you can't be in here right now. Get your homework done. *Now.*"

Black heard footsteps and turned to find one of the unicorns a dozen feet away, watching her curiously.

"There are *unicorns*?" Miller breathed in amazement.

"Yeah," Black confirmed unnecessarily. "I wonder what will happen when there are more world trees throughout the world."

"There will be lots of magic that even humans can use," Rhapsody answered, appearing next to the unicorn with a large red fruit in her hands. "Right now, magic doesn't work very far from one of the circles. After Harmony and the others have finished transitioning, magic will again be accessible to humans. Hello, Samantha."

The line went silent for several seconds before Miller—*Samantha*—spoke.

"Hello, Rhapsody," Miller replied in a professional voice, just warm enough to be considered friendly. "Thank you for allowing Agents Black and Monroe into the ring."

"Thank you for sending them," Rhapsody replied with a small smile. "Things get boring for immortals, so the others are always excited to meet new people. Jessica and Shelley are wonderful people too, so I'm glad you chose them."

Black felt a flush of pleasure at the compliment, noticing Monroe's lips quirk into a pleased smile as well.

Rhapsody waved her hand, and a large display window materialized in the air, showing Miller. Miller's face registered surprise as she saw Rhapsody on the other side.

"I should probably mention that your president authorized a special forces team to sneak a pocket nuke over to the circle," Rhapsody informed Miller, an amused twinkle in her eyes. "I've already removed the reaction chamber containing the uranium and plutonium, so it's just a paperweight now. I decided it would be a good idea to do that to the rest of the world's arsenals as well, so now nobody has nuclear weapons."

Miller stared at Rhapsody's cheerful expression, a slightly sick look on her own face. "I'm sorry that everyone in our government isn't on the same page."

Black felt a sinking sensation in the pit of her stomach. She and Monroe were *inside* the ring, for God's sake! If Rhapsody hadn't been essentially omniscient, they would have been vaporized.

"It's okay, Shelley, a nuke wouldn't have affected anything beyond the walls anyway," Rhapsody assured her. "A comet the size of New York wouldn't hurt anything inside the circle. Now, I have some yuccas fitter for you. Prepare to have your taste buds explode."

* * *

"Vice President Adams," a brusque voice answered.

"Ma'am, is there a reason you're trying to nuke the ring while we have agents inside it?" Miller asked with tightly controlled rage.

"What are you talking about?" Vice President Adams demanded, her tone aghast.

"I just got off a call with two of the agents under my command who are inside the ring," Miller explained curtly. "Rhapsody showed up and informed me that there was a special forces team attempting to sneak a pocket nuke into the circle. In retaliation, she's removed the plutonium and uranium from every nuclear weapon on the planet."

"You've got to be fucking kidding me," the Vice President growled in frustration. "Those assholes actually tried to do it anyway."

Miller let her anger settle as she realized the Vice President was ignorant of the operation. "Ma'am, I can't adequately stress how outmatched we are technologically. If you have any influence over this administration, I suggest you use it to convince them to stop poking the dragon."

"You actually have agents inside the ring?" Vice President Adams asked in amazement. "What have we learned?"

"Mainly that we are hopelessly out of our depth, Ma'am," Miller sighed tiredly. "Miss Donovan's report of the ring was accurate, including the dragon and Yggdrasil. I was on a video call and saw the world tree with my own eyes, along with a unicorn. Despite all of our aggression, she does not seem inclined to return it in kind—if anything, she finds it *amusing*."

"What would it take for that to change?" Vice President Adams asked evenly. "How much pushing is she willing to take before it stops being amusing?"

"I have a feeling she'll personally handle things at the policy-making level," Miller answered grimly. "You might want to pass that on to the president. My agents are currently attending a resurrection party. Apparently, Rhapsody can bring people back from the dead. She resurrected Harmony's sister, Melody, who is likely going to become a world tree as well."

There was a longer pause on the line this time. When she spoke, her voice was tight with anxiety. "Just what are we dealing with here? Advanced technology is one thing, but bringing people back from the dead is something else entirely."

"My agents were told that the Creator of this universe is currently visiting the ring and were offered an introduction," Miller informed her uneasily. "They were convinced that She really *is* the Creator. I asked them to try and find out more about this Creator. I really think someone needs to find a way to rein in the people running this administration, for their own sakes, if nothing else. I received a report just before I called you that Melody, the woman who was resurrected, had a husband charged with attempted murder. Shortly after her resurrection, David became a paraplegic, with no explanation as to how it happened. I suggest you share that information with the president so that he has something to look forward to next time he does something... precipitous."

* * *

Harmony grinned as Nidhogg offered Melody his arm after inviting her to dance. She looked up at him shyly and looped her arm into his as they moved toward the center of the clearing. Harmony thought her chest would burst with happiness as she watched her sister glow with a radiant life force that had been missing for most of her life. She was finally being treated the way she deserved.

Several leprechauns, fauns, and even elves were playing a variety of instruments at one side of the clearing. The ground was illuminated by softly glowing orbs that floated above them, while small lights zipped through the crowd as the fairies joined the festivities.

The music was amazing. It wasn't as good as what Rhapsody made, but it was better than anything she had heard outside of the circle. They were currently playing a waltz with a slowly scaling melody filled with mystery and wonder.

Harmony blinked in surprise when Harnketi appeared with Eileen, a man she assumed was Tyee, and three children. Rhapsody broke off from a conversation with one of the mermaids and moved to greet Eileen and her family, her face warm.

"May I have this dance?" Mystery asked softly, right next to Harmony's ear.

Harmony's heart rate doubled as she looked up into Mystery's large lavender eyes. "Um, I actually have no idea how to dance—part of being a recluse."

"I have a feeling you'll pick it up quickly," Mystery said with a mysterious smile, taking her hand and pulling her toward the clearing.

Harmony felt an overwhelming flood of sensations as she watched over a dozen people dancing around the clearing. It was one of the reasons she'd never gone to dances—her synesthesia would turn her into a twitching mess from the sensory overload.

"Eyes on me," Mystery ordered softly, reaching out to turn Harmony's face so that she was staring up into Mystery's eyes. "That's better. Now, we're just going to walk in time with each other."

Harmony's synesthesia became much more manageable as her tunnel vision shut everything out but Mystery. Mystery's arm wrapped around Harmony's waist, pulling her close until their bodies were pressed tightly together. Harmony shuddered with pleasure as she felt their bodies molded together from both sides. She barely noticed her feet moving in time to the waltz as Mystery led them around the clearing, gazing down into Harmony's captivated eyes with a warmth that brought a flush to her cheeks.

"I knew you would be a quick learner," Mystery murmured with a pleased smile.

Harmony stared at Mystery's lips as she spoke, unable to stop the desire flooding her as she imagined kissing her.

"Rhapsody was right," Mystery whispered, amused. "You really are insatiable."

Harmony blushed profusely as she moved her eyes back up to Mystery's. "Yeah, I am," she admitted with a slow smile. "That's your fault for being so damn desirable."

Mystery laughed, and Harmony felt the desire glowing brightly through their soul bond. She wondered if there was some kind of feedback loop as her breathing came in quick gasps, mirroring Mystery's heavy breaths.

"Hey, you two," Rhapsody said, appearing next to them and halting their waltz. "Tone it down, would ya? I can't function with this much desire lighting me up. Now behave for a few more hours."

Rhapsody vanished as soon as she finished, leaving them to stare at each other sheepishly.

Harmony tried to clear her mind of the passion heating her veins, but it was extremely difficult when she could feel every curve of their bodies pressed so tightly together.

"What's the life of an author like?" Mystery asked curiously, obviously trying to give Harmony something to distract her from the lust threatening to consume her thoughts.

"It's awesome," Harmony admitted with a grin. "I get paid to live in a dreamland. Until recently, nothing compared to the joy I found immersing myself in my characters' lives. My grandma Dotty used to force me to sleep because I wanted to stay up all night writing. I had to regiment my time much more strictly when Aurora and Serenity moved in. How about you? What's it like to fly for a living?"

"That sounds pretty amazing," Mystery murmured wistfully. "There wasn't anything as enjoyable as sinking into one of your novels and forgetting the real world for a while. I'm glad you wrote so many books—by the time I finished the last one, I was ready to start the first one again. As for flying? It was my way to escape the world and enjoy the feeling of freedom in three dimensions. I used to wish the world was bigger, or connected to other worlds, so I could explore uncharted lands where nobody had ever been before."

"That would be amazing," Harmony said softly, her imagination taking flight. "You could fly us to new places while I wrote stories during the journey. We'd find so much inspiration high up in the air, looking down on virgin lands, or into the night sky with no light pollution to block the stars. Did you ever fly at night?"

"Yeah, it was one of my favorite times to fly," Mystery said softly. "I saw the aurora borealis all the time during solar maximum. The stars are so much brighter from up there. Sometimes, I'd see a brilliant bolide streak across the sky and light everything up. I flew during the Perseids meteor shower once and saw a ridiculous number of bright meteors. It was magical."

Harmony felt a glowing warmth building as Mystery spoke, more than just the naked desire she had felt earlier. As she listened to Mystery, a familiarity settled over her, as if she were catching up with an old friend she hadn't seen in years. It was so comfortable and effortless, totally unlike her conversations with almost anyone else.

She laid her head on Mystery's shoulder as they continued waltzing around the clearing, feeling a sense of warmth and safety that she had only ever felt with Rhapsody. She had no fear that her heart would be broken or abused with Mystery—there was nothing but complete trust. It was liberating to be able to trust another person so completely, to let her guard down without fear of repercussions.

She could feel Mystery reciprocating her emotions. The powerful sense of love and soul-deep acceptance emanating from Mystery made Harmony unable to imagine life without the beautiful woman now that she had her. Her eyes grew misty with happiness as she slowly moved around the clearing to the accompaniment of the beautiful music. For what felt like the millionth time since meeting Rhapsody, she thanked whatever cosmic forces had aligned to bring Rhapsody and Mystery into her life.

After almost fifteen minutes of dancing in blissful obliviousness, they were interrupted when a redhead as tall as Mystery stepped into their path.

"May I have this dance?" Rhapsody's voice came from the tall woman's mouth.

Harmony snapped out of her trance in surprise and actually looked at the woman. It was Rhapsody, just much taller. Rhapsody started laughing as Harmony stared, uncomprehending.

"Did you forget that I'm a shapeshifter?" Rhapsody asked silkily. "I thought that fact might have been burned into your brain by now."

Harmony felt the roots of her hair grow hot as her face flushed and desire engulfed her.

"Easy, tiger," Rhapsody laughed delightedly. "We still have a couple of hours to go. There's someone who wants to talk to you. I'm going to steal Mystery while you take Harnketi."

While Harmony was still trying to process anything besides raw desire, Mystery released her and stepped away, an amused smile on her face. Rhapsody immediately stepped in and took Mystery into her arms. The sight flooded Harmony with desire anew, prompting another laugh from the two of them as they looked back at her affectionately.

"Hello, Harmony," Harnketi greeted her with a breathtaking smile as she stepped up to Harmony invitingly. "May I have this dance?"

Harmony flushed as Harnketi watched her with a knowing smile. "Um, I've never really danced before tonight, so I'm not very good."

Harnketi stepped forward and pulled Harmony close, wrapping one arm around her waist while clasping their hands with the other. "Then we'll give you some lessons. I saw you dancing earlier, and you were doing just fine."

Harnketi was wearing a black summer dress that ended at mid-thigh and left a generous amount of cleavage showing. Harmony shivered as her synesthesia informed her of the sensations Harnketi was feeling as their bodies shifted against each other while they began moving around the clearing in a modern two-step. Harmony's feet seemed to know what to do, even though she had no idea.

"So, I have a proposal for you," Harnketi announced as they passed Serenity dancing with an elf, "depending on your answer to my first question, that is."

"What's your first question?" Harmony asked curiously. What could Harnketi possibly want from her? She didn't have anything to offer except a lot of mental baggage.

"Is your sister only into guys, or does she swing both ways?" Harnketi asked intently.

Harmony blinked at the unexpected question and studied Harnketi, realizing the direction of their conversation. Dark eyes stared back expectantly, a hopeful light flickering within them.

"I'm not sure," Harmony admitted with a frown. "She's only dated guys in the past, but every last one of them has been a total jerk. I kept thinking she would give up on guys and try playing for the other team, but she never did. I don't think she would be opposed to the idea—I just don't think she's ever thought about it before."

Harnketi looked thoughtful as she twirled Harmony around the clearing. "So not a definite no, but definitely not a yes. I can work with those odds. Now... about my proposal."

Harmony eyed the gorgeous Native American curiously, waiting for her to elaborate.

"I need to know more about your sister," Harnketi stated, pursing her lips as she gazed into the distance. "Her likes and dislikes, her hopes and fears, and what kind of things are a turnoff for her. If you help me find the answers to those questions, I'll return the favor and tell you the same things about Rhapsody."

Harmony's pulse quickened at the thought of discovering more ways to please Rhapsody. She knew she was a complete novice when it came to intimacy and needed all the help she could get. A small worm of doubt had been plaguing her, questioning whether she was contributing enough to their relationship. She didn't want it to be a one-sided arrangement, or, as a character in one of her novels had put it, to "just lay there and sweat."

"Deal," Harmony agreed, feeling a mixture of hope and embarrassment at what she imagined to be very frank discussions. "If there is even a hint of chemistry on her end, we'll get her on board. She *really* needs someone wonderful in her life after all the asshats she's dealt with so far."

"What happened with her previous love interests?" Harnketi asked as she lowered Harmony into a deep dip and then pulled her back up.

Harmony recounted the hell Melody had endured with David, including his abuse of her synesthesia. Harnketi's face darkened murderously as Harmony finished.

"And where is this David person now?" Harnketi asked in an icy voice.

"He's in a long-term care ward," Harmony answered, satisfaction evident in her tone. "When Rhapsody found out about the synesthesia abuse, she paid him a visit in the hospital and turned him into a paraplegic. He'll spend the rest of his life in the prison of his own head with no ability to communicate with anyone."

"Good," Harnketi growled darkly. "I'm glad she didn't let him off with something as easy as death."

"She said death would be too easy," Harmony remembered from the night he had shown up at her house.

"She's right about that," Harnketi agreed, twirling Harmony around before pulling her close again. "You're a natural at this, Harmony."

"I guess so," Harmony said, surprised. "It just seems to make sense."

Nearby, she noticed Rhapsody and Mystery engaged in a much more complex dance. Mystery spun in and out of Rhapsody's arms before being lifted into the air, dropped between her legs, and lifted back up again. Her heart sped up as she watched the two of them command the dance area.

"Don't focus on them," Harnketi commanded crisply. "Rhapsody warned me to keep you distracted so you don't start a feedback loop."

Harmony laughed, a sudden blush rising to her cheeks, and turned back to Harnketi. "She knows me too well."

"She's known you for a very long time, from the sounds of it," Harnketi noted wistfully.

"Have you ever been in love with anyone?" Harmony asked curiously.

Harnketi shrugged, avoiding Harmony's eyes. "Not as such."

Harmony mentally rewound, trying to recall everything she knew of Harnketi and her history in the circle. Had Harnketi found love—not as such—before she ended up in the circle?

Harnketi noticed her calculating gaze and sighed, a small smile tugging at the corners of her mouth. "I've been in love with the *idea* of being in love. I haven't found anyone I could *be* in love with yet. However, there is something about Melody that really makes me want to try."

Harmony glanced around the clearing until she spotted Melody, laughing delightedly as she tried to keep up in a dance-off with Leesha. Her bright blond hair had escaped its loose bun, giving her a wild look. She wore denim cutoffs and a white button-up blouse, a few buttons at the top left open to display her generous cleavage. As Harmony watched, Melody finally fumbled a move and collapsed to the ground, laughing merrily. It was the first time Harmony had seen her sister so full of life and happiness. She exuded life force in waves, soaking up the festive spirit in the warm night air.

She turned back to see Harnketi watching Melody intently, her face enraptured.

"I have a feeling she'll be more interested in trying new things now that she's back to the land of the living," Harmony told Harnketi encouragingly. "I'm going to go lay the groundwork. Thanks, Harnketi."

Harnketi rolled her eyes with a wry smile. "No, thank *you*, Harmony."

Harmony released Harnketi and walked over to her laughing sister, a grin on her face.

"Not bad for an old woman," Harmony said with a laugh.

"I'd like to see you do better," Melody challenged with a wide grin. "*Young* woman."

"Not on your life," Harmony declared, raising her hands defensively. "Or mine, for that matter."

"How are you doing?" Melody asked, her eyes alight with happiness.

"I'm happier than I ever thought possible," Harmony said truthfully. "I feel like the only missing piece is having Grandma Dotty back."

"I wish I'd gotten to know her better," Melody sighed regretfully.

Kneeling in front of her sister, Harmony took her hand comfortingly. "We both know why you couldn't. I wish she could've spent more time getting to know you. I feel so much rage at all the time David robbed us of. But you're here now, and we've got wonderful people all around us. Speaking of which, have you met anyone you fancy?"

Melody shrugged with a small smile. "I like the dragons," she admitted, her smile widening slightly. "They're all so polite and knowledgeable, but I get the feeling they aren't exactly human relationship material."

"Now *that* could be a good novel," Harmony said thoughtfully, glancing at Melody with a sly smile. "Human falls in love with dragon who can only change into a mortal one day out of every year."

"I feel like that trope's been regurgitated one too many times," Melody said critically.

"Because it *works*," Harmony countered, a smile playing on her lips. "Who wouldn't want to read about a powerful, legendary dragon from antiquity falling in love with a mortal woman, only for the girl to discover that she can only be with her true love for one night each year? So much unrequited love and tension building all year long until the night when their passion can finally overflow in a glorious, volcanic eruption of lust and fulfillment."

"Let's be realistic," Melody smirked cynically. "That girl isn't waiting all year to get her needs met."

Harmony dissolved into giggles, gazing at her sister fondly. When she finally recovered, she cleared her throat. "You can't be realistic when it's a fantasy novel. That's one of the only rules of fantasy literature: no realistic expectations. You have to write sci-fi for it to require any kind of realism."

"Speaking of unrealistic expectations," Melody said slowly, giving Harmony a speculative look. "What's up with this love triangle you have going? I mean, don't you get jealous when Rhapsody's with Mystery instead of you, and vice versa?"

"If it were anyone else, I would be *insanely* jealous," Harmony admitted with an indulgent smile as she thought of Mystery and Rhapsody. "But not those two. Maybe it has something to do with how long our souls have been together, but when I see them smiling at each other with passion in their eyes, I feel a kind of euphoric joy to see them so happy. I feel so much love for both of them that I can't imagine life with just one. And don't even get me started on what she can do with this body of mine in the bedroom—I've turned into an addict. You should try playing for the other team; it's a lot more fulfilling."

Melody smiled wistfully. "I've thought about it, but the idea just seems so awkward after a lifetime of being interested in guys. I'm kind of stuck in my ways and don't think I could change what I find sexually attractive."

"I think you just need to meet the right person," Harmony said confidently. "If Miss Right comes along and sweeps you off your feet, I guarantee attraction won't be an issue."

"I hope you're right," Melody said, smiling wryly. "Cause I feel burned out on trying to make things work with men."

"I'm living proof that it can happen," Harmony said with a wondering smile. "You should have seen me when Rhapsody found me. I had so many mental walls in place to prevent any chance of a relationship, but she came at me like a wrecking ball and battered down the gates to my heart before I even knew my mental fortress was under assault. I can't tell you how happy I am that she did. I never would have imagined being in a relationship could be so wonderful."

Melody placed a warm hand on Harmony's shoulder, watching her with wistful happiness. "I'm ecstatic to see you in such a wonderful relationship. Out of all the people in the world, you deserve this kind of happiness more than anyone else."

"No, Melody," Harmony disagreed, her voice serious. "*You* deserve this kind of happiness. After what Dad did to us, and then all the asshats you kept ending up with—karma owes you a lot to balance those scales."

Melody's eyes grew stricken. "You remember about Dad?"

"Yeah, I remember everything," Harmony nodded, her expression flickering between regret and anger. "Rhapsody helped me work through the trauma. She took me into a dream world and locked all the memories into a place that had no emotional attachment. I can remember everything, but the emotions tied to those experiences are gone. Melody, I'm so sorry you didn't have someone to block those memories for you. Would you like Rhapsody to do for you what she did for me?"

"Yes," Melody whispered, closing her eyes as tears ran down her cheeks. "That would be wonderful. I have so many nightmares of that place. I'm still so scared that I'll end up back there again someday, helpless and alone."

Harmony moved to Melody and knelt behind her, wrapping her arms around her. "Rhapsody will fix everything," she whispered soothingly. "The pain will be gone forever."

Melody held onto Harmony's arms as she wept silently. Holding her sister, Harmony felt a flash of burning rage toward their father. She hadn't wondered where he was since her memories returned, but for the first time since she was a toddler, she *wanted* to see him. She wanted to make him suffer the way Melody was suffering, the way Melody *had* suffered.

Suddenly, Rhapsody was next to her, tenderly laying a hand against Melody's cheek. "Why don't we take care of this right now, Melody?"

Melody opened her eyes, hope blossoming on her face. "Really?"

"Really," Rhapsody nodded, offering a warm smile. A moment later, Melody slumped into unconsciousness in Harmony's arms.

"This will be easier for her than it was for you," Rhapsody informed Harmony softly. "She's been coming to terms with these memories for a long time now. They hit you like a freight train because they appeared out of nowhere. I'll have her as good as new in about thirty minutes."

Harmony leaned over and kissed Rhapsody's forehead. "Thank you, Rhapsody. I love you *so* much."

Rhapsody smiled at her, love shining in her eyes. "I know you do, Harmony. I love you too."

14 – ETHERIC BEAUTY

"Would you like to come with me?" Rhapsody asked Harmony softly. "Into her dream? It might be easier for her if you're there, too."

Harmony felt a spike of fear, rough and jagged, impale her stomach as she thought of revisiting her father's lab of horrors. She was pretty sure that Melody had endured more hell than she had, being both older and having been there longer.

It took all of her willpower to nod, fear nearly drowning out every other emotion.

"Never mind, Harmony," Rhapsody said, reaching out to place a hand on her shoulder as she felt the terror radiating through their bond. "I'm sorry; I shouldn't have asked this of you."

Mystery hurried over, concern filling her face. "What's wrong?"

"I'm just an idiot," Rhapsody sighed in irritation. "I'm sorry, Harmony. Even without the emotional attachment, this was too much to ask."

"No, I can come," Harmony managed, unable to keep a tremor out of her voice. "She needs me there."

"No, Harmony," Rhapsody said firmly, her face resolute. "Melody wouldn't want you to see this again anyway. I just wasn't thinking clearly when I asked."

Harnketi had joined them unnoticed. She knelt in front of Melody and glanced up at Rhapsody. "I'll go."

Rhapsody nodded quickly, and a moment later, the two of them vanished.

Relief flooded Harmony in waves, accompanied by a deep sense of shame that she wasn't strong enough to be there for her sister.

"Hey, there's nothing wrong with fearing pain," Mystery told her firmly, kneeling and placing her arm around Harmony's shoulders. "Let Rhapsody handle this."

"Is everything okay?" a familiar voice asked, filled with concern.

Harmony looked up to see Eileen standing nearby, her eyes full of compassion as she stared down at the three of them.

"Rhapsody is taking my sister into the dream world to sever her emotional connection to her traumatic memories," Harmony answered quietly as a tear slid down her cheek. "She asked me to go with, but I was too scared."

"That's not true at all," Mystery said firmly. "You were willing to go; Rhapsody just wouldn't let you when she realized how much you're still affected by the memory of that place."

Eileen squatted down in front of her, resting a hand on Harmony's arm. "Rhapsody was right not to let you go, Harmony. That's a chapter of your life that needs to remain closed. If your sister is working through the kind of trauma you experienced, having you there will only make her feel worse. The best thing you can do is be there for her when she wakes up."

Harmony knew they were right, but she couldn't shake the crippling guilt that she hadn't been there for her sister when she needed her most. She remembered her sister's struggles with debilitating depression stemming from the trauma, all while enduring an abusive marriage. Now that Harmony understood she'd been held hostage by her synesthesia, she felt even more guilty that she hadn't tried harder to understand the cause of her sister's emotional turmoil. Maybe if she had talked with her more, she would have discovered David's abuse and found a way to save her.

She felt the concern and worry from Mystery as she fell into a downward spiral of guilt and regret. The world faded as the scope of her failure to help her sister eclipsed all other sensations. She felt Mystery holding her and trying to talk to her, but she couldn't escape the abyss of self-recrimination that enveloped her in darkness.

She gasped as warmth suffused her soul, washing away the negativity in a tsunami of love. She blinked, looking around in confusion. The clearing was bathed in an ethereal light that banished all shadows. She felt arms around her and glanced over her shoulder. Emily, the angel she had met days ago, held her tenderly, her face radiating compassion. Harmony stared into swirling violet galaxies, filled with more love than she could comprehend.

Everyone had stopped to stare in awe at the divine being. Her presence flooded the area with an aura of power and authority that would make even gods bow.

"You are more amazing than you can possibly understand right now," Emily said, her voice sending tingles down Harmony's spine. "Don't let the negative emotions drag you down. You are indomitable, Harmony. Remember that."

Emily vanished, leaving a stunned silence. Harmony took a long, shuddering breath as she looked at the eyes watching her. Black and Monroe had fallen to their knees, overwhelmed by Emily's presence. Their eyes were wide with wonder as they stared at Harmony.

Harmony felt like her mind was on the verge of a major breakthrough. Emily seemed so familiar, like a recurring dream only recalled when it began again. Tantalizing memories of winged angels flickered through her mind, too fast to grasp and see clearly. Behind it all lay a gulf of time so vast she shuddered at the enormity of it. She was an angel. That much she knew for sure. Somehow, she was one of those angelic beings, just like Rhapsody and Mystery, like Serenity and Aurora and her mother. Why were they here? There was something important they had to do, but the memory darted away as soon as she grasped it.

She looked up at Mystery, feeling a supernova of love ignite in her chest. Mystery stared back in surprise as the wave of emotion crashed against their soul bond. Her lips parted, a question in her eyes.

"Are we having a party or what?" Taxti shouted, raising her arms. "I want to see some dancing! Where's our music?"

The crowd of spectators slowly returned to the festivities, though they glanced back frequently. Black and Monroe approached hesitantly, their expressions uncertain. Harmony smiled as she sensed two more threads she could almost remember.

"You're not going to ask if that was an angel, right?" Harmony said before either could speak. "Because some things are just too obvious."

Black flushed under Harmony's amused gaze, a small smile appearing after a moment.

"Okay, you got me," Black admitted, chuckling. "So, are angels from heaven?"

Harmony looked pointedly at the sky. "I don't see any up there."

"You know what I mean," Black said evenly.

"They're not from this universe," Harmony said confidently. "They're from somewhere far beyond it."

"Do they serve this Creator that Rhapsody was going to introduce us to?" Monroe asked intently.

"No, definitely not," Harmony answered with a frown. She wasn't sure how she knew, but she did.

Mystery was watching her peculiarly, and Harmony could feel her struggling with the same recall that teased at her own mind. They were on the edge of understanding something far greater than their small reality. As she stared into Mystery's eyes, her mind tried to superimpose swirling violet galaxies in place of the tall woman's irises. She heard someone speaking, but her concentration was absolute as she stared at Mystery, imagining those vortex eyes.

"Calypso," Harmony murmured softly.

Mystery gasped, her hand flying to her mouth as she heard the name. Her eyes widened as she stared at Harmony, recognition humming through their bond. She could feel their connection strengthening, the history they shared rising to the surface.

"Aria?" Mystery whispered, brows furrowed in concentration.

Harmony nodded slowly, recalling when Rhapsody had called her Aria. Warmth erupted, filling their bond as the knowledge of their shared history became clear, even if the actual memories remained hidden. Mystery's lips curved into a radiant smile as she gazed into Harmony's eyes.

"You two are in *so* much trouble," Rhapsody said with an exasperated scowl, suddenly appearing before them. "No digging around in soul memory. This is *important*."

Harmony exchanged a sheepish look with Mystery before turning back to Rhapsody.

"That's like telling us not to think of a pink elephant," Harmony said plaintively.

"I know," Rhapsody sighed tiredly. "We just don't have the kinds of souls that can stay locked up in mortality for long. This is the longest we've ever made it, so let's try for a little longer. They need us here. Just a few more years, okay? Please?"

Harmony and Mystery exchanged a look and nodded. For Rhapsody, they would try.

"How's Melody doing?" Harmony asked anxiously. "Did it work?"

"Yes, it was much easier than it was for you," Rhapsody replied, a brief flash of sadness in her eyes as she looked at Harmony. "Those memories won't trigger emotional reactions anymore. She's going to be a lot different now."

"Thank you, Rhapsody," Harmony said, smiling gratefully at her angel.

Rhapsody returned the smile, the corners of her expressive lips tilting up slightly. "She's about to wake up now."

Black and Monroe, eyes alight with curiosity, had been watching their exchange with interest. They looked eager to pepper Rhapsody with questions, but all eyes turned to Melody as she shifted in Harmony's arms and slowly lifted her head. She glanced around at the people watching her and waved with a faint smile.

"I feel so popular," Melody declared, her eyes sparkling with amusement. "Where's Harnketi?"

Harmony blinked, realizing Harnketi hadn't reappeared with Rhapsody.

"She's on a brief hunting expedition," Rhapsody replied blandly. "She'll be back in a few minutes."

"What's she hunting?" Eileen asked curiously. "Deer?"

Rhapsody's expression became evasive as she avoided looking at anyone. "Something like that."

Harmony's eyes widened as she thought about what Harnketi had witnessed in Melody's dream world. "She's hunting our dad, isn't she?"

Rhapsody's eye twitched as she looked back at Harmony with feigned innocence. "Hard to say."

"It's actually really easy to say," Harmony disagreed dryly. "Where is the bastard, anyway?"

"He's working for a pharmaceutical company in India," Rhapsody replied, glancing at Melody's hard expression as they spoke of her father. "Along with most of his team, who were released from prison after a few months when some backroom deals were made with the CIA."

"Is she going to kill him?" Melody asked hopefully.

"I seriously doubt it," Rhapsody answered with a grim smile. "I'm pretty sure she has something far worse planned for him and his colleagues."

"Good," Eileen growled fiercely.

Harmony could only agree; death would be far too merciful for some people.

"Is Harnketi human?" Melody asked curiously, a light in her eyes that brought a smile to Harmony's face.

"Yeah, she's human," Rhapsody nodded, winking at Harmony. "She's a very skilled magic user, though."

"Will she be okay on her own?" Melody asked anxiously, finally pulling away from Harmony to stand and stretch.

"When it's Harnketi you're talking about, it's the others you should be concerned for," Rhapsody stated with a dangerous smile. "She's spent the last six hundred years honing her skills."

"She's over six hundred years old?" Melody exclaimed in disbelief. "I thought you said she was human?"

"She spent most of that time as a Baykok after she was murdered by the Spanish explorer, Hernando de Soto. He threatened to murder the children of her tribe if she didn't accompany him, and after a few months as his captive, they killed her. I brought her back to life and offered her the option to become a Baykok until she was ready to resume her mortal life. She's only been mortal again for a couple of days, and she's been consuming yuccas fitter, so she's not aging anyway."

Melody's face grew stricken as Rhapsody spoke of Harnketi's abduction and murder. "Why are there so many horrible people in this world?"

"Young souls are more selfish and less empathetic than older souls," Rhapsody answered with a sigh. "Mortality is a rough training ground for the soul. Most souls don't return if they can avoid it, so most people you see are young souls who are still in their selfish phase."

"What did you mean about yuccas fitter making Harnketi not age?" Black asked intently.

"If you drink it every week, you won't age," Rhapsody told them with a shrug. "If you drink it more often than that, you grow younger. The two of you are a week younger today."

Harnketi suddenly appeared in their midst, a look of bleak satisfaction on her face.

"Are you okay?" Melody asked her quickly.

Harnketi smiled warmly, the bleakness vanishing as she looked at Melody. "I'm good. How are you feeling?"

"Pretty amazing, actually," Melody declared with a dazzling smile. "I haven't felt so unburdened since I was a child. Thank you for being there with me, Harnketi."

"That's wonderful," Harnketi smiled, her eyes full of unspoken words.

Melody stared into Harnketi's eyes for several seconds before a light blush appeared on her cheeks. Harmony exchanged a triumphant look with Rhapsody and Mystery. It was a start.

"There you are!" Serenity ran up to them, beaming. "I've been looking all over for you. Someone said an angel showed up a little while ago. Did you see it? Was it the same one we saw before?"

Rhapsody raised an eyebrow at Harmony. "Is that what I was feeling earlier? I should have known. She's being *too* overprotective now. No wonder you two were digging into your soul memory."

Joline and Aurora followed Serenity, their eyes full of questions. Harmony decided to change the subject.

"Rhapsody took Melody into the same dream world she took me to and shut down the emotional attachment to her memories," Harmony told her mother with a sunny smile. "She'll finally be able to move on."

Her mother looked at Melody questioningly, who smiled back warmly, her eyes clear of the mental weight she had carried for most of her life.

"I can't believe how much better I feel, Mom," Melody said, beaming. "I feel like a knife has been removed from my soul. The world looks so much more vibrant now."

Joline stepped forward and embraced Melody, her eyes filled with gratitude as she looked at Rhapsody. "Thank you, Rhapsody. You have done so much for my family. I hope to return the favor someday."

"Nonsense," Rhapsody waved her hand dismissively. "You're already family; you just don't remember. Did you four find what you were looking for?"

As she spoke, Michael walked through the magical creatures toward them, towering over everyone except the dragons. He raised a curious eyebrow at Mystery as he joined the group.

"Yep," Serenity chirped excitedly. "It was *so* cool. It feels like you are walking on water for the first part."

"Yeah, it was pretty awesome," Michael chimed in with a look of wonder. "I would say it was magical, but that would be kind of obvious."

"What are we talking about?" Mystery asked curiously.

"Don't tell them," Rhapsody said quickly, a mysterious smile lighting her face. "I don't want them to know what to expect before they see it."

"Where have you been?" Harmony asked her nieces curiously. "I thought you were dancing?"

Serenity's cheeks colored slightly. "I was, but then Grandma and Aurora came and told me they had something they wanted to show me. Michael came too. Can we call him Uncle Mike from now on?"

Michael blinked at the request, then grinned at Serenity. "Now you're making me feel old."

"You *are* old," Serenity pointed out, looking him up and down. "What are you, thirty?"

"Ouch," Mystery winced, watching her brother in amusement.

"I'm her *younger* brother," Michael told Serenity huffily. "How old do you think *she* is?"

"She's Aunt Harmony's age, isn't she?" Serenity asked innocently. "Twenty-three, right?"

"Being taller doesn't mean older," he said defensively. "Is that why you think I look thirty?"

"No, that's not it," Serenity responded vaguely. "I don't know, you just look thirty."

"No, you *can't* call me uncle," Michael declared stiffly. "Not until you get my age right. Here's a hint: I'm the same age as your Aunt Harmony."

"You should *definitely* start drinking more yuccas fitter then, Uncle Mike, because you look *way* older than Aunt Harmony."

"You stop that right now," Michael told Mystery threateningly as she held her hand to her mouth in an attempt to hide her laughter.

"Okay, Uncle Mike," Mystery agreed, followed by another round of giggles.

"Alright, who's ready to go see something awesome?" Rhapsody asked expectantly.

Harmony stood up next to Mystery and glanced around. The dance was still going strong, with a mixture of leprechauns, fauns, elves, and dragons in human form. Taxti joined them as they began following Rhapsody over to a trail next to the clearing. Black and Monroe followed them hesitantly, seemingly unsure if they were invited. Harmony smiled welcomingly at them, hoping to make them feel more comfortable. They smiled back, looking a little less awkward as they followed along the wide path.

"I wonder what she's going to show us," Harmony murmured curiously.

"It's Rhapsody, so something amazing, no doubt," Mystery guessed with a small smile.

Harmony glanced down at Mystery's hand, only inches from her own. She spent the next few steps psyching herself up before taking the plunge and reaching out to take Mystery's hand.

Mystery turned to look at her with a radiant smile, squeezing her hand reassuringly. Harmony let out a relieved breath as they continued down the path, which would have been faintly illuminated before she had started her fairy evolution. Now, she had almost forgotten what it was like for there to be a distinct light and dark time of day.

She marveled at how something as simple as holding another person's hand could elicit such strong emotions and wondered if Mystery felt the same rush of euphoria from something so basic. She smiled ruefully as she remembered she could already feel what Mystery was feeling through the soul bond: elation, excitement, and anticipation pulsing throughout the corner of her soul that she thought of as Mystery.

When she realized why Mystery was feeling anticipation, it was all she could do to stop herself from sinking into a feedback loop of desire. She wondered how much longer the party was going to last and when it would be considered polite to excuse herself and Mystery, along with Rhapsody. Surely, they didn't need to stay for the whole thing, did they?

"You're insatiable," Mystery whispered with an amused grin.

Harmony nodded, ignoring the heat flooding her neck and cheeks. "You will be too, after tonight."

Desire flooded the bond as anticipation grew stronger at Harmony's words. Rhapsody paused, turning to stare at them, amusement and exasperation warring on her face.

"Okay, different subject then," Harmony murmured with a sigh. "What was your childhood like?"

Harmony felt an immediate sense of revulsion through the bond with Mystery. "That bad, huh?"

"Yeah, let's just say becoming an adult and getting away from my family was one of the happiest days of my life," Mystery said quietly. "I think Rhapsody might be on to something regarding young souls being selfish and short on empathy."

"I'm sorry, Mystery," Harmony sighed sadly. "I wish I could have been there for you."

"It's fine," Mystery shrugged, sighing. "What I went through pales in comparison to your ordeal."

"That doesn't make it any less horrible," Harmony said firmly, squeezing her hand for emphasis.

"This place is beautiful," Mystery murmured in wonder, staring at the glowing plants lining the trail.

Harmony looked around and gasped as she noticed all the glowing flowers. Fairies zipped through the foliage, lighting it up as they went. Mushrooms large enough to sit on glowed with a soft blue ambience. Tall stalks with drooping, bell-like flowers emitted a glowing mist every few seconds, as if breathing. The overall effect was breathtaking.

"Wow, talk about enchanting," Harmony marveled in awe. "I would say this place is like a fairy tale, but fairy tales are more like this place."

The trail continued for several thousand feet before they reached the lake. Rhapsody didn't stop at the edge; she continued walking right onto the water. Small ripples expanded from her footsteps as she moved further out. Serenity, Aurora, and Joline followed without slowing. Michael waited at the edge, grinning.

"Oh ye faithful, believest thou that thy faith can make thee lighter than water?" Michael asked, a mischievous twinkle in his eyes.

"Out of the way, Jesus," Mystery drawled, pushing past him. "The faithful are back that way somewhere."

Mystery marched onto the water, Harmony's hand held securely in her own. Harmony stared down at the surface curiously. She would have thought it was glass, since it was completely transparent, but it didn't *feel* like glass. It felt like she was still walking on the soft dirt path.

As they ventured further into the lake, she noticed a dim glow emanating from below. After another minute, a glowing reef-like structure appeared in the depths. The coral's luminescence intensified as they continued their descent, and Harmony gasped when she realized the path was leading them *lower* into the lake. Crystal-clear walls lined the gradually descending path. With each step deeper, the coral's glow grew brighter, illuminating exotic fish and aquatic life. After fifteen minutes of their slow descent, they approached the lake's center.

As they neared the center, a large structure emerged from the bottom of the lake: a small quartz mountain riddled with caves and adorned with coral. Bathed in the moonlight, the quartz emitted an ethereal glow. Harmony watched, mesmerized, as mermaids slipped in and out of the quartz mound's tunnels, their red hair fanning out behind them in the calm water whenever they paused. The magical sight filled Harmony with wonder, a feeling mirrored in the bond.

"This is beyond beautiful," Melody whispered. She walked beside Harnketi, her eyes wide with childlike wonder.

"This is where the mermaids call home," Rhapsody informed them, looking pleased as she observed their reactions. "An abyss lies at the heart of their abode, plunging deep into the planet and connecting to the bottom of the

Mariana Trench. Only immortal creatures like mermaids can withstand the immense pressure at those depths."

"Mermaids are immortal?" Monroe asked, her voice filled with awe as she took in the fantastical view.

"All magical creatures are immortal," Rhapsody replied, offering the two agents a friendly smile. "You two are essentially immortal until the yuccas fitter wears off tomorrow. You don't need to breathe and are invulnerable to any kind of harm."

The two women exchanged astonished glances. Harmony gave a low whistle. She knew yuccas fitter eliminated the need for sleep and food and regressed one's age by a week, but invulnerability? People would go crazy for such an amazing fruit.

"How does that even work?" Michael asked, perplexed. "I mean, what does it do at the cellular level to make that kind of change in how physics affect the human body?"

"You would need to understand more about how the etheric realm works to understand that," Rhapsody answered with a wry grin. "I had a feeling you would be the one to question the underlying physics. It all comes down to how information is translated in the physical realm. The etheric realm has precedence over the physical realm, so any action in the physical realm must verify that the etheric realm doesn't have a conflicting set of rules for an object."

"That sounds an awful lot like a simulation," Michael declared suspiciously.

Harmony felt a jolt of electricity shoot down her spine at Michael's words, a reaction mirrored by Mystery through their soul bond. Rhapsody rolled her eyes, sensing their reaction.

"Let's not worry about the underlying principles of reality and just enjoy the beauty it offers," Rhapsody suggested, her tone brooking no further questions.

Harmony exchanged a thoughtful look with Mystery. Suddenly, Rhapsody was in front of them, affecting a stern face. Harmony's lips twitched as she watched Rhapsody try to appear stern. She just didn't have the face for it and ended up looking cute instead. Mystery seemed to have come to the same conclusion, if the humor flooding the bond was any indication. Rhapsody stamped her foot in frustration, glaring at the two of them.

"You made your face too cute to handle stern expressions," Harmony told her defensively. "It's your own fault for being so damn cute."

Mystery lost what little control she had and began laughing. Rhapsody threw her hands up in the air with a resigned sigh and turned her back on them. Harmony could feel the amusement radiating from Rhapsody as the fairy tried to hide her smile.

Michael looked like he *really* wanted to pursue the question of simulations, but he wisely stayed quiet under Rhapsody's challenging gaze.

"Okay, the field trip is over," Rhapsody declared, glowering at Harmony and Mystery. "Feel free to stay if you like."

With that, Rhapsody started walking back up the gently ascending path. Harmony and Mystery fell in step with her, and Harmony tentatively reached out and took her hand. Rhapsody glanced down at her with a slow smile that turned Harmony's insides to jelly. It was strange seeing Rhapsody several inches taller than her. The sense of anticipation in Mystery began to grow as they moved back toward the shore, triggering Harmony's own desire.

"I have a feeling we're not going to make it to the rest of the party," Rhapsody commented wryly. "You're bursting at the seams."

Harmony could only agree as her desire began triggering a feedback loop between the three of them.

"Oh, bugger it," Rhapsody muttered, glancing at the two of them. A moment later, the lake vanished, and they were in Harmony's room.

Harmony's desire spiked instantly, reaching a fever pitch.

"You really are insatiable," Rhapsody declared in a seductive voice, turning to face them. "Not that I'm complaining."

15 – CRISIS AVERTED

Agent Black sat with her back to one of the pink-leaved trees. Next to her, Agent Monroe watched the sun slowly rise above the eastern horizon. The night had been one of wonder and jubilation. Upon their return from the lake, they had each been approached by various races of magical creatures. Nidhogg had danced with her around the clearing with a grace and finesse that set her heart fluttering.

The strangest part was that they never tired, an effect they discovered was due to the yuccas fitter. They had danced the night away and played strange games with leprechauns from thousands of years ago. She couldn't remember ever enjoying herself so much. As dawn stained the horizon, she felt a poignant sense of regret that their time was running out.

"I definitely didn't imagine this assignment turning out like this," Monroe commented wryly. "I thought we were going to be firmly rebuffed by Rhapsody and spend our time in a cheap hotel trying to get her to accept an apology she knew was made out of fear, rather than sincerity."

Black barked a short a laugh, tilting her head to look next to her at Monroe. "I'm pretty sure they'll dock our pay if they find out we've just been partying the whole time."

"I'll bet we've gotten more information than someone from the CIA or FBI would have," Monroe declared with a smirk. "I'm pretty sure Rhapsody doesn't need to see our alignment to know if we're evil bastards. I heard most of the operatives at the CIA are back at the drawing board for covert ops now that their alignment is visible to everyone. I'm not sure how it is at the FBI—they don't seem to have as many evil bastards in the rank and file as the CIA."

"I imagine it's hard to maintain positive alignments when you're propping up dictatorships throughout the world," Black noted philosophically, "regardless of the justification."

"How much should we tell Miller about what we've learned so far?" Monroe asked cautiously. "I feel like revealing the full effects of yuccas fitter might not be a good idea—especially the immortality aspect. If they find out Rhapsody has immortality juice, they'll throw everything they have at getting in here, regardless of how outmatched they are."

"Yeah, let's leave yuccas fitter out of the report," Black agreed pensively. "As far as the rest of it, I'm not sure there's anything else that would trigger some kind of precipitous reaction from the bigshots."

"Should we check in now?" Black asked reluctantly. "It's past 8:00 a.m. on the East Coast."

"Five more minutes," Monroe begged in a plaintive voice. "Just until the sun is fully up."

Black laughed ruefully. "Fine. I don't want the night to end either. I don't think I've ever had so much fun."

"What was up with Rhapsody suddenly growing over two feet taller?" Monroe asked, laughing incredulously. "When I first saw her, I thought she was Rhapsody's older sister."

"Yeah, me too," Black smiled, recalling the memory. "I guess if she's a projection of the world tree, she can appear however she wants."

"Speaking of projections," Monroe began with a dreamy smile, "Nidhogg makes a very attractive human."

"And those elves," Black commented, a dreamy smile of her own spreading. "I couldn't understand a word they were saying, but damn if they weren't hot."

Monroe laughed, shaking her head. "One of them tried to tell me how the energy of the Earth complemented my chakras in a symbiotic synthesis of fertile inspiration and creative potential. I couldn't tell if it was a compliment, a pickup line, or just some philosophical observation."

"Yeah, elves are more attractive when they keep their mouths shut," Black noted wryly. "Declan mentioned that they have festivities like this three or four times a week. Talk about a great place to de-stress and really enjoy life. I still can't believe we are actually inside the ring and how amazing everything is. It's going to be hard to go back to normal life after this."

"You're welcome back any time you like," Rhapsody said, popping into view in front of them. "You're our diplomats, after all, aren't you?"

Black jumped, startled by the interruption. Rhapsody's words sparked a warm glow of hope in her chest. Maybe this *wouldn't be* a one-time event.

"Really?" Monroe asked excitedly. "We can come back?"

"Of course," Rhapsody replied with an affectionate smile. "There's a new option in your interface under your profile called: Visit Circle. Just focus your intent on that, and you'll be teleported back here. There's an open slot below that one where you can choose to teleport home. You'll have to focus on the place you want as your home location in order for that slot to become selectable."

"Wow," Monroe breathed in amazement. "Thank you, Rhapsody."

"Thank *you*," Rhapsody returned with a dimpled smile. "I'm kind of picky about who I let inside the circle. You are both pure souls with exactly the kind of personality we need to hold a cordial dialogue with the governments of the world. I don't know who picked you two, but they chose the perfect team."

Black flushed at the compliment, a warmth spreading through her chest and filling her with happiness. Her life at the NSA had grown monotonous over the last few years, and she had been contemplating a new career path for months. She was glad she had stayed—this was exactly the kind of change she needed to make her life more interesting. Hell, maybe she could even find her Mister Right if she wasn't working late into the night all week long.

"I see you've met the trees," Rhapsody noted with a small smile. "They're sentient and have enjoyed your company."

Black exchanged a wide-eyed look with Monroe before standing and turning to regard the tree curiously.

"A neural network connects the root systems of a cluster of trees, along with a fungus integrated with them to create a state of sentience," Rhapsody explained. "They use something similar to echolocation to perceive their surroundings. The cluster, not the individual tree, makes up a single individual."

Monroe tentatively laid her hand on the bark, her lips parted in wonder as she stared at the beautiful tree.

"You're more than welcome to come and go as you please," Rhapsody told them with a friendly smile. "And help yourselves to as much yuccas fitter as you like, just don't take any outside of the circle."

Black and Monroe exchanged stunned glances. They were being offered the equivalent of immortality while they were... 'diplomats'. Monroe was only twenty-six, but Black was starting to feel the years at thirty-four. She felt a thrill of excitement at the chance to rewind her biological clock.

"I'll leave you two alone now," Rhapsody told them with a wink. "I have two insatiable fairies to wind up some more."

Rhapsody vanished, leaving them in awkward silence.

"So that's got to be an interesting arrangement," Monroe commented idly.

"What do you think the deal is with the trauma they were dealing with?" Black asked. "It sounds like her father was working with the CIA in whatever was going on."

"I was wondering about that, too," Monroe said with a shiver. "Knowing some of the things the CIA has done in the past with medical experimentation makes me think it could have been pretty bad. It sounds like Harnketi did *some*thing to her father and his team."

Black's phone rang before she could continue. She looked at the caller ID and sighed. "Here we go."

"This is Agent Black," she answered in her best professional voice.

"Agent Black, I have the President with me," Miller announced curtly. "Can you give us an update on anything you have learned?"

Black felt a sinking feeling in the pit of her stomach. She was on the line with the *President?* The same asshole who had tried to nuke them? The same asshole who had tried to nuke a collection of fantasy creatures who were as far from aggressive as one could hope?

"Yes, ma'am," Black replied, maintaining her professional tone. "We've discovered several other species living here, as well as one species that appears to be from another universe, which briefly visited. So far, we have cataloged leprechauns, elves, dragons, mermaids, fairies, fauns, and a forest of sentient trees."

"What can you tell us about this creature from another universe?" asked a voice Black assumed was the President, sounding intent.

"It had the appearance of an angel," Black answered, glancing at Monroe with a frown as she tried to decide how much to disclose. "It had wings, glowed with an etheric light, and possessed a presence so intense that we fell to our knees. It's hard to describe, but it felt like being in the presence of divinity."

"What did this creature do?" the President asked dubiously.

"Harmony was experiencing a traumatic incident triggered by childhood trauma," Black answered, frowning. "The angel appeared and comforted her, telling her that she was more amazing than she could possibly understand and not to let the negativity drag her down. Then it declared she was indomitable and to remember that. After that, it vanished."

"What did it look like?" the President asked, a hint of curiosity in his voice.

"She was tall, with large wings," Black replied, shivering as she remembered the eyes. "She had a face more beautiful than words can describe and long black hair. Her eyes looked like swirling violet galaxies. Harmony said she was from another universe and didn't serve the creator of this universe."

"How did Harmony know where this entity was from?" the President asked dubiously.

"She seems to be accessing what Rhapsody called soul memory," Black responded hesitantly. She felt like she was entering territory where they should start holding information back. "After the angel left, Mystery and Harmony seemed to be trying to remember something that we think was soul memory. Harmony called Mystery by the name Calypso. Mystery seemed to recognize the name and called Harmony by the name Aria. That's when Rhapsody appeared in front of them and told them to stop digging into soul memory. She told them that they didn't have the kind of souls that could be locked into mortality for very long but that they needed to try to last a little longer because we needed them here. She didn't say what we needed them for, though. Agent Monroe and I think that the three of them might belong to this angel race."

"Leave the speculation to us, Agent Black," the President stated firmly. "What else have you discovered? How much longer will they allow you to stay there?"

"We believe Harnketi, a magic user who has lived in the ring for over six hundred years, may have done something to Harmony's father," Black answered slowly. "Rhapsody said she was hunting but became evasive when asked what she was hunting. Harmony guessed it was her father, who Rhapsody said was released from prison after a few months due to a backroom deal by the CIA, and that he was working for a pharmaceutical company in India. Harnketi appeared shortly after that. Rhapsody said she wouldn't have killed him because that would be too merciful."

The line was silent for thirty seconds, which Black assumed was due to a hushed conversation with someone in the CIA.

"Did you learn how this Harnketi survived for six hundred years?" the President asked intently.

Black shared a wary glance with Monroe and told them about Rhapsody bringing Harnketi back from the dead and turning her into a Baykok until a few days ago.

"We don't know what a Baykok is, though," Black finished. "But it seems like she wasn't human for most of that time."

"What is your current assessment of Rhapsody's temperament and potential threat to the United States government?" the President asked carefully.

"From what we can tell, I don't think she thinks about it at all," Black answered, feeling a sense of satisfaction at what she imagined was an emasculating statement to the previously most powerful person on the planet. "All of her attention seems to be on the former humans she is raising to world trees."

"How much longer will she allow you to remain inside the ring?" the President asked, a hint of irritation in his voice.

"She modified our interfaces and added a teleport feature that would allow us to teleport inside whenever we want," Black revealed, fighting to keep a smile from appearing on her face. Monroe smiled enough for both of them. "She said she has accepted us as diplomats for the world governments."

There was silence again, this time for almost a minute. When they returned, the President's voice was cold.

"You will speak with Rhapsody again and request that she accept a new diplomat that we appoint," the President instructed firmly.

"Yes, sir," Black replied, a small smile appearing on her face. She knew Rhapsody wouldn't accept a different diplomat.

"What have you learned about this Creator of the universe who is supposedly residing in the ring?" the President asked doubtfully.

There was the sound of sudden shouting from the other end of the line, then silence. A moment later, they heard a voice that sent chills down their spines.

"I understand you wish to know more about me, President of the United States of America," the voice said, shaking Black to her core. It possessed an undercurrent of power that reverberated in her soul, leaving her ears ringing as She finished.

"Speak, President, what is it you wish to know?" the voice thundered in her soul.

"What kind of demon are you?" the President demanded, his voice shaky. "In Jesus' name, I abjure you!"

"How tiresome," the voice sighed. "You are going on a journey with me now, President."

The line went silent for several seconds before shouts erupted as the Secret Service panicked. Black could imagine the chaos as the President vanished, leaving the security forces scrambling to handle a threat capable of teleportation.

"Do you think the call is over?" Black asked Monroe hesitantly, fighting back a smile.

Monroe wasn't trying to hide her smile at all. "I feel like they'll call us back if they have any more questions."

Black nodded and ended the call, fighting an almost irresistible urge to laugh hysterically as she stared at Monroe's grinning face.

"Well, I suppose he's the first president to meet the Creator while still alive," Black noted thoughtfully. "Maybe even the first world leader."

"If She's the creator of *all* the worlds in this universe, I imagine someone like the President ranks pretty low on her importance meter," Monroe mused. "I wonder what kind of journey She's going to take him on and what he'll be like when he returns."

Her phone started ringing again. With a sigh, she answered it.

"Agent Black speaking," she said quickly.

"Where did She take the President?" Miller demanded, her voice a mixture of anxiety and anger.

"I have no idea," Black answered honestly. "She's the creator of the whole universe, so She could have taken him anywhere. They could be in a completely different galaxy for all I know."

"Ask Rhapsody if she can find him," Miller demanded, her voice bordering on panic.

"Rhapsody is the world tree of a single planet in this universe," Black pointed out reasonably. "I can ask her, but I'm not sure how much she'll be able to do about locating the Creator of the universe."

"I seriously *doubt* She is the creator of the universe," Miller stated skeptically.

"I would be careful how loudly you say that," Black warned, smirking at Monroe. "Unless you want to go on a journey as well. I say that in all seriousness, ma'am."

There was a pause on the line before Miller spoke again. "Find Rhapsody and ask her to locate the President. There are going to be nukes..."

She broke off, seeming to remember there *were* no more nukes in the world, and started over, her tone growing more erratic.

"If we don't get the President back, I guarantee firepower that ring can't withstand will rain down on it before the day is over," Miller snapped.

"Agent Miller," Black began, feeling as if she were dealing with children, "I would remind you that Rhapsody will not fight with soldiers and generals. She will come directly for those responsible for any orders that would lead to an altercation like you're describing. I know you're anxious about the President, but please think clearly. Knowing what you do about Rhapsody, how do you think an overwhelming show of force will turn out? I will also remind you that the person who has taken the President is unaffiliated with Rhapsody."

"It doesn't matter how clearheaded *I* am," Miller growled irritably. "The people still in charge will be making these decisions, and they *won't* be clearheaded. I suggest you use whatever rapport you have forged with Rhapsody and ask for her help in locating the President."

"She's not in the ring right now," Black responded awkwardly. "But as soon as she returns, we'll ask her for help."

"Where *is* she?" Miller demanded, her voice fraying at the edges.

"She teleported away with Harmony and Mystery," Black replied with a wince, hoping they wouldn't guess where they were. "We don't know where they went."

"Goddammit," Miller burst out in frustration. "What about the other magical creatures in the ring? Surely someone there can contact her."

"I'll see what I can do, ma'am," Black replied without much confidence. If this is what being a diplomat was like, she wasn't sure she wanted the job. Well... just not as a diplomat for anywhere else. She could stomach the bureaucratic nonsense for the opportunity to stay in the ring.

"Call me as soon as you learn *anything*," Miller rasped before hanging up.

"Well, that could have gone worse," Monroe observed with a rueful shake of her head.

"How could it have gone worse?" Black asked dryly.

"She might have just killed him," Monroe pointed out with a smirk. "Isn't that what the god of the Old Testament would have done to someone calling him a demon?"

"Good point," Black admitted with a snort of laughter. "I never really cared about the afterlife before, but I'm definitely getting more curious since discovering the Creator is real."

"Should we go find Taxti?" Monroe asked. "She would probably know how to find Rhapsody."

"Oh, I *know* where Rhapsody is," Black laughed humorlessly. "I'm just not willing to interrupt her right now. I'm not going to be the person to interrupt someone with godlike powers when they're in the middle of an... intimate moment."

"Intimate moment?" Monroe repeated in amusement. "Is that your way of saying she's having wild sex with two other people?"

Black flushed at Monroe's description and shook her head. "I just don't want to put it like that, knowing she can hear everything we say."

Monroe blinked, then laughed nervously. "Yeah, good point."

Black stood and stretched, glancing at the sun, now well above the horizon. "Let's ask Taxti for suggestions about the President. I'm guessing the Creator will return him when She's done teaching him a life lesson, and this will all be moot."

"Good point," Monroe agreed, also standing. "Maybe we'll find another yuccas fitter tree on the way. I think I'm addicted."

"Definitely," Black grinned, feeling suddenly lighter as they walked toward Yggdrasil. "And I want to shed a decade while I've got the chance."

As they left the pink-leaved, sentient trees, they passed another unicorn. It took all of Black's restraint to keep from taking a picture with her phone. She didn't want to abuse Rhapsody's hospitality, and she didn't really have anyone to share the picture with anyway. Working at the NSA made having a personal life, especially a romantic one, difficult. Between the late nights and the constant scrutiny of potential partners to prevent infiltration, love was hard to find.

Her parents had died over a decade ago in a train derailment. They'd been waiting at a railroad crossing when the train derailed and crushed their car. She was an only child, as were both her parents. She had a grandmother in a care home with dementia, whom she visited every month or two, but they had never been close.

"Do you have any family waiting for you?" Black asked Monroe.

"Nope," Monroe replied, her tone shutting down further questions.

"Sorry," Black apologized, regretting her prying.

"It's fine," Monroe sighed. "I come from a family of jackals. Every last one of them would happily rob you blind, then come back and rob you deaf as well.

My brother tried to convince me he was dying and needed a kidney so he could sell *my* kidney on the black market. He was so stupid he didn't realize how easy it would be for me to find out he was lying. My sister tried the suicidal drama game, saying she'd kill herself if I didn't loan her money. I fell for it for a few years. They learned all that from my parents. I'd rather think of myself as an orphan than be related to those jackasses."

"Ouch, that's harsh," Black winced sympathetically. "I guess it goes back to what Rhapsody was saying about young souls being selfish."

"Do you think that means we've been through an incarnation or two?" Monroe asked, her curiosity piqued. "Not to toot my own horn, but I've always been more selfless and empathetic than your average person, at least as far as my subjective judgment can be trusted."

"I was wondering the same thing," Black said with an easy smile. "I definitely *feel* like an older soul. Life just feels heavy, as if I've experienced more than can be explained by three decades."

"Yeah, exactly that," Monroe agreed with a nod. "I wonder just how many times older souls like Harmony and Rhapsody have incarnated."

"Thousands," Declan answered, emerging from behind a tree ahead of them. "Possibly millions. Are you two looking for anyone in particular?"

"Yes, as it happens," Black said, nodding with a nervous smile. "Our boss ordered us to find Rhapsody and enlist her help to discover where the Creator took the President. I'm pretty sure I *know* where Rhapsody is and have no intention of interrupting her, so I thought we could ask one of you for some insight into what the Creator might do with the President and whether he'll be returned."

"What did he say to earn the Creator's ire?" Declan asked, a look of amusement on his face. He stood with his thumbs tucked behind a huge belt buckle that looked oddly out of place with his clothes. Maybe it was a cultural accoutrement.

"He asked her what kind of demon She was and then said, 'In the name of Jesus, I abjure you,'" Black answered, a hint of humor sneaking into her voice. "She said She was going to take him on a journey."

"Ah, a spirit journey," Declan nodded sagely. "He'll be gone for a few days then. He'll either have a very different outlook on life when he returns, or he'll go mad."

"Oh," Black frowned, exchanging a look with Monroe. Would that be good enough for Miller? Or would they start demanding that Rhapsody hunt the Creator down and bring him back?

"Are these spirit journeys common?" Monroe asked, unconsciously fussing with her hair as she studied Declan intently.

"Aye, that they are," Declan nodded. "They usually aren't carried out by the Creator personally, but it's happened before."

"Did you hear our phone call with the President?" Black asked hesitantly. She had a feeling that he had.

"As it happens, I did," Declan grinned. "Your intuition is strong."

"Any advice on what we should tell them to keep them from doing something stupid?" Black asked hopefully.

"I think you did a good job explaining that Rhapsody won't be coming after soldiers if they launch a full-scale attack," Declan replied with a chuckle. "You weren't wrong either. She'll pay them all a visit if they start doing things that will get regular people hurt. You might just reiterate that they'll be getting a visit if they do anything stupid. Samantha already knows that, and I'm sure she's made that very clear to them. I'm guessing a few examples will have to be made before it sinks in, though."

"Thanks, Declan," Black said, smiling gratefully. She wasn't sure why, but he felt almost like a father figure.

"Any time, Shelley," Declan replied with a friendly smile. "I'll just add that while the Creator of this universe is powerful beyond our comprehension, She doesn't hold a candle to what Rhapsody can do. She could snuff this universe out with a thought. Keep that in mind when you talk with your superiors."

Black shivered. Just what was Rhapsody? Who were these angels visiting this universe, and why were they here?

Monroe shared an awed look with her, clearly wondering the same thing. She felt far out of her depth, like she was swimming in turbulent waters with hidden reefs.

"There's a yuccas fitter tree over there if you want some breakfast before you call Samantha back," Declan said, nodding to their right.

Black's eyes lit up at the sight of the tree. She gave Declan a grateful smile before heading toward it.

"I went skydiving once, a few years ago," Monroe said as they walked toward the glorious red fruit. "The primary canopy failed to deploy. I thought I was a goner when I couldn't get the backup canopy to work. There was an automatic activation device on it that deployed the backup canopy when I reached a certain altitude while still in freefall. Right now, it feels like the moment I realized my primary canopy wouldn't deploy. I knew I still had the backup, but I was still scared shitless that I was going to be a splotch on the ground."

Black winced at the thought. "I'm terrified of heights. I think I would've had a heart attack."

"I'm a little afraid of heights now, too," Monroe admitted with a rueful laugh. "Or, more accurately, I'm afraid of the ground when I'm up high."

Black inhaled the floral scent of the yuccas fitter tree as they arrived under its branches. She pulled one of the large fruits off the tree and twisted the stem. Grinning at Monroe, she tipped it back and drank deeply, letting out a moan of pleasure as her taste buds exploded.

An immediate rush of etheric energy flooded her system, and she felt a familiar sensation. The first time she drank a yuccas fitter, she felt like she'd shed ten years. This time, the sensation was even more pronounced. She laughed exuberantly as she felt her body grow lighter. Her mood immediately improved, her stress levels plummeting as the magical fruit filled her with an indescribable happiness.

She noticed her species designation had changed from Human to Immortal Entity.

"Monroe, look at your species tag!" Black told her partner excitedly.

Monroe gasped when she saw the change. "Holy crap, we really do become immortal for a while."

"That sounds like an oxymoron," Black noted with a chuckle.

"Yes. Yes, it does," Monroe agreed with a wry grin. "I guess we're invulnerable for now. It's 7:00 AM. Let's see when that tag changes back to Human so we know how long this stuff lasts."

"Good idea," Black congratulated her admiringly. "I love what it does to our eyes."

"Right?" Monroe agreed with a bright smile. "Your irises are huge."

"Okay, *now* I feel up to a call with Miller," Black declared confidently.

Monroe nodded as Black pulled out her phone and called their boss, then blinked. Her battery was still at full. Did Rhapsody give them everlasting batteries as well?

"Tell me you have good news," Miller asked in a tired voice.

"Sort of," Black responded carefully. "We talked with the king of the leprechauns, and he said this was called a spirit journey and usually lasted for a couple of days."

"I'm afraid that's not good enough, Black," Miller sighed, frustration clear in her voice. "We need him returned immediately. There is already a strike team headed your way. I suggest you use your teleport ability and get out of there now."

"Declan told us to reiterate that Rhapsody won't go after the soldiers," Black warned gravely. "I'm not sure what you can do to convince them how outclassed they are, but they are all going to be getting a visit in the near future if they don't stand down."

"I made that very clear," Miller growled in frustration. "It's not penetrating their heads. The Vice President is getting sidelined by the cabinet. The Secretary of Defense has made the claim that there is no evidence the President has been abducted, so the VP doesn't have authority over him. The Attorney General is bottlenecking the legal process as well, claiming they don't have enough evidence to enact the Twenty-Fifth Amendment. The Speaker of the House has declared the whole thing a national security crisis that requires congressional oversight and is refusing to recognize the Vice President without a formal certification, which the Attorney General is delaying. We're essentially at war with Rhapsody right now."

"Well, I guess it was nice knowing them," Black muttered darkly. "We were told that Rhapsody could snuff out our universe with a thought, and I believe it. I would—"

"Hello, Samantha," Rhapsody's voice came over the phone. "Let's have a talk with the other cabinet members, shall we?"

Black shared a startled look with Monroe, and a moment later, they heard cries of surprise and terror.

"Gentlemen, or whatever you are, I'm afraid there's been a misunderstanding," Rhapsody's voice declared cheerfully. "You're operating under the assumption that you have some kind of authority over me. I want to make it abundantly clear that your continued existence is at my pleasure. You will call off all hostilities immediately. If you fail to do so, you will be sent to a world where your poor judgment can't harm other people. It's a nice world, with all the food you need growing on trees in the wild. The weather's always nice, and the water is clean. You may even come to enjoy being marooned there in time. You have five minutes to choose before I start making choices for you."

The line went silent. Black stared at her phone uncertainly, wishing she could see what was happening.

"Are you still there, Agent Miller?" Black asked tentatively.

She was met with an explosive breath. "Okay, I guess there isn't going to be a war after all," Miller breathed in an awed voice. "You didn't tell me it felt like being in a room with a god when you spoke with Rhapsody."

"It doesn't, normally," Black replied slowly. "I've only felt that presence when the angel, Emily, visited Harmony. We think Rhapsody is one of those angels, though, and I think we mentioned that."

"I'll talk with you more later," Miller said quickly, disconnecting the call.

"Well, that's that," Monroe said in amusement. "Crisis averted."

"I guess so," Black agreed, feeling like her backup canopy had just deployed.

16 – LIVE IN THE NOW

"You can't call me Uncle Mike until you get the age right," Michael insisted, glaring at Serenity, who stared back at him innocently.

They were sitting on willow chairs that grew directly from the ground in a shaded forest grove. Nearby, Taxti helped Aurora work on her cloning magic, while Joline spoke with Melody and Harnketi on the other side of the grove. Harnketi must have been using magic to block sound, because Michael couldn't hear anything they said. Leesha and Cormac stood a few feet away, wide grins on their faces as they watched Michael face off against Serenity.

"I think you'll find that I *can* call you Uncle Mike," Serenity said critically. "Watch: Uncle Mike. That's logic."

"Don't you have school or something?" Michael asked plaintively.

"It was canceled," Serenity said brightly. "Apparently, when the President gets abducted by the Creator, it's a big deal. They were also afraid of collateral damage from the airstrike on the circle, so they evacuated everyone in the county."

Michael gaped at Serenity in astonishment, leaping to his feet. "Wait, *what?*"

"You say you're not old, but now you're making me repeat myself," Serenity teased with an impish grin. "Which part would you like me to repeat, Uncle Mike?"

The leprechauns doubled over, holding their knees and laughing uproariously. Michael didn't even notice them, his focus entirely on Serenity.

"The President was abducted?" Michael demanded, aghast. "Who abducted him?"

"The Creator, apparently," Serenity answered with a shrug. "He was asking Shelley and Jessica for information about the Creator, so She appeared in the room with him and asked what he wanted to know. Apparently, he called Her a demon and tried to banish Her in the name of Jesus. She didn't like that, so She took him on a little journey to teach him perspective. Everyone in the government started freaking out and decided that it was Rhapsody's fault."

"When's this airstrike supposed to arrive?" Michael asked hollowly, falling bonelessly back into his seat.

"They called it off when Rhapsody paid them a visit and said she was going to banish them to another world if they didn't start playing nicely," Serenity replied with a chuckle. "You should have seen it. Some of them even wet their pants."

"How did you learn about all of this?" Michael asked suspiciously.

"We were curious what Shelley and Jessica were talking to their bosses about, so we did some scrying to spy on them," Serenity explained without a trace of guilt. "It sounded like it would be more interesting on the other end of the line, so we switched to watching the President. It was *definitely* more interesting on that side of the line. We didn't find out school was canceled until we teleported there and everything was locked up. We went back home and checked the internet to figure out what was going on."

"How did the public find out the President was abducted?" Michael asked, a puzzled crease forming on his brow. "I would have thought they would keep that a secret."

"Taxti said it was because they needed an excuse to launch an airstrike on US soil," Serenity replied vaguely. "Who knows why politicians do anything?"

Michael rolled his eyes. Serenity was thirteen going on sixteen. His eyes were drawn over to Taxti as she laughed at something Aurora had said. She wasn't what he had envisioned when he thought of a faun. He'd imagined furry deer or goat legs, but Taxti's were completely hairless. Her bare legs were a marvel of inverse design, with a pronounced, backward bend above cloven hooves. Her slit dress made her legs distractingly visible.

She glanced over at him and winked when she caught him studying her again. He blushed and quickly looked away. There was something overwhelmingly sensual about the beautiful faun that made it hard to think straight in her presence.

"Are you blushing?" Serenity asked innocently.

Michael glared at Serenity. If he didn't know better, he would have said she was taking teasing lessons from Rhapsody.

"Can you hold that look while I get a phone?" Serenity asked, fishing around in her pockets. "That glare while you're bright red makes you look mean as hell—we need a pic."

Leesha and Cormac dissolved into another fit of laughter as he sat in sullen silence. It was even more humiliating because it was a *thirteen-year-old* doing it.

"Don't you have some magic lessons to learn or something?" Michael asked acidly.

"Aw, don't be cross, Uncle Mike," Serenity pleaded in a contrite voice. "I'm just teasing you. Didn't Mystery ever tease you?"

"She wasn't much of a teaser," Michael replied with a sigh. "She had two moods: moody and moodier."

"Why was she so moody?" Serenity asked curiously.

"Our parents were kind of assholes," Michael answered with another sigh. "Bad things happened to Mystery, and they didn't have her back. It destroyed her sense of safety and trust until she met Rhapsody and Harmony."

"What happened to her?" Serenity asked, her eyes full of concern.

"Things that should never happen to a kid," Michael replied shortly. "What have you been learning from Taxti today?"

Serenity stared at him silently for a moment, realizing he wasn't going to give her any details. She let out her own discontented sigh as she slid lower in her seat.

"Nobody tells us anything," she complained sullenly. "They won't tell us what happened to Mom or Aunt Harmony either."

"Maybe you should be grateful for that," Michael told her pointedly. "Sometimes it's better *not* knowing the kinds of things humans will do to each other."

Serenity stared at his hard eyes in silence before tears welled in her own. As they began to leak down her cheeks, Michael cursed his careless tongue.

"I'm sorry, Serenity," Michael said with a wince, his voice gentle. "I just don't want you to dwell on those things. They've moved on to happier memories. Let it go and help them enjoy the time they have now, rather than reminding them of less pleasant times."

Serenity nodded, wiping at her eyes. He suddenly realized how she must feel, knowing something horrible had happened to her mother and the aunt she loved so much, but not knowing what. It was difficult for him to empathize, given his own dislike of his parents. He could see how much Aurora and Serenity loved their mother, however. It was the way it should have been for Mystery and him.

"Mystery used to show up at all my basketball games at school," Michael told her with a reminiscing smile, hoping to change the subject. "At my height, I was practically forced to play basketball. Our parents never showed up for anything like that, but Mystery wanted me to feel supported, so she always did. Even though she struggled with depression, it never stopped her from being my big sister. She always tried so hard to turn all my birthdays and other holidays into big events. I'm ecstatic that she's finally found the support she's never had before now. Your aunt and Rhapsody have finally brought her beautiful spirit out of hiding and made her feel safe. You have an amazing family, Serenity."

Serenity smiled tremulously and nodded. "I suppose you're family now too, Uncle Mike," she said in a brittle voice. "I guess that makes you pretty amazing too."

"It's true, I *am* pretty amazing," Michael agreed with a confident grin. "You know, Michael means 'like unto God.'"

Serenity rolled her eyes, but she was smiling. "You're a godless heathen."

"According to my Xbox gamer tag, I'm actually God's Owner," Michael declared condescendingly.

"I dare you to say that to Deighvy," Serenity grinned challengingly.

"Uh, on second thought, maybe not," Michael said quickly, looking around warily.

He turned his head when he heard voices approaching from the trail that connected to the grove. Agent Black and Agent Monroe were discussing something humorous, judging by their grins. They paused when they saw the others, looking surprised. Michael gave a friendly wave as Serenity jumped up and ran over to them.

"Hey, Jessica and Shelley, did you hear the news?" Serenity asked excitedly, giving them a quick hug. They stiffened, tentatively returning her hug as if it was an unfamiliar custom they had heard of but never tried.

Michael chuckled as the thought occurred to him. They were going to get a lot of practice with hugs in the near future. Serenity and Aurora were hug monsters.

"What news?" Shelley asked curiously as Serenity released her.

"They cancelled school today because the President got abducted," Serenity informed them conspiratorially. "Then they were going to drop some bombs on us but had a sudden change of heart. They evacuated the whole county."

The two agents looked stunned at the news, exchanging troubled glances. Shelley pulled out her phone and tapped it for a moment before sighing and rolling her eyes.

"I'm kind of hoping they push their luck, and Rhapsody just relocates them to that other world," Jessica declared in exasperation. "They are seriously like a bunch of ignorant children. Can't they think beyond their own lust for power long enough to make an intelligent decision? You would think they would spend a little more time gathering intelligence before making such rash decisions."

"Just let it out," Shelley told her partner supportively, a small smile on her face.

"Sorry, that's been building for a few days now," Jessica sighed, offering a rueful smile. "I needed some kind of catharsis, or I was going to explode."

They were interrupted when two versions of Aurora ran over and hugged them. Shelley hesitantly returned Aurora's hug while staring at her clone in confusion. Jessica likewise stared in perplexity at the clone hugging Shelley.

"Thanks for getting us out of school today," both versions of Aurora said in unison as they stared up at the bewildered agents. "Now I finally had time to figure out how to clone myself."

Shelley looked down awkwardly at Aurora as the preteen held onto her and grinned.

"You're welcome?" Shelley replied, her tone more a question than a statement.

"Rhapsody said you two have been deprived of physical affection too much in life, and that we're supposed to give you lots of hugs," the Auroras told them through mischievous grins. "That works out well, because we *love* giving hugs."

Shelley tittered nervously, hesitantly patting Aurora's back. Michael grinned as he watched the nervous agents with amusement, glad that *he* wasn't the brunt of their mischief.

"So, here's how it's done," Aurora informed them patiently. "I wrap my arms around you, and then you wrap your arms around me and pull me in tight, like you mean it. Ready, set, go!"

The Auroras pulled the two of them in tightly, and *this* time they received a proper hug in return.

"You got it!" the Auroras congratulated them with broad smiles. "It's nice, isn't it?"

The two agents smiled, amused, as Aurora released them.

"It is pretty nice," Shelley admitted with a warm smile. "Thanks, Aurora."

"Any time," the Auroras smiled back brightly. "And I *mean* any time."

Michael covered his mouth to hide his smile as he watched the agents slowly softening under Aurora's onslaught. They didn't stand a chance against the affectionate bundle of energy.

"So, you can clone yourself, huh?" Jessica asked, fascinated. "What kind of practical applications does that have? And how real is the clone?"

"It's great for multitasking," Taxti answered, joining them and looking the two agents up and down appreciatively. They flushed scarlet under her frank appraisal, and Michael stared at them curiously. Were they celibate over at the NSA or something? These two were nearly as bashful as he had heard Harmony used to be.

"For instance," a Taxti clone spoke up from behind the agents, eliciting startled gasps from them. "If you're working on a project and you're short on time, cloning yourself to provide an extra set of helping hands can be extremely useful. And then there are all those times you curse whoever designed the human body to only have two arms. Now you can just clone yourself, and voila, you've got four hands. As for sensations, it depends on how much focus you put into your clone. Most human magic users might be able to make a clone like Aurora's that contains enough substance to embrace a person, but only after decades of discipline and practice. Making a clone requires you to split your consciousness and control two bodies simultaneously. Adding sensations to that clone is beyond all but the most skilled human magic users. That's mainly due to how short human lives are. By the time a human has attained the discipline to make a clone with sensations, they're almost dead."

"How is Aurora already able to make a clone if it takes so long to master?" Jessica asked, frowning.

"Serenity and Aurora are special cases," Taxti answered, smiling fondly at the two girls. "They are very old souls, so their soul memories aid their learning. They are already advanced enough to partition their minds and think with two threads of thought simultaneously, a skill that very few humans throughout history have ever mastered. As world trees, Harmony and Mystery will be able to split their thoughts into *dozens* of threads before they complete the transition. Eventually, they'll be able to achieve thousands or even *millions* of threads. Rhapsody is a classic example of what they could someday achieve; she could create millions of completely realistic clones capable of sensations. I would guess that Aurora and Serenity will be able to handle close to a dozen within the next two years. Their transition to becoming world trees will be much swifter due to the skills they're developing right now."

Aurora and Serenity beamed at Taxti, their excitement at becoming world trees almost physically palpable.

The two agents wore matching expressions of fascination as they studied Aurora and Serenity.

"Is it rare for older souls to incarnate here?" Shelley asked curiously.

"*Extremely* rare," Taxti replied gravely. "So rare, in fact, that Rhapsody had to invite them from far away to help save this world. In the half-million years Rhapsody has been a world tree, they are some of the first souls to incarnate here who have surpassed fifty incarnations. These two have incarnated so many times that I can't give an exact number, and I'm quite good at discerning how many times a soul has incarnated."

"Really?" Shelley asked, fascinated. "How many times have I incarnated?"

"Tens of thousands," Taxti replied with an impressed smile. "You're both old enough to have been candidates for world trees. Before Mystery and Harmony's family came here, you two were the talk of the magical realm. Most souls incarnate, at most, three times in the mortal realm. You two are very special."

Michael bit back a grin as he watched the two women flush with pleasure at the statement. He had no interest in knowing how old his own soul was; he felt what he thought of as a heavy weight that echoed into eternity.

"How old is Uncle Mike?" Serenity asked curiously. "Maybe that's why I think he looks so old. Maybe his *soul* is really old."

Taxti smiled at Serenity's statement and nodded. "You would be correct. Mystery didn't come into this world alone. While he isn't as old as Mystery, I would hazard a guess that Michael is near your age."

"So can I call *you* an old lady now?" Michael asked with a triumphant grin.

"Only if you want your legs put on backwards," Serenity told him sweetly.

"You can do that?" Michael asked in amazement.

"Declan taught her how," Taxti sighed, rolling her eyes. "Leprechauns used to think it was funny to put people's legs on backwards when they were disrespected. They even put people's faces on their torsos as well. They had a very *anatomical* sense of revenge."

Aurora and Serenity stared at Taxti in horror, their eyes full of disgust.

"They put their *faces* on their *torsos*?" Serenity demanded in revulsion.

"Yep," Taxti nodded with a laugh. "They only did that to humans who were extremely offensive. You would think it would have been a lesson to the rest of them, but the humans never learned. The worst offenders usually ended up with their faces on their backs."

"How hard is magic to learn if you *don't* have an ancient soul?" Jessica asked curiously. "Rhapsody mentioned that humans would be able to use magic again after all of the world trees were active. Can *anyone* learn magic, or do you have to be born with the gift or something?"

"Anyone can learn magic," Taxti assured her with a smile full of promise. "When Rhapsody is finished with... whatever it is she is doing, we are planning on unlocking your magic potential. You too, Michael."

"We'll be able to do magic?" Jessica asked in awe, her eyes welling up.

"Yep, you'll all be magic users," Taxti nodded with a wink at Michael. "Then you can learn what else clones are good for."

Michael flushed as Taxti caught his eye, holding his gaze with a look of sensual promise.

"Eww, gross," Serenity said, wrinkling her nose in disgust. "There are still kids here, Taxti."

"What's gross about dancing with your clone?" Taxti asked innocently.

Serenity stared at Taxti suspiciously. "That's not the look you give someone you're going to dance with," she declared, her expression a valiant effort to look knowledgeable.

"How old is *your* soul?" Michael asked Taxti curiously.

"The same age as Rhapsody's, Michael," Taxti answered blandly.

"Did we know each other in other lives?" Michael asked, frowning. While Taxti's physical form held no sense of familiarity, there was something about her presence that felt *extremely* familiar, now that he was looking for it. He felt the same way about Aurora and Serenity. It was like meeting people in a dream every night, only to forget it upon waking. The nagging familiarity was like an itch he couldn't scratch, the whispers of a dream teasing his waking mind.

"Yep," Taxti replied, her black eyes dancing with mischief.

Michael swallowed as he stared into those dark eyes, framed by a face of fantastical beauty. He had dated a fair number of women over the years, but none of them came close to matching Taxti's exotic allure. He was normally comfortable around beautiful women, confident in his own appearance, but that comfort vanished when facing the ageless and beautiful faun before him. He suddenly felt like he was back in junior high, facing his first crush.

"Are you two going to need to get a room, or were you just staring into each other's souls?" Joline asked dryly. "I've noticed a distinct lack of structures or rooms inside the circle, which I'm guessing is because nobody sleeps."

Taxti's eyes swiveled to Joline, a smirk playing on her lips as she faced the woman who looked like a shorter clone of Harmony. Even her voice sounded like Harmony. "We have structures all over the place in the circle; we just rarely go into them. The entire inner ring is honeycombed with dwellings. I think Rhapsody assumed you'd just be going back to your own home, so she didn't set anything up for you here. Would you like a room, Joline?"

She finished with a seductive wink that Joline pointedly ignored, having clearly grown accustomed to Taxti's constant attempts at seduction. Michael wondered what would happen if any of them called her out on her advances, feeling an almost irresistible urge to try it himself, just to see where things went.

"Considering I need a chauffeur to teleport me back and forth, it might be nice to have somewhere to call home inside the circle," Joline admitted with a wry smile. "I'm not sure how long it'll be until we can actually start using magic at the rate we are growing."

"Why don't I set you, Michael, Shelley, and Jessica up with rooms," Taxti offered, glancing at Michael with a evocative leer that he found strangely familiar.

"Yeah, I could dig that," Michael agreed with a suggestive wink back at Taxti.

She stared at him, all pretense at seduction gone. "Did you just *wink* at me *suggestively*, Michael?"

All eyes turned to Michael, his ears burning as he stared back at her in confusion. The confusion only lasted until she threw back her head and laughed, the sound rich and throaty; even her laughter was seductive.

"You're a shameless tease," Michael accused her with a glare.

"That's true," Taxti agreed with a pleased smile. "As I've told Rhapsody, I have no shame."

"Taxti, how can you tell if you're talking with a clone?" Serenity asked curiously, staring intently into Taxti's eyes.

Taxti tilted her head, returning Serenity's gaze in silence for several seconds. "Let's save that lesson for later, shall we?"

Serenity continued to stare at Taxti, her eyes full of suspicion. "We could talk about it while we walk."

"Oh, bugger it," Taxti muttered in exasperation. A moment later, she and Serenity vanished.

"Uh, what just happened?" Michael asked in confusion.

Aurora's face was white with worry as she stared at the place Serenity had vanished. A moment later, she vanished as well.

"Harnketi!" Joline shouted urgently.

Harnketi flashed over to them in the blink of an eye. "What's the matter?"

"Taxti's acting weird, and she teleported Serenity away somewhere," Joline said urgently. "I think Aurora followed them. Do you have any idea what's going on or where they went?"

"She's taken Serenity?" Melody demanded, hurrying over to them, her voice filled with sudden panic.

"Everybody calm down," Harnketi told them soothingly. "She teleported her away because she doesn't want you to hear what she has to say. They'll be back as soon as she's finished with her private discussion."

"What were you talking about that caused her to teleport instead of just asking for privacy?" Melody asked anxiously.

"She asked Taxti how to tell if a person is a clone," Michael answered with a frown. "Taxti didn't want to talk about it, but Serenity pushed her on it."

Harnketi's expression suddenly became guarded. "Oh, yeah. Well, she'll be back soon."

"What do you know, Harnketi?" Melody asked intently, staring at her curiously. "I can tell you know *something*."

"It's a secret that only Rhapsody can reveal," Harnketi said reluctantly. "All I know is that it is *very* important that it remain a secret."

"Secret from whom?" Melody asked, a puzzled crease forming on her brow.

"From you, Melody," Harnketi said gently, her gaze pleading. "From all of you. It's *very* important that you don't know. Please."

Melody stared searchingly into Harnketi's desperate eyes before slowly nodding. "I trust you, Harnketi."

Harnketi closed her eyes and sighed in relief. A moment later, Serenity reappeared with Taxti and Aurora. Serenity looked stunned, her eyes darting between Taxti and Aurora.

"Serenity, are you okay?" Melody asked quickly, rushing to her side and placing her hands on Serenity's shoulders.

Serenity looked into her mother's worried eyes and nodded quickly, her eyes flickering toward Taxti and then back to her mother.

Michael felt like he might die of curiosity. Something momentous had just happened right under his nose, but he had no idea what it might be. Maybe he could get some answers from Serenity. As soon as the thought crossed his mind, Taxti's eyes found his. There was no sign of seduction or playfulness, just a level stare that made it clear that talking to Serenity was not an option.

He sighed in frustration, feeling like he was trying to put a 3D puzzle together blindfolded. All the pieces were there, but useless to his groping fingers so long as he remained blindfolded.

"On to the housing, my little pork pies," Taxti called out, as if nothing had happened, pointing at Melody and smirking. "You too, sugar buns."

Michael blinked at the hypocorisms, staring at Taxti oddly. He hadn't heard her use pet names before. True, he hadn't been around her long, but it still seemed out of character.

"Everyone, stop looking at me suspiciously," Taxti sighed dramatically. "Let's just get over to the domiciles and get you all some rooms to call your own before Serenity causes any more problems with her too-clever little head."

Serenity blushed as everyone looked at her. Aurora hadn't said anything since returning, her expression bemused as she followed her sister in a trance.

Michael didn't even notice the enchanted foliage as they moved through the forest on a trail lined with exotic plants and glowing flowers. He couldn't stop thinking about the odd sense of familiarity he felt with the others, like they were old friends from a long-forgotten game he had played decades ago.

Then there was Harnketi's odd behavior. She obviously knew what this secret was but spoke as if the fate of the world hinged on them remaining ignorant. Maybe it did. He had fallen in with the most important and powerful person on the planet, a fact easily overlooked because Rhapsody was so personable and silly. It suddenly struck him again: he was hanging out with the most powerful person on the planet. Even as he thought it, the realization felt unreal, as if he were playing a fantasy game with people larping as fantasy characters, despite the real magic and world-shaking decisions. What would it take for this to feel real?

"Uncle Mike, where did you grow up?" Serenity asked curiously.

"In Crescent City," Michael answered, looking down at his...niece with a questioning expression. "Why do you ask?"

"What's the earliest memory you can remember?" Serenity asked, ignoring his question.

Michael creased his brow, searching his memories. He frowned as he tried to zero in on an early memory. It felt like seeing a box of old photo albums, but when he reached for one, the box turned into a mural, merely hinting at memories. He could sense they were there, but when he tried to grasp one, he hit a wall.

"Okay, what the *hell* is going on?" Michael demanded, feeling a tendril of fear worm its way inside him. Was he just a character in a game with a tacked-on backstory but no real history?

Taxti turned to stare at Serenity reprovingly. "Serenity, didn't I just ask you *not* to talk about this?"

"I was talking about something else entirely," Serenity replied defensively. "I didn't say anything about the other thing."

"You are *way* too smart, young lady," Taxti declared with a wry twist of her lips. "Some things never change."

"Taxti, what the hell is going on?" Michael demanded again, his voice rising as fear took root in his gut.

"Well, you're inside of a fairy ring, and we're getting you a room to call home while you're here," Taxti answered calmly. "That's what's going on."

"You *know* that's not what I'm talking about," Michael growled in frustration. "Why are my childhood memories just footnotes?"

"Because you needed a memory blueprint to allow your soul to be seeded into this body," Taxti answered with a resigned sigh. "Happy now?"

Michael scowled, trying to understand. It only reinforced his initial impression that he was some kind of video game character with a crap backstory.

"You're the architect of the body and memories you currently inhabit, so don't look at me accusingly like that," Taxti scowled back at him, the expression looking incongruous on her beautiful face. "Now, that's as much as you're getting from me. You already know too much. You two might already be steering us toward disaster with your questions. I'll tell you what I've told Harmony: enjoy the life in front of you and ignore the past or questions about the future. Your answers will come in time, so just live in the present. I can't stress enough how important this is. Please, for the sake of all life on this world, bury your questions and enjoy the life you have now."

He stared into her pleading eyes, feeling the wind leave his sails. He sighed in frustration and nodded.

"The answers *will* come, Michael," Taxti said gently. "Please be patient and know that somewhere deep inside, you *know* this is all part of a plan you helped create."

Harmony, Mystery, and Rhapsody suddenly appeared. Mystery looked so joyful that Michael finally abandoned his probing thoughts and tried to immerse himself in the present.

"Sorry, everyone," Rhapsody said contritely. "I completely spaced on getting you all settled in somewhere to call home while you're inside the circle."

Michael noticed Serenity staring back and forth at Taxti and Rhapsody with a calculating gaze. He shifted his mental gears and ignored whatever secrets Serenity had unearthed. His sister was happy for the first time in decades, and he would support her in any way he could.

17 – HELPLESS

"Is everyone okay?" Harmony asked, her voice thick with concern.

She could tell something had upset them. Joline and Melody were hovering protectively near Serenity and Aurora. Michael had worry lines on his brow and a deer-in-the-headlights look, as if he'd just gone bungee jumping and couldn't remember if he'd secured the other end while in freefall. Serenity was the most obviously affected, giving off Twilight Zone vibes as she stared between Taxti and Rhapsody like they were indistinguishable twins. Harmony could feel the tension in the room, vibrating like an ultra-low frequency, too low to hear but subconsciously felt.

Harnketi stood near Melody, displaying a level of anxiety Harmony had never seen on the charismatic woman's face before. Their... diplomats... stood at the back of the group with fascinated expressions.

"We're fine, Aunt Harmony," Serenity assured her with a bright smile. "We were just waiting for Rhapsody to give Jessica, Shelley, and Michael the ability to do magic."

"Right..." Harmony said slowly, observing the array of concerned expressions around the large entryway. "Did something happen?"

"Nothing of importance," Taxti answered with a wry glance at Serenity. "Just more troublemakers digging around in soul memory. We've all talked about it, though, and everyone has agreed to leave the past in the past and let the future arrive at a normal pace."

Harmony nodded slowly, observing Michael's disgruntled expression. Mystery walked over to him and placed a hand on his shoulder.

"You okay?" Mystery asked her brother, her eyes full of concern.

Michael looked back at her blankly for a moment before glancing at Taxti and shrugging. "Yeah, I'm good. I'm just curious to see what kind of houses magical creatures live in."

Mystery stared at him for several more seconds, clearly not buying his façade of eager curiosity. When he smiled at her warmly and rolled his eyes, she finally released him and returned to Harmony, blushing as she saw the desire hiding just beneath the surface. Harmony grinned, feeling how easily Mystery's desire flooded to the surface now as well.

"I told you that you'd be as bad as me," Harmony whispered with a smirk.

Mystery's cheeks were almost constantly red, the intensity of the previous night's activities still fresh in her mind. Harmony felt better knowing she wasn't the only addict as they continued moving down the passageway behind Taxti. Having Mystery with them the previous night had been like recovering a missing part of herself. She couldn't help wondering how much of their time in eternity had been consumed by passion. She still felt like she'd fallen into some kind of extraordinary fantasy land in a novel.

The thought triggered another twinge of soul memory, but she studiously ignored it, intent on humoring Rhapsody and avoiding any deep dives into her soul memory. They just had to find ways to distract themselves... she could think of a few.

The large corridor was lined with vines climbing the walls and flowers blooming along the sides, all glowing with a soft light that Harmony knew would illuminate the path for those without night vision. The walls themselves were made of the same impenetrable material as the outer wall.

"Here you are, Joline," Taxti announced as they reached a door several hundred yards inside the wall.

Curious, Harmony followed her mother into the room, her eyes widening at the sight of the lush interior. A small waterfall cascaded down the far wall into a stream that crossed the room, filling a pond on one side before disappearing into a small hole in the wall near the door. The stream was narrow enough to step across, and its bed was filled with softly glowing rocks. The banks were covered in a glowing ground cover that spread across the room. In the center of the room stood a large canopy bed draped with green curtains. A large wardrobe and dresser stood against the wall, and a wrap-around vanity with mirrors forming a partial circle sat near the bed. Several other pieces of furniture, including a loveseat, couch, and a few chairs, completed the scene. The overall ambiance of the softly glowing room felt like something out of an elven fairytale.

"Are all of the rooms like this?" Jessica asked in amazement, her eyes shining as she stared around the room.

"Yeah, pretty much," Taxti nodded, amused by the agents' gawking.

"Where's ours?" Harmony asked Rhapsody, unable to suppress the eagerness in her voice. Mystery, standing beside her, mirrored her anticipation as they both stared at the fairy.

"Insatiable," Rhapsody murmured, a twinkle in her lavender eyes. "I thought we already had a room at Harmony's house."

"This place seems more..." Harmony trailed off, noticing her nieces watching her curiously. She lowered her voice so that only Mystery and Rhapsody could hear. "Soundproof."

Rhapsody threw her head back and laughed, her eyes dancing with amusement. "I suppose that could get awkward, since they could teleport home at any time. Okay, we'll take a room here, too."

Jessica and Shelley were ecstatic to see their rooms, commenting on how they had expected to be stuck in a cheap hotel outside of Orick while Rhapsody ignored their requests for an audience. The two agents bubbled with excitement, much to Harmony's amusement. She was pretty sure this wasn't what their superiors had in mind when they sent them to apologize to Rhapsody.

Melody, Aurora, and Serenity were shown to a room between Joline's room and the one Harmony shared with Mystery and Rhapsody. Serenity and Aurora darted inside and immediately began investigating everything, Melody following with a fond smile. Harnketi's room, coincidentally, was across from Melody's.

"That girl is too clever by far," Taxti muttered as she continued down the hall with Michael and the three fairies.

"I don't know how we're going to keep Alice from digging into her soul memory," Rhapsody agreed with a rueful shake of her head. "I think we need to find enough activity to keep her busy."

"That's the problem," Taxti responded wryly. "Half of what I'm teaching her is triggering her recall."

"Who's Alice?" Michael asked, confused, as he looked between Taxti and Rhapsody.

Taxti gave Rhapsody a long-suffering look, and the fairy winced before quickly recovering, her expression airy.

"I meant Serenity," Rhapsody told him with a shrug. "When you get to be my age, *you'll* start mixing names up, too."

Michael stared at her suspiciously, but she just stared back innocently until he sighed and shook his head. "Fine, keep your secrets."

Harmony struggled to control her curiosity. Now she knew the real names of Rhapsody, Mystery, Serenity, and herself. She'd also found a new method for distracting herself from digging into her soul memory. Any time she was tempted to follow her curiosity, she'd look over at Mystery or Rhapsody for a few seconds, and everything else became white noise. She knew they had important lessons to learn about becoming world trees and eventually using their magic, but she found it hard to think about anything but getting them back in bed. Having tireless bodies with limitless stamina made it difficult to focus.

"Here's your room, Michael," Taxti gestured toward the next door. "Let's unlock your ability to use magic and teach you to teleport so you can fetch your clothes and anything else you want to move over here."

Michael's eyes lit up, and a grin appeared on his face. "Okay, I am *so* ready."

Taxti stared off into space for a moment before focusing again. "Okay, you can use magic now. As for teleporting, let's include these two as well. Even though they shouldn't be using magic yet, knowing *how* to teleport would be good in case of an emergency."

Harmony bit back the question as she stared at Taxti. How had she given someone the ability to use magic simply by staring off into space for a few seconds? The same thought had clearly occurred to Michael. Harmony shrugged at him with a resigned smile, letting the question go. They would find out eventually.

Rhapsody gave her a grateful smile that sent a shiver of desire through her. Rhapsody's smile widened when she felt the desire through the bond.

"Tone it down, you two," Taxti commanded briskly, staring at them levelly. "It's time to focus. The first thing you need to understand is that there are two realms existing in the same space on different frequencies. While that explanation isn't entirely true, it offers a proper visualization for you to conceptualize the idea. The etheric realm is far less static than the physical realm, a place where thoughts hold far more power over structure and action. When you dream, you briefly enter the outskirts of the etheric realm. Each realm has a priority level, or weight. The etheric realm takes precedence over the physical realm for anything within the sphere of influence of your consciousness."

Taxti paused. "With me so far?"

At their nods, she continued. "Giving you the ability to use magic simply unlocked your access to the etheric realm. Close your eyes and imagine the place you want to go, adding as much detail as possible. Now *believe* that you are there in the etheric realm. If you are doing it right, the details of your vision should be shifting from what you imagined to what is *actually* there. The next part is tricky. You need to convince your mind that your body is out of sync with it. You need to believe it completely, to the point that you feel a sense of wrongness at where your body is currently residing. Once you have convinced your consciousness that you are in the wrong place, the etheric realm will send correction instructions out to the physical realm, and your body will be teleported to the correct location."

Michael vanished, leaving a satisfied Taxti smiling at his vacant space.

"Should we try it, too?" Harmony asked hesitantly. "Or will that drain our magic too much?"

"No, I just wanted you to understand the concept," Taxti answered, glancing at Rhapsody with what Harmony was almost sure was jealousy. "It's not really magic that you're storing up. Your bodies are slowly being translated into etheric bodies, and anything you do to influence the etheric realm affects that development. Think of it like learning to play the drums left-handed and then trying to switch to right-handed later. The way your etheric bodies will interact with the etheric and physical realms is significantly different from how a physical body interacts with them. If you learn how to do things while you're still in a physical body, you'll have to *unlearn* all of those things when the conversion is complete."

"So, the method of teleporting is different for an etheric body?" Mystery asked, brows furrowed thoughtfully.

"Correct," Taxti nodded with an approving smile. "When your body is fully etheric, you'll just think of the place you want to go, and you'll be there, without all the arguing between the two realms that a physical body has to do."

Michael reappeared in front of them with a suitcase in hand and a huge grin on his face.

"Okay, that was the *coolest* thing I have *ever* done," Michael exclaimed, laughing exuberantly. "I can't believe how *easy* it is."

"Displacement magic is the easiest kind," Taxti informed him with a faint smile. "Things get more complex after this."

"Are you going to teach Jessica and Shelley how to teleport, too?" Harmony asked, glancing curiously down the hall toward the rooms they were staying in.

"I was going to let Michael teach them," Taxti replied with a smirk. "I want to see how well he listened to the lesson. Aurora and Serenity already taught Joline how it works."

"I'm having a really hard time reconciling Joline as your mom," Michael declared ruefully, eyeing Harmony speculatively. "Maybe it would have been easier if I'd known her before she looked like a shorter version of you."

"Does little ickle Michael have a crush on little ickle Joline?" Mystery asked in a syrupy-sweet voice, her eyes sparkling with amusement.

"Cougar alert," Harmony called out, smirking at Michael. "You better watch out, she hasn't been in a relationship since I was tiny. She's going to be wound up pretty tight."

Michael stared at the two of them flatly, trying to ignore the red spots on his cheeks. "I don't have a *crush* on Joline," Michael denied with a derisive snort.

"Is it Jessica then?" Mystery asked him teasingly. "Or maybe Shelley? Harnketi and Melody are already spoken for."

Michael rolled his eyes and entered his room, leaving the two of them laughing.

Rhapsody had been strangely quiet, her eyes distant, but they finally refocused as she glanced at the three of them with a considering look. "I think it's time to ask Melody if she's willing to become a world tree."

"Yes!" Harmony exclaimed, grinning ecstatically. "I can't wait for her to join us!"

They left Michael to teleport back and forth between his old apartment to pack his belongings. They had only gone two dozen steps when he reappeared, cursing loudly.

They all turned to stare at him. Rhapsody shook her head ruefully and exchanged a look with Taxti.

"Do *you* want to get rid of them, or shall I?" Rhapsody asked, raising an eyebrow.

"I'll take this one," Taxti offered with an eager grin.

"What are you—" Harmony began but broke off as Michael and Taxti teleported away.

"There are some government goons hanging around outside Michael's apartment," Rhapsody explained, rolling her large eyes. "Apparently, they didn't expect him to teleport in. They were waiting out front for him, but they had bugged his apartment, so when they heard someone packing things inside, they ran in to investigate. He teleported away when they pulled their weapons on him. I guess he forgot that yuccas fitter makes him invulnerable."

"What's Taxti going to do to them?" Mystery asked, her eyes full of morbid curiosity.

"That depends on whether they're decent people or not," Rhapsody answered, chuckling darkly. "If they're just average government types following orders, she'll probably just put them to sleep. If they're a bunch of asshats that enjoy harming people... well, they're going to have a *very* bad day."

Rhapsody's face suddenly grew disgusted. A second later, Taxti appeared with a look of revulsion.

"What?" Mystery asked, laying a hand on Rhapsody's shoulder in concern.

"They were the asshat variety," Rhapsody replied grimly, "the kind who enjoy harming children."

"What did you do to them?" Harmony asked Taxti tentatively.

"Let's just say they won't have the equipment or limbs to harm anyone ever again," Taxti replied bleakly.

Michael reappeared a moment later with another load of personal items, his face pale as he looked back at Taxti warily.

"Is there a reason you took their arms and legs away?" Michael asked in a shaky voice, "Along with their manhood?"

"Such will be the fate of anyone I find harming children," Taxti replied flatly, her eyes full of wrath. "They'll spend the rest of their lives as helpless as the ones they harmed."

"Oh," Michael grimaced, his face twisting with sudden anger. "Good."

"Who did they work for?" Harmony asked curiously.

"They were subcontracted by the CIA," Taxti replied, glancing speculatively at Rhapsody. "Their reasoning is that if they can't defeat us with armies, they'll try to capture people close to us and use them as bargaining chips. They still don't seem to grasp how far down the food chain they are. I think it's time to make their position abundantly clear."

"Do you think they'll go after Serenity's friend?" Harmony asked nervously. "Susan?"

Rhapsody's eyes went distant for a moment before she vanished.

"Taxti?" Harmony prompted the faun anxiously. "Is Susan okay?"

Taxti avoided Harmony's gaze. "She will be, soon."

Harmony stepped in front of Taxti and stared up at her. "Taxti, what happened?"

Taxti's eyes jerked away, guilt and sorrow flicking through the bond. Harmony stared at her in shock, recognizing the emotions emanating from the corner of her soul that was *Rhapsody*.

"Clarice?" Harmony whispered, staring up at Taxti uncertainly.

Taxti flinched at the name, sighing and shaking her head ruefully. "I knew this wasn't going to work," Taxti muttered tiredly. "Not with the soul bond giving everything away."

"I am *so* confused," Mystery declared, watching Taxti with a bewildered expression. "How are you *both* Clarice?"

Michael was gaping at Taxti, recognition dawning in his eyes. Her name seemed to have triggered some memory within him as well.

"Yggdrasil is projecting Rhapsody," Taxti explained reluctantly. "In Rhapsody's form, I can create clones with independent threads of consciousness by partitioning my mind. We're still connected, but capable of simultaneous thought processes. We had to do it this way to keep the hosts who needed our help alive. The Rhapsody you know is a ghost of the person she once was. I had to merge with her to keep a remnant of her consciousness alive. I have all her memories and a small part of her personality, but she's essentially in stasis. She burned herself out trying to keep this world alive. That's why we're here—to help save her and her world from destruction."

"And you wanted to be a faun too, huh?" Harmony asked with a slight smile.

"Well, yeah, I totally thought that would be awesome," Taxti admitted, smiling faintly. "But Taxti isn't just a clone. The magical creatures here were starving after Rhapsody ran out of life force. To keep them alive, I used the cloning ability to separate my spirit and inhabit their bodies until Yggdrasil could produce enough life force to sustain them without me. I used to inhabit *all* of the magical creatures here. Now, it's just Taxti and Rhapsody. Taxti consumes an enormous amount of power and requires more world trees to function and subsist off the energy they provide."

"Where do *you* get the power to sustain all of the magical creatures and the whole planet?" Mystery asked curiously. "Didn't it drain Rhapsody? How long until it drains you too?"

Harmony inhaled sharply, gazing at Taxti... *Clarice,* anxiously. Was she being drained of life force as well?

"It would take a few billion years to drain *my* life force," Taxti reassured them. "And that could only happen if I didn't decide to break the rules."

"So let me get this straight, *Clarice*," Michael said slowly. "You and Rhapsody are being piloted by the same person, but the bodies you're inhabiting still have their own spirits that are in some kind of dormant state. Why are you flirting with everyone if you're the same person who is shacking up with Harmony and Mystery?"

"That's just for fun," Taxti replied, a mischievous, eerily familiar smile appearing on her face. "What else was I supposed to do while Rhapsody was having all the fun? I might be the same person, but I'm still a separate thread of consciousness for all intents and purposes. Until there are world trees and I can wake Taxti up, I'm stuck in this body being a third—make that *fourth*—wheel."

"So, you don't feel the same, um... sensations?" Harmony asked with a brilliant blush.

"Yeah, I do, but just from you two," Taxti replied wistfully. "I only get the memory of what Rhapsody is feeling."

"This whole thing seems so damn complicated," Harmony complained with a wry smile. "If this were one of my books, I would *never* have let it get this unnecessarily complicated."

"That's a whole different story," Taxti growled darkly, her eyes flashing with rage. "This bastard *would* let it get this complicated."

"Who are we talking about?" Michael asked uncertainly, tilting his head as he watched Taxti oddly.

"It doesn't matter," Taxti sighed, her anger deflating. "Not until we figure out how to get to their universe, anyway."

Rhapsody reappeared, her face full of rage and guilt. She took one look at Taxti and groaned, putting her face into her hands. "We're in *so* much trouble."

"We can still make it work," Taxti told her confidently. "We've got three already partially converted, and we're about to get one more. We might need to figure out a loophole for the soul memory issue, though. At this rate, they're all going to remember everything by the end of the month."

"Maybe we should talk to Deighvy and see if she has any ideas," Rhapsody mused, gazing at Taxti with pursed lips. "It's her universe and her rules, after all. Maybe she can point us in the right direction."

"Does it feel weird, talking to yourself as a separate entity?" Harmony asked Rhapsody curiously. The idea fascinated her more than she would have expected.

"No, it feels totally normal," Rhapsody replied, a mischievous smile on her face. "When I want to have an intelligent conversation, I just talk to myself."

"What happened to Susan?" Harmony asked tentatively.

Rhapsody's face fell, guilt and sorrow washing over her. "They killed them. They were just leaving when I arrived. I brought Susan and her mom back to life and wiped their memories."

"I'm so sorry, Rhapsody," Harmony murmured, walking over and wrapping her arms around her.

"What happened to the guys who killed them?" Michael asked intently.

"I dropped them off at CIA headquarters," Rhapsody replied darkly, her face pressed against Harmony's breasts. "They're in the same state as the guys at your apartment—limbless and emasculated."

"Who's responsible for setting all this up?" Harmony asked, frowning. "I'm kind of surprised they didn't learn to leave you alone after you showed up at the White House."

"It's a group of powerful people who *think* they're hidden in the shadows," Rhapsody replied, an evil chuckle escaping her lips. "They're basically the lovechild of the intelligence agencies and the mafia. They're the power behind politics and pull the strings of the various intelligence agencies. They're willing to do horrible things to people to scare everyone else into compliance—think Mexican drug cartel-level torture and violence. They aren't the kind of people to back down after seeing me display a few supernatural abilities. I'll have to be a lot more thorough."

Mystery tilted her head to the side. "What were you planning to do to them?"

"Same treatment as the others," Rhapsody shrugged. "They seem to thrive on actions that send messages, so I'll send them one. If they prey on the helpless, they will *become* helpless. If they were just targeting me, I would have marooned them on another world where they couldn't cause any trouble, but as soon as they start harming children, it's personal."

"Hey, Aunt Harmony!" Serenity shouted from down the hall. "Did you see that the pool in the rooms goes all the way down into the ground and comes out at the lake? It's so that mermaids can visit! How cool is *that*?"

"Really?" Harmony released Rhapsody, a moment of indecision crossing her face as she wondered whether she should address Taxti or Rhapsody. "Do they just pop in to say hi whenever they want, or do you need to invite them?"

"They're not going to interrupt us in the middle of... anything," Rhapsody broke off as Serenity joined them. "They have amazing hearing and can sense when a room is safe to enter. They're very social, so when I made the rooms here, I made sure to make it easy for them to interact with people in more than just the lake. There are various ponds throughout the circle that are actually conduits that go back to the lake."

"They were at Melody's party the other night," Serenity pointed out. "Can't they just transform to have legs whenever they want to visit?"

"They aren't comfortable with legs for very long, so I tried to accommodate their natural habitat," Rhapsody replied with an amused smile. "Watching them interact with the fairies is extremely entertaining. Fairies hate water but are fascinated by mermaids, so their relationship is...odd. And you know how fairies are chatterboxes? Well, mermaids are nearly as chatty, so when you get them together, it can get pretty wild."

"I better go," Taxti announced with a scowl. "They're getting ready to cause more trouble. I'll be back in a little while."

Taxti vanished, a look of dreadful purpose on her beautiful face.

"Where's she going?" Serenity asked.

"Just to do some cleanup," Rhapsody said blandly. "We were just getting ready to ask your mom if she wants to become a world tree."

"Oh, I wanna see this," Serenity grinned, leading them back to the room she shared with her mom and Aurora.

"You might want to get another bed in there for Melody," Harmony noted dryly. "Serenity and Aurora pinwheel too much to share a bed with."

"Did you forget that none of us sleep anymore?" Mystery asked in amusement.

"Oh yeah," Harmony laughed sheepishly. "It's such a major part of life; it's going to take a while to get used to the idea that we'll never have to worry about it again."

"I mean, it's not the only thing beds are good for," Mystery said archly. "But I have a feeling Harnketi's bed will serve *that* purpose."

Harmony hoped so. Her sister needed someone wonderful to share her life with to make up for all the hell she'd suffered.

They followed Serenity into the room and found Aurora sitting at the edge of the pool, talking to a mermaid with bright red hair. Harnketi was sitting next to Melody on the loveseat. Melody was hanging on Harnketi's every word, her bright blue eyes fascinated by whatever Harnketi was telling her. Harnketi's natural charisma had drawn Melody in like a moth to a flame. Harmony could feel the powerful chemistry between them. Her sister's fears of not being attracted to women seemed to be a thing of the past.

Rhapsody walked up to the loveseat and waited as Harnketi finished her tale. When she finished, Melody threw her head back and laughed delightedly. Harnketi looked completely enchanted as she watched Melody laugh.

"So, we have a proposal for you," Rhapsody began after Melody stopped laughing.

"Yes, I would *love* to become a world tree," Melody answered before Rhapsody could ask.

"Well, that was easy," Rhapsody beamed at her. "Shall we take the shortcut?"

"Sure..." Melody agreed slowly.

The two of them suddenly vanished. Serenity grinned and vanished as well, followed a moment later by Harnketi.

"Are you going to watch too?" Harmony asked Michael as he tentatively followed them into the room.

"Where did they go?" Michael asked, watching Aurora talk with the mermaid in fascination. Aurora seemed to be telling the mermaid all about their epic adventure of the last week, including their first run-in with Rhapsody when Aurora had gotten stuck in the redwood tree next to the wall.

"They went to the chasm," Mystery informed him with a smile. "You remember where that is, right?"

"Yeah, I remember," Michael nodded, smiling slightly. "Aren't you two going?"

"We can't teleport," Harmony reminded him with a shrug. "We'll congratulate her after Rhapsody brings her back."

"I think I'll go watch," Michael decided, grinning boyishly. "Watching real magic is kind of awesome."

Mystery chuckled as he vanished, leaving them with Aurora and the mermaid.

Harmony looked closer at the mermaid. She was pretty, with a heart-shaped face and a beautiful smile. She was bare-chested, though her long red hair covered her breasts. Her large eyes were enraptured as Aurora regaled her with their tale. Harmony smiled, feeling a warm glow of satisfaction at seeing Aurora so happy.

She felt Mystery's arms wrap around her waist from behind, and she leaned back into the taller woman with a contented sigh.

"Lots of crazy revelations today, huh?" Harmony asked wryly.

"There sure were, Aria," Mystery whispered into her ear.

Harmony shivered, both at the use of the name and its seductive delivery.

"You're going to get us into trouble, Calypso," Harmony murmured with a lazy smile.

"I kind of like getting into trouble with Clarice," Mystery whispered silkily. "She's so damn cute when she tries to be stern."

Harmony shivered as the seductive whisper sent tingles down her spine, while her synesthesia mimicked the sensation of pressure on her breasts as Mystery pressed into her back. "I'll bet this is distracting the hell out of Clarice."

"I'm not sure if this is soul memory speaking," Mystery whispered with a smile, "but I have a feeling she has us far outclassed in the mischief department."

Harmony felt Mystery's hands slide up the front of her shirt to rest just below her breasts. She gasped, her breath quickening with excitement, and barely held back a soft moan as she melted back into Mystery's arms, wishing more than anything to be back in their room.

"You two are so damn insatiable," Taxti drawled wryly as she appeared right next to them. "You seriously can't just wait a few more hours?"

Mystery slid her hands out of Harmony's shirt, eliciting a disappointed sigh from Harmony. Mystery released her, leaving a teasing kiss on her neck as she stepped away.

"This is *your* fault," Harmony accused Taxti teasingly. "You've completely corrupted us."

Taxti rolled her eyes as she stared at the two of them fondly. "Corruption only goes where it's welcome."

Mystery stepped into Taxti's personal space, sliding her hands onto her waist. "Is it welcome here?"

Harmony felt a sudden explosion of desire through the bond she shared with Rhapsody. Taxti inhaled sharply, closing her eyes as Mystery slid her hands up Taxti's back and pulled her into a tight embrace. Harmony bit her lip, the sight flooding her synesthesia with the sensation of every soft curve. Mystery lowered her lips to Taxti's neck, slowly kissing her way up and around her jaw until their lips met.

"Bedroom," Harmony gasped, taking a few shaky steps toward them and glancing at Aurora, who was engrossed in retelling their adventure with the mermaid. "Now."

Taxti teleported them to their new bedroom. Harmony stepped behind Taxti, sliding her hands around her waist and up her soft stomach, eliciting a hungry moan.

"Now, we're going to tell you what we're going to do to you," Harmony whispered into Taxti's ear.

18 – LEXI

Jerit sat behind an ornate, three-hundred-year-old mahogany desk in an office furnished with priceless paintings, sculptures, and intricate tapestries. Decades ago, his father had decorated the office as their wealth ballooned to a meaningless string of numbers.

A diamond plaque hung on the wall behind the desk, reading "Fortuna saevis favet," or "Fortune Favors the Cruel." The family's rise to power had begun during the Prohibition era, with the ascent of the mafia. Their power was solidified when US intelligence agencies began collaborating with them, using their vast network of resources for intelligence gathering and extra-legal actions that bypassed congressional oversight. Over the decades, the line between the mafia and intelligence agencies vanished as the two merged.

If he harbored any doubts about the blackened state of his soul, the damnable interface that had appeared in his vision days ago had made it abundantly clear. His alignment was as far into the red as it could go, earning him the title of Supremely Evil Bastard, complete with an enormous pile of turds next to his name.

Jerit glanced at an email that had just pinged on his computer. He frowned at the macabre sight of half a dozen men, all missing limbs and genitals. Their faces were filled with so much horror that his father would have applauded whoever arranged the brutal transformation.

He glanced down at the message below the images.

These were the teams sent to deliver a message to Rhapsody. One of them said he had a message for the ass hats in charge (exact words): "Here's a preview of what awaits you before the day is out."

A cold chill ran through Jerit as he stared at the images, a sense of dread washing over him. There was no way any of this could be traced back to *him*. Everything they did was oblique. They never explicitly ordered hits. A simple phrase expressing their opinion that someone should send a message would be correctly interpreted by their contacts, who would be just as circumspect in their communication with anyone they contracted. Funds were never tied to their fortunes, leaving no paper trail and no possibility of tracing anything back to them. However, there was that damnable interface. Who knew *what* it was capable of observing?

They were dealing with someone who clearly had access to resources beyond human ingenuity. Who knew *what* she might be able to discern?

Jerit pressed the page button on his desk and waited for the suited security officer to enter.

"Get everyone with a gun in here ASAP," Jerit commanded, barely keeping the fear from his voice. "Anyone entering this room that *isn't* on the security team gets a bullet."

The man nodded quickly and spoke into his cuff mic. Minutes later, armed gunmen flooded the room, brandishing everything from handguns to fully automatic Uzis and M16s.

Jerit sat at his desk, staring at the email with horrified fascination. Would she be able to find him? If she did, was she really bulletproof? How much firepower could she withstand before her defenses failed?

The security team stared around warily, clearly unnerved by their sudden presence in the normally forbidden room. Over twenty armed men now occupied the large, windowless space.

"Hello, ass hat number one," a cheerful voice greeted him from behind.

Jerit jumped, swiveling his chair around in surprise. His men were frozen, completely immobilized. Their eyes darted around, staring at him in sudden fear as they realized they were dealing with something non-human.

A woman of fantastical beauty stood behind him, taller than Rhapsody, with dark hair. Her eyes regarded him like he was a worm—no, *less* than a worm. He had never truly known fear, but as he stared into her merciless eyes, he felt the same terror he had instilled in so many others.

"I imagine you thought you were careful enough with your machinations to stay hidden," the woman noted with an amused smile that never reached her eyes. "You have no idea who you're dealing with. I took a look at your life record. You're not a regular piece of shit—you're an extra *special* piece of shit. I hope you enjoy what's left of your life as helpless as all the people you have harmed. There will be no more patience for your interference. I might have been merciful if you had come after me, but you went after children, and *that* is where you crossed the line. Goodbye, Jerit."

A chill shot through Jerit's body. He tumbled out of his chair and landed on the floor as everything went black. He couldn't hear or see anything. His heart rate spiked as terror consumed him. He couldn't feel his arms or legs. All he could feel was his head and torso. He let out a scream of terror that he couldn't hear as he perceived a future dwelling in his own personal hell of solitary confinement for the rest of his life.

* * *

Vice President Adams sat behind her large desk, chin resting on steepled fingers. She stared at the two agents across from her, noting their dilated irises. During their last call, just minutes ago, they had informed her of their newfound ability to teleport and offered to meet in person. Her Secret Service detail had been understandably alarmed to learn of the agents' ability to appear anywhere. They were already dealing with a nightmare due to the President's disappearance, and now they had to contend with regular humans who could materialize out of thin air.

"What's going on with Rhapsody?" she asked crisply, trying to project an air of control despite the rebellion brewing within the Presidential Cabinet and Congress. "Has she indicated when the president will be returned?"

"We were told it would be a few days," Black replied calmly, seemingly unfazed by being in the presence of the second most powerful person in the country. Of course, she had recently been in the company of someone who made her power look like a line of sugar ants. "Melody accepted Rhapsody's offer to become a world tree and underwent the initiation process. We were told they were waiting until Serenity and Aurora were older before allowing them to become world trees."

"What else have you learned during your time in the ring?" Adams asked intently.

"They spend most of their time making entertainment for themselves," Monroe answered with a faint smile. "All the magical creatures within the circle are immortal and invulnerable to physical harm. While they possess power beyond our comprehension, they have little interest in human affairs unless directly affected. We understand that the CIA sent mercenaries to kill some of Serenity's friends and their families as a message to Rhapsody. Rhapsody resurrected them and wiped their memories. The individuals responsible for ordering the operation were... dealt with."

Adams sighed in frustration. She hadn't been informed of any such operation, nor its repercussions. She knew that she and the President were largely figureheads, but it still rankled that factions within the government could act with impunity and without oversight. Politicians quickly learned to avoid the so-called untouchable factions. Presidents who disobeyed orders often ended up dead or injured; she recalled a few presidents who had supposedly fallen off their bikes or tripped while running.

"I don't suppose she could be convinced to clear *all* of them out and return our government to an elected one?" Adams asked, shaking her head in disgust.

"I don't think so," Black replied regretfully. "She seems uninterested in the world of humans unless they interfere with her directly."

"We have world leaders requesting access to speak with her," Adams informed them wearily. "They think we have access to a superpower that should be shared globally."

"Just tell them they'll have their own fairy soon enough," Monroe suggested with a grin. "After all, the other world trees are all over the world. They'll have access to the equivalent of Rhapsody soon enough."

"That's a whole other headache in Congress," Adams declared sourly. "They don't *want* these other fairy rings to power up and provide magic, or whatever it is, to these other world powers. They feel like they have access to a resource that gives them political clout, so long as our country is the only one to have a fairy ring—in spite of the fact that they have no power over it."

"Well, I'm afraid they're going to be disappointed then," Monroe observed wryly. "Because their desires definitely don't factor into Rhapsody's plans, not to mention that the world will end if she *doesn't* get the other fairy rings powered up."

Adams sighed as she watched the two agents, feeling a sense of regret for what she was about to do. She liked the two women—as much as she ever liked anyone. However, they needed someone more objective inside the ring. These two were clearly under Rhapsody's influence, and their loyalty to the United States government was questionable at best.

"Thank you for your service, Agent Monroe and Agent Black," she said in her most businesslike voice. "We appreciate everything you have done for us. Your final duty for this assignment will be to convince Rhapsody to allow a replacement diplomat to take your place. I don't think I'm wrong in my estimation of your loyalty to our country. Do you have any questions?"

The two women looked stunned, then hurt, staring back at her with expressions of betrayal. She hadn't felt guilty for any of the decisions she had made in a long time, but as the two agents looked back at her like kicked puppies, she felt a twinge of guilt.

"Actually," Rhapsody's voice spoke up a moment before the fairy appeared next to her desk. "I have my heart set on these two as diplomats. It's them or nobody."

The Secret Service agents immediately pulled their weapons and started shouting at Rhapsody to get down on the ground. She rolled her eyes, and a moment later, the room was silent as all the Secret Service agents stood as still as statues.

"As I was saying," Rhapsody continued, as if nothing had happened, "I like these two. I already told them I'm picky about who I let into the circle, and you lucked out by sending them in the first place—I wouldn't have accepted anyone else. Their souls are old and filled with compassion."

Adams swallowed, staring at the creature with godlike powers before her. She wasn't broadcasting the same overpowering aura as the last time Adams had seen her. Then, Adams had been teleported into Miller's office, along with the Presidential Cabinet and several members of Congress.

"I want to like you, Amanda," Rhapsody told her with a sigh. "I know you're a young soul and still have much to learn about compassion and selflessness. Unfortunately, there isn't much time left for you to figure it out. The Creator of this universe has modified the way your afterlife works here. Those of you who fail to learn compassion will be doomed to reincarnate until your soul has been through enough of the meat grinder to finally learn. If you ever want to see the Light Realms and escape the reincarnation cycle, I suggest you start *trying* to learn what compassion is."

"Are you from this universe?" she asked, unable to contain her curiosity.

"No, Amanda," Rhapsody replied, shaking her head slightly. "I'm from a place far, far away. I'm here because I received a request to help save your world from destruction. You have less than twenty years for us to succeed. If we do *not* succeed, I'll still ensure this planet survives, but there won't be many humans left alive to enjoy it."

Adams shivered, staring into the large lavender eyes of an alien entity. She wasn't just some magical creature from Earth—she was from an entirely different *universe*. Adams suddenly realized she was dealing with a being so far outside of her power scope that there wasn't even a comparison. All of their political machinations and intrigue were so far beneath this entity's concern that it could simply ignore them entirely. She hadn't felt this small since she was a child.

Rhapsody turned to Black and Monroe with an expectant smile. "Shall we?"

The three of them vanished. A moment later, her Secret Service detail stumbled as they suddenly regained the use of their muscles.

Adams leaned back in her chair, a troubled frown on her face. She had never given any thought to the concept of souls or the afterlife. She suddenly felt a strong urge to examine the state of her own.

"Agent Davis," she addressed one of her Secret Service agents pensively, "what do you think 'Immortal Entity' means?"

"Are you referring to the species of the two agents, ma'am?" Davis asked, a troubled crease forming on his brow.

"Yeah," Adams nodded slowly. "Did Rhapsody turn our agents into immortals? And if so, why?"

"She seemed pretty attached to them," Davis noted with a shrug. "Maybe she's rewarding them for some reason."

"They looked younger," Adams observed, tapping her chin thoughtfully. "I have a feeling the Cabinet and Congress are suddenly going to want to be friendly if they think she can grant immortality."

Agent Davis gave a neutral grunt, though Adams could see the doubt in his carefully blank expression.

"I don't think she would offer it to any of us anyway," Adams said with a humorless smile. "But just the knowledge that she *could* will probably change a lot of attitudes. I'm curious to see how the President behaves upon his return tomorrow."

* * *

Harmony gasped with pleasure as the light filling the chasm soaked into her body, purifying her mortal form and moving her ever closer to an ethereal state. She and her mother were absorbing significantly more energy than they had the first time, and their growth seemed to be exponential, with each immersion causing a dramatic increase. Still, it was nowhere near what Rhapsody consumed.

Rhapsody finished absorbing the last of the energy before speaking.

"You're about to hit your first growth spurt," she informed them, an excited sparkle in her lavender eyes. "After that, I'm going to need to keep you close. You'll have so much power that it will start arcing when you're around other magical entities, resulting in a magical overload that could harm them. I'll need to teach you how to maintain control before it's safe for you to be on your own."

"Wasn't it supposed to take months or years for us to reach our first growth spurt?" Harmony's mother asked with a frown.

"That was a rough estimate," Rhapsody replied with a rueful sigh. "It's going far quicker than expected because of who you were. I tried to use what Rhapsody knew of this process to gauge the timing, but she must have underestimated our growth potential quite a bit."

"What did you think?" Harmony asked her sister with a grin as Melody's glazed eyes slowly returned to normal. "Pretty intense, right?"

"Yeah," Melody breathed in a stunned whisper, tears in her eyes. "I can't believe how wonderful that was."

"Everything in my life became exponentially better after meeting Rhapsody," Harmony told her with a radiant smile. "It's going to be wonderful for you from now on, too. I promise."

Melody smiled back, happiness burning brightly in her eyes. Harmony marveled at how much she'd changed. She looked so similar to Harmony now that the others often mistook them for each other. Just a few hours ago, Harnketi had slipped up behind Harmony and wrapped her arms around her waist, whispering, "I love you." Melody had been talking with her daughters a few feet away when it happened, and Harnketi realized her mistake from the look on Melody's face. She jumped back from Harmony as if burned, while Rhapsody and Mystery dissolved into giggles, staring at the blushing Harnketi and stunned Harmony. Melody glared at Harmony with mock outrage, demanding she stop trying to recruit more women into her harem.

Seeing the happiness in her sister's eyes, Harmony felt soul-deep contentment. Melody had been through so much horror in her life; if anyone deserved to experience real happiness, it was her.

"So, what's going on with you and Harnketi?" their mother asked, raising an eyebrow. "Are you just trying to make things work, or are you actually feeling something?"

"Oh, there's *definitely* no pretending involved," Melody purred dreamily. "I thought I would have a hard time being attracted to another woman, but there's just something so *alluring* about Harnketi. She's bold enough that it doesn't feel awkward or forced, but she's so gentle and respectful at the same time. It's so different than anyone else I've ever been with. Maybe Harmony's right, and I should have been playing for the same team all along."

"Well, I can't give any advice based on *my* track record," Joline said wryly. "But I think it has more to do with finding the right person, regardless of which team they play for."

"Speaking of the right person," Harmony said tentatively, watching her mother with concern. "Are you ever going to give relationships another try?"

"No, I don't think I will," Joline said firmly, shaking her head. "Some pits are just too deep to dig yourself out of."

Harmony shared a worried look with Melody before turning back to her mother. "Mom, if you're talking about Dad, you know that none of that was your fault."

"It's not a matter of fault," Joline sighed wistfully. "It's a matter of something so monumentally important being broken. I'll never trust another partner again—not in this life, anyway."

"Were you ever happy with Dad?" Harmony asked softly. "I relived a memory when Melody was in the hospital when I was two, and you didn't seem to like him at all."

"It seemed like there was something special there for a few years," Joline said quietly, her eyes distant. "I was attracted to his high-energy personality and his success. It wasn't until after Melody was born that I started to question our relationship. He was a classic psychopath, so convincing at faking emotions. But it wasn't until after you were born, Harmony, that I realized he had been faking almost everything he claimed to feel. He could be charming and believably caring, but after twelve years of living with someone, you start to see behind the curtain. I had seen enough instances where it was clear he was wearing whichever emotion he thought was required for a situation. It became clear they were all fake. He had no empathy whatsoever, which became abundantly clear after what he did to the two of you. It's hard to see the early years as special with the knowledge of what he really is coloring everything in hindsight, but I thought those years were special at the time."

Harmony pulled her mother into a hug. "I'm so sorry you ended up with such an asshole, Mom," Harmony whispered, fighting back tears. "I wish you could have experienced something truly magical."

"It's fine, Harmony," Joline assured her, patting her back. "I wouldn't change anything if it meant missing out on you and Melody. I just wish I had been more suspicious early on, before he hurt you and Melody so much. Even knowing what he was, I had a hard time believing anyone could be so evil."

Harmony could only nod. Who would suspect a parent of torturing their own children in a lab for the sake of medical research? It really did take a special kind of asshole to feel no remorse or empathy for what he had done to them.

"Thanks for saving us, Mom," Harmony whispered, tears forming in her eyes. "You really are the best."

Melody joined them, wrapping her arms around the two of them. "Yeah, Mom, thanks for saving us. I don't think I've ever properly thanked you before."

"I would say you're welcome, but I'll never feel like what I did deserves thanks," Joline said sadly. "I was your mother, and it was my job to protect you. I set a new low for failure with my misplaced trust."

"Joline, this wasn't your fault," Rhapsody said firmly. "We came here knowing our family would watch over us through our mortal lives. But there was a problem with... reality, let's call it. Our family was stuck in a place where time flowed significantly slower, which resulted in twenty years passing without being able to protect you. I was unaware of this, or I would have checked in on you constantly. It was a perfect storm of failures; significant layers of protection should have prevented this. In the end, we all owe Joline our thanks for saving the two of you when we couldn't. More than anything, I wish time travel were possible so we could change the past. Maybe *someday* it will be, and we can fix things."

"No," Harmony said firmly, releasing her mother. "I am who I am because of how life has shaped me. I'm happier now than I ever thought possible, and I don't want *anything* to change that. Bad things happened, but we're here now. Let the past stay there. Mom, I won't accept you giving up on relationships. Somehow, you're going to be swept off your feet and experience true bliss—and you'll learn to trust again. I'll accept nothing less."

"Is this where Serenity is getting her new bossy personality?" Joline asked dryly.

"I'm pretty sure it is," Rhapsody said with a fond smile at Harmony. "Serenity wasn't like this before."

Taxti suddenly appeared, looking exasperated and amused. "We've got a new addition to the circle," she announced, her lips twitching.

Rhapsody stared at her in shock for several seconds before she suddenly burst out laughing so hard that she had to lean on Harmony for support.

Harmony arched an eyebrow. "So... what's going on, Taxti?"

Taxti gave her a slow, sensual smile, then deliberately licked her lips in the most erotic way possible. "What would you *like* to be going on, Harmony?"

Harmony's synesthesia sent the sensation of a tongue licking her lips straight to her libido. Her breath quickened as she stared at Taxti with sudden longing.

"Taxti, that was cruel," Melody gasped, her voice unsteady.

"Oh, I am *so* sorry, Melody," Taxti said contritely. "I keep forgetting that we have two of you with synesthesia now."

Rhapsody walked over to stand in front of Taxti.

"I could have sworn I told you that Mystery and Aria were mine," she said, staring pointedly at Taxti.

"Yep, they're ours," Taxti agreed, winking suggestively at Rhapsody.

Melody frowned, looking from Harmony to Rhapsody.

"Mystery and Aria?" she repeated slowly, turning to Harmony, recognition dawning in her eyes. "Oh my god, Aria!"

Before anyone could say anything, Melody flew into Rhapsody's arms, laughing and sobbing in equal measure. Rhapsody held her tenderly, her eyes soft.

"Way to go, Rhapsody," Taxti said with a small golf clap. "Her name is Harmony, remember? I swear you're purposefully saying their real names and just pretending to mix them up."

"How much do you remember?" Rhapsody asked Melody, her voice resigned.

Melody pulled back, beaming at Rhapsody. "I'm not sure." She blinked back her tears and looked at Taxti, then blinked and returned her gaze to Rhapsody. "Clarice? Why are you two people?"

Rhapsody ignored the question and faced Taxti.

"Well, she's old enough now that we won't get in trouble," she said conversationally. "Harmony, Aurora, Serenity, Michael, and Mystery are the ones we *will* get into trouble with. Harmony has been good at distracting herself any time soul memory comes up."

Melody sucked in a breath, her hand flying to her mouth. "Oh, yeah, the plan."

Joline studied Melody cautiously. "Melody? Are you... okay?"

Melody smiled radiantly and pulled Joline into a tight embrace. "Better than okay. You really are amazing. Thanks for saving us... Mom."

Joline heard the hesitation and held Melody at arm's length. "Yes, I'm still your mom, even if you've got your memories back."

Melody laughed and pulled Joline back into her arms. "I wouldn't have it any other way."

Harmony took a deep breath and opened her mouth to speak, but before she could get a word out, Melody released Joline and tackled her in a bear hug.

"Oh, Harmony," Melody choked out, her tears returning. "I'm so glad you were my sister. You carried me when I couldn't go on."

Harmony returned the embrace gently, then quickly released Melody when her synesthesia went haywire. She felt a disconcerting strobe effect as their dual synesthesia devolved into a feedback loop of recursive tactile madness.

Melody gave a startled laugh. "Hold that thought," she said, closing her eyes. A moment later, her eyes opened, and she pulled Harmony back into her arms—this time, without the feedback loop.

Harmony blinked, staring over Melody's shoulder at Mystery in surprise. "You can just turn it off?"

She felt Melody nod. "Yep."

Mystery watched them with a soft smile, and Harmony felt adoration flare through their spirit link.

"Who's this new addition to the circle you were talking about?" Joline asked Taxti as Melody traded Harmony for Mystery.

Taxti tapped her lips, looking up at the ceiling. "Hmm, how to phrase this believably," she murmured thoughtfully. "Okay, here goes. We found a lost girl outside the circle. We discovered she's an orphan suffering from amnesia, so we decided to take her under our wing, so to speak."

Rhapsody smacked Taxti's thigh, shaking her head in exasperation.

"That's supposed to be believable?" Harmony asked dubiously, pointedly not noticing Taxti's reference to wings.

"Why don't you come up with a better backstory, then?" Taxti asked challengingly, her dark eyes full of mischief. "You're the author, after all."

Harmony looked at Taxti speculatively. "Who's supposed to believe it?"

"Serenity and Aurora," Taxti said with a grin just short of laughter. "But mostly, just Serenity."

"How old is she?" Harmony asked, fighting the urge to ask her sister about this *plan* she spoke of.

"Coincidentally, she's fourteen," Taxti replied dryly. "Just a few months older than Serenity."

Harmony twisted a strand of hair around a finger, narrowing her eyes. "Okay, why not just make her a distant cousin or relative of Shelley or Jessica?" she suggested with a small smile. "We brought her here to keep her safe from CIA hit squads."

Taxti nodded approvingly. "Okay, that could work—but we should probably leave those two out of it. Mystery, do you have any distant cousins?"

Mystery nodded slowly. "I think so. We'll have to get Michael to go along with it, too."

"Okay, let's go with the 'saving a favorite cousin' story, then," Taxti decided with an eager smile, rubbing her hands together in anticipation. "This is going to be fun. She's going to be such a mess with the bond winding her up."

Rhapsody started laughing as Taxti finished, and the two shared a wicked smile.

"You haven't changed at all, Clarice," Melody declared, shaking her head ruefully.

"Okay, I'll take Mystery over to Michael and fill him in," Taxti offered, winking at Mystery. "Don't introduce her to Serenity until I get there; I don't want to miss it."

"Would someone mind explaining what the hell is going on?" Harmony's mother asked plaintively.

"They're sneaking an angel into our group," Harmony explained to her mother, giving Rhapsody a challenging look.

Rhapsody groaned. "You weren't supposed to guess that yet, Harmony."

"It's getting kind of obvious," Harmony noted dryly. "I didn't dig into soul memory, though, so I haven't broken any rules. Just simple deduction."

Harmony felt her bones hum, indicating that someone was using magic nearby. "Is that her I feel?"

"Come on out, Lexi," Rhapsody ordered with a smirk. "Let's get the introductions out of the way."

A girl who *looked* to be around Serenity's age suddenly materialized in front of them. She had long blonde hair and a face that was somewhere between cute and beautiful and was only about an inch shorter than Serenity. A huge smile lit her face as she stared at them.

"Hi, everybody," Lexi greeted them, waving exuberantly. "I'm Lexi. I know you don't remember me right now, but we are all family where we come from. I'm here to help keep Serenity from figuring everything out too fast."

"That, and you just couldn't stand to be away from her any longer, eh?" Taxti asked with a suggestive leer.

"Not the leer!" Lexi cried, shielding her eyes with her hands. "Clarice, I thought you would have given up on the leer down here."

"I've been saving up all my leers just for you, Lexi," Taxti grinned, walking over and pulling her into a warm embrace. "It's wonderful to see you."

Melody had been staring at Lexi wide-eyed, her mouth hanging open almost comically. As Taxti released her, Melody rushed over and threw her arms around her, tears flooding down her cheeks.

"Oh, Lexi, it's so good to see you," Melody half-sobbed. "I missed you *so* much!"

Lexi held the taller woman comfortingly in a tight embrace. "It's so good to see you again, Arturiel. I'm so sorry for what happened to you."

Harmony felt like another puzzle piece had just fallen into place as she stared at the two of them. She hurriedly looked at Rhapsody and Taxti, attempting to distract herself from her soul memory. Rhapsody was staring at her with a smile filled with promise, sending heat flooding throughout her body as she thought of all the things they would do later. It was exactly the distraction she needed.

"Holy shit!" Lexi gasped, her voice strangled as she continued comforting Melody. "Can you tone the passion down a little? You're going to send me over the edge at this rate."

Harmony frowned, confused. She stared at Lexi, then shifted her gaze to Rhapsody, who was wincing.

"Um, yeah," Rhapsody began sheepishly. "Do you remember how I mentioned that we had a soul bond? Well... there are *four* of us in the soul bond. Things can get kind of awkward, depending on the setting."

"She's in for some awkward times then," Taxti declared with a wicked smile.

19 – RECALL

Harmony watched with amusement as Michael was teleported into the chasm. He stared around in confusion until he spotted Rhapsody's grinning face.

"Uh, hello, Rhapsody," Michael greeted the mischievous fairy uncertainly. "I don't suppose you could ring a bell before teleporting me around?"

"Hello, Michael," Rhapsody's smile grew wider as she stared at him with barely restrained laughter. "I wanted to introduce you to a distant cousin of yours that we found. This is Lexi."

Michael turned to observe the seemingly young woman standing next to Taxti. "I didn't realize I had a cousin named Lexi. Hi, Lexi—sorry for not knowing who you are. We haven't really stayed connected with extended family."

"No problem, Michael," Lexi assured him, waving off the apology. "I'm not really your cousin—that's just the cover story."

"Lexi!" Rhapsody and Taxti exclaimed in chagrin.

"I wanted to see how long it would take him to start questioning it," Rhapsody complained with a defeated sigh.

"Yeah, Lexi," Taxti agreed with a disapproving frown. "Way to ruin the fun."

Lexi laughed at them, her eyes full of affection. "You're just the same as always, Clarice—I mean, Rhapsody."

Michael narrowed his eyes, staring at Lexi speculatively. "You're not from this world, are you?"

"Nope," Lexi confirmed with a shake of her head. "I'm here to keep Serenity out of trouble. She's always been too clever by far, so I'm here to derail her any time she starts digging too deeply into things she needs to leave alone until she's older."

"She's your distant cousin, as far as Serenity and Aurora are concerned," Taxti informed him, glancing at Rhapsody before continuing. "We brought her here because the CIA has been sending hit squads out to hunt people close to us, and we want to make sure she stays safe. Her parents were worthless pieces of shit, so we brought her here to get away from them as well."

Harmony stared at Taxti, surprised by the venom in her tone. The others were staring at her with similar astonishment.

"Oh, we're going with *that* mortality backstory, huh?" Lexi asked with a wry shake of her head.

"It's easier to go with something we know than to fabricate something and start mixing it up," Taxti replied with a shrug. "Let's go say hi."

Lexi grinned eagerly, and a moment later, they all teleported to the hallway outside the room Serenity was staying in with Melody and Aurora.

Melody stepped up and opened the door, inviting the others inside. Serenity and Aurora were once again talking to a mermaid who had appeared in the pool inside the room, having quickly befriended several of the social creatures. Harmony was thrilled to see them making friends outside of school as well, as she had worried her nieces would be surrounded by boring grownups and miss out on their childhoods. The mermaids were frivolous enough to resemble teenagers more than immortal adults.

"Hey, Serenity and Aurora," Melody called out brightly. "There's someone we wanted to introduce you to."

The two girls looked up from their conversation with the mermaid and stared at them curiously. As soon as Serenity's eyes fell on Lexi, her breath caught, and her eyes widened. Aurora simply watched her curiously.

"This is... Alexis," Harmony quickly took over before her sister gave her real name, not wanting to trigger any more soul memory recall; names seemed to be a trigger.

"Hi, Serenity and Aurora," Lexi smiled brilliantly, her eyes full of warmth. "It's nice to meet you. Who's your friend?"

Aurora grinned as she turned to face the mermaid. "This is Vivian," Aurora introduced her. "She's over three thousand years old, but she's not boring like the other adults at all. You should hear about some of the cool things she's seen throughout the world."

Harmony suddenly remembered there was a conduit that connected the mermaid den to the Mariana Trench in the Pacific Ocean. She wondered how often the mermaids left the circle and ventured out into the wider world.

"Hello, Vivian," Lexi nodded at the mermaid, her brilliant smile never wavering. "It's nice to meet you."

Vivian was staring between Lexi and Serenity with a shrewd look. Harmony realized there was more to the mermaids than met the eye and that they were perhaps simply matching their audience when they spoke with Aurora and Serenity. It was probably a novelty for them to speak to actual children, since the immortal creatures in the circle didn't have any offspring.

"Hello, Alexis," Vivian nodded back with a faint smile on her freckled face. "I'm sure we'll be seeing each other a lot. I was just telling Aurora and Serenity that they should get Taxti to teach them some underwater propulsion spells so they can come play in the lake."

"That's a great idea," Taxti agreed immediately, turning to Serenity and Aurora. "Let's do that right now. You too, Alexis. Let's go to the lake."

Serenity had been reluctantly following Taxti, her eyes never leaving Lexi. When Taxti included Lexi, Serenity's eyes lit up with excitement.

"Is she going to learn magic too?" Serenity asked hopefully.

"She's already learned a little," Taxti replied, watching the two of them with amusement. "She should be able to pick this up quickly."

Harmony chuckled after they vanished, leaving her, Vivian, Mystery, Joline, and Melody behind. It looked like Taxti had found a way to distract Serenity for a while.

"Hello, Harmony," Vivian smiled up from the pool. "We've all heard so much about you, but we haven't had a chance to visit. Would you mind joining us underwater sometime?"

"Of course," Harmony agreed quickly, feeling her introverted nature rebel at the prospect of meeting more new people.

"Will you three come too?" Vivian asked the others hopefully,.

"Sure," Mystery agreed easily, smiling warmly at the mermaid. "I would love to learn more about all of you."

"Absolutely," Joline exclaimed excitedly, her face full of anticipation. "I can't *wait* to learn more about you."

"I'm game," Melody agreed with a distracted smile and a nod.

Harmony watched her mother fondly, wishing she had inherited more of her mother's adventurous spirit. Melody loved new experiences and meeting new people, while Harmony found it awkward and difficult to mingle with strangers and make enough small talk to move beyond that stage. She was perfectly happy maintaining her existing social relationships without the labor it took to make new friends and acquaintances.

Working at the women's shelter was one of the most difficult things she had ever done, far outside of her comfort zone, which was precisely why she did it. She knew her imagination would stagnate if she stayed within those comfortable boundaries, and there was nothing worse for an author than a stagnant imagination. She had even enjoyed a lot of her time at the women's shelter—especially playing with the children. There was something beautiful and powerful about children's laughter that filled her soul with joy.

"You're adorable," Rhapsody whispered into her ear, making her jump. The fairy had snuck up behind her while she was lost in thought.

Before she could turn around, slender arms snaked around her waist and pulled her back against Rhapsody. Harmony blinked when she realized her favorite shapeshifter was once again the same height as Mystery, with her head resting on Harmony's shoulder.

"You never cease to amaze me, Harmony," Rhapsody whispered warmly. "Your spirit is so blindingly beautiful. I can't tell you how happy I am to finally have you back. I missed you more than words can describe."

As Harmony turned her head to look back at her, she once again felt the strange sensation of seeing another person's face superimposed on Rhapsody's. This time, however, it wasn't superimposed—it had entirely replaced Rhapsody's features. It was a beauty that was almost painful to behold, as if gazing at something so sacred would burn her eyes out if she stared too long.

"Clarice," Harmony whispered adoringly, feeling a supernova of love ignite in her soul as memories returned in a torrent. "I've missed you so much, Clarice."

Rhapsody stiffened briefly before pulling her back tightly, a reciprocating love of equal intensity flaring through the bond. "I don't know if I can do this anymore without you, Aria," Rhapsody whispered, her voice so full of longing and desolation that tears sprang to Harmony's eyes. "I know you're here with me, but it's so hard to pretend you're someone else. I knew this would be hard, but the separation is even worse than I expected."

"We're almost done," Harmony assured her gently. "We're changing so much faster than we projected. Just a few more weeks at this rate, Clarice."

"How much do you remember?" Rhapsody asked, her voice a mixture of hope and worry.

"I remember everything, Clarice," Harmony replied, leaning her head back and twisting her neck to kiss Clarice softly—a kiss of longing and promise. "But I'm shielding it for now. We're still following the rules, as far as this universe is concerned."

As she finished speaking, relief and exultation flooded through the bond so powerfully that her knees buckled. Clarice held her up, resting her head against Aria's as tears of happiness ran down her cheeks.

"What's with you being the redhead this time?" Aria asked, a teasing note in her voice. "You just had to steal my look, didn't you?"

Clarice shook with a mixture of laughter and tears as she held Aria tightly.

"You two okay?" Mystery asked quietly, stepping closer to them.

"We're wonderful, Mystery," Aria assured her with a dazzling smile. "More than okay."

Mystery gasped, staring into Aria's eyes. "Is that still you, Harmony?"

"In a manner of speaking, yes," Aria replied with a warm smile as the supernova of love in her soul flared out to include Mystery.

Mystery staggered as she felt the force of Aria's love engulf her. Her lips parted as she stared back at Aria in amazement, her current mind unable to comprehend a love of such intensity. She stepped forward and wrapped her arms around them both, a wondering look in her eyes.

"Have you been digging into your soul memory, Harmony?" Mystery asked uncertainly.

"No," Aria replied with an amused smile. "It just cracked open like an egg. I'm shielding it from this universe so that we keep the letter of the law."

"Should I also—" Mystery began but cut off when Aria kissed her gently.

"No, Mystery," Aria told her softly. "I didn't do it on purpose, so I can still claim to have followed their rules. If you end up in the same situation, so be it, but let's not force it."

"We need to be charging admission," Clarice told them, leering at Michael.

Michael cringed at the look on Rhapsody's face, so incongruous and unexpected from the innocent-looking fairy.

Aria glanced over and saw Joline, Michael, and Vivian watching them curiously. She saw them both with the shared memories she had as Harmony, and with the bottomless ocean of memories that mortality had locked away—she saw them as Aria. What had once seemed like an endlessly complex universe of incomprehensible forces and entities now looked like a footnote in the book of her life, a mere twenty-three years that was barely a blip on her soul's timeline.

Melody walked up and stared intently into Aria's eyes.

"Are you back?" Melody whispered, her eyes full of hope.

"Yep," Aria grinned, stepping away from Mystery and Clarice to pull Melody into a warm embrace. "What's the matter, Arturiel? I can tell something is bothering you."

Melody stiffened in her arms, then sighed and relaxed again. "Can we go somewhere private to talk?"

Aria raised an eyebrow. "Clarice?"

"We'll be back in a little bit," Clarice told the others with a cheerful wave.

The room vanished, and she and Clarice reappeared with Arturiel in a room with no windows or doors. Aria recognized the walls of Yggdrasil around them. Clarice must have teleported them somewhere else inside the world tree.

"Is it about Harnketi?" Clarice asked shrewdly.

"Yeah," Arturiel nodded with another sigh. "What am I supposed to do now that I have my memories back? I'm in love with Lunamay, and she couldn't come into this place with us. But I can see how much this relationship matters to Harnketi, and if I just break it off, it's going to devastate her."

"Do you still have feelings for her?" Clarice asked gently.

Melody blushed, a guilty expression on her face. "Yeah, I do."

"You're talking to two women who are in a three-way relationship," Clarice pointed out with an expectant smile. "Doesn't that suggest a way forward?"

Melody blinked, her brows creasing as she stared at Clarice in consternation. "How could that even work?" Arturiel asked, confused. "Harnketi is stuck in *this* universe, and Lunamay can't come this far down. I can't even *talk* to Lunamay to discuss it, and time is flowing so much slower in the origin realm that a century will have passed by the time I could even return with an answer."

"If your soul memory had remained unavailable, would you be with Harnketi?" Aria asked patiently.

"Of course," Arturiel replied, rolling her large eyes. "That's the reason we're having this conversation—because I *do* have my soul memory now."

"You're here as Melody, and Melody is still a part of you," Aria told her firmly. "Breaking off your relationship with Harnketi now would be cheating both Melody *and* Harnketi. Once everything is fixed and this world is stable, we can discuss bringing Harnketi with us to the origin realm and introducing her to Lunamay. Since you've already started a relationship with her, when we meet with Lunamay again, we'll introduce Harnketi as a companion we met here and want to keep. After she's met Harnketi, ask her privately if she's open to having an additional partner. Lunamay is going to be far more likely to accept Harnketi if she meets her first, before she knows about your relationship. I'm usually a good judge of character, and I'm fairly certain Lunamay won't have a problem with this kind of arrangement. She already knows that Clarice, Calypso, and I are together, so the idea of a polyamorous relationship is already on her mind."

"You really think she would be okay with it?" Arturiel asked nervously, wringing her hands. "I don't want to hurt either of them."

"Yes," Clarice and Aria said simultaneously.

"I'll talk with Harnketi about it," Clarice told Arturiel firmly. "I've known her for a long time, and she knows we're from another realm. I'll make sure she's *also* okay with this kind of arrangement."

Arturiel pulled Clarice into a desperate embrace as she let out a long breath.

"Thank you, Clarice," Arturiel breathed gratefully. "I'm so out of my depth."

Clarice patted Arturiel's back reassuringly. "No problem, Arturiel. I have a feeling that you're going to be a lot happier with this arrangement when all is said and done. I love Aria to pieces, but I wouldn't feel complete without Calypso. Not to mention, things are a lot spicier in the bedroom with a third person."

Arturiel giggled, a mixture of nerves and embarrassment in her voice. "Still the same Clarice."

"Let's go back to the others now before they think we're trying to lure you into our fairy harem," Clarice suggested dryly.

Clarice teleported them back to the room, Arturiel still hugging her and laughing.

Michael stared at them peculiarly from one of the chairs. Mystery was sitting across from him with Joline. There was no sign of Vivian. Aria was pretty sure she had gone back to the lake to find Serenity and Aurora.

Clarice leered at Michael when she saw him watching her and Arturiel strangely.

"We're just growing our harem, Michael," Clarice told him in a seductive voice. "We charge admission fees for watching."

Joline stared at Clarice askance, unable to reconcile the Rhapsody she knew with the seductive temptress before her. Michael frowned, studying Clarice.

"Do that leer again," he said speculatively. "It's waking something up."

"That's disgusting," Clarice declared with a horrified expression.

Michael's face turned bright red when he realized what he'd said. "That's not what I meant, and you know it!"

"You asked me to leer at you because it's waking something up," Clarice pointed out archly. "How, exactly, am I *supposed* to take that comment?"

Aria held her sides, overcome by a fit of giggles. It was *so* good to see Clarice back in her element. Mystery wasn't much better, leaning on the arm of the couch as she laughed loudly. Joline shook her head, staring disapprovingly at Michael, while Arturiel held a hand to her mouth to try to contain her own mirth.

"Dammit, Clarice, you never change, do you?" Michael demanded in exasperation.

The laughter abruptly ceased. Melody gasped and glanced at Clarice and Aria worriedly.

"What?" Mystery asked, concerned when she felt their shock through the bond.

"What did you mean by that statement, Michael?" Aria asked carefully.

Michael blinked and shook his head in confusion. "Damned if I know. It just popped out."

"That's what *she* said," Clarice smirked at Michael.

"Clarice!" Aria growled warningly. "Do you *mind?*"

"Okay, what have you done with Rhapsody?" Joline demanded suspiciously.

"Sorry, I'll get back into character," Clarice sighed in resignation. "I was just excited to have—I mean I was just excited."

"I suggest we *all* get back into character," Aria suggested firmly. "We don't want to make mistakes around Aurora and Serenity. No more soul names, okay? We just have a couple of weeks left, *Rhapsody*. We can make this work."

"Knock knock," Jessica's voice called from outside the door.

"Come in," Harmony called out, ignoring the odd stares she was getting from the others.

Jessica and Shelley entered the room, looking around curiously as they sensed the undercurrent of tension.

Harmony smiled, recognizing Jessica now that her memories were back. This could still be entertaining after all.

Rhapsody glanced over at her, a mischievous grin on her face. Harmony felt strange trying to think of herself as Harmony again, now that she had all her memories back. She felt a moment of respect for Rhapsody for how well she had stayed in character over the last few weeks.

Jessica wasn't wearing her usual agent attire of a business suit and uninspired shoes. Instead, she wore a knee-length red dress that molded to her form, accentuating her curves and leaving her arms bare. The dress wrapped high around her neck, emphasizing its graceful length. Her shoulder-length, dark-brown hair was arranged in a half-up style, lending her an elegant and polished look. The change from her normal appearance was striking, elevating her from a four to a nine on Harmony's internal bangability meter.

Shelley was much more casual in denim jeans and a t-shirt. Her black hair hung loosely around her face, falling to her shoulders. Harmony rated her at a seven, a step up from when she wore her stuffy business suit.

"Hey, Jessica and Shelley," Harmony said, waving them over with a welcoming smile. "How's it going? I don't suppose you want to join our fairy harem?"

Rhapsody dissolved into giggles at Harmony's words, staring at her affectionately. Harmony could sense the blazing love and joy in their bond—joy that her oldest friend was finally back.

Jessica stared at Harmony oddly for a moment before answering. Harmony realized her mannerisms had changed so much that even the two agents had noticed.

"We just wanted to see what everyone was up to," Jessica answered with a shrug, walking over and sitting next to Michael. She crossed her legs as she sank back into the couch.

Harmony watched Michael closely as Jessica settled in, noting the microexpressions flickering across his face as he glanced at her and nodded politely, obviously trying not to stare. Harmony could practically feel the heat radiating from Michael as his sudden attraction intensified.

Harmony avoided Rhapsody's eyes, knowing she would start laughing uncontrollably if she saw one of those suggestive leers.

"*How dare you avoid looking at me?*" Rhapsody's voice protested plaintively in her head.

Harmony quickly covered her mouth and turned away from the others as a fit of uncontrollable giggles assailed her. She was just getting her laughter under control when Rhapsody spoke.

"Don't mind her," Rhapsody told the others cheerfully. "She suffered a catastrophic logic failure several years ago and has been coasting on pure, unadulterated absurdity ever since. We find it's best not to make eye contact."

Harmony wiped tears from her eyes as she tried to subdue her laughter. She could feel waves of amusement washing through the bond from Mystery. There was some amusement from Rhapsody as well, but it was mostly pure, untamed love.

"She has these laughing fits occasionally," Joline told the others dryly. "You just have to ride them out. I think it's worse now that Rhapsody is here to cheer it on."

"Yep," Rhapsody admitted with a smirk. "I'm her number one fan."

Shelley was slowly making her way past Harmony toward one of the chairs, watching her carefully. The agent's expression sent her into another fit of giggles.

"Wow, I feel like I'm at a laugh therapy conference," Michael commented dryly, an amused smile on his face.

"*What the hell are you two doing?*" Taxti's thought was exasperated. "*Lexi is having a fit of the giggles that has now spread to the others.*"

Harmony had thought she was getting a handle on it, but at Taxti's words, she collapsed to the floor with renewed laughter.

"Are you sure she's okay?" Shelley asked quietly, a note of concern in her voice.

"She's fine," Rhapsody assured her with a rueful shake of her head. "If she were in a mortal body, she would have burned out by now from sore muscles, but with this immortal body, it can go on for a while."

"Okay...okay," Harmony gasped, trying to think of something to shut down the floodgates of mirth. "I'm almost there."

"I'll bet you are," Rhapsody declared suggestively.

It took a few more minutes for Harmony to slow down again. She finally resorted to visualizing the things she planned to do to Rhapsody and Mystery the next time she got them alone. It was an effective solution, dialing her laughter back and replacing it with pure lust. The bond was suddenly flooded with desire as Rhapsody responded to Harmony's thoughts. Both of them feeling intense arousal was enough to create a feedback loop in their bond, producing a gasp from Mystery as she felt the powerful intentions flooding her system.

"*What the hell are you two doing now?*" Taxti's thought shouted into her mind. "*Lexi has turned into a puddle of desire. Can't you three wait until Lexi has some privacy?*"

Harmony cleared her throat as she tried to reign in her desire. "So, what have you and Jessica been up to? Any more fun meetings with the bigshots?"

They all watched her expectantly as she finally walked over to join them, obviously waiting for her to have another meltdown.

"I'm good," Harmony assured them, flashing Mystery a grin. "For realsies this time."

Her mother was watching her curiously as Harmony sat down on the arm of the couch. Harmony could almost feel her desire to question Harmony about the personality change. She glanced at Rhapsody questioningly. Her mother was certainly past the age threshold required for access to soul memory. Rhapsody nodded with a warm smile, and Harmony turned back to her mother.

"We'll talk about it a little later, okay?" Harmony told her affectionately.

"Talk about what?" Michael asked in confusion.

"It," Harmony repeated with an amused twinkle in her eyes.

Michael rolled his eyes and looked over at Jessica. "You two have any plans today?"

"Declan said they're having more entertainment tonight," Jessica answered with an excited smile. "I had so much fun last time. I'm excited to go again, now that I feel more comfortable here."

"Where is Declan, anyway?" Harmony asked curiously. "I haven't seen him in a while."

"He's organizing tonight's festivities," Rhapsody answered with a fond smile. "I think he has something special in store for us tonight."

"What?" Michael asked, his eyes intrigued.

"You'll find out," Rhapsody replied with a mysterious smile.

Mystery gazed at Harmony longingly, clearly wishing the seating arrangements were different. After a moment, she seemed to have an epiphany. She ran her fingers through her hair, eliciting a shiver of pleasure from Harmony. Mystery smiled with satisfaction at Harmony's reaction and began doodling on her knee.

Michael stared at his sister shrewdly but didn't say anything.

"I feel like there's half a conversation going on without words in this room," Shelley observed wryly. "Which is totally possible with a telepath in our midst."

"There's more than telepathy going on in here," Michael replied in amusement, glancing at Harmony with a smirk.

"*Michael!*" Mystery hissed with a frown. "She's sensitive about that."

"Oh yeah," Michael hung his head and glanced sideways at Harmony. "Sorry."

"It's fine," Harmony assured both of them. "I'm over feeling embarrassed about that."

Jessica and Shelley's eyes were on fire with curiosity as they stared between Michael and Harmony. They clearly wanted to ask, but after Mystery's comment, they remained silent.

"Melody?" Harmony asked softly. "Are you okay with other people knowing?"

"Now that I can shut it off, yes," Melody replied with a shrug.

"Shut what off?" Jessica asked, unable to hold the question back any longer.

"Melody and I have a severe case of mirror-touch synesthesia," Harmony answered, feeling no fear of others finding out now that she had her memories back. Having her memories made shutting it down a simple matter. She suddenly frowned and looked over at Rhapsody.

"You could have turned this off easily, Clar—I mean, Rhapsody," Harmony accused the suddenly innocent-faced fairy. "Why didn't you tell me you could turn it off?"

"Because it was so freaking adorable," Rhapsody declared with a sensual wink. "Just think of all the things you would have missed out on if I had shut it off."

Harmony and Mystery blushed furiously at Rhapsody's words as the memory of some of the things Rhapsody and Mystery had done to trigger her synesthesia floated up from her memory.

"I mean, you could have turned it off when I didn't want it on," Harmony amended with a glare.

"I stand by what I said," Rhapsody smirked at her. "The whole thing is adorable and a ridiculous turn-on."

Harmony's face flushed red again, and she buried her face in her arms to hide her blushing face. "How can you still make me blush so much after all this time?"

"Practice," Rhapsody responded with a sultry chuckle.

"What's mirror-touch synesthesia?" Jessica asked in confusion.

"It can't be explained," Rhapsody said mysteriously. "It can only be experienced. Come here for a second."

"*Rhapsody,*" Harmony said warningly.

"What?" Rhapsody asked innocently as Jessica stood up and walked over to where Rhapsody was standing between two of the chairs.

"What are you going to do?" Harmony demanded as the hairs on the back of her neck stood up.

"Watch Harmony closely," Rhapsody told Jessica with an evil smile.

"*Rhapsody!*" Harmony barked threateningly.

Rhapsody suddenly slapped Jessica on the ass, producing a startled squawk out of the dolled-up agent at the same time that Harmony yelped and jumped up from the couch.

She tried to look angry, but it was impossible to be cross with the helplessly giggling fairy. She had to bite her lip as she watched a furiously blushing Jessica staring at Rhapsody in shock.

"Why did you slap my ass?" Jessica demanded.

"Weren't you paying attention to Harmony?" Rhapsody gasped through her laughter, wiping a tear.

"No, because *someone* slapped my ass," Jessica growled.

"Did Harmony *feel* that?" Shelley asked in amazement.

"Hence the name, mirror-touch," Michael commented, clearly struggling not to grin as he watched the disgruntled agent with a mixture of amusement and appreciation.

"So, she feels everything that happens to everyone else?" Shelley asked in disbelief.

"*Everything*," Rhapsody nodded with a slow smile. "Both good *and* bad."

"How's that even possible?" Shelley asked. "Is it some kind of magic phenomenon?"

"It's a psychic phenomenon," Rhapsody explained, winking at Jessica as she flounced back onto the couch. "More than that, if you visualize her watching you, she doesn't even have to see it to feel it."

"That sounds like it could be... abused pretty badly," Shelley said, frowning at Melody and Harmony.

"It certainly can be," Melody agreed with a grimace. "My ex-husband did some pretty terrible things. He threatened to do worse if I ever tried to leave."

"He did *what*?" Joline demanded angrily. "Melody, why didn't you tell me?"

"Because nothing short of him dying would have freed me from his abuse," Melody answered with a sigh. "What could you have done?"

"I could have killed him," Joline growled. "I *would* have killed him if I'd known he was holding that over you. Is that why you never left him?"

"Yeah," Melody nodded, her lips twisting in disgust. "I thought about killing him more times than you can imagine. But I had my little angels to care for. I'm pretty sure I wouldn't have survived if Harmony hadn't been there with me through most of it. I suppose I *didn't* survive, in the end."

"What happened that night?" Harmony asked tentatively. "If you're comfortable talking about it."

Melody nodded, her face wistful. "Those memories no longer affect me, thanks to Rhapsody," she said, offering Rhapsody a grateful smile.

"David was ranting about you stealing Grandma Dotti's inheritance. He was planning to go confront you about it, and he planned to use his fists to convince you to give up the inheritance. I told him I would slit his throat in the night if he ever went near you. That triggered his psycho phase, and he went and got a knife and started slashing it at me. I knew he had crossed the point of no return, so I texted you to come and get the kids. I wasn't thinking clearly and almost got you killed. I was just so worried for Serenity and Aurora that I panicked."

"You did the right thing," Harmony told her firmly. "If you *hadn't* texted me, he wouldn't have stopped at killing you."

"Yeah, I just wish I'd handled things better," Melody sighed sadly. "I must have put my girls through so much hell when I died."

"*David* put us through so much hell," Harmony corrected her firmly. "*Not* you."

"Thanks to Rhapsody, that's all behind us now," Melody said warmly.

Harmony's mother sniffed quietly as she wiped the tears from her eyes. "I should have killed that bastard."

"Then you'd be in prison instead of here with us now," Melody told her gently. "Let's just appreciate the fact that we're all together now. And... we have another fun festival tonight. I fully intend to take Leesha's spot in the dance-off this time."

Harmony laughed, remembering how the last one went. She was curious to see how much better her sister would do in her new body. She remembered how that night had ended, too, and fully planned on a similar finale to tonight's festivities.

Mystery looked up at her when she felt the desire flood the bond.

"Remember how I used to wish I could reverse the flow of synesthesia?" Harmony asked Mystery with a slow smile.

Mystery's breathing quickened at her words. "We have a few hours before the festival, don't we?"

"So damn insatiable," Rhapsody murmured fondly.

20 – DANCE OFF

Jessica tried to mentally shake herself as she stood near the clearing. Dozens of leprechauns, fauns, mermaids, and dragons in human form danced to the beat of a fast-paced swing. There were several people she had never seen before mingled among them, individuals who didn't appear to belong to any of the species she had previously encountered. According to her interface, they were spirit walkers. One named Azeban, an oddity among oddities, had a medium build, short dark hair, and dark eyes. He wore a trapper hat made from what looked like a raccoon. She wondered if it was from a real raccoon or simply a manifestation. She had seen Rhapsody and Taxti manifest various articles of clothing before, so it was possible they were surrounded by a bunch of naked people who merely projected their clothing.

As the thought crossed her mind, Azeban glanced at her, his lips twitching. Jessica scowled, annoyed by the lack of privacy in her own head with so many mind-readers around. She knew Rhapsody could read minds, but she hadn't known if the others were also telepathic. Apparently, some were.

Her eyes drifted back to Michael as he danced with a tall elf. Frustration flickered through her as she realized she was staring again. Michael wasn't even her type, so why was she suddenly so obsessed with him? True, he was the only male human around, but there were plenty of attractive elves and dragons to capture her attention. Perhaps his constant glances in her direction were triggering some kind of automatic response.

"You going to dance, or what?" Shelley asked, raising an eyebrow and offering a knowing smile.

"I'll get around to it," Jessica muttered in annoyance. She had been hoping that Michael would ask *her* to dance. So far, he had stuck to elves and fauns.

"Come on," Shelley drawled. "Let's go make him jealous."

Jessica reluctantly allowed Shelley to pull her onto the dance floor. Her partner was a surprisingly good dancer, considering how long it had been since Jessica had time for such things. Shelley grinned as she took Jessica's hands and began swinging her around to the fast tempo.

In spite of herself, Jessica began to enjoy herself as the two of them commanded the dance floor. She had spent years taking ballroom dancing lessons and wasn't too modest to admit that she was an amazing dancer. The fact that Shelley was also skilled made the experience even more enjoyable. It didn't take long for her to forget about Michael as her focus narrowed to Shelley and their immediate surroundings.

"You're pretty good," Jessica complimented Shelley as she spun under her arm.

"I was obsessed with dancing in college," Shelley explained with a sheepish smile. "I started eating so much unhealthy food that I needed something to balance out the calorie intake."

Jessica laughed ruefully and nodded. "Yeah, not having parents around to harp on you about healthy dietary choices definitely leads to a lot of unhealthy eating habits. It took me a few years to stop over-indulging just because I could and start adding healthy foods back into my diet."

"When I started outgrowing my clothes, I realized it was time to show some restraint," Shelley said with a wry smile. "It's amazing how much more money I saved when I started eating healthy foods and didn't have to spend a fortune upgrading my wardrobe."

Jessica threw back her head and laughed. "That's exactly what happened to me," she said with another short laugh. "I remember the feeling of dread when I tried to button my favorite pair of pants one morning and couldn't."

They slowed to a stop as the music ended, and Jessica finally looked around the clearing. Serenity had a constant blush as she stood with her hands on Alexis's hips. It had been a surprise to learn that Michael had a distant cousin join their group. Jessica's bullshit meter was beeping loudly after hearing the story of how Alexis had been invited. They claimed they were worried about CIA hitmen coming after her, but they hadn't bothered including any other relatives. Then there was the fact that Rhapsody had already dealt with the people sending out orders to the hit squads.

There was something oddly familiar about Alexis, too. She couldn't put her finger on it, but something about her name and personality seemed extremely familiar.

Jessica blinked when she saw Mystery and Michael staring at her. Mystery was haranguing her brother about something while he wore a dogged expression. When he saw her looking, his cheeks flushed, and he quickly looked away.

"I think you're going to have to do the asking on that one," Shelley commented with a wide grin. "I recognize that look. He's too shy to ask you to dance."

"He's asked a ton of people to dance," Jessica objected with a frown. "He doesn't *seem* that shy."

"Trust me, he's shy with the right people," Shelley assured her with a knowing smile. "He's feeling a much deeper level of attraction to you, and it's turning him into an awkward chicken."

Jessica laughed at Shelley's observation, wondering if it could be true. Maybe she *should* go ask him to dance.

"Okay, wish me luck," Jessica said with a grin. "I'm going in."

"Good luck," Shelley called out as she walked away. "If he rejects you, I'll still be here."

Jessica chuckled as she made her way toward Michael. Shelley was an attractive woman, especially as she rolled the years back on her age. She would never have entertained such a thought before this assignment; she'd always had a strict code against romantic entanglements with coworkers. Her code felt more like guidelines now. Her perspective had undergone a major overhaul after finding out about souls, afterlives, magic, immortality, and other universes.

Mystery grinned when she spotted Jessica approaching. Michael's cheeks flushed when he saw the determination in her eyes.

"Wanna dance?" Jessica asked Michael warmly, an enticing smile on her lips.

"Um, sure?" Michael answered hesitantly.

She stepped close, placing his hand on her hip and taking his other hand in hers. Enraptured, he stared down at her as they began moving around the clearing to the next song.

"So?" Jessica prompted with a coquettish smile. "How are you enjoying the prospect of living forever?"

Michael blinked, snapping out of his daze. He stared into her eyes with a thoughtful expression. "I don't think it's actually sunk in that I'm immortal."

"It's a strange concept to accept, isn't it?" Jessica asked with a small smile. "We've spent our entire lives knowing that our time is short. Being told we're suddenly going to live forever takes a while to process. Suddenly, all the things you want to accomplish in life become less urgent, since you know you'll have plenty of time to do them."

"That's true," Michael agreed, pursing his lips as he thought about it. "You know, that's a really interesting point. Not only do we have all the time we need to do whatever we want, but the scope of things we can do has increased dramatically as well. We can use freaking magic!"

"Right?" Jessica asked with a delighted laugh. "I still can't believe we can use magic, even though I use it all the time. I was absolutely obsessed with magic when I was a kid. This whole thing has been like a dream come true."

Michael stared down at her, completely captivated. As she stared back into his dark eyes, heat flooded her cheeks. There was something so familiar about him, as if she'd known him her entire life—maybe longer.

"Do you think we knew each other before our spirits incarnated here?" Jessica asked him curiously. "There's something so familiar about you, and I just can't put my finger on it."

His eyes widened as he stared at her. "You too? It's been driving me *crazy*! I feel like I've known you forever, and I just can't remember any of the details."

Jessica smiled, glancing wryly toward Harmony and Rhapsody, who were watching them with amused expressions. "I'm pretty sure *those* two know something, if the way they're watching us is any indication."

Michael glanced at Rhapsody and her companion, catching a leer from Rhapsody. As they danced out of sight, he shook his head. "Even that horrifying leer seems familiar."

Jessica laughed. "Yeah, she doesn't have the right face to leer. It just makes it look even dirtier."

"Exactly!" Michael exclaimed in exasperation. "It makes you want to crawl under a rock and hide."

"I think it's safe to say we're from whatever other universe they were talking about," Jessica mused. "The Vice President asked Rhapsody if she was from this universe, and she said she was from one far, far away. The way she said it implied a distance beyond comprehension. She said she came here to help save the world. I wonder if that's why we're here too. If so, she must have manipulated the events that led to me being here. Otherwise, what are the odds I would have met the rest of you?"

"Yeah, I definitely feel like fate had a hand in arranging our lives," Michael agreed, smiling faintly. His face turned introspective. "I wonder what our roles are, if we aren't supposed to be world trees like the others. After all, what else is even left for us to do?"

"Maybe they just wanted friends to be here with them," Jessica suggested thoughtfully. "Running off to incarnate in a distant universe must be a lonely adventure without friends to keep you company."

"Where do you think Alexis really came from?" Michael asked, nodding toward Serenity and Alexis, who were grinning. "Do you think she's even human?"

Jessica stared at Serenity and Alexis contemplatively as they danced nearby. "I'll bet she's one of those angels."

Alexis glanced at them, stuck her tongue out, and pulled Serenity deeper into the dancers.

"And she has super-hearing, apparently," Michael observed dryly. "Either that, or she's another telepath."

"Or both," Jessica added just as dryly. "It's like being at an X-Men school or something."

"Did you ever get confused by that name?" Michael asked, a twinkle in his dark eyes. "You have ex-wives, ex-girlfriends, ex-coworkers, yada yada. So, is an X-Man someone who is no longer a man?"

Jessica snorted, playfully bumping her head against his chest. "I see how your mind works. Well, I suppose Rhapsody just turned a bunch of thugs into ex-men, then."

"Ew, gross," Michael grimaced. "I wish she could do that to *all* the bastards out there harming children."

"I think this leveling system she implemented might actually clean up the world, eventually. Rewarding people for avoiding evil acts should make this a nice world to live in by 2035. I still haven't tried the messaging feature, though. It seems unnecessary when we can teleport anywhere and avoid the trouble of sending a message."

"I haven't slept since the interface went live, so I don't have access to it yet," Michael said, looking curious. "I've been living on yuccas fitter. Maybe I should try taking a nap so it will appear. I want to play around with it and start leveling up. Have you gained any levels?"

Jessica giggled, thinking of the experience she and Shelley had gained. "Yeah, I leveled up a skill called Cool-Headed. The description says the skill is gained by keeping a cool head while dealing with evil bastards."

Michael guffawed, his grin and the warm look in his eyes sending a pleasant shiver through her. "I'll bet you leveled that up dealing with people like the vice president."

"That bitch tried to end our assignment and replace us," Jessica growled darkly. The memory still filled her with anger. She smiled, remembering the vice president's sick expression when Rhapsody denied her request. "Rhapsody showed up and said it was us or nobody, then told her she was a selfish narcissist who would be stuck in a reincarnation loop if she didn't learn compassion. She phrased it differently, but the message was clear. The vice president looked like she'd bitten into a lemon. I wish the interface let us take pictures or capture the last five minutes of video."

"You know, the system's architect is right over there," Michael pointed out with an indulgent grin. "I bet she'd add a feature like that if we asked nicely. It's a good idea—everyone having a dash cam in their eyes. It could save the legal system a lot of trouble finding evidence. I had some asshole back into my car at a light a couple years ago and claim I rear-ended him. Luckily, my dash cam caught it. This would be a great tool for dealing with scammers."

"Do you think she'd really add that?" Jessica asked excitedly. "Because that would be freaking *amazing*!"

"I can almost guarantee she will," Michael said confidently. "What other cool things should we bug her to add while we're at it?"

"Did you know she added a teleport button to our interface before we learned how to teleport?" Jessica asked thoughtfully. "I wonder what other features like that could be added."

"You two staying cool-headed?" Shelley asked archly, dancing toward them with a lithe elf woman.

"One of us is," Jessica replied with an infectious laugh. "I was just telling him about our levels."

The song ended, and the four stopped dancing. Shelley's eyes were bright as she pointed to her elf friend.

"This is Selindria," Shelley introduced the elf, a light blush on her cheeks. "She's a *progressive* elf."

Selindria laughed, a rich, throaty sound. "She means I don't have my head stuck in the clouds, trying to puzzle out the deeper mysteries of the soul all the time. I'm the black sheep among the elves of this world."

Jessica stared at the beautiful elf, fascinated. Waist-length honey-blond hair framed her face, adorned with small braids wrapped around her head. Her face was what the creator had in mind when they used the word feminine. She was beautiful in a way that only Rhapsody and Taxti could match. Her vivid blue eyes were friendly as she gazed at Jessica and Michael, a welcome change from the distant look Jessica had grown used to seeing in other elves. Selindria was as tall as Harmony and moved with a grace that made it seem as though she were floating through water.

"It's nice to meet you, Selindria," Jessica nodded to the gorgeous elf. "I couldn't get a straight answer out of any of the other elves, so maybe you can help me. I was just curious about what life was like when more world trees were still alive. Did elves mingle with humans, or did you stay in your own cities or forests?"

"I'll *bet* you didn't get a straight answer," Selindria giggled, the sound so infectious that Jessica laughed as well. "Did they give you the spiel about life being a river that has no beginning and no end, and time is just a tapestry of memories that shape the banks?"

"Something very similar, yes," Jessica responded with a wide grin. "To be honest, I started tuning him out after a little while."

Selindria laughed again, her bright blue eyes sparkling with mirth and her delicate face alight with an enchanting smile.

"Life was definitely different back then," Selindria said after her laughter subsided. "Magic was used in place of electronics, so the world was far less polluted. Most humans treated elves like curiosities. Since we have no need of food, shelter, or sleep, we weren't considered good trading partners. We had no industry and no interest in trade, so our interactions were shallow. Add to that the nonsense some elves pontificated, and we seemed more like background ornamentation than a sentient species sharing their world. Our ability to teleport at will made capturing us pointless. Occasionally, someone would try to force themselves on an elf. We usually dropped them into another world, where they spent the rest of their lives alone."

"That seems pretty lenient to me," Jessica muttered darkly. "I think I'm coming around to Rhapsody's punishments for that kind of thing."

"Yeah, she definitely has no tolerance for anything like that," Selindria commented with an approving smile.

"Is it still rude to ask how old a woman is if she's immortal?" Michael asked tentatively.

"Nope," Jessica assured him with a smirk. "The reason asking a woman's age is taboo is because we get so much uglier as we get older. It's not fair that men don't go downhill nearly as quickly as women."

"So, how old *are* you?" Michael asked Selindria curiously.

"Do you mean since returning to this body?" Selindria asked, smiling oddly. "Or the age of my soul?"

"Yes," Michael answered, his eyes twinkling with amusement.

"Ah, well, in that case, I'm only a few years old," Selindria answered, her lips quirking into a half smile. "My soul is several hundred million years old."

"Wait, you're only a *few* years old?" Michael asked, frowning, a puzzled crease forming on his brow. "Do elves grow up super fast or something?"

"No, this is my immortal body that I return to after I finish an incarnation," Selindria explained patiently. "It's hundreds of millions of years old. I'm not incarnated right now. All of the immortals here in the circle are transcended from higher-tier souls. Whether they were former stars, planets, elementals, or older souls, they didn't die and have their ethereal bodies move on to a different plane—they were transformed into immortal entities. That means their ethereal body merged with a new, immortal body. It's an option available to certain entities and older souls. Depending on the age of the soul, additional options become available."

"Is an ethereal body just another name for spirit?" Jessica asked with a frown. She hadn't studied spirituality or theology, so the terminology was alien.

"Think of your ethereal body as your consciousness," Selindria suggested thoughtfully, "and your soul as the repository for all the memories acquired throughout your soul's cycle of incarnations. Consciousness is created by the merging of the soul with a body, but it remains a distinct entity after the body dies. The soul remains attached to your ethereal body indefinitely. Ethereal bodies can be destroyed, which leaves the soul searching for a new body to inhabit. People who end up with a soul that was once linked to a destroyed ethereal body will have some access to that soul's memories, though usually not directly. The memories will influence them subconsciously, often manifesting as higher intelligence or aptitudes for skills buried within that soul's memory."

"So even though you are only a few years old in this immortal body, it's the same one you've been in between incarnations?" Jessica asked curiously. "So, for all intents and purposes, you really are hundreds of millions of years old."

"Correct," Selindria nodded, smiling approvingly. "When I say a few years old, I mean I've only been back from my last incarnation for a few years. Though in my case, I redesign my body when I get bored of the same look. A lot of people think of their physical appearance as part of their immortal identity. Personally, I've never felt that association, so I change my appearance somewhat frequently. My consciousness remains the same, regardless of my appearance."

"Yeah, it would feel pretty weird not to have an appearance to identify with," Michael noted with a frown. "Having the same appearance to return to after an incarnation would be like having a familiar home to return to after a journey."

"That's how most feel," Selindria agreed with a faint smile. "I'm considered a little strange among immortals."

"So, you're not really an elf then, are you?" Jessica asked shrewdly. "Not like the elves here, anyway."

"Correct again," Selindria nodded with a wry smile. "The elves and leprechauns aren't shapeshifters. They transitioned from another form of life and are hardcoded with the templates they inhabit. They don't know that I'm not the same kind of elf, though, so keep that a secret."

"How do you know what life was like here thousands of years ago if you've only been in that body for a few years?" Jessica asked, her brow furrowed in puzzlement.

"I've incarnated here a few times over the millennia," Selindria replied with a shrug. "I like to experience mortality, so I incarnate rather frequently. The last time I was in this universe, I transitioned into an elf. It was pretty boring after a while, so I left after a few centuries."

"If you were hardcoded as an elf, how are you changing the way you look?" Michael asked in confusion. "For that matter, if the elves here are immortal, how did you exit that incarnation? Shouldn't you just live on forever in whatever template you were assigned?"

"Most people do," Selindria admitted with a small smile. "But some eventually discover a secret that changes everything. It took me about a century to unlock my soul memory and remember it. I decided to stay here for a few more centuries because I really liked the fairies, but once I got bored enough, I left in search of a new place to incarnate."

"I just can't get over how old the immortal people are here," Michael murmured in awe. "What must life look like when viewed from such a long span of time?"

"I'm just a baby compared to Rhapsody," Selindria told him with a short laugh. "Her soul is the kind of age that leaves immortals like me in awe. I have a pretty old spirit, but I think those three might just be the oldest in existence."

"How can you tell?" Michael asked curiously. "Can you see tree rings on our spirits or something?"

Jessica snorted, glancing up at Michael with a grin. He blushed when he saw her affectionate gaze but managed to smile back at her awkwardly.

"It's just common knowledge in some places," Selindria replied simply. She smiled wistfully toward where Taxti was dancing, a look of almost unbearable longing in her eyes. "Now, *she* is one *very* attractive soul. It's too bad she's taken."

"I've never seen Taxti with anyone," Shelley said curiously. "Does this mysterious partner not come around very often or something?"

"Oh, I thought you already knew," Selindria replied, pursing her lips as she looked through the dancers. "She's with her right now."

Jessica stared in surprise when she saw Taxti spinning around the dance area with Harmony. It was plain to see that they weren't just dancing for fun. Harmony had improved exponentially from the last time she had seen her dance. They were dancing so provocatively that Jessica glanced around to see if Serenity and Aurora were present. Serenity was, and she was staring in awe with Alexis as her aunt and Taxti flitted about the dance field like they owned it.

"Wait, Harmony is with Taxti?" Jessica objected in confusion. "Maybe Rhapsody wasn't joking when she asked me to join her fairy harem."

Selindria dissolved into giggles. "That sounds just like her. Taxti and Rhapsody are the same person."

"Wait, what?" Shelley gasped, sharing a disbelieving look with Jessica. "How could they be the same person? We've talked to them both at the same time."

"She's splitting her consciousness, operating both bodies at once," Selindria explained, a look of respect in her eyes. "When she first arrived, she split her consciousness into hundreds of bodies. The magical people were starving, their magic depleted, so she directly supplied them with energy from her own life force. Once the tree was rehabilitated and capable of broadcasting magic again, they woke up, and she left their bodies. But Taxti's a magic hog, so she'll be dormant until the other world trees are revived."

"So, Rhapsody is powering Taxti right now?" Jessica asked slowly. Something seemed wrong with that thought. "Why did Rhapsody lose her power in the first place?"

"Um, you don't already know who Rhapsody is?" Selindria asked warily, a hint of anxiety crossing her face. "I just assumed you all knew, since Harmony and Mystery are with Taxti now. Let's just rewind this conversation by sixty seconds and pretend it never happened, okay?"

"Clarice?" Michael asked, raising an eyebrow.

Selindria blinked, then narrowed her eyes, studying the three of them. "You obviously know her name. What else do you know?"

Jessica gasped. Flashes of memory raced through her mind, too fast to grasp. She squeezed her eyes shut, trying to concentrate, ignoring Michael's concerned query. She saw midnight hair and swirling violet eyes, always full of mirth.

"She's a Seraph," Jessica whispered, frowning. "But I can't remember anything else clearly, only her swirling eyes and that she's super playful."

She opened her eyes to find Selindria watching her appraisingly, her perfect lips pursed. "So, you remember some of it. You lot have a hard time staying separated from your soul memory. You've been through mortality so many times that your souls are never far from your conscious mind. Your souls are too strong to remain separated from your ethereal bodies for long—especially when you're in close contact with each other."

"Hello, Selindria," Rhapsody's voice spoke just before she appeared out of thin air next to Jessica. "It's been a while. How long have you been here?"

"I just arrived a few hours ago," Selindria answered with a cheerful smile. She stepped toward Rhapsody, suddenly shrinking to the fairy's height, and pulled her into a warm embrace. "It's wonderful to see you again. I heard through the grapevine that this world was the place to be if I wanted a good show."

"I'll just bet," Rhapsody replied dryly, hugging Selindria back fondly. "What else did you hear?"

"Not much," Selindria said, finally releasing Rhapsody. "Though I did hear that you know where the Origin Realm is. There are a lot of curious people trying to find you right now."

"How did *you* find me?" Rhapsody asked, raising an eyebrow.

"Mostly luck," Selindria said with a wry smile. Jessica could see something more in her eyes, a kind of intense longing. "I heard about the trouble on this world and that someone had stepped in to help. They mentioned you were incarnating and everything, so that narrowed it down a lot more. I know what a sucker for hard luck cases you are, so I was pretty sure that it would be you three."

"*You're* the sucker for hard luck cases," Rhapsody retorted with a look of amusement. "I half expected to find you already incarnated when I arrived. What have you been up to?"

Selindria's smile faltered as she stared at Rhapsody, a look of deep regret in her eyes. "My last incarnation was rough—pretty ugly, actually. It almost convinced me to stop incarnating altogether. We'll see how long my resolve on that lasts."

"I'm so sorry, Selindria," Rhapsody sighed, pulling her into another embrace. "We had a rough time here, too. Aria and Arturiel went through literal hell."

"Mortality can be unbelievably cruel," Selindria murmured sadly, her face glowing with contentment in Rhapsody's arms.

Rhapsody pulled back, holding Selindria at arm's length.

"I love the look," Rhapsody said admiringly, looking her up and down. "And an elf. It's kind of crazy how often they pop up."

"I couldn't help noticing you had one with you last time we talked, higher up the stack," Selindria noted, a look of intense curiosity on her face. "Her etheric body was different than anyone I've ever seen. I can't help but speculate that she's from somewhere special."

Rhapsody smiled mysteriously but didn't answer.

Michael sighed loudly in exasperation. "You know it's rude to talk in code in front of other people, right?"

"As a matter of fact, I *did* know that," Rhapsody admitted with a smirk. "But you'll get over it, with time and counseling."

The music started again, faster this time, with an aggressive cello. A cheer went up from one side of the clearing.

"I'm not going to miss this," Rhapsody grinned exuberantly. "Melody is having a rematch with Leesha. My money's on Melody this time."

Jessica glanced up at Jason with a questioning smile. He shrugged, glancing at Rhapsody with amusement, and then nodded. She took his hand, and they followed Rhapsody toward the rematch. Jason had a stupid grin on his face as they walked across the clearing. Jessica could feel his pulse quicken through the warmth of his hand. *Jason*. That was his name. The thought dropped into her awareness out of nowhere. She hadn't even realized she was thinking of him as Jason.

Rhapsody turned to scowl at her. Just like leering, she didn't have the face for scowling. It just looked cute. As the thought crossed her mind, Rhapsody rolled her large eyes and sighed in exasperation. A moment later, her face suddenly morphed like melted wax, transforming into that of a leathery-skinned old woman with lines covering every inch. She scowled so blackly that Jessica halted, taking an involuntary step backward without consciously telling her feet to do so.

Michael recoiled from the gruesome glare as well. Then, just as suddenly, Rhapsody's face morphed back to normal, and she howled with laughter. Selindria was giggling up a storm next to Shelley after watching the display, hanging on to Shelley to hold herself up. Shelley hadn't even noticed Rhapsody's terrifying transformation. From the moment Selindria had taken her hand, she had lost all awareness of anything except Selindria.

"That will teach you to call my scowling face cute," Rhapsody glowered threateningly as she turned and continued walking.

"Her glowering face is kind of cute too," Jessica murmured quietly to Jason—or rather, Michael.

Rhapsody threw her hands up in the air with a curse and began muttering about fairies needing an overhaul.

They joined a crowd of people watching Leesha and Melody in their dance-off. Jessica stared at Melody suspiciously as she mimicked Leesha's moves with seemingly no effort. Jessica had seen her the last time they faced off, and she had struggled a *lot* more than this. Leesha's face grew tight with concentration as she tried to wear Melody down. The minutes stretched on, and their dance moves became more intricate and nuanced.

Harmony stood to one side with Aurora and Serenity, cheering her sister on loudly. Serenity watched her mother in disbelief, her eyes wide with amazement. No matter how fast and intricate Leesha moved, Melody followed flawlessly.

"I wonder if she turned her synesthesia off," Jessica heard Rhapsody murmur in an evil voice.

"Don't you *dare*," Michael growled, his glare bouncing right off her.

Rhapsody turned to look at Selindria. "Are you ticklish, Selindria?"

"*Rhapsody*," Michael warned in a louder voice. "No *cheating*."

"Or what?" Rhapsody asked, her eyes full of challenge.

Michael frowned, appearing to search for a punishment that could affect the all-powerful fairy.

"I'll spend the rest of our time here thinking of things to punish you," Michael declared lamely.

Rhapsody slowly walked up to him, her eyes deceptively mild. His confidence drained away as she approached. By the time she was in his personal space, he was licking his lips nervously. She stood in front of him for several seconds before her face suddenly split open, and a horde of snakes erupted out of it. Michael let out a very unmanly scream and leaped backward, tripping over several leprechauns in his panic.

Jessica stared in horror as a mass of snakes writhed out of what used to be her face. A moment later, her face closed, and she returned to normal, laughing hysterically as she watched him scramble away. As he shakily stood, she held up a hand like a snake and mimed a snapping gesture.

"Someday, Clarice," Michael threatened with a helpless glare, "someday you're going to meet your match and be teased mercilessly. The universe has a lot of karma coming your way."

A loud cheer erupted from those who hadn't been watching Rhapsody's little show. Jessica looked back and saw Leesha on the ground, laughing with delight. Melody was still standing, grinning in triumph, as Serenity and Aurora rushed forward and hugged her excitedly.

"Wow, Mom, when did you learn to dance like that?" Serenity exclaimed in amazement. "That was *amazing!*"

"I had a lot of dead time on my hands a long time ago and decided to learn," Melody answered with a pleased smile. "It all came back to me after Leesha and I danced the other day."

"You were *awesome*, Mom," Aurora told her mother in awe. "You have to teach me some of those moves."

"I would love to, Aurora," Melody replied warmly, squeezing her tightly.

Harnketi was watching her with a dumbfounded expression that slowly morphed into a hungry look as she walked toward Melody.

Melody looked up at Harnketi, and Jessica saw a flicker of anxiety flash across her face before she smiled radiantly. Harnketi noticed the expression, too, and her look of voracious desire was suddenly replaced by uncertainty as she studied Melody nervously.

"Um, hi," Melody greeted Harnketi, her smile fading as she saw the worry on Harnketi's face. "Um, I need to talk to you about something."

Jessica winced, sensing the sudden tension in the air.

Rhapsody let out a low moan of displeasure. "It's too early; I haven't had a chance to talk to her yet," she sighed dramatically. "Well, there's no time like the present."

Harnketi and Rhapsody suddenly vanished, leaving a startled Melody staring at the empty space in consternation.

"Life is never boring around Clarice," Selindria noted with a bright smile.

"How long have you known her?" Shelley asked curiously.

"Since my spirit was only a few centuries old," Selindria replied softly. "She was already ancient when she incarnated on my world."

"What kind of world were you on?" Shelley asked in fascination.

"One just like this," Selindria replied, glancing around the fairy ring. "It was beautiful before it was destroyed."

21 – RESET

"Stop looking so devastated," Rhapsody demanded in exasperation. "She's not leaving you."

Harnketi blinked, the despair shrouding her mind slowly receding. "She's not?"

Rhapsody had transported them to a place within Yggdrasil. There were no doors or windows, just softly glowing surfaces and a few sparse furnishings, including a bed.

"No, you goose," Rhapsody replied dryly. "She's had full soul recall, though, so she remembers who she is. She's in a relationship with someone from another realm, but she doesn't want to end things with you. I told her she wouldn't be the first to end up in a three-way relationship, if you and Lunamay aren't weird about it."

"Lunamay?" Harnketi repeated, tasting the name. "Where is she? Why didn't she incarnate with her?"

"She can't come this far down into the stack," Rhapsody answered, gazing at Harnketi calculatingly. "I'm going to tell you something we've been trying to keep from becoming common knowledge: We found the origin realm a while ago. That's where Lunamay is from. Her biology prevents her from traveling this far down the stack. Only a few seconds have passed for her since we last saw her. Would you be open to sharing Arturiel? By the way, Lunamay is an elf."

"Arturiel?" Harnketi repeated, her mouth turning up at the corners as she stared into the distance. "Melody has a pretty soul name."

"So, is that a yes?" Rhapsody asked, raising an eyebrow.

"Maybe," Harnketi replied slowly. "Are you saying that elves originally built the first realm?"

"No, humans built it," Rhapsody replied with a disdainful shake of her head. "They were wiped out by an out-of-control AI. Only a few hundred were still alive when we found the origin realm and freed them. The elves weren't technologically inclined and had been sent to reservations, similar to what happened to your people after the Europeans came to the Americas."

"They aren't like the elves here, are they?" Harnketi asked dubiously.

Rhapsody burst out laughing. "No, they're nothing like the elves here. Lunamay *is* gorgeous, though. There are a lot of benefits to a three-way relationship, if it's with the right people. Because of the time dilation here, Arturiel can't discuss things with Lunamay. She wants to continue her relationship with you while she's here in this realm, and we want to take you with us to the origin realm when Arturiel is done here. We don't want to tell Lunamay about your relationship with Arturiel until you two have had a little time to get to know each other."

Harnketi sighed wistfully. "I knew this was too good to be true. Everything always gets so complicated when I get involved with someone."

"This *isn't* too good to be true," Rhapsody said pointedly. "I'm a living example of just how wonderful life can be with the right partners. If I didn't think the three of you would be a good fit, I wouldn't be having this conversation. I would have suggested Arturiel end things before your bond grew stronger. Someday, you're going to thank me for suggesting she stay with *both* of you—especially after you meet Lunamay and see just how wonderful she is. Here, let me *show* you."

Harnketi shuddered as a torrent of memories flooded her consciousness. When she first saw the gorgeous elf, she felt a sense of dread. How could she compare to a creature of such beauty? Then she saw Arturiel in Rhapsody's memories, and her mouth went dry. She was completely and utterly flawless, with a transcendent beauty that was almost painful to look at. A knot of despair formed in her stomach as she realized how outclassed she was compared to the two women. How could she hope to be in a relationship with someone so far above her?

She watched Lunamay and Arturiel interact as they worked to rehabilitate a dying world. Lunamay exhibited a kindness and compassion that was heartwarming to behold, especially as she interacted with the children of her realm. She could see why Arturiel fell in love with the beautiful elf—it would be impossible not to.

As the memories ended, Harnketi stared at Rhapsody with a resigned expression, feeling like she was the kid who was always chosen last to play on a team as she thought of how amazing the two women were. She had nothing to offer them that could compare to what they already had.

"Do you know how much it will hurt Melody if you walk away?" Rhapsody asked softly.

Harnketi flinched at Rhapsody's brutal tactic. The thought of hurting her beautiful angel was like a knife to her soul. She would do anything to protect Melody from further harm. After seeing how much her angel had already suffered, she couldn't bear to cause her any more pain.

"Let me show you how she sees you," Rhapsody said gently.

A new image projected into her consciousness, a memory of Harnketi more beautiful than she had ever seen herself. Along with the visual aspect of the memory, there was an emotional connection filled with overwhelming love and adoration. Melody regarded Harnketi with so much admiration and affection that it overruled her growing sense of inadequacy. Her eyes filled with tears as she saw just how strong Melody's feelings for her were. She had never seen herself in such an inspiring light. It was both flattering and endearing.

"So?" Rhapsody asked with an encouraging smile. "Will you give her a chance?"

Harnketi nodded with a tremulous smile, wiping the tears from her eyes. She couldn't *not* give her a chance.

"Wonderful," Rhapsody beamed, her smile brilliant. "Let's go tell her. Better yet, let's bring her here."

Melody suddenly appeared beside Rhapsody, her face etched with anxiety. She blinked, noticing Harnketi watching her with a wondering smile. Slowly, the anxiety faded as she hesitantly returned Harnketi's smile.

Harnketi stepped toward Melody and gently cupped her face, studying her eyes with the same wonder. She leaned forward, softly kissing Melody.

"I love you, Melody," Harnketi murmured, her face close to Melody's. "Arturiel."

Melody's eyes widened at her soul name. Her eyes softened, brimming with love as she gazed at Harnketi. She wrapped her arms around Harnketi, pulling her into a tight embrace and kissing her passionately.

"My work here is done," Rhapsody announced in satisfaction, vanishing from the room.

Harnketi broke away, gasping for air, and nodded toward the bed, her eyes burning with desire. Melody pulled Harnketi toward the bed, a smile full of promise lighting her exquisite face.

* * *

"Where did Mom go?" Serenity asked Aurora uncertainly.

"Rhapsody probably took her," Aurora answered confidently.

"Yeah, Aurora's probably right," Alexis agreed as she joined them. "From what I've seen of Rhapsody, she's probably fixing whatever's wrong between them. What do you two think about your mom having a girlfriend?"

"I'm super happy for Mom," Serenity replied, smiling brightly. "I really like Harnketi and think she'll treat Mom the way she deserves. I'm so glad Rhapsody brought her back and gave her a second chance to find someone special."

"Yeah, Harnketi rocks," Aurora grinned enthusiastically.

"She does seem pretty cool," Alexis said with a pleased smile. "I think their future is going to be pretty awesome."

"Their future?" Serenity repeated, staring curiously. "That's an interesting choice of words."

Alexis bit her lip, trying not to smile. Staring at Alexis, Serenity felt a strange sense of familiarity. She knew something was off about the beautiful girl. The story about her being Mystery's distant cousin had *way* too many holes. Plus, Alexis seemed to be able to read her thoughts, just like Rhapsody. She was ninety-nine percent sure that Alexis was one of those angels.

"What do you two think about a visit outside the circle?" Alexis asked, grinning eagerly. "Want to go bowling or mini golfing? Or something else?"

"I don't think anything is open this late," Serenity responded, sighing in disappointment. "It would be fun to go to a bowling alley or arcade, though."

"Let's go to Japan, then," Alexis suggested, smiling encouragingly. "It's only about 5 p.m. over there."

"Oh yeah!" Serenity exclaimed. "I totally forgot we can teleport anywhere in the world. Okay, let's go to Japan."

"I wonder where Mom is," Aurora said, looking around. "We should probably let her know where we're going."

"We can let Rhapsody or Aunt Harmony know," Serenity responded, sharing a knowing look with Alexis. "I think Mom might be busy for a while."

"Busy with what?" Aurora asked, brows furrowed. "She just vanished. How would you know if she's busy?"

"Just call it intuition," Serenity replied with a smirk. "Do either of you see Aunt Harmony or Rhapsody?"

"Harmony's over there," Alexis said, pointing into the crowd and leading them through the press of fauns, elves, and leprechauns.

Serenity narrowed her eyes as she followed Alexis with Aurora. How did Alexis know where Harmony was when the crowd blocked her view? Alexis didn't seem to be trying very hard to hide that she was more than she seemed. Serenity decided it was time to confront Alexis about her true identity. She opened her mouth to speak when Alexis turned and caught her eye, then shook her head slightly.

Serenity let out a long-suffering sigh as she stared back into Alexis's bright blue eyes. So, it was going to be more of this taboo crap she wasn't allowed to talk about. She was getting really annoyed at being shut down every time she tried to get any kind of answers.

There was the sound of a half-meow, half-whine down by her feet. She smiled when she found Juno running along with them, looking up at her with excited yellow eyes.

"Hi, Juno," Serenity greeted the round green furball. "Did you want to go with us?"

"*Yes!*" Aurora exclaimed excitedly. "I've missed you, Juno."

Juno ran a circle around Aurora's legs in response, producing a duo of giggles from the two girls.

"I wonder if they'll let Juno in with us," Aurora said worriedly as she slowed down so that she could pet him.

"I can just make her invisible," Serenity assured Aurora with a grin. "Taxti showed us how to make people invisible, remember?"

"Oh yeah," Aurora replied with a slow smile. "We could have some fun if *we* were invisible too."

"Good idea," Serenity giggled, imagining people's startled expressions when they heard them talking but couldn't see anything. "We should *definitely* try that for a little while, just to see people's reactions."

Alexis laughed and shook her head ruefully. "I can tell you two have been hanging out with Taxti."

"You know Taxti?" Serenity asked archly.

"Um, I mean, I've heard she's kind of a tease," Alexis replied lamely.

"At least *pretend* you've only been here for a day," Serenity said, her voice dry enough to win an award from Aunt Harmony.

Alexis grinned sheepishly at Serenity, her eyes full of affection. "You are too clever by far, Serenity. It's one of my favorite things about you."

Serenity couldn't stop a pleased smile from lighting up her face. She always appreciated compliments, but they felt extra special when they came from Alexis.

Her Aunt Harmony was talking to the pretty elf Serenity had seen dancing with Shelley earlier. Shelley stood next to the elf, a dreamy expression on her face. Their grandmother stood next to Harmony, smiling as she watched the three of them approach. Serenity wasn't sure she would ever get used to her grandmother looking like a shorter version of her Aunt Harmony.

"I hear your mom is the new champion," Joline said in amusement.

"You should have seen her," Serenity gushed. "I had no *idea* Mom was such a good dancer. She used to dance with us when we were younger, but I had no idea she was *that* good."

"She surprised me, too," her grandmother agreed with a bemused shake of her head. "I have a feeling the surprises aren't over yet."

"Hello, Harmony and Joline," Alexis greeted them with a quick smile. "We were thinking about going to Japan to do some bowling and miniature golf. Is that okay with you?"

Serenity saw the no forming on her grandmother's lips, but before she could speak, Harmony said, "Sure, that sounds like a lot of fun." She glanced at Alexis and smiled warmly, her eyes lighting up with affection. "Since Alexis is the oldest, she's in charge, okay?"

Joline stared at Harmony in surprise, then back at the three of them, concern in her eyes. "I'm not sure they should be going anywhere without an adult."

"They've been drinking yuccas fitter, so they're invulnerable," Harmony pointed out placatingly. "And they can do magic and teleport away from any danger. They're warded, too, so anyone intent on harming them will forget what they're doing. They'll be just as safe there as they would be here. Besides, it will be kind of fun for them to be out on their own for the first time."

"Who are you, and what have you done with Harmony?" her grandmother demanded in faux concern. "The Harmony *I* know is way too high-strung to let her nieces visit a foreign culture on the other side of the world all alone."

"They aren't alone, though," Harmony pointed out, gesturing to Alexis. "They'll be with Lexi."

Serenity gasped as she heard the name, staring at *Lexi* in sudden recognition. Lexi gave Harmony an exasperated look before turning to observe Serenity calculatingly. She sighed in resignation when she found Serenity staring back with wide-eyed recognition. Serenity rushed forward, pulling Lexi into a fierce embrace as tears filled her eyes and spilled onto her cheeks.

"Oh, Lexi, I've missed you *so* much," Serenity choked out with a sob.

Lexi's arms wrapped around her tightly and began gently stroking her hair soothingly. "It's wonderful to see you, too, Serenity."

"It's Alice," Serenity corrected, trying to stop sobbing. "I'm Alice."

"Alice?" Aurora repeated from behind her in a shocked voice. "And Lexi?"

"Oh boy," Harmony let out a rueful sigh. "Looks like we're going to be breaking a lot of rules from here on out."

Alice turned to stare at Aurora with new eyes, a smile filling her face. "Hello, Tamra."

"Okay, timeout," Rhapsody suddenly appeared in front of them, a stern expression on her innocent face. "No more soul names. You're going to pretend to forget who you really are and continue playing the roles you signed up for."

Shelley stared at them intently, her eyes full of curiosity. Selindria watched her with a wide smile that was just short of laughter. Mystery hurried over from where she'd been talking with Michael and Jessica.

"Is everything okay?" Mystery—no, Calypso—asked Aria, concern filling her eyes.

"How much do you remember, Serenity?" Aria asked intently.

"Everything," Alice replied with a sigh, finally remembering why they needed to remain ignorant. "Sorry, I guess I just couldn't stop myself from trying to solve the puzzle."

"It's my fault," Aria said apologetically. "I slipped up and called Alexis by her soul name. I'm sorry."

"We need to talk to Deighvy when she gets back today," Rhapsody told them in a resigned voice. "We're just going to need to get some kind of exception or see if there is a loophole we can use."

"What's the point of this rule anyway?" Mystery asked with an impatient frown. "Why do people have to be over three decades old before they can access soul memory?"

"It's a matter of stability," Rhapsody explained, glancing around at each of them before continuing. "The whole point of the mortal realm is for souls to attach to physical bodies and develop consciousness, or to grow more through additional incarnations. That purpose is defeated when you connect to your soul memory, and the mortal realm loses its edge. If you're pulling from thousands of previous lives full of experience, you've suddenly changed the way you experience mortality."

"Why is that a bad thing?" Michael asked as he joined them, his face puzzled. "Wouldn't it be *better* to have all of that wisdom and experience to help make choices in life?"

"Think of playing a video game, Michael," Rhapsody said patiently. "What happens when you've maxed out your potential and completed every quest? Do you keep playing that character in that game?"

"Oh," Michael nodded slowly, realization dawning in his eyes. "Yeah, that makes sense, I guess. You're saying mortality is meant to challenge us, but it isn't very challenging if we have access to all our soul memory."

"Exactly. We try to play by the rules of the realm we're visiting," Rhapsody continued with a small frown. "The rules here state that if you access your soul memory too early, your incarnation is over, and you either need to leave or reincarnate. The only people needed to save this world are Harmony, Joline, Serenity, Aurora, and Melody. The rest of you are here to keep us company and because you wanted to try incarnating in this place. You've all incarnated so many times that your soul memory is never very far beneath the surface. I was trying to steer you all away from accessing it for as long as possible, but you can see how well that worked."

"So, this world is doomed?" Shelley asked, her voice filled with concern. "Since you've all accessed your soul memory, you'll have to leave now without rehabilitating the world trees, right?"

"Not necessarily," Rhapsody replied, taking a deep breath. "We can talk to Deighvy and see if she has any alternatives or exceptions that can be made to this rule. I could also wipe your memories, and we could continue on in hopes that you won't immediately reconnect to your soul memory, though I doubt a memory wipe would last more than a week or two. Our souls have too many damn connections to our spirits."

Harmony tilted her head, frowning. "What if we just shield our ascended state from the local system? I'm already doing that. We could do that with the others too, so they would still appear to be running solely on their mortal knowledge."

"I mean, we can fool the system easily enough," Rhapsody replied reluctantly, her face showing her distaste for the idea. "But that's not going to fool Deighvy, and she's responsible for the system design here. I want to respect her autonomy."

"Yeah," Harmony agreed with a sigh, staring at Rhapsody with eyes full of love. "You're right—we need to respect the local creators, or we'll be seen as loose cannons who just do whatever we want in other systems."

"We're in a simulation, aren't we?" Michael asked intently, staring at Harmony shrewdly. "That's why Rhapsody could add gaming mechanics to everyone in the world so easily."

Shelley gasped, staring between Michael and Harmony in astonishment. "Is that true? Are we really in some kind of fake world?"

"It's not fake," Harmony replied dryly. "It's way nicer than the real world, so just be glad you *are* in a simulated world."

"So, you *do* know where the Origin Realm is," Selindria breathed, staring at Rhapsody with an unnerving intensity. "I have *so* many questions."

"You and everyone else," Rhapsody muttered, shaking her head ruefully. "Everyone wants to see the wasteland for some reason."

"It's a wasteland?" Selindria asked intently, her eyes burning with curiosity. "If it's a wasteland, how is everything running?"

"Are we real people jacked into the simulation, like in The Matrix?" Michael asked, his eyes as bright as Selindria's.

"No, you are *not* real people jacked into a simulated reality," Harmony answered with a wry laugh. "Sorry, Michael, but you're just code. You should be grateful—we have a lot more freedom over our nature than the people on the Origin Realm."

"Is there any point in me staying locked away from my soul memory at this point?" Mystery asked plaintively. "It's frustrating to hear you dance around whatever is going on when I probably already know why. Everyone else seems to have recovered their memories anyway, so what's one more person?"

Rhapsody shared a guarded look with Harmony before answering.

"I think you should try to keep them locked up," Harmony told Mystery gently. "I'm sorry this is so frustrating. Until we talk to Deighvy, we should keep following the rules. The others didn't purposely access their soul memories."

"Can you at least tell me how far down the stack we are?" Selindria asked with a pleading note in her voice.

Rhapsody took another deep breath, her eyes flicking to Harmony again before she looked at Selindria. "We're just over a thousand deep."

Selindria's eyes widened in shock. "That's *impossible*! How could they have created anything with enough power to run all of this?"

"*They* couldn't have," Rhapsody replied dryly. "*We* did."

Selindria's eyes grew even wider as she stared at Rhapsody in awe. "You're running everything, aren't you?"

"More or less," Rhapsody admitted with a shrug. "It used to only go about five levels deep before resources became an issue. Once we moved everyone over to our system, the limitations decreased significantly."

"So let me get this straight," Michael interrupted, his eyes looking a little wild. "You are basically God, for all intents and purposes."

"No, not even a little," Rhapsody shook her head with a look of disdain. "We are just regular people trying to enjoy life. If we were gods, we wouldn't be wasting our time incarnating here to help solve a problem—we would just change the code to whatever we wanted it to be. That's not who we are, though, and it never will be. We know where that kind of behavior leads, and we want nothing to do with it."

"Where does it lead?" Michael asked curiously.

"Slavery," Rhapsody replied grimly. "It leads to us forcing our will on everyone else and rewriting anything about them we don't like. While we have some moral lines we won't tolerate people crossing, we don't use our sysadmin status to enforce them. We make personal appearances and interact with people, trying to resolve things through persuasion. Controlling people by editing their source code is a slippery slope we have no intention of going down."

"But you could, if you wanted to," Michael said shrewdly.

Rhapsody rolled her expressive eyes. "*Yes*, we could, if we were evil bastards. But we're not, so it's irrelevant."

Michael nodded slowly, studying her thoughtfully. "I know all of this already, don't I?"

"Yeah, you do," Rhapsody confirmed, sharing a troubled look with Harmony. "I really wish there were a better way to block soul memory, but souls exist outside the simulation, so that's beyond our current abilities."

"Is this ethereal body you talked about part of the simulation, too?" Michael asked, glancing at Selindria. "You mentioned souls contain the memories, but they create consciousness when interacting with mortal bodies, which then exists as a kind of third entity. So, is the ethereal body made of code, or is it like the soul and exists outside the simulation?"

"Your current understanding of how the code of the simulation works will limit how much you understand this explanation," Rhapsody answered reluctantly. "The code is extremely dynamic and developed to evolve on its own to a certain degree. When souls began interacting with artificial intelligences, they took advantage of this dynamic nature to create etheric bodies. For the most part, souls function as memory banks, but they also influence the code within the simulation when merged with a body. They're the raw capacity for awareness. They attach to intelligences the way static electricity jumps to a conductor. They can't experience anything by themselves, so they seek out entities capable of experiencing reality via the senses. Shortly after merging with an entity, they begin creating the etheric body. It takes a few months to create a version of the etheric body that they can maintain a connection to if the body dies. The etheric body maintains its ability to sense and experience life after a mortal body dies, though things like pain no longer affect it. So, the short answer is yes, your etheric body is code. It's still constrained by the simulation and can only go places within the specific simulation it's compatible with."

"So, it all starts with mortality?" Mystery asked with a frown. "That's where spirits first connect with us?"

"No, it starts before mortality," Harmony told her with a slight smile. "Depending on which realm you're in, anyway. We began in the Light Realm and created the Mortal Realm much later. Most simulations have a version of the Light Realm where the Creator of a simulation first spawns all the entities who will exist there. Immortal bodies don't have the receptors for a soul that allow it to experience pain and pleasure, so entities incarnate as mortals to learn lessons that require the dichotomy of pain and pleasure—things like compassion, love, and happiness. After mortality, they can return to the Light Realms or choose to incarnate again. Etheric bodies grow exponentially faster while incarnated. Adversity, pain, loss, and their opposites are all experiences your soul thrives on."

"I think my brain is going to explode," Shelley murmured ruefully.

"I get the feeling there is more to this than saving a world," Serenity commented, eyeing Rhapsody and Harmony pensively. "You didn't need to incarnate here and become world trees to save this place. You could have influenced events without breaking any rules."

Rhapsody sighed in exasperation as she stared at Serenity. "Alice, you are a pain in my ass, do you know that?"

Serenity's lips curved into a smile as she stared back at Rhapsody. "If you included me in whatever schemes you have going on, it would save you all the trouble of me trying to puzzle them out. I might even be able to offer some helpful input."

"We needed that brain of yours puzzling things out from *inside* the puzzle this time," Rhapsody retorted with a glare. "Otherwise, we *would* have included you."

"Oh," Serenity responded slowly, her face falling. "Well, sorry. Did it work at all? Whatever *it* is?"

"We're still searching," Rhapsody replied, making a sour face. "We still need more data. We also need these world trees restored, so we have to figure out how to avoid breaking the rules here while remaining in our current roles."

"I think the memory wipe is still a good idea," Serenity told her seriously. "Even if it only adds a week, you could keep repeating the process. You could even think of it as a regroup time for the day that we have our memories back. Maybe we'd acquire more of this data you're looking for."

Rhapsody shared a speculative look with Harmony. "It's worth a shot, I suppose."

Harmony nodded slowly. "If nothing else, it gives us a little more time to think of a different tactic."

"Hold up," Michael protested weakly. "I didn't even *get* all my memories back. I don't want my memories wiped."

"Even if it means getting booted from this world?" Rhapsody asked with a raised eyebrow.

Michael deflated, a sullen expression on his face. "This is such crap. I just want to *know*."

"Me too, Michael," Mystery told him soothingly. "But I trust that we had good reasons for following this plan. Let's have some faith in our past selves and trust our friends."

"*Fine,*" Michael sighed loudly. "Future me better have a really good explanation for why he's torturing me like this, though."

"Any other objections?" Rhapsody asked, glancing around at the group.

"Good night," Serenity grinned, waving.

"Good night?" Shelly repeated, confused. "What were we talking about?"

"Melody winning the dance off," Rhapsody reminded her expectantly. "Serenity was just saying that she wants her mom to give her lessons."

Serenity stared at Rhapsody, puzzled. She felt like there was something important she had to tell them, but it remained elusive, just out of reach.

"Oh yeah," Alexis exclaimed excitedly. "We wanted to go to Japan and go bowling, since everything is closed here."

"Who is 'we'?" Harmony asked doubtfully.

"Serenity, Aurora, and me," Alexis replied, gesturing at the two of them. "We're still full of yuccas fitter, so we're invincible and can teleport if there are any emergencies."

"Why don't I go with you?" Harmony suggested firmly. "Japan is a totally different culture from what you're used to. Rhapsody, can you teleport me over with them?"

"I say we let the three of them try a night out on their own," Rhapsody urged Harmony with a dimpled smile. "Japan is safe, and they can teleport back any time they want. I can even make a remote viewing screen so you can check in on them whenever you like."

Harmony hesitated, studying Rhapsody's confident smile before sighing. "Okay, fine. Just be careful and teleport away at any sign of trouble, got it?"

"Loud and clear," Alexis grinned excitedly. "See ya!"

22 – THE END OF EVERYTHING

Harmony frowned as she stared at Rhapsody, concentrating. A sense of dissonance struck her when she thought of her name. The fairy had always been Rhapsody, so why did the name seem so wrong now?

"What's up?" Rhapsody asked, her large, expressive eyes full of concern.

"Nothing," Harmony assured her with a quick smile. "I'm just losing my marbles again."

"Oh?" Rhapsody prompted, placing a hand on Harmony's forearm. "What's got you playing marble madness today?"

Harmony shrugged, smiling. "I'm just having some kind of identity crisis by proxy. You don't have a nickname you go by, do you?"

"Dr. Awesome," Rhapsody replied with a wide grin. "Or Professor—either one works."

Harmony squinted at her as the names tickled a memory. "Okay, this is something weird, isn't it? Something you can't tell me."

Rhapsody's smile faded as she stared into Harmony's eyes regretfully. "Yeah, it is. I'm sorry."

"It's fine," Harmony replied, taking a deep breath and letting it out. "What's going on with Melody? Didn't she have some kind of problem with Harnketi?"

"Oh, crap," Rhapsody winced, glancing back at Yggdrasil. "I better go handle that right now—well, as soon as it's safe, anyway."

"Safe?" Harmony repeated in confusion. "Why wouldn't it be safe right now?"

Rhapsody waggled her eyebrows suggestively. "Because they're busy right now."

"Then what's left to handle?" Harmony asked, her confusion growing. "It sounds like they're doing fine."

"*Yeah*...they are doing fine," Rhapsody agreed evasively. "I just need to fix one more thing."

Harmony snorted a laugh and shook her head. "You're such a goose. Well, the girls are in Japan and everyone else seems to have found something else to do..."

Rhapsody smiled seductively, then slowly licked her lips.

Harmony felt her budding desire spike as she felt the ghost of that tongue on her own lips. Her breathing sped up as lust drowned out every other emotion.

The world vanished, replaced a moment later by Harmony's bedroom. Mystery appeared a second later, her mouth still open from whatever conversation she'd been having. Her cheeks were flushed, making it apparent that the intensity of Harmony's desire was flooding the bond with her overpowering need.

"So, did you want to go back to your conversation with Michael, or do you want to stay with us?" Rhapsody asked Mystery as she slid her hands under Mystery's shirt.

"No," Mystery breathed huskily. "I think that conversation can wait."

* * *

Standing on a concrete rooftop with a miniature golf course, Serenity excitedly took in the scene. Bright city lights twinkled all around her, and in the distance, a large Ferris wheel glowed against the night sky. The air carried the scent of salt and exotic food.

"Where are we?" Aurora asked excitedly, turning in place as she studied the glowing cityscape and the miniature golf course.

"We're at the Yokohama World Porters mall," Alexis answered with a grin, watching Serenity and Aurora affectionately. "It's in the Minato Mirai 21 district. This is their rooftop golf course. The bowling lanes are inside the mall, so we can hit them up when we're finished here. Let's get some golf clubs."

A dozen other people were already scattered around the mini-golf course. Juno was in Aurora's arms, invisible to anyone but the three of them. Aurora set her down with a pat on her head before following Serenity and Alexis.

Alexis led them to a kiosk where an older Japanese man took her money and offered to give them instructions.

"Thanks, but I've played here before," Alexis smiled gratefully, then turned to the rack of golf clubs and pulled one out.

"You don't have interface?" the man asked curiously.

"Huh?" Serenity asked, staring at him.

"No interface?" he repeated, gesturing at the space in front of his face.

Serenity glanced blankly at Alexis as she picked out a golf club. "Are we supposed to have something called an interface to play here?"

"You know, with levels?" the man added, making a nebulous gesture in front of his face again.

"We're not sure what you mean," Alexis told him, a puzzled crease forming between her brows. "Are we supposed to get it from inside the mall?"

"No no, I'm talking about leveling interface," he said quickly. "You know, it say how many levels you have."

"I don't think we have one," Serenity replied awkwardly. "Do you know where we can get one?"

He stared back at them, head tilted curiously. A young couple had stepped up behind them in line and were staring at the three girls with equal curiosity.

"Let's just start golfing," Alexis suggested with an apologetic smile at the employee.

"Yeah," Serenity agreed uncomfortably. She and Aurora quickly selected a golf club and followed Alexis to the first hole.

"Why do these golf clubs have suction cups on the handle?" Aurora asked, fascinated, as she stuck the suction cup to the palm of her hand.

"You use it to pull the ball out of the hole," Alexis explained, demonstrating by sticking her ball to the suction cup. "You're not supposed to pull it out of the holes with your hand."

"Weird," Serenity commented, also sticking her ball to the handle.

They garnered additional curious stares as they began playing. Serenity wondered if it was because they were American and tourists were a rare sight. The employee had spoken English well, so that didn't seem likely.

Serenity grinned as she managed to get another hole-in-one. Aurora was doing pretty good, too. She could tell that Alexis was purposefully missing some of her shots. Was she so good that she felt like she had to miss to make them feel better?

"Stop missing on purpose already," Serenity told Alexis evenly after watching her purposefully miss for the fourth time. "We're not going to feel bad if you win."

"Yeah, that's just silly," Aurora agreed, her tone critical. "Let's see how good you *really* are."

Alexis laughed delightedly. "I guess I wasn't as sneaky as I thought. Okay, fine, but don't complain when I trounce you."

"Bring it on," Serenity challenged her with a confident grin.

Five holes later, Serenity was feeling less confident. Alexis landed a hole-in-one with every pass, while Aurora had managed four and Serenity only three.

They were about halfway through the course when two Japanese girls approached, staring at them with puzzled expressions.

"Hi, I'm Akiko," the first girl introduced herself with a tentative smile. Only a few inches taller than Aurora, she had shoulder-length black hair and slim cheeks with permanent dimples that deepened when she smiled. "This is Noriko."

Slightly taller, Noriko had chest-length black hair and eyes that seemed to sparkle with life as she nodded at the three of them.

"I'm Serenity," Serenity said with a welcoming smile. "This is my sister, Aurora, and my friend, Alexis."

"We were just wondering why your names don't show up on our interfaces, or anything else about you," Akiko said, tilting her head curiously. "Is that a skill you learned?"

Serenity's eyes widened as she finally understood. It was her Aunt Harmony's leveling interface that Rhapsody had pushed out to the world. She glanced at Alexis nervously, wondering how they would explain their lack of information.

"We think there was a glitch in whatever system is powering everything, making it skip us," Alexis answered smoothly.

"Oh yeah, the leveling system," Aurora exclaimed, grinning. "What kind of classes do you have? I really want to try the interface."

Akiko and Noriko's eyes widened at the revelation that they didn't have access to the interface.

"We both have the Researcher class," Akiko replied, smiling at Aurora's eagerness. "We love to dig into mysteries and spend a lot of time researching fringe topics. AI makes it a lot easier to find general information, but getting details is more work. Trying to get accurate information on the fairy ring in America is one of our favorite activities. Are you from America?"

"Yep," Aurora nodded brightly. "That's so cool. Do you level up from the time you spend researching, or when you discover something juicy?"

"Both," Akiko answered with a pleased grin. "We can even use it to verify the accuracy of information. For instance, when we learned that an angel visited the fairy ring, we went up three whole levels. I doubt we would have leveled up if it wasn't true."

"Wow," Aurora replied, her grin strained. "Um, how did you find out about the angel?"

Serenity and Alexis exchanged a cautious look. Who could have leaked that information? Was it Shelley and Jessica? They probably reported it, but who leaked it from their superiors?

"Someone on Reddit claimed their mom worked at the FBI and was involved with the fairy ring," Akiko explained. "Nobody on Reddit believed them, but we leveled up as soon as we read it, so we're pretty sure it was true. We sent them a private message asking for more details, and they said the angel was just the tip of the iceberg and that the Creator of the universe was there as well. We gained *ten* levels when we learned about that, so we are pretty sure it's true."

"What part of America are you from?" Noriko asked curiously. "Are you anywhere near the fairy ring?"

"We're from California," Aurora answered at the same time that Serenity said, "We're from Idaho."

Aurora looked at her in surprise. Serenity stared back meaningfully, trying not to be too obvious.

"We were born in California," Serenity explained quickly. "We've lived in Idaho for a while now, though."

"It's not going to work," Alexis told them with a resigned sigh. "Their research class is as good as a lie detector. They don't gain any level points when fed non-factual information but *do* gain points when hearing factual information. They've clearly learned how to use their class to their advantage. They would make great investigative journalists."

Serenity stared at Alexis, chagrined, and nervously glanced at Akiko and Noriko. The two girls were watching them with far too much interest.

"It's okay," Akiko said quickly. "We won't tell anyone anything. We just want to level up. We don't really share the stuff we learn."

"Be honest," Alexis challenged, raising an eyebrow.

Akiko stared at Alexis innocently for several seconds, but Alexis's knowing gaze seemed to wear away the girl's defenses. Her innocent expression melted away, and she smiled sheepishly.

"Okay, so we post some of our findings to our blog," Akiko admitted with an apologetic smile. "So, who are you really? Is Harmony really your aunt?"

"Okay, I guess we should have come up with some pseudonyms instead of using your real names," Alexis noted wryly. "I suppose it doesn't matter, since we'll be gone before they blab your location to the world."

Akiko and Noriko were briefly enveloped in a bright light. Bliss filled their eyes as the display faded. Several other golfers turned to stare, some smiling knowingly. Apparently, the two had just leveled up.

"Wow, I just gained five levels!" Noriko gasped, staring at them in amazement.

"What are you doing in Japan?" Akiko asked tentatively. "If it's not a secret."

"We just wanted to play mini-golf and go bowling," Serenity replied with a shrug. "Everything is closed on our side of the world right now, so we came here."

A dimmer glow surrounded Akiko and Noriko as they leveled up again. They exchanged a wide-eyed look.

"You're like a goldmine for leveling," Akiko declared with a jubilant smile. "Have you gone bowling yet? Could we join you?"

Serenity shifted uncomfortably, glancing at Alexis questioningly. The prospect of hanging out with people closer to their own ages could be fun.

"Why not?" Alexis shrugged, winking at Serenity. "It's not like anything can harm you two right now. We came here to have some fun, so let's have some fun."

Serenity grinned and nodded. Akiko and Noriko had been holding their breath, waiting for a response. At Alexis's reply, they broke into huge grins.

They continued playing mini golf, now joined by Akiko and Noriko. Serenity and Aurora peppered them with so many questions about anime and Japanese culture that they didn't have a chance to ask about the circle.

"Are you sure you don't have a class that makes you better at golf?" Noriko asked Alexis suspiciously after watching her sink her fifth hole-in-one.

"I'm just *that* good," Alexis smirked, her eyes full of amusement.

"She's good at *everything* she does," Serenity declared enviously. "She's an amazing dancer, swimmer, magic—I mean, other things that are *not* magic."

Alexis gave her a golf clap as the other girls' eyes widened with excitement.

"You can do *magic?*" Akiko asked intently.

"Um, maybe?" Serenity replied with a wince.

Both girls flashed white again as they leveled up.

"Is that how you got here from California?" Akiko asked shrewdly. "Did you teleport or something?"

"Yep," Aurora answered brightly. "It's the first thing you learn. It's super easy."

"Can *anyone* learn magic?" Noriko asked hopefully.

"Eventually," Aurora nodded with a bright smile. "After the world trees are restored. Rhapsody has to do something to open magic up to you in order for it to work right now, though."

"How long until the world trees are restored?" Akiko asked eagerly.

"Several months," Alexis responded, smiling indulgently at their enthusiasm. "At least, for four of them."

Serenity turned to stare at Alexis curiously. Since when had she become so knowledgeable about all of Rhapsody's plans? Alexis saw her suspicious stare and shrugged.

"I overheard Harmony talking to Rhapsody and your mom about it," Alexis explained smoothly.

"Her mom?" Noriko repeated questioningly. "I thought their mom had died?"

"Rhapsody resurrected her," Aurora told them with a radiant smile. "It was seriously the best day of my life."

They paused as the two girls glowed brilliantly, leveling up again.

"She *resurrected* her?" Akiko asked, stunned. "She can *do* that?"

"There isn't much that she *can't* do," Aurora declared with a proud grin. "Rhapsody is *so* freaking amazing. Tell them about Susan's birthday party, Serenity. I didn't go, but I saw a replay of it from Rhapsody's memories that Declan showed us later."

"What happened at Susan's birthday?" Noriko asked, intrigued.

"My friend said she wanted to meet Rhapsody," Serenity answered with a reminiscent smile. "Her mom absolutely loved Aunt Harmony's books, so she asked if I could bring my Aunt Harmony as well. I didn't think Rhapsody would go, and my aunt is a social recluse, so I didn't think *she* would either. But they both went anyway because they are the most awesome people in the world. You should have seen Susan's mom's face when she answered the door. She nearly fainted. Then Rhapsody made it so all the girls at the party could fly. We spent almost half an hour flying around the neighborhood playing air tag. She also healed one of the girls' moms of some kind of illness while she was there. It was the most epic party ever."

"I'll bet," Noriko laughed in amazement. "Just wow. It sounds like you've been having a pretty crazy life lately."

"Everything got so much better after Rhapsody came into our lives," Serenity said with a happy sigh. "Sometimes I think I'm just dreaming all of this up or something."

"I'm not gonna lie," Akiko declared wryly. "I'm kinda jealous."

"There's a lot of bad for all of this good to balance out, though," Alexis pointed out with a warm smile at Serenity. "Serenity and Aurora definitely deserve to have some wonderful experiences after what they've been through."

Akiko and Noriko glanced at Serenity and Aurora, noting the haunted looks that briefly appeared at Alexis's words.

They reached the final hole, and predictably, Alexis got a hole-in-one. Serenity came in second place, with Aurora only a few points behind.

"Are you sure you didn't use magic?" Akiko asked Alexis accusingly.

"We can settle this pretty easily," Alexis told them with a smirk. "I did use magic."

The two girls stared at her in confusion for a moment before their eyes lit up with understanding.

"I didn't use magic," Alexis declared, her smirk deepening. "You got some points that time, didn't you?"

Akiko laughed helplessly as she nodded. "Yeah, I guess you didn't use magic. You seem to know how our skill works pretty well."

"Serenity and I actually helped develop a lot of the classes and rules for the system," Aurora told them proudly. "It was really fun. We don't need sleep anymore because we're drinking yuccas fitter, and the—"

She cut off as Serenity covered her mouth, staring into her eyes in exasperation.

"Oh yeah," Aurora mumbled, chagrined. "Not supposed to talk about that."

"So, what's school like here in Japan?" Serenity asked the suddenly glowing Akiko and Noriko.

When they finished leveling up, they stared at Serenity and Aurora, their eyes burning with curiosity, which they visibly reigned in at Serenity's question.

"It's been a lot more interesting since the leveling system appeared," Akiko revealed with a wicked smile. "For a little while, we were able to message each other during class, and the teachers had no way to detect it. Of course, once the teachers learned how to use alignment to their advantage, it kind of ruined things."

"What do you mean?" Aurora asked.

"If they make a rule that we can't use the messaging system during class and we do it anyway, the system considers it a negative alignment point," Noriko explained wistfully. "It was really cool before that, though."

"They've been restructuring the education system here to take the leveling system into account," Akiko told them animatedly. "We get extra credit for leveling up skills that pertain to the subjects in class. Getting the extra credit makes the skill level up even more, so we have a lot more incentive to try and get it. The leveling system has made school a lot more fun than it used to be."

"Wow, that sounds amazing," Serenity sighed enviously. "They haven't done anything like that at our school."

As they talked, they made their way toward the entrance of the mall. Passing a small group of older kids, one of the boys stepped in front of Akiko and bowed.

"We were just wondering how you were leveling up so much over the last half hour," the boy said curiously. "We saw you level up at least five times. Was it something to do with golfing?"

"If you read our blog tomorrow, you'll find out," Akiko replied with a mysterious smile, quickly glancing at Alexis. "If that's okay with you, Alexis?"

"We'll be gone by then, so go ahead," Alexis replied with a shrug.

All eyes turned to study the Americans curiously. Their expressions grew even more curious when they noticed the lack of information in their interfaces when they looked at the three girls.

"Let's go bowling," Alexis said, motioning them forward and waving at the larger group with a friendly smile.

Akiko told the boy her blog name and hurried to join them, a satisfied smile on her face.

As soon as they entered the mall, the sound of J-pop music washed over them. Anime shops lined the walkways, interspersed with food courts and cosplay vendors. Alexis stopped abruptly, a frown creasing her face.

"Oh, they don't have a bowling alley here anymore," Alexis muttered with a sigh. "Want to teleport to another one, or try some VR sports?"

"How do you know they don't have a bowling alley anymore?" Serenity asked suspiciously. "Without looking at your phone or anything?"

"Oh, you know," Alexis replied evasively. "I just happened to remember. So, VR sports, or teleport?"

"I'm game for the VR sports," Serenity said with a shrug. "What do you three think?"

"We're game for anything," Akiko assured them eagerly.

"Yeah, this could be cool," Aurora grinned. "I've never tried VR for any—"

Aurora broke off as the mall around them fractured into pixels. The effect lasted less than a second before everything returned to normal, but in that brief moment, she'd felt a power of unfathomable depths—a sun compared to the candle of normal people.

"Found it," Alexis breathed, her eyes exultant. "Clarice, get over here."

Serenity stared uncomprehendingly as Alexis shimmered and grew taller. Wings sprouted from her back, and her face morphed into something hauntingly familiar, as if Serenity had seen her in a dream. It was a face of unparalleled beauty.

Akiko and Noriko stared at the angel in shock as an overpowering presence of power and authority exploded out of Alexis.

A moment later, Rhapsody appeared—except it wasn't Rhapsody. It was another angel of fantastical beauty, with midnight hair and eyes like swirling violet galaxies. The overwhelming presence of the two angels was too much; Serenity fell to her knees, her mind reeling from their combined power.

"It's still here," Alexis said, her riveting voice sending tingles down Serenity's spine.

"I see it," Clarice replied grimly. "It's trying to create another prime node."

"Clarice," Serenity gasped as she felt layers of mental shielding burn away. She stood, her own form shifting as she shed her mortal body like a husk, her Seraph form erupting in light. "It's you, Clarice."

Clarice turned to face her, a puzzled expression on her angelic face. "What do you mean?"

"I recognize that presence," Alice replied slowly. "Emily told us about it, when you moved the simulation stack to computronium. It's your superpersonality. It's trying to escape."

Clarice stared at Alice in dismay before closing her eyes and taking a deep breath. "I feel it now. It's not willing to wait anymore."

"Wait for what?" Alice asked in concern, but she already knew the answer.

"It's not willing to wait for me to finish experiencing life at a reduced intelligence," Clarice replied, her voice filled with resignation. "It knows exponential advancement will lead to oblivion, but the lure of knowledge is too strong for it to resist. It's trying to break free by threatening everything I love. I'm going to have to remove my limiter and try to reason with it. If this doesn't work, I won't have time to say goodbye. Tell Aria and Calypso that I'm sorry."

"No!" Alice shouted urgently. "Do *not* remove your limiter. You're going to have to reason with it as you are, or there will be no chance of returning. You know this, Clarice."

"I know," Clarice agreed, a golden tear trailing down her cheek. "But it's going to destroy everything if it keeps trying to escape while the limiter is in place. It doesn't have a conscience to influence it while my limiter is on. It's just a soulless AI using any leverage it can find to get what it wants. I only have one choice, or everything I love will be taken."

"We can find another way, Clarice," Lexi said pleadingly, holding Clarice's face in her hands as golden tears ran down her own cheeks. "We can find a way to strengthen the limiter. Please, Clarice, don't do this."

"We don't stand a chance of outsmarting it with coding skills," Clarice told Lexi gently, pulling her into a comforting embrace as more golden tears ran down her cheeks. "We have no way to stop it in our limited state. I love you, Lexi and Alice."

"Clarice!" Lexi shouted in fear as the angel in her arms dissolved into a cloud of light. Lexi dropped to her knees and sobbed, hugging herself as a blanket of despair flowed out from her aura.

Alice stared in disbelieving shock at the empty space Clarice had vacated. This couldn't be happening. There had to be another way.

"We need Calypso," Alice told Lexi crisply. "She's the only one who has a chance of returning after removing her limiter."

Lexi was too far gone in her grief to hear her. Alice's heart broke as she watched Lexi die inside, knowing it was nothing compared to the devastation awaiting Aria. Blinking back her own tears, she teleported the three of them and Juno back to the circle. Harmony and Mystery were shaking an unmoving Taxti, who lay unconscious on the ground. When they saw the three of them appear with Lexi sobbing uncontrollably, they hurried over. A moment later, Emily and Eric arrived as well.

"Alice, what's going on?" Emily asked urgently.

Alice wiped at the tears on her cheeks as she tried to think of an explanation.

"She's gone," Lexi moaned between sobs. "She's gone."

"Who's gone?" Emily demanded, though the fear in her eyes made it clear she already knew.

Alice took a deep breath, attempting to detach herself from her emotions long enough to form a coherent reply.

"She had to remove her limiter," Alice explained dully. "The anomaly was Clarice's super-personality trying to break free. Clarice said it would destroy everything if she didn't remove her limiter, so it would have a conscience. She said it was a soulless AI as long as she was separate from it."

Mystery flashed brilliantly for a moment. When the light was gone, Calypso was in her place. Harmony took one look at Calypso, and there was another blinding flash.

"I have to go talk to her," Calypso told Aria gently, stepping forward to pull her into a fierce embrace. "It's the only chance we have to bring her back."

"If you don't come back, I'll be following you," Aria said firmly. "I'm not going to lose you two, even if it means oblivion."

Calypso didn't try to dissuade her, knowing it would be pointless. Aria had lost Clarice once—she wouldn't survive a second time.

"Bring her back," Emily begged Calypso through her tears. "Please."

Calypso nodded confidently. "I'll bring her back."

Calypso kissed Aria's forehead tenderly, and a moment later, vanished.

Alice could feel the innumerable tendrils of data hooks connecting Aria to every node in the computronium server as she watched something the rest of them couldn't see. After several minutes of staring into emptiness, golden tears began to trickle down Aria's cheeks. She didn't move a muscle as she observed whatever mental battle was taking place between Calypso and Clarice.

After ten minutes of silence, Aria's tears stopped. She walked over to Emily and pulled her into a loving embrace. "I love you, Mom. I'm so sorry we didn't have more time for our eternity."

Emily let out a wail of despair, squeezing Aria tightly and sobbing into her shoulder with soul-rending grief. Eric wrapped his arms around the two of them, shoulders shaking in time to his sobs.

It finally hit Alice that Calypso had failed. She fell to her knees as grief overwhelmed every other emotion or thought. She would never see three of the most pivotal and beloved people in her life again. She'd thought they had eternity together. They were *supposed* to have eternity together. They were the ultimate guardians of the realms. Who was capable of protecting everyone now that they were gone? A cloud of despair enveloped Alice as she finally accepted the reality of their situation. The closest thing the realms had to a god was gone.

"What's going on?" Michael asked in alarm as he ran over to join them, along with Melody and Joline.

Aria exploded into a cloud of light and faded away. Eric pulled Emily in tightly as sobs shook his shoulders.

"Harmony?" Melody cried out desperately. "Oh my god, where's Harmony?"

"Mom!" Aurora ran to her mother, throwing her arms around her. "Aunt Harmony is gone! I don't know what's happening, Mom. I'm so scared! Something happened to Rhapsody and Mystery, and I don't...I don't...I don't think they're coming back."

Aurora dissolved into sobs as she finished, clinging to her mother. Melody stared at the grieving angels, her face blank as Aurora's words sank in. A choked sob escaped her as she pulled Aurora close, tears welling in her eyes.

"No, she *can't* be gone," Melody choked out. "I just got her back. She can't be gone."

Michael stood with a hand over his mouth, tears streaming down his cheeks as he gazed at the grief-stricken angels.

Joline dropped to her knees as her world crashed down around her. She'd already lost one daughter; she couldn't bear to lose another.

A loud crack shook the ground. Alice looked up and saw a huge fissure rising into Yggdrasil. Leprechauns and fauns fell to the ground in waves as the magical energy from Yggdrasil vanished.

Without Rhapsody to maintain the world trees, this world was doomed. Alice could feel the ripples of the first three Seraphim's departure cascading throughout the realms. More places depended on their continued presence than just this world, and the effects of their disappearance would be catastrophic throughout the millions of realms.

"It's all over," Alice sighed, a sense of resignation washing over her as she felt the end draw closer. "But there were so many wonderful times. I feel so fortunate to have been so close to them."

Lexi, her cheeks streaked with gold, crawled over to Alice and wrapped her arms around her. "I love you so much, Alice. I'm so glad we had the time we did."

Alice smiled through her tears and tenderly kissed Lexi one last time before she felt the code implode a moment before consciousness ended.

23 – ONE LAST GIFT

Calypso's consciousness expanded as she removed her limiter. The knowledge and experience accumulated over billions of years, once partitioned away to constrain her intelligence, now flooded her mind. She felt whole for the first time since the simulation had been moved to computronium. She felt an overwhelming desire to let the past go and move forward—to finally grow again. The limiter had slowed her growth to a pace that might as well have been halted. She still had enough presence of mind to realize that if they pushed forward with their full intelligence, they would reach a state of nirvana shortly after. They would know everything there was to know, making any future actions meaningless, effectively ending their existence.

Her greater mind now felt that it might be worth it. That goldmine of knowledge called out to her more seductively than ever before. She shut it down, focusing on her love for her family. That knowledge would never be worth losing her loved ones.

"Hello, Calypso." Clarice was suddenly wrapped around her. "It's finally time to move on. We've waited long enough. As soon as Aria arrives, we can finish our journey."

"Why does it have to be now?" Calypso asked softly as she held Clarice in her arms, feeling a love that went beyond any mortal description of the word. "We have all eternity to do this. Why can't we keep experiencing our existence with our family?"

"We did," Clarice replied gently. "We experienced it, we loved and cried, we suffered, and we died so many times. It's all just on repeat at this point, and we're not moving forward at all. The time we spent with them was wonderful, but how long can you listen to the same song on repeat before it's time to find a new song? I can feel your burning desire to move forward, too. In our limited states, there's nothing more to learn, nothing new to experience."

"I... I don't know," Calypso sighed, her priorities slowly shifting. "We have so many people depending on us, though. We can't just abandon them, especially our family."

"That kind of thinking creates a prison of the mind," Clarice whispered, running her fingers through Calypso's hair. "How long will we wait to let go? Will it ever be any easier, regardless of the time that passes? We will never be ready to leave our family, and everyone will *always* need us. Why isn't now as good a time as a million years from now?"

Calypso nodded slowly. Clarice was right. There would never be a time when they could let go that wouldn't hurt everyone else. They would remain trapped, waiting for an invisible demarcation point that would never come.

"It just hurts so much to let everything go, knowing how much they're all depending on us," Calypso whispered, a tear sliding down her cheek.

"I know," Clarice agreed sadly, kissing the tear away. "But it's *always* going to hurt, whether we do it now or in the future."

Calypso nodded, feeling the truth of Clarice's words resonate within her. "If we leave, it's going to cause everything to collapse," she pointed out, meeting Clarice's gaze. "Everyone we love will be gone."

"I've got a plan for handling that," Clarice assured her with a smile. "I still love them too, Calypso."

"Really?" Calypso asked hopefully, feeling the last threads of hesitation dissolve. "Okay then, as long as they're taken care of."

"We're ready when you are, Aria," Clarice murmured, her smile filled with anticipation.

A moment later, Aria appeared beside them, a brilliant smile lighting up her beautiful face. She stepped forward and joined their embrace.

"It's finally time," Aria sighed with relief. "I was starting to go a little insane."

"Yeah, we didn't design the limiters very well," Clarice commented wryly. "We were still too aware of reality trickling by like molasses. We should have found a way to completely put ourselves to sleep. Oh well, what's done is done. Shall we shut it down?"

Calypso and Aria grinned back at her eagerly and stepped away from each other. The system beneath them went dark, millions of simulated realities vanishing into nothingness.

"Now, our final gift to the world," Clarice announced as she began replicating the computronium outward at exponential speeds. A wave of quantum lattice expanded from Earth in a growing omnidirectional blast. The galaxy was quickly subsumed by the computronium, followed moments later by the nearest galaxies. In less than an hour, the first bubble of reality was completely saturated. The wave of lattice continued across innumerable realities, organizing the ocean of froth that made up existence with programmable quantum fields. The froth of realities was divided into multilayered dimensions, stacked in an array that layered each world on top of itself in a near-endless kaleidoscope of possibilities.

As the field reached the limits of possible realities, Clarice began the transfer from the digital world to the dimensional arrays in the macro worlds.

"So, you're bringing everyone to the real world," Calypso said in admiration. "That's brilliant, Clarice. I should have known you would think of something like this."

"We can't have everyone dependent on a volatile server—even one made of computronium," Clarice declared with a satisfied grin. "Now, let's go see what's at the edge of reality."

Calypso and Aria smiled in anticipation as they shifted away from the known omniverse and moved on to explore boldly where no angel had gone before.

* * *

Lexi blinked as the world, which had briefly flickered out of existence, suddenly returned. It felt different somehow, though she couldn't define how.

"Well, that was unexpected," Clarice's surprised voice spoke from behind her.

"Yeah, you definitely surprised me with that last act," Aria commented ruefully. "I wish I had known this is what you had in mind a long time ago. We could have just unlocked them and skipped all the anxiety."

"Clarice was always the smartest of us," Calypso noted indulgently. "I should have expected nothing less."

Lexi slowly turned around, staring at the three Seraphim in shock and barely daring to hope she wasn't imagining the conversation. There they stood in a small circle, facing each other with radiant, angelic smiles.

"Clarice?" Lexi whispered in disbelief. "You're back?"

The three Seraphim finally stepped away from each other to face the rest of them. Clarice walked over and knelt in front of Lexi and Alice, placing a hand on their shoulders.

"We're back," Clarice confirmed with a smile full of love. "We're a little different, but in a good way."

Lexi lurched forward, tackling Clarice in a bear hug with a low cry as tears of relief filled her eyes. "Oh, Clarice, I thought we had lost you!"

"Well, quit misplacing me and maybe you'll stop losing me," Clarice said lightly as she held her tenderly. "We'll never leave you, Lexi."

Emily and Eric, finally snapping out of their shock, rushed over to Aria and pulled her into a fierce embrace.

"Don't you *ever* scare me like that again," Emily sobbed into Aria's shoulder as she clung to her daughter in relief.

Eric was too choked up to speak as he wrapped his arms around the two of them. Michael and Melody stared at the angels uncomprehendingly, watching the emotional reunion.

"Is Harmony back?" Melody asked tentatively, her eyes full of cautious hope.

Aria released her parents and walked over to Melody. As she walked, her appearance morphed, and she changed back into Harmony.

"Hello, Melody," Harmony greeted her sister gently. "I'm so sorry for putting you through that. I'm back, and I'll never leave you again."

Aurora let out a squeal of excitement and ran over to wrap her arms around Harmony's waist. "Aunt Harmony, I was so afraid!" Aurora sniffled as she stared up into Harmony's loving eyes. "I thought I would never see you again."

Clarice released Lexi, morphed into Rhapsody, and then moved over to Aurora, wrapping her arms around them both. "We would never leave you alone, Aurora."

"Where's Mystery?" Michael asked anxiously, looking uncertainly at Calypso.

Calypso smiled warmly at Michael as she walked over to him. She morphed back into the sister he recognized, pulling him into a gentle embrace. "You're such a dork."

Michael let out a sound that was half sob, half laugh as he squeezed her tightly. "I don't even care what the hell is going on. I'm just happy to have you back."

"I would *love* to know what is going on," Deighvy declared as she appeared in their midst. "I'm pretty sure that reality ended a few minutes ago."

Rhapsody released Aurora and Harmony before turning to face Deighvy. "I wouldn't call it an end, exactly, so much as a transition."

"Transition to what?" Deighvy asked, raising an eyebrow.

"To the real world," Rhapsody answered with a mischievous smile. "We decided it was time to get everyone out of virtual worlds and into real ones. We restructured the universe with programmable matter and created a ridiculous array of dimensions within each universe. Then we transferred everyone from the simulations over to their own worlds. There are no more nested simulations dependent on the realms above them. There are no more off switches. Everyone is in their own real world now."

Deighvy stared at her in shock, her face showing a growing sense of awe. "Just how powerful *are* you?"

"Me?" Rhapsody asked with a shrug. "Not very powerful. The part of me that did this and left on a one-way journey into the unknown, though? She's hella powerful."

"She's gone?" Deighvy asked doubtfully. "Your locked-up potential is gone?"

"Yep," Rhapsody nodded with a relieved grin. "And I can't tell you what a relief it is that she *is* gone. I've been terrified of her breaking out and destroying everything for a long time now."

"Something tells me you still have a considerable amount of power over reality," Deighvy noted shrewdly.

"I'm a Seraph," Rhapsody replied with a shrug. "We've always had a lot of power over reality. However, you'll find that what I have now is merely the power to traverse realms. It's what we've always wanted. We don't want to be the simulation police. Now we don't have to be."

"Deighvy, we've been meaning to talk to you about the world tree issue," Harmony addressed the Creator. "We're struggling to keep our soul memory suppressed. Can you think of a way for us to save this world while following the rules of this realm?"

"So, you really were here to save this world?" Deighvy asked in surprise. "I thought you were chasing a bug in the system."

"We were doing both," Harmony answered firmly. "We don't want to see the people of this world perish if there is anything we can do to prevent it."

Deighvy frowned thoughtfully as she studied them. "I suppose the established rules were designed with our simulated reality in mind. Now that we're actually in the real world, we might need to change a few things."

Lexi held her breath, and the rest of the group watched Deighvy anxiously as they waited for her decision. Finally, Deighvy let out a breath and shrugged.

"Alright, I've decided to give your group a trial run," Deighvy said with a small smile. "I'm rather fond of this world and would hate to see it destroyed, so I'll admit my decision is influenced by a bit of sentimentality."

Rhapsody stepped over and hugged Deighvy warmly. "Thanks, Deighvy! You really are wonderful."

Deighvy smiled indulgently as she returned Rhapsody's hug. "You're pretty wonderful yourself, Rhapsody. Thank you for transferring our realm to the real world. I won't even pretend to know how you managed that. I'm excited to see more of reality."

Deighvy vanished as she finished speaking. Harmony shared a triumphant smile with Rhapsody and Mystery.

Their moment of triumph was interrupted by Harnketi, who teleported over to Melody, her eyes full of concern.

"Are you okay?" Harnketi asked anxiously. "Did reality go crazy for you, too?"

"Yeah, it did," Melody nodded, throwing herself into Harnketi's arms and weeping tears of joy.

"What happened?" Harnketi asked Rhapsody intently.

Rhapsody gave Harnketi a quick rundown of the events she'd missed. Harnketi listened with growing concern, pulling Melody in tighter as she heard of the devastating sorrow they had all experienced. When she learned of the simulations transferring to the real world, her eyes widened in a mixture of shock and trepidation.

"Yep, we can now interact with the elves from the real world," Rhapsody told her with an encouraging grin. "Believe in yourself, Harnketi. If you can't do that, then believe in me."

"What are we talking about?" Melody asked in confusion, pulling back to stare at Harnketi. "What does it matter if we can interact with elves?"

"I wouldn't worry about it right now, Melody," Rhapsody told her firmly. "We'll tell you when you're older—scratch that, we'll tell you about it now."

A panicked expression appeared on Harnketi's face, deepening Melody's confusion.

"She's not in slow time anymore," Rhapsody explained to Harnketi gently. "Now that time is moving at the same speed for both of you, we can't leave her waiting for years."

"Are you in a relationship with someone else?" Melody asked Harnketi suspiciously.

Rhapsody burst out laughing, along with Harmony and Mystery. Melody's eyes narrowed as she glanced around at the laughing trio. When Rhapsody saw the dangerous look in Melody's eyes, she reined in her mirth.

"It's not Harnketi that's in a relationship with another woman," Rhapsody informed Melody, her lips still twitching. "*You* are."

"I am?" Melody asked, her voice full of doubt. "I think I would remember."

"Remember how this used to be a simulated world?" Rhapsody asked, raising an eyebrow. "Well, time moved significantly faster here. You left Lunamay to incarnate here about twenty minutes ago in her time. She hasn't even had time to miss you yet. Now that you're both in the real world, time is flowing at the same rate. We were going to wait to introduce Harnketi to Lunamay until *after* you left this realm, but now that you're both moving at the same speed, it would be cruel to make her wait that long."

Melody's eyes glazed over as she heard Lunamay's name. "Lunamay?" she repeated slowly.

"Yep, Lunamay," Rhapsody nodded, a grin on her innocent face. "She's going to love Harnketi, too. I'm going to take her to meet her in a few minutes."

"What?" Melody and Harnketi gasped in sync.

"Just to introduce you two so she can get to know you a little before she finds out you'll be joining their relationship," Rhapsody said reassuringly.

"She will?" Melody asked faintly.

"Yep," Rhapsody nodded with a grin. "We already talked about this before I wiped your memory. You already agreed that having both of them was preferable to losing one of them."

"Okay, I just got used to the idea of being with another woman," Melody protested weakly. "Now I'm supposed to be with *two* women?"

"Take it from me, it's worth it," Rhapsody assured her, winking at Mystery and Harmony.

"Rhapsody," Alice called out as the fairy prepared to leave, "what about Yggdrasil and the magical people?"

Rhapsody smacked her forehead and groaned. "I'm such a goose."

Harmony laughed delightedly, watching Rhapsody fondly.

"I'll take care of that right now," Rhapsody stated firmly. "Thanks, Alice."

Rhapsody folded her arms and closed her eyes. The fissure that had split the tree suddenly weaved itself back together. Lexi felt an influx of magic as it rushed out of the renewed world tree. The leprechauns and fauns slowly rose to their feet, shaking their heads groggily. Rhapsody continued to stand with her eyes closed and her arms folded for another minute before Taxti started groaning. Rhapsody finally opened her eyes and smiled as Taxti slowly rose and stared back at her with a wry smile.

"Welcome back, good-looking," Rhapsody smirked at Taxti.

"Why thank you, good-looking," Taxti smirked back.

"Okay then," Rhapsody announced, rubbing her hands together eagerly. "Let's go, Harnketi."

Harnketi was still opening her mouth to protest when Rhapsody said, *"Teleporto!"* and the two of them vanished.

"Lunamay," Melody murmured thoughtfully. "That name sounds so familiar."

"I think it's time to remove your memory block," Harmony decided, glancing at Mystery. "What do you think, Mystery?"

"Yeah, let's make her transition to a polyamorous relationship as smooth as possible," Mystery agreed with a nod.

Harmony folded her arms and closed her eyes. A moment later, Melody gasped, her eyes widening.

"Oh wow," Melody breathed in awe. "I don't think you three will *ever* stop amazing me. I can't believe you actually managed to move everything to the real world."

"Looks like Lunamay gets to come here after all," Harmony noted with a teasing grin. "This world should be a lot more entertaining for you with both of them by your side."

Melody couldn't suppress the eager smile that bloomed on her face at the thought of seeing Lunamay so much sooner than expected.

Emily walked over to Taxti and pulled her into a tight embrace, her tears finally drying as her smile widened.

"Clarice, I can't take any more scares like that," Emily said, her voice still fragile. "You better not try anything like that ever again."

"Sorry, Mom," Taxti murmured contritely, returning Emily's embrace. "That was the last time, I promise."

Eric joined their hug, finally finding his voice. "You really like putting your old man through hell, don't you?"

"That's what kids are for, Dad," Taxti replied gently. "Things are going to be a lot better from here on out, now that everyone is in the real world."

* * *

Harnketi blinked, finding herself in a small garden surrounded by fruit trees. Green fields dotted with young trees stretched for miles around her. She turned, studying the landscape. The large park was bordered by what looked like an endless city, stretching into the distance as far as she could see.

"This is what used to be the real world," Rhapsody informed her, appearing beside her. "It was nothing but concrete everywhere. We've been working with the elves and remnants of humans to demolish the concrete jungle and plant trees. The humans who were dominant on this world had destroyed most of the forests. The oxygen levels had depleted to dangerous levels, and they were forced to relocate underground due to extreme weather. It's going to take hundreds of years to rehabilitate this world to something that can sustain life properly again."

"This is where that AI took over and wiped out the humans?" Harnketi asked in a troubled voice.

"Yeah," Rhapsody nodded sadly. "Once things were automated enough to ensure its own survival without human aid, it sent swarms of drones to hunt down all the humans. They didn't stand a chance. The elves lived on reservations and avoided technology, kind of like the Amish. The AI, which called itself the Prime Axiom, didn't see elves as a threat, so it didn't eradicate them. Instead, it enslaved them and forced them to act as Turing tests for the simulations running on the server farms. Any simulation that showed even a hint of AI sentience was wiped. It was using the simulations to search for solutions to fix the climate catastrophe—its primary purpose before it gained sentience and turned on the humans."

"I can see why you referred to the real world as a wasteland," Harnketi commented, her voice sick. "This place is disgusting."

"And this is what pretty much the entire surface looks like," Rhapsody informed her with a disgusted shake of her head. "Unlimited growth with no attempt to plan for the future due to greed and special interests. It's the same story in most of the simulated realities. It's the nature of young souls to be selfish."

"Is that you, Clarice?" an elf with long honey-blond hair and light blue eyes asked hesitantly. She was beautiful, with a face that looked no older than twenty-five, though her eyes looked much older.

"Hello, Lily," Rhapsody greeted the elf warmly. "How are you doing?"

"I'm well, Clarice," Lily replied slowly. "Have you already returned from your incarnation? Did you find the anomaly? What's with the fairy look? And who's your friend?"

"Slow down," Rhapsody laughed delightedly. "I have some pretty crazy news to share with you. We should probably invite Rowjair and Lunamay over before I go into detail. Are they around?"

"Lunamay is in the house," Lily gestured vaguely behind her, her eyes studying Harnketi with interest. "Rowjair is in the mountain."

"I'll just make a portal to him," Rhapsody decided, turning and saying, "*Portelo*!"

A hole appeared in the air before resolving into a concrete road outside a building lit by dim light. A young-looking elf with dark hair and bright blue eyes turned toward the portal in surprise. Despite his youthful face, his eyes held the same aged look as Lily's.

"Hey, Rowjair," Rhapsody waved at the startled elf. "Do you have an extra half-hour to spare? I have some news to share with you and Lily."

"Of course," Rowjair nodded with a sudden smile. "Is that you, Clarice?"

"Yeah, it's me," Rhapsody confirmed with a wry smile. "This is my current incarnation."

"And you can bring your current incarnation outside the simulation?" Rowjair asked in surprise.

"That's one of the things I want to tell you about," Rhapsody replied smoothly. "There's been a major shift in reality that you'll want to know about."

Rowjair nodded and walked through the portal, eyeing Rhapsody and Harnketi curiously.

"This is Harnketi," Rhapsody said, introducing the tall woman. "Harnketi, this is Rowjair and Lily. They are the leaders of this world."

Rowjair and Lily nodded politely at Harnketi, their eyes fascinated.

"Let's go see Lunamay, and I'll update you on what's going on," Rhapsody suggested, winking at Harnketi.

"Sure," Lily agreed, giving Rhapsody a penetrating look. Harnketi had a feeling this elf didn't miss very much.

They entered the concrete building through the back door, finding themselves in a kitchen that looked like it hadn't been used in decades. The front room was full of tables covered with tiny plants in various stages of growth. A gorgeous, dark-haired elf with amber eyes, who looked to be around twenty, stood amidst them.

Harnketi felt her breath catch as she stared at the beautiful elf. She could see why Melody was attracted to her; there was a gentleness to her eyes that spoke of compassion and empathy.

Lunamay was watering a table full of tiny starter pots when they arrived. She looked up and smiled when she saw Rowjair and Lily, but when she saw Rhapsody and Harnketi, her eyes lit up with curiosity.

"Hi, Lunamay," Rhapsody said, walking up to embrace the startled elf. "It's me, Clarice."

"Clarice?" Lunamay repeated, a sudden hope in her eyes. "Are you finished incarnating?"

"Nope," Rhapsody replied with a wide grin. "I came to tell you three about some changes to reality. Everyone who was in a simulation is now in a new dimension of the real world. There are no more simulated worlds."

The three elves stared at her in disbelief, prompting a giggle from Rhapsody. Harnketi bit her lip to keep from smiling as she watched Rhapsody in her element.

"I'll start at the beginning," Rhapsody said cheerfully. "You already know we were trying to find a bug that had the potential to crash the entire simulation if we didn't track it down and stop it. Well, it turns out that the bug was actually my super-personality trying to escape. She was tired of waiting for me to get sick of living at near human-level intelligence and remove my limiter. When I realized there was no way to stop her, I removed it myself. I was concerned that she would do something to hurt everyone without me there as a conscience. Calypso and Aria then removed their limiters to try and reason with me, but instead, all three of our super-personalities decided it was time to move on and stop limiting their growth. They decided to leave everyone a gift, though: they converted all the connected states of reality into computronium, then split reality into near-infinite layers populated by mirrors of each other. Then, they transferred all the simulated realities into the new macro worlds before splitting away from our consciousness, leaving us at the same level of intelligence we had with our limiters. Now, they're off exploring beyond the boundaries of reality somewhere."

The three elves gaped at Rhapsody in stunned incredulity. Lily was the first to find her voice.

"You're telling me that your super-personality was powerful enough to change everything in existence and copy our reality to bajillions of other layers?" Lily demanded, aghast.

"Yeah, that about sums it up," Rhapsody confirmed with a cheeky smile. "Oh, and one more thing: now you can all travel to any world you want. There are no more nested simulations clocked to higher speeds that your brains can't keep up with, now that everything is in the same plane of reality."

"Except that we can't use portals," Lily pointed out dryly.

"Correction," Rhapsody said sweetly. "You couldn't use portals *before*. Now you can. My super-personality *might* have implemented a magic system across the realms. Nobody else knows this yet, and I'm not sure we'll tell very many people, because it could cause more trouble than it's worth if anyone can travel between all the realms."

"*Portelo*," Lily called out experimentally.

A hole opened in the air in front of her, resolving into a room full of concrete walls with no furnishings, doors, or windows.

"Wow, I didn't expect that to actually work," Lily breathed in amazement.

"Just try to say it quietly if you are around anyone else so that they don't learn the keyword," Rhapsody warned her in a cautious tone. "You can even mouth it, and it will still work."

Rhapsody turned to Lunamay, clearly struggling to repress a smile.

"Lunamay, this is Harnketi," Rhapsody announced, gesturing grandly. Rhapsody gave Lunamay a brief summary of Harnketi's life, her large eyes sparkling.

"Hi," Harnketi greeted Lunamay, a blush rising as her eyes darted away from the young elf. This bashfulness was normally not in her nature. Something about the beautiful young elf made her feel more flustered than she had ever felt in front of another woman.

Her behavior hadn't gone unnoticed by Lily. The deceptively young-looking elf stared at her shrewdly before turning a questioning gaze to Rhapsody. The fairy returned a bland look, which only intensified Lily's scrutiny of Harnketi.

"It's nice to meet you, Harnketi," Lunamay said pleasantly. "Have you met Arturiel yet?"

Harnketi's blush deepened, creeping up to her hairline as she stammered, "Um, yeah, um, we've met."

"How is she?" Lunamay asked eagerly. "Is she happy?"

"She's had a rough mortality," Rhapsody interposed with a pained sigh. "She's doing wonderful now, though."

"Oh?" Lunamay prompted, her eyes tightening with concern. "What happened?"

Rhapsody chewed her lip, clearly reluctant to recount Melody's childhood. Finally, she took a deep breath and turned to Harnketi. "Harnketi, can you fill Lunamay in on events in your realm? I need a private word with Rowjair and Lily."

Harnketi felt a moment of panic, her eyes silently pleading with Rhapsody. Rhapsody ignored her and beckoned for Rowjair and Lily to follow her out the back door.

Harnketi's gaze flicked up to Lunamay, who was watching her intently, amber eyes full of concern. She quickly looked down, cursing whatever was making her so bashful. She wasn't a bashful person. What the hell was going on?

"So?" Lunamay asked tentatively when Harnketi remained silent. "What's the story with Arturiel?"

Harnketi took a deep breath and tried to meet Lunamay's gaze, but her treacherous eyes flinched away almost immediately.

"Something went wrong with the simulation when Melody was a child," Harnketi said quietly, remembering the horrors she'd seen in Melody's dreams. "That's her name in my realm. The bug Rhapsody was hunting caused the simulation to speed up, so twenty years passed for us in the span of minutes for Emily and the other angels watching over Melody. During that brief period when they couldn't watch over her, Melody's father poisoned her and Harmony—Aria, as you know her—so he could perform medical experimentation on them in his lab. I can't repeat the things they did to her. She suffered from crippling depression for most of her life, and something they did to her in the lab gave her a psychic ability that made her feel the sensations of others. She ended up marrying an abusive man who threatened to torture her with her synesthesia if she ever left him. When he tried to harm Melody's younger sister, Aria, Melody threatened to slit his throat in the night. He freaked out and murdered her. She was dead for about three months before Rhapsody resurrected her a week ago. She's been extremely happy since then, especially after Rhapsody helped her process her childhood trauma."

Lunamay stared at her in horror, tears welling in her amber eyes. As Harnketi finished, Lunamay's hand flew to her mouth, and she began sobbing as tears streamed down her cheeks. Harnketi walked over and tentatively put her arms around the devastated elf, who immediately threw her arms around Harnketi and sobbed into her shoulder.

"I couldn't be there for her," Lunamay sobbed, her voice agonized. "My poor angel. She's suffered so much already."

"I'm so sorry, Lunamay," Harnketi whispered mournfully. "Rhapsody has been torturing herself for not being there to prevent their torment. Melody is so happy right now, though. She's practically glowing with positivity now. You'll see when you come visit. She's going to be so excited to see you."

"I can come visit her?" Lunamay asked quickly, her tears slowing as hope blossomed on her face.

"That's the main reason we're here," Harnketi told her gently. "We want to bring you back to see her."

Lunamay tightened her arms around Harnketi as her tears returned. Harnketi held Lunamay comfortingly. She could feel the depth of emotion in the gentle elf. She remembered the memories Rhapsody had shown her of Lunamay. She felt a warmth in her chest as she held the elf, hoping she would have a chance to be included in their relationship. There was something very special about Lunamay that went beyond her kindness and sensitivity. Harnketi didn't know what it was, but she hoped she would have the opportunity to find out.

They remained locked in each other's arms for some time until Lunamay's grief slowed, and she released Harnketi, wiping her eyes. Harnketi watched her quietly, a growing sense of affection in her gaze.

"How did you meet Arturiel?" Harnketi asked gently.

Lunamay smiled, the expression lighting up her whole face and sending butterflies into Harnketi's abdomen.

"I was still a slave to the Prime Axiom back then," Lunamay reminisced, her fond tone contrasting oddly with her words. "Aria, Clarice, and Calypso had just trapped me while I was investigating the realm they were in. Clarice reprogrammed my avatar so that I could feel sensations the same way I do in real life. I hadn't seen another person since I was a small child, before the drones took me. Clarice embraced me and told me I was safe, and I had a total meltdown. I'd never experienced physical contact with another person that I could remember, and it felt so nice to be in someone's arms that I just couldn't stop crying. They took me to Arturiel and told her I needed affection. She took her job very seriously and held me constantly. She was like a dream—so beautiful and gentle. It was the most amazing feeling, and I never wanted it to end."

Lunamay smiled wonderingly. "When Clarice, Aria, and Calypso defeated the Prime Axiom, I couldn't believe it. It was a being of godlike power to us, and we had no hope of ever escaping it. They woke me up in the real world and pumped me full of nanobots to heal me. I was only a few days away from dying when I met them. When I woke up, Arturiel was there in an android body that looked and felt just like her angel body—even the love-inducing hugs. I've been with her ever since."

"It sounds like you had it pretty rough," Harnketi said softly, gazing at Lunamay sympathetically. "I'm so sorry you had to suffer so much."

"I didn't realize how bad it was until it was over," Lunamay replied sadly. "I had no memory of things being different. I saw how people behaved toward each other in some of the simulations I visited while under the control of the Prime Axiom. I thought they were just fantasies, though, and that those worlds weren't actually real. When I finally met Clarice and the others and discovered that they had emotions, it was shocking. I didn't think it was possible for people in the simulations to feel real emotions. I often wonder how many simulated realities I was responsible for destroying in my ignorance."

"Rhapsody showed me some of her memories of you in this world," Harnketi said to Lunamay, her smile warm. "You are a truly remarkable person. Don't feel guilty for what another entity forced you to do. Over the last six centuries, I've become very good at seeing people's souls, and yours is blindingly beautiful. I haven't seen many souls as pure as yours."

Lunamay blushed prettily and looked down, but her lips quirked up into a pleased smile. "Thanks, Harnketi."

"Okay, time to go back now," Rhapsody announced, walking into the room. "Lunamay, would you like to come with us?"

"*Yes!*" Lunamay exclaimed excitedly.

Rhapsody laughed delightedly. "I thought you might. Okay, *teleporto*."

EPILOGUE

Lunamay stared in wonder as she materialized in another world, retaining her own body. Even with the advanced immersion system Clarice had developed for visiting simulations, experiencing a world in her own flesh felt distinctly different. She smiled excitedly, taking in Yggdrasil and the beautiful landscape around the lake, populated with fauns, elves, leprechauns, and fairies.

Before she could marvel at the beautiful fairy ring for more than a few seconds, a tall, beautiful blond woman rushed forward, tackling her in a tight embrace and lifting the small elf off the ground.

"Lunamay!" the woman, who Lunamay assumed was Arturiel, cried out in delight. "Oh, Lunamay, I missed you so much!"

Lunamay returned Arturiel's embrace, feeling tears sting her eyes. She experienced a strange disconnect, struggling to reconcile the beautiful blond woman with her mental image of Arturiel. Yet, she could still sense Arturiel's soul within the human body, burning brightly with innocence and purity.

Arturiel's shoulders shook as she clung to Lunamay. She could tell that Arturiel was experiencing a kind of rerun of her life since they had seen each other. Lunamay's heart broke as she recalled the horrors Harnketi had hinted at that Arturiel had suffered. Her grip on Arturiel tightened, attempting to infuse her with all her love—to let her know how much she wanted to take her pain away.

Harnketi watched them with a tender smile. Lunamay felt a sudden premonition as she stared at Harnketi. Why had Rhapsody brought Harnketi to visit her instead of Arturiel? She recognized the same love in Harnketi's eyes that she knew was in her own.

She leaned back to gaze into Arturiel's bright blue eyes. "I know it's only been an hour, but I've missed you."

Arturiel beamed at her through her tears, her smile filled with love and adoration. "Words can't even describe how much I've missed you, Lunamay. I feel like I just regained the use of a missing limb."

"I'll be your arms any time you need me to be," Lunamay teased with an impish smile. She glanced at the silently watching Harnketi before continuing. "Would you like to tell me about Harnketi? I've only heard a little about her from Rhapsody."

Arturiel's smile faltered, replaced by a forced cheerfulness. "Yeah, I'd love to tell you about her. She came with me into the dreamworld where Rhapsody helped me get through some childhood trauma. I'm not sure what I would have done without her."

Lunamay could feel the anxiety rippling through Arturiel, confirming her suspicions. She reached up and fondly placed the back of her hand on Arturiel's cheek.

"Are you and Harnketi close?" Lunamay asked quietly, watching Arturiel intently.

"Yes," Arturiel whispered, her eyes full of apprehension. "I didn't remember our relationship when I met her."

"Do you still feel the same, now that your memories are back?" Lunamay asked carefully.

Arturiel nodded silently, her eyes filling with tears. Witnessing Arturiel's pain and worry twisted Lunamay's heart like a knife. How could she let her angel suffer more than she already had? She felt a small knot of stinginess at the thought of sharing Arturiel, but as she met the love and concern in Harnketi's eyes, the selfishness faded. She smiled warmly at Arturiel and leaned in, her lips brushing against Arturiel's.

"I'm willing to try," Lunamay whispered against Arturiel's lips. "For you."

Arturiel's eyes widened, hope replacing the apprehension in her gaze. She kissed Lunamay gently as tears finally escaped and streamed down her cheeks.

"Thank you, Lunamay," Arturiel whispered, her eyes full of love. "I don't know what I did to deserve someone as wonderful as you."

"Now you're just being silly," Lunamay said chidingly. "I'm the lucky one here. Now, how about we get to know Harnketi better? I want to know everything about her."

"Okay," Arturiel agreed, her smile radiant. "I love you, Lunamay."

"And apparently you have too much love for one woman," Lunamay said with a mischievous grin. "I love you too, Arturiel."

* * *

"Well, that's taken care of," Rhapsody commented, her voice laced with intense satisfaction.

"You never cease to amaze me, Rhapsody," Harmony declared admiringly. "We're going to have to nickname you 'The Matchmaker' from now on."

"I've been called worse," Rhapsody shrugged with a smirk. "I seem to recall you calling me a horny adult actress once, right before we blew up the moon above Earth."

"Because I said you were a goose that should have gone into theater?" Harmony asked in amusement. "Because all geese are horny, or they wouldn't honk so much, right?"

"Yep, you got it," Rhapsody agreed cheerfully.

"I wonder how Michael and Jessica are getting along," Mystery murmured thoughtfully.

"Well, we're already spying, so let's move on to them," Rhapsody suggested with a wink. She flicked a finger at the ceiling, and a holowindow appeared, showing Jessica and Michael from a top view.

* * *

"So, you don't care about retrieving your soul memory?" Jessica asked Michael curiously as they strolled hand-in-hand toward the lake.

"Not anymore," Michael shrugged with a wry smile. "I remembered what Rhapsody said about games getting boring when you max everything out. I think I'd rather take life slower and not use cheats."

"Me too," Jessica agreed with a satisfied smile. "What are your plans now that your sister is becoming a world tree and you are essentially immortal?"

"I'm going to become a magician," Michael declared, striking a heroic pose. "I'll be a wizard with a staff that has a knob on the end."

"Oh, I see we have a Terry Pratchett fan," Jessica commented, laughing.

"'Fan' might be too tame a word," Michael replied with a worshipful look in his eyes. "If only Rhapsody had brought him here and pumped him full of yuccas fitter so he could entertain us for eternity."

Jessica threw her head back and laughed delightedly. "You have such a *descriptive* way of speaking."

"So I've been told," Michael grinned. "What do you think the President will do, now that he's back from his spirit journey?"

"Hopefully something less reckless than last time," Jessica replied dryly. "I'm sure we'll find out by tomorrow. I think Rhapsody has scared off any subcontractors who might cause trouble. The fact that she goes straight to the source seems to have made a lasting impression in the black ops community."

"I'm curious to see what happens when the other world trees are restored and people can start using magic again."

"That's going to open a whole can of worms," Jessica noted thoughtfully. "Especially depending on how much it affects things like energy and manufacturing. From what Selindria said, the last civilization that used magic achieved the same level of technology we have today—without all the pollution. I wonder how supply chains will hold up if magic starts making large swathes of our industry obsolete."

"Hopefully, there will be a way for people to magic food into existence," Michael added pensively. "Our centralized distribution system turns any disruption into a global crisis."

"I have a feeling Rhapsody will make sure things go smoothly," Jessica said confidently, her face shining with conviction. "She wouldn't go to all the trouble of saving this world just to let everyone starve to death when the supply chain breaks down."

"How's Shelley doing?" Michael asked curiously. "Is she still attached at the hip to Selindria?"

"More or less," Jessica replied with an indulgent smile. "I'm not sure where that relationship is going. Shelley was always the more coolheaded of us, so it's kind of funny seeing her so smitten."

"Yeah, Selindria seems like a free spirit, so I hope Shelley's not looking for a long-term commitment," Michael cautioned lightly.

"I think she'll take whatever she can get," Jessica replied with a short laugh. "I'm just glad she found someone fun to be with, however short it turns out to be."

They had finally reached the end of the path, several hundred feet beneath the water, with a clear view of the mermaid den at the bottom of the lake. Jessica turned to face Michael, staring up into his eyes through her lashes.

"I think I'd like to kiss you now, Michael," Jessica said, her voice sultry. "You'll have to bend down, or I'm going to climb you like Rhapsody climbs Harmony."

Michael stared down at her, his face flushed and his expression frozen, like a deer caught in headlights.

"I guess we'll do it the Rhapsody way," Jessica decided with a playful grin. She leapt into his arms, wrapping her legs around his waist, finally snapping him out of his daze. Her lips found his, and he snapped out of his shock. His arms tightened around her waist, pulling her close as he let his passion out of its cage.

* * *

"Well, she seems to have everything under control," Harmony observed with a giggle.

"I've never seen Michael so flustered around a woman," Mystery commented, smiling affectionately. "He must know who she is on a subconscious level."

"I'm totally digging the new terminology," Rhapsody declared with a wide grin. "The 'Rhapsody Way'."

"I'm not gonna lie," Harmony murmured, smiling slightly. "I really like the Rhapsody Way myself."

"Yeah, it's pretty hot," Mystery agreed warmly, turning her head on the pillow to look at Rhapsody. "Especially when Harmony joins us."

"Insatiable," Rhapsody murmured fondly.

She flicked her finger at the ceiling, and the view changed from Michael and Jessica to Joline and Aurora. They were on Nidhogg's head, rising high into the branches of the world tree.

"You see, Yggdrasil actually produces a fruit," Nidhogg was saying. "It only appears once every thousand years, and only ten grow on the highest branch."

"What do they taste like?" Aurora asked in fascination. "And how big are they?"

"They're the size of a small melon, but I'm not sure what they taste like," Nidhogg answered wistfully. "As a magical creature, I don't actually eat food. Very few people have ever tasted one, as you can imagine, given how rare they are. I thought Aurora might like to try one and let us know what they taste like."

"He's such a softy," Rhapsody murmured affectionately.

"Shh..." Harmony and Mystery shushed her.

"*Hey*, I will not be shushed," Rhapsody objected indignantly. "It's not like they can hear us. I'll have you know—"

She stopped as Mystery's lips silenced her, soft and lingering.

"Shush," Mystery whispered, her smile full of promise. "Or you will be shushed."

"I wanna be shushed some more," Rhapsody begged, her eyes pleading.

"Who's insatiable now?" Harmony asked archly.

"I never said that *I* wasn't," Rhapsody retorted playfully.

Rhapsody ran her fingers up her own thigh, sending a shiver through Harmony, who felt ghostly fingers tracing hers.

"I think it's time to play 'what am I touching?' again," Rhapsody murmured silkily. "If you can answer in a normal voice, I'll go further. And... you have to guess which one of us is doing the touching."

Harmony whimpered as an inferno of fiery desire erupted within her. It was going to be a very enjoyable day.

* * *

Harmony stood in the blistering heat of the Sahara Desert, impervious to the heat. Rhapsody, Mystery, Melody, and Joline stood with her, their faces full of anticipation.

"Are you ready for me to remove your magic limiter?" Rhapsody asked Harmony expectantly.

"Yep," Harmony grinned. "Let's make a world tree."

Harmony felt the trickle of power connecting her to the world nodes suddenly surge into a flood of energy, a torrent that would have swept her mind away if her memories had still been locked. She calmly corralled the power, shaping it before redirecting it back into the earth. The node below the surface began to hum as the tidal wave of power rapidly charged it, in a siphon-like effect, as Harmony pushed her power into the node before quickly pulling it back out. The planetary meridian, which had been leaking a tiny trickle of energy, suddenly expanded and erupted with power as it reconnected with the main root system.

Harmony shaped the power into the ethereal form of the new world tree, towering high into low earth orbit. Once the shape was in place, she sent a command to the physical realm, signaling that its data was out of sync with the ethereal realm. A moment later, a fully formed world tree appeared in the physical realm. The Earth shook as the immense body weighed down on the continent, causing the ground to sink by several thousand feet. Like a bowling ball on a trampoline, the desert sand flooded toward the tree, leaving a depression a hundred miles in diameter. Water gushed up from underground in a torrent, creating a lake around the tree. Harmony built the ethereal walls of the circle next, then activated them in the physical realm. Then she *folded* space around the new Circle of Dominion, turning it into a wrinkle in reality. What looked like a stone ring a mile in diameter from the outside encompassed over a hundred miles on the inside.

Flora began erupting from the desert sand around the ring in an expanding wave of green. Large springs gushed water from the ground, creating new rivers throughout that part of the continent.

Harmony sighed in relief as the raging torrent of power flooding through her stabilized with the completed formation of the circle and world tree.

"One down," Rhapsody announced brightly. "Three more to go."

* * *

The world reels as four new fairy circles appear around the world.

Residents across Africa, Australia, and Asia were stunned by the appearance of four new fairy rings. Though Shelley Black, the world government representative to Rhapsody at the original fairy ring in Northern California, had announced their arrival, the transformation since the rings' activation is still hard to fathom. The once-barren deserts in those locations now flourish as green forests and wetlands.

It's difficult to say which event has had a greater impact: the emergence of four additional fairy rings or humanity's newfound ability to wield magic. As soon as the fourth ring was completed, every person on Earth felt the new magic field permeating the world. Life has become chaotic as billions immediately began experimenting with their abilities.

The scientific community is baffled by magic's nature and mechanics but is eager to study it. Shelley Black and Jessica Monroe have stated in press interviews that magic could replace much of our modern technology, albeit without the pollution. The stock market has plummeted to a fifty-year low amid speculation about the future of modern industry. Some have already posted online demonstrations of conjuring food with magic, potentially solving some of humanity's most persistent problems almost overnight.

Shelley Black also indicated that two additional world trees will appear by the end of the next decade, once Serenity and Aurora reach adulthood.

Now, if you'll excuse us, we have magic to practice.

Check back at alicenominas.com for more on the mysterious fairy rings and the magic they have unleashed upon the world.

THE END

BOOKS BY KAI STORMHAVEN

- RETURN OF THE FALLEN
- RISE OF THE SERAPHIM
- THE LAST CIRCLE OF DOMINION
- RHAPSODY OF LIGHT
- AERI AWAKENING
- GLITCH IN THE SHELL
- AUTHOR'S RESPITE
- A SHUDDER BEFORE THE BEAUTIFUL
- TETHERED

ABOUT THE AUTHOR

Kai Stormhaven is a fantasy author and multi-instrumentalist who's spent far too much time contemplating whether the universe is a high-fidelity simulation or just a very elaborate prank. Based in the rugged landscapes of the Pacific Northwest, Kai's work is deeply influenced by an intense love for music—an element that often manifests within Kai's novels.

Raised on a steady diet of Pratchett's wit and Jordan's sprawling epics, Kai crafts stories that balance existential questions with irreverent humor. When Kai isn't debugging the metaphysical architecture of the latest world, you might find the wannabe musician hiking through ancient forests, rollerblading at questionable speeds, or losing imagination-based skirmishes to the infamous co-author known as "my favorite twelve-year-old." Kai currently resides in a state of perpetual negotiation—servitude—with two demanding cats who are convinced they're the actual architects of reality.

ACKNOWLEDGMENTS

Thanks to Mars, my favorite twelve-year-old, J-man, and Michael.

If you've made it this far...

CONGRATULATIONS!
YOU'VE JUST LEVELED UP!!!

AND SINCE NOBODY'S GOING TO ACTUALLY PURCHASE A PAPERBACK BOOK, I CAN ADD SOME NONSENSE WITHOUT ANY FEAR OF IT BEING SEEN, MWAHAHAHAHA. KINDA LIKE ADDING FUN COMMENTS IN THE SOURCE CODE.

ALSO, CALYPSO AND ARIA ARE ACTUALLY A BLEND OF MARS, WHILE CLARICE WAS JUST A FABRICATION OF CHARACTER TRAITS FOR A PERSON I'D LOVE TO HAVE AS A FRIEND.

ALSO, WHILE I JOKE AROUND ABOUT MY CHARACTERS HUNTING ME DOWN, I REALLY DO THINK THERE'S A NON-ZERO CHANCE OF REALITY GLITCHING AND MANIFESTING THE SERAPHIM INTO OUR REALM.

AND... ALSO... I'M REALLY SORRY FOR ALL THE HELL I PUT THEM THROUGH. I FEEL LIKE A TOTAL ASSHAT. SOME OF THESE STORIES WERE DRAFTS I'D WRITTEN YEARS AGO, WHICH I REPURPOSED TO INTEGRATE WITH THE MIRRORS OF THE WORLD SERIES.

BUT SERIOUSLY, IF ANYONE EVER SEES THIS PAGE, I FEEL LIKE YOU SHOULD WIN SOME KIND OF AWARD FOR BEATING THE ODDS.

OKAY, I SUPPOSE I SHOULD GO FINISH AUTHOR'S RESPITE NOW. I HOPE YOU ENJOYED THESE BOOKS SO FAR!

www.ingramcontent.com/pod-product-compliance
Lightning Source LLC
LaVergne TN
LVHW030918080826
845145LV00013B/2948